Chasing red

ISABELLE RONIN

sourcebooks
casablanca

Published by Sourcebooks Casablanca, an imprint of Sourcebooks, Inc.
P.O. Box 4410, Naperville, Illinois 60567-4410
(630) 961-3900
Fax: (630) 961-2168
www.sourcebooks.com

The author is represented by Wattpad.

Library of Congress Cataloging-in-Publication Data

Names: Ronin, Isabelle, author.
Title: Chasing Red / Isabelle Ronin.
Description: Naperville, Illinois : Sourcebooks Casablanca, [2017]
Identifiers: LCCN 2017026610 | (softcover : acid-free paper)
Subjects: LCSH: Women college students--Fiction. | Basketball
    players--Fiction. | GSAFD: Love stories.
Classification: LCC PR9199.4.R654 C48 2017 | DDC 813/.6--dc23 LC record
    available at https://lccn.loc.gov/2017026610

Printed and bound in the United States of America.
WOZ 10 9 8 7 6 5 4 3 2 1

To my Wattpad readers. Pancakes?

CHAPTER

one

Caleb

THE DANCE FLOOR GLOWED AS RED AND GREEN LASER BEAMS SHOT out from the rotating lights in the ceiling. It was Friday night, and the club was packed with people dancing and jumping to the DJ's throbbing music. The floor pulsed beneath my feet, and the heat radiating from the mass was inescapable. My eyes roved over the tightly packed crowd. They reminded me of penguins huddled in the cold—on crack.

"What the hell's wrong with you?" Cameron yelled in my ear, giving me a friendly punch to the arm. His ice-blue eyes glittered in the dim light. "That was the fourth chick you turned down tonight, and we just got here."

I shrugged. Saying that I was bored with the meaningless sex and monotonous flirting seemed pretty pathetic. All right, the sex I didn't mind, but I was feeling restless, looking for something else lately. A challenge, maybe. The thrill of the chase.

I chugged my beer. "If you ate the same shit every day, you'd get bored of it too," I replied.

Justin barked out a laugh. His blond, gel-soaked hair stayed in place as he comically motioned with his head and then with his beer to the dance floor. "Check that out, man. Holy shit!" he exclaimed, letting out a high-pitched whistle.

In the middle of the dance floor, a girl was dancing—no, scratch that—*gyrating* so sensuously that I couldn't help but stare. She moved like… Sex comes to mind. Her short, tight dress covered her hourglass body like a second skin, seducing the dozens of eyes turned on her.

And it was in make-me-sin red. Damn.

I might have drooled a little as she bent over and did something dreamy with her hips. Her long ebony hair swayed against her tiny waist, and her legs looked a mile long in those spiky heels. There was something captivating in the way she danced, a defiance that flowed with the silky movements of her body. I felt my heart skip one fast beat against my chest when she looked up and our eyes met.

"Shit. I'm going to take this girl home with me," Justin yelled excitedly.

That was low and annoying enough to distract me. I hated cheating, and Justin had a girlfriend.

Cameron shook his head at Justin, looking up when a redhead asked him to dance. He laughed and whispered something in her ear. The redhead giggled. Cameron nodded to me and they left.

"Hello, team captain."

A soft body sidled up to me, reeking of intense floral perfume. I looked down into the heavily made-up eyes of Claire Bentley. I can appreciate the magic makeup does to a girl's face, but not when she looked like she was punched and was now sporting two black raccoon eyes.

"Claire. How's it going?" I gave her a small smile, but it only encouraged her to grab on to my arm.

Ugh, no. Why did I sleep with her again?

"Oh, you know, nothing much." She batted her eyelashes, pushing her breasts into my side. I couldn't help but glance quickly at her cleavage. Her breasts were staring at me. Ah, one drunken night and those lovely things must have been enough reason for me at the time.

The strap of her dress slid down her shoulder. She looked up at me from beneath her lashes, and I wondered if that was a practiced move. Still, I thought it was kind of sexy. If she were someone else, I might be interested. My eyes strayed past her shoulder to the dance floor, searching for that girl in the red dress. Claire's grip on my arm tightened, yanking my gaze back to her.

"You owe me a drink, Caleb. I dropped mine when you walked by." Her tongue snaked out to touch her top lip.

I hid my wince. She was trying too hard, and I didn't want to be trapped in her claws all night. Racking my brain on how to shut her down without offending her, I desperately looked around for Cameron or Justin. Neither was in sight. Assholes.

"Hey, baby." My eyes widened in surprise as the girl I'd been shamelessly ogling on the dance floor earlier wrapped her arms around my waist, maneuvering me out of Claire's grasp. When her eyes shifted to mine, I forgot how to breathe.

She was stunning.

"He's with me," she told Claire, but her eyes were still locked with mine. I was mesmerized by the way her mouth moved. Her lips were wide and full, colored a very, very hot red. "Aren't you?" Her voice was soft and low, reminding me of dark rooms and hot, smoky nights.

I felt my heart leap inside my chest for one insane second—it might have been a full minute or two. She wasn't beautiful in the classic sense. Her face was striking and eye-catching, with high, sharp cheekbones and long, dark brows above catlike eyes filled with secrets. I wanted to know every one of them.

When I didn't respond and just stared, her brows drew together in confusion. The dusky gold of her skin glowed under the dim light, making me wonder how it would feel. I caught her arms quickly before she moved away, placing them around my neck. I was right. Her skin was soft and smooth. *More* was all I could think.

Leaning close to her, I let my lips brush her earlobe and whispered, "Where have you been?" A smug smile split my lips as I felt her shiver. "I've been looking for you my whole life." Leisurely, as if I had all the time in the world, I glided my mouth from just under her ear to the hollow of her throat.

Before I could do anything else, she stepped away.

"She's gone. You're safe," she said, smirking. "Now you can buy me a drink for saving you."

I placed my hands in my pockets to stop myself from reaching for her again. I already missed the feel of her in my arms. "Sure, what would you like?"

She shook her hair back, and I couldn't stop watching her. I was captivated. "Something strong. Tonight, I want to be someone else. I want to…forget."

That was my cue. I slid my hand around to the small of her back, pulling her toward me so our faces were only inches apart. "You can be anyone you want with me." Her scent seduced me. It was addicting. "Why don't we leave this place and go somewhere I can help you forget, Red?"

Her eyes turned cold before her palms flattened against my chest. She pushed me away. "Nice meeting you too, asshole." She turned on her heel, waved, and left me staring after her like a lost puppy.

What the hell just happened? Did she just reject me?

The feeling was so unfamiliar that all I could do was watch her until she disappeared in the crowd. She swayed a little, like she'd had too much to drink. I almost ran after her to make sure she was all right, but she'd probably just spit at me. I figured her friends would take care of her.

But what the hell did I do wrong? She was sending all the right signals that she was interested. Maybe I should have actually gotten her the drink first.

"Caleb!" Another girl yelled behind me, but I was no longer in the mood for anything but my bed.

Funny how I had been wishing for a challenge tonight, but when one stared me in the face, I screwed it up like an idiot.

I closed my eyes and inhaled the refreshing air as I stepped out of the club. I had parked my car at the end of the lot and walked hurriedly to it, afraid someone would see me and drag me back inside. I'd rather chew my arm off than go back in there.

My steps faltered as I spotted the silhouette of a woman leaning against one of the filthy brick walls of the club parking lot. She'd probably had too much to drink. I would have been happy to leave her in peace, but when I glanced at her again, I noticed a man leering at her from a few feet away. My protective instincts kicked in as the man straightened and walked toward her.

The woman shifted, and the dim light from the streetlamp touched her face. My pulse kicked up a notch as I recognized her—Red.

I didn't need to think twice and went straight for her. The man hadn't noticed me yet because his gaze was concentrated on her. On the prize. The only prize he was getting tonight was a bloody nose if he didn't stop and turn his ass around.

When his hand closed around her wrist, I nearly growled. The anger surprised me, but I had to shake it off or this night would turn into a shit show. I took a few steps forward, and the man froze. He finally saw me.

"Hey, baby! Where have you been?" I exclaimed, fighting to keep my voice light as I approached. I refused to look at her face for fear of what I'd see there. If she looked even remotely scared, I was going to hit this dumb shit in the face. "I've been looking everywhere for you." I touched her shoulder and nodded at the dirtbag, meeting his gaze straight on. "I got her now."

When he refused to let go of her, I straightened to my full

height, widened my stance, and turned my hardest do-*not*-fuck-with-me gaze on him. The pervert let go and moved back a step, two, three, until he whipped around and started running in the opposite direction.

"Dumb shit," I said under my breath.

"What d-did you call me?"

Surprised that she'd heard me, I studied her face. How drunk was she?

"Not you. Although I guess *dumb* is debatable. What are you doing here alone?" My hands shot out to hold her up as she swayed on her feet again. "Whoa. You all right?"

It had been too dark inside the club to notice, but now I could see her face was pale, her eyes glassy. Without waiting for her reply, I scooped her up in my arms. She let out a weak protest.

"Do you need to throw up?" I asked, shaking her a little when she didn't respond.

That wasn't a smart move on my part, I realized. She moaned in distress, covering her mouth with her hands, as I headed to my parking spot. When she looked like she wasn't going to puke, I settled her carefully inside my car.

"I just got this car. You're not going to throw up in here, are you?" I started the ignition. She looked like she'd passed out already. "Where do you live? I'll drive you."

"H-homeless," she whimpered, surprising me that she'd responded. "Kicked out of my p-place."

Leaning against the headrest, I took a deep breath and rubbed my face. Homeless? Now what? I could drop her off at a hotel and pay her lodging for a few days so she'd have a place to stay while she found a new place. It was more than a stranger would do. But then I glanced at her and that plan evaporated.

Her eyes were closed, her breathing even and shallow, but even in sleep, she looked troubled. This girl who was so fierce on the dance floor looked so vulnerable now. Her face seemed familiar to me, like a barely remembered picture from a long time ago, but I couldn't place where I'd seen her before. I wouldn't forget a face like hers.

My brother, Ben, always liked to point out that I was a sucker for damsels in distress, and when I decided to take her to my apartment, I proved him right. I told myself she would not be safe in a hotel, especially in her current state. God knows what would have happened outside the club if I hadn't shown up.

It was spring, but the temperature was still dropping a few degrees at night. Fog covered the windshield and the windows of my car. When she shivered, I turned the heater on full blast, shrugged out of my jacket, and covered her with it. She was going to have a hell of a hangover when she woke up in the morning. We were a few minutes away from my apartment when she suddenly jerked up in her seat, covering her mouth.

Shit, no.

She threw up all over my car.

I nearly cried. My brand-new car! The sound of her retching was bad enough, but the smell was so putrid I nearly gagged myself. Desperately opening the windows and sunroof, I let out the breath I was holding and frantically gasped for air.

"Damn, girl. One good deed and—"

She threw up again.

"Maaan!"

Pissed, I debated if I should drop her off at a hotel. I didn't know this girl. Even my savior complex had a limit.

But I knew I couldn't do it.

Resigned, I guided my car into my apartment building's garage, parked in my spot, and warily approached the passenger seat. Holding my breath, I cleaned her as much as I could with an extra towel I kept in my car for basketball practice, then picked her up in my arms. She stank to high heaven.

I carried her through the lobby, and the concierge pressed the elevator doors for me since my hands were full. "Your girlfriend had too much to drink, sir?"

"Now, you and I both know I don't do girlfriends, Paul."

He chuckled.

As soon as I keyed in the code to my apartment, I went straight to the guest bedroom. She whimpered when I gently laid her on the bed, curling up like a little kitten. "Mom," she sobbed.

Glancing at her face, I hesitated beside the bed. Whatever this girl had gone through hadn't been pleasant. I knew I should probably clean her up and change her clothes, but I didn't think she'd appreciate it when she discovered a stranger had stripped her. I might lose an eye or a hand if I did. Better not risk it.

Her breathing eventually evened out. I don't know how long I stayed there watching her sleep.

CHAPTER
two

Veronica

THE SOFT WARMTH OF SUNLIGHT ON MY SKIN WOKE ME. I SAVORED the clean, white sheets covering me, thinking of how sweet my mom was for changing them. Content, I smiled and burrowed.

My mom. It wasn't possible. My mom was dead.

I shot up from the bed, dazed. Blinking several times, I looked around the unfamiliar room and swallowed the panic climbing up my throat. *Where the hell am I? And what is that horrible smell?*

"It would really help right now if you don't panic," I muttered, taken aback by the foul taste in my mouth. I took several deep breaths to calm my pounding heart and tried to assess my situation.

At least I still had my clothes on, even though they were soiled with dry...vomit. That stink was coming from me. *Good God.*

I could recall everything that happened yesterday, but what happened at the club was a blur of fuzzy images. Getting kicked out of my apartment because I couldn't pay the rent for two months was brutal. Leaving most of my belongings wasn't so hard since most of them were old and cheap anyway. I had only taken my good clothes and mementos of my mother, stowing everything in my campus locker.

For the first time in my life, I'd stepped into a club not to serve drinks or wipe tables but to get drunk. It was my version of giving life the finger. I was a lightweight, and it hadn't taken long for the alcohol to hit my system.

Since paranoia was my best friend, I inspected my arms and was relieved that I still had all my fingers. A dark-blue duvet covered my legs, making me wonder if I still *had* legs. I wiggled my toes. Great—still worked. Lifting my dress, I made sure I didn't have any fresh stitches or feel any pain. Someone could have stolen my precious organs. Satisfied that all my body parts were intact, I studied the room more closely.

To call it a room seemed an understatement. It was larger than my whole apartment, furnished with expensive, tasteful things. A wide window with heavy, pale-blue curtains encompassed almost the whole wall to my right, showcasing a prime view of the city. I realized I must be in a high-rise building.

Did I do something wilder than getting drunk last night? Like maybe—God forbid—sleep with a stranger? Lifting my butt, I did some Kegel exercises as if that would tell me if I had lost my virginity. Well, I wasn't sore.

I was panicking again…

"Deep breaths, Veronica. Deep breaths," I muttered, looking around the room again.

I scooted to the edge of the bed and stood, my bare feet sinking into a plush rug. Whoever owned this place must be loaded—and I had no intention of meeting him. What if he was a drug lord? Someone this rich must be. What if he wanted to fatten me up before selling my organs?

Calm down!

I spotted the en-suite bathroom and took advantage of it. When I was done, I slowly crept to the bedroom door and peeked out. Even in my panicked state, I couldn't help noticing the incredible surroundings. Everything looked sleek and modern. The space was wide and open. Bright sunlight slanted through the tall, wide windows. Paintings hung strategically on industrial-gray concrete walls, and an enormous flat-screen TV sat in front of an L-shaped black leather couch. Hardwood floors gleamed.

I sneered at the luxury of it.

Life is unfair, I mused as I walked through a hallway that opened into another wide-open space.

Where is the front door?

I stopped when I reached the kitchen. It had the same modern industrial feel as the rest of the place. There was a bar on the left side of the room with barstools tucked underneath. Crisp, white cupboards, granite countertops, glass pendant lights hanging from the vaulted ceiling, stainless-steel appliances—the whole works. My breath caught as I set eyes on someone standing in the corner. He was tall, his shirtless back showing he had tan skin, and I could see his muscles were rippling when he moved his arm.

I stood there, nervous and scared. As if he sensed my presence, he turned around. His eyes widened and his jaw fell open as he took in my appearance.

I knew that face.

Caleb. Caleb Lockhart!

Oh no, not him! This was not happening. I'd woken up in the lair of the campus man whore.

A piece of bread fell out of his mouth as he continued to gape at me. His wavy brown hair was mussed and sticking up everywhere, as if he too had just woken up. His chest and stomach were well defined. The long counter in front of him ended just below his waist so I couldn't see if he was—

Please, God, I hope he's wearing something down there.

And then he grinned. As if he had all the time in the world, his gaze leisurely traveled from the top of my head to my toes, then back up to my face. I felt my toes tingle.

"Hey, baby, you look like you've had a busy night," he drawled.

Oh God.

"Did we…? Did you…?" I stuttered, crossing my arms to hide my chest from his lascivious gaze.

One dark brow lifted as he waited for me to finish my question. My mouth felt dry, and my head was starting to throb. I looked down at my naked feet and wondered where I'd put my shoes. Silly, silly girl.

"Just tell me," I said finally.

"Tell you what exactly?" His eyes were laughing at me, and I could see his dimples. He knew exactly what I was talking about, but he seemed to find joy in torturing innocent people. *Jerk.*

When he stepped around the counter, I moved a step back and yelled, "Stay away from me!" At least he was wearing sweatpants.

He frowned, holding his hands up. "What the hell is wrong with you?"

My eyes frantically searched for a weapon nearby, in case he decided to attack me. I could grab one of the pans on the hanging pot rack if needed.

"Why am I here?"

"You don't remember?"

I had a sudden urge to pull my hair. "Remember what?"

His face darkened. "Some pervert nearly attacked you last night. I saved you." He shook his head. "He could have raped you."

My head started to throb. Memories from last night were starting to come back.

"And you threw up all over my car." He paused. "Twice."

"R-raped me?" I vaguely remembered resisting a guy's advances. What if it was him?

Caleb nodded, staring at me intently. The way his green eyes bored into me triggered a memory. A low, masculine voice murmuring, *I've been looking for you my whole life...*

I shook my head to clear it and glared at him. "How do I know you're not that guy?"

"Oh please," he scoffed, rolling his eyes. "I don't have to force a girl to sleep with me."

He stepped back, leaned against a butcher block behind him, and crossed his arms against his impressive chest, studying me with his head tilted to the side. The muscles in his arms flexed.

"Thank you," I said quietly, but I was still suspicious. Growing up in a rough area meant suspicion came naturally to me. "I don't remember much from last night."

"You were drunk," he stated.

"I think I remember that part."

"And you're not hungover?"

I shook my head.

"Amazing," he said, sounding impressed.

"Look, if you don't mind giving my shoes back, I can get out of your way." I assumed he knew where they were. I didn't find them in the bedroom.

"Not so fast."

"What?" My eyes shot to an espresso machine sitting on the counter five feet away. I could use that in case he decided to grab me. Could I lift it?

"You threw up all over my car, and I just got it a few weeks ago."

Oh. I bit my lip. "Isn't your dad rich?" I gestured uselessly at the luxury surrounding us. "Can't you just have somebody clean it for you?"

His eyebrows shot up. "So you're going to have someone else clean up your mess?"

I clenched my teeth. "What do you want from me?"

Leaning back, he pulled himself up to sit on the butcher block, his glorious body on uninterrupted display. I gulped.

"Do you have anywhere to go when you leave?" There was

a basket filled with apples beside him. He reached for one. How fortunate he was to reach for food whenever he wanted. He didn't have to fear being hungry…or homeless.

"What kind of question is that? I'm going home." I had no clue where home was, but he didn't know that.

Without removing his gaze from mine, he tossed the apple in the air, caught it, tossed it again. "And where is that?"

My stomach quietly growled. "It's none of your business."

"Well, I quite possibly saved your life. I believe in conserving energy, so I want to make sure you don't waste mine. I asked you last night where you live, and you told me you're homeless. Frankly, right now, you look like someone just stole your last dollar."

My mouth opened in shock.

He placed the apple back in the basket and crossed his arms again. Was he flexing in front of me?

"Why do you care?" I demanded.

It was a moment before he answered. "Do you really have somewhere to go?"

The mild, sympathetic tone did it. I felt my throat close and my eyes tear up. I could tell he was uncomfortable with my sudden display.

He jumped off the butcher block and went to open the fridge.

"Here," he said quietly, handing me a bottled water.

I tried to say thank you, but my throat was too tight. When I looked up, he was backing away from me.

"You know you stink, right?"

I laughed. I laughed so hard that I was almost hyperventilating. Then I started crying. I couldn't stop if I wanted to.

To keep myself from falling on my face, I squatted where I was and sat on the floor. My crying turned to ugly hiccup-sobbing. He must have thought I was insane.

"Why don't you stay here for a bit until you find an apartment?"

Shocked, I could only stare up at him.

He shrugged. "I know when someone is at the end of their rope," he added.

At the end of their rope? I glared at him, quickly wiping at my tears. I hated looking up at someone when I talked to them so I got back on my feet, struggling to pull my dress down. He was still taller, which made me angrier.

"Listen, pal, I may be homeless, but I am not accepting your charity."

We both fell silent.

The sound of the water bottle crinkling in my hand was followed by that of a steady stream of water spilling onto the floor.

Embarrassed, I closed my eyes. When I heard him clear his throat, I tried to calm my breathing by counting to ten before opening my eyes.

His eyebrows were raised as if he was waiting for me to say something. When I didn't, he continued.

"Where else will you go? A homeless shelter? Listen." He raised his index finger. "One, I live by myself, so you'll only have the pleasure of my company. Two"—he raised a second finger—"you're certainly safer here than at a shelter. And three"—he raised a third finger—"*ding, ding, ding*! You can stay here for free."

I narrowed my eyes. It all sounded too good to be true. "Why are you helping me?" Life had beaten me enough that I knew nothing came free.

He opened his mouth, but nothing came out. Then he shook his head. "I don't know."

Live with Caleb Lockhart. In this huge place. For free. My only other options were the shelter or live on the streets. "I'm not going to be your prostitute."

He looked insulted. "Do you really think I need one? Woman, have you seen this body? Besides," he added, grinning, "when you decide to sleep with me, you'll be the one paying *me*."

Wow. The size of his ego must constantly give him a headache. I gave him a disgusted look and pretended to yawn. "Everything that's coming out of your mouth sounds interesting. I don't know why I keep yawning."

Those green eyes widened and homed in on my face. I thought I'd pissed him off this time, but the most unexpected thing happened. He started laughing. "I like you," he said, chuckling. "I mean you're a knockout, but I didn't think it went beyond that."

Did he just insult me?

"I'm offering you a way out of your misery. Why don't you take it?" He pinched his nose with his fingers. "And could you please take a shower? You might be gorgeous, but I ain't spending time with a girl who smells like the sewer."

I huffed. He was right though—I smelled really, really bad. But… "Then what do you want in exchange?"

"Not everyone wants something from you," he replied grimly.

"Oh, is that what you think?" I laughed bitterly. "Everyone wants something one way or another. Haven't you learned that yet?"

He tilted his head to the side and studied my face again. I wondered what he saw when he looked at me. My looks and the shape of my body usually made people think I was always looking for *fun*. Fun was the last thing on my mind. I was too busy staying alive, too busy working for my next meal to think about anything else. Last night had been an anomaly.

I had no other good options—just shelter or street—and he was offering me a way out. He at least looked sincere. It was about choosing the lesser of two evils. I took a deep breath.

"I could clean," I said quietly.

Was I really doing this? Why not? The world hadn't given me a free ticket in so long. I was overdue for one.

"Sorry?" He blinked at me, and I wasn't sure if he was teasing or serious. "I didn't hear what you said."

I took another deep breath, and this time my voice was stronger. "I could clean your place in exchange for my stay."

"I already have someone come in three times a week for that," he answered.

"I can cook."

He frowned. "Don't string me along like that. That's not very nice."

I rolled my eyes.

"Can you really cook?" His face lit up. He looked like a little boy who had found the last cookie at the bottom of the jar.

"Yes," I answered, ignoring the crazy effect his smile had on me.

"Deal!"

This was too easy. "You said you live by yourself, but how can you afford this place?"

His expression shuttered. I hoped he didn't think I was trying to find out how much money he had. That I was a gold digger. But why *wouldn't* he think that? He didn't know me from Eve.

I might have been poor, but I wasn't a freeloader. My hands proved how hard I worked, and I was proud of that. One more year and I would get that diploma. I'd work my ass off to have a good life. I didn't need much—a steady job, a simple house, and a serviceable car would be more than enough to make me happy. And I would never go hungry again. I'd get there without help from anyone.

"Look," I hissed angrily. "I was only curious. If you think I'm some gold digger—"

He held a hand up. "Will you stop putting words in my mouth? Do you really think I want this life? This...this." He gestured to the whole room. "You think this makes me happy?" His jaw was set, his hands fisted.

"Yes!" I answered. I fell silent, incredulous. He had no concept of what it meant to go hungry, to not know where he was going to sleep next, to live in fear. We were worlds apart.

This was never going to work.

We both stood there awkwardly, but after a few seconds, he opened his mouth again, waggling his eyebrows as if nothing had happened. "Know what? You do my homework while you're cooking my dinner tonight."

So much for that moment. I opened my mouth, but nothing came out.

"Hold on," he said. "I didn't even get your name."

"Veronica Strafford."

"I'm Caleb Lockhart."

I didn't smile back, didn't tell him I already knew who he was. Who didn't? Everyone in our college knew about him.

"Which university do you attend?" he asked.

How did he know I was even attending one? "Letting me stay here doesn't mean I have to spill my guts, does it?"

"You actually did already. In my car, remember?" he pointed out dryly. "Can you please take a shower? Feel free to borrow my clothes. Even"—he grinned—"my underwear."

I snorted. We stood facing each other, unsure, lost in our thoughts. Was I doing the right thing by staying here? Where else would I go?

"You can stay in that bedroom where you slept last night. It has its own bathroom." He went back behind the counter, distancing himself from me. "I'm leaving soon. Make yourself at home."

I nodded, feeling awkward. Was this really happening? How could he leave me alone in his place when he didn't even know me? I could rob him blind, for all he knew.

"Thank you. I…" I paused, unsure. "Thank you," I repeated, meaning it.

He nodded.

I turned away from him, biting my lip. Where the hell was that room again? I looked to my left, then to my right. His apartment was enormous, and I had been in a panic when I left the bedroom.

"Problem?" he asked.

I jumped, spinning back around. I looked up—and up—to find him standing right behind me, smiling. This close and in my bare feet, he towered over me. "I-I forgot where the room is. Just tell me where it is, and I'll stay out of your way." I could feel myself blushing.

When he didn't reply, I glared at him. He was still smiling.

"What?" I demanded.

"Jeesh, hostile much?" He moved in front of me. "Follow me."

I walked behind him, trying not to stare at his body too much. I almost yelped when he suddenly glanced back over his shoulder. He winked at me and said, "Welcome to my place, Red. I hope you enjoy your stay."

CHAPTER
three

Caleb

Girls were my weakness.

I knew this, but I had never broken my rules for any girl.

Until last night.

Sweat trickled down my face as I gripped the ball in my hands, raised my arms, and took my shot. I cursed under my breath when I missed the second time.

What the hell was I thinking?

I'd already decided I'd give her money so she could rent her own place, but the second I saw her this morning—with the defiance in her dark eyes, but most of all, the sadness she tried so hard to hide—my plans had disappeared like a puff of smoke.

On the way back to the locker room, I caught the fresh towel Cameron threw at me and wiped my face with it. I was distracted, and practice had been brutal.

Justin appeared in front of me, jogging backward. "Did your

mommy forget to breastfeed you this morning, Lockhart? Your game sucked, dude."

I threw the towel at his face.

"Where'd you go last night?" Cameron asked, ignoring Justin's whiny complaints.

"Yeah," Justin piped up. "I saw you talking to that hot piece of ass at the club. Did you score?"

Why did I feel like punching his face? Justin always talked like his mouth came from a garbage dump. It hadn't bothered me before, but I found that I didn't like him talking that way about *her*. Besides, his stone-hard, gelled blond hair irritated me today.

I pulled off my sweat-soaked shirt, balled it up, and, without guilt, threw it at Justin's face. It boggled the mind how his blond hair stayed in place. He must have used epoxy.

"What the fuck, dude!"

Cameron laughed, but he sobered as he turned to me, his gaze piercing mine. He had the eeriest blue eyes I'd ever seen.

"Everything good?" he asked.

Opening my locker, I reached for my bag and straddled the bench to rummage for a fresh shirt and jeans.

"Yeah. Just need to get laid."

Justin snorted. "Like you'd have a problem in that department."

If he knew how hard I was shut down last night, he'd laugh his ass off. God, if he knew I couldn't even get Red's *phone number*, I'd never hear the end of it.

This morning on my way out, I'd stopped by her room and

suggested she give me her number so I could text her the lock code to my apartment door. Simple request. But *nooo*.

"Just tell it to me," she said.

"What if you forget it?" I waved my phone at her. "It's easier if I text you."

"I can memorize it," she insisted, raising her chin in challenge.

"Don't you have a phone?"

"I have a phone," she huffed. "But it's only for emergencies. Texts cost me a dollar each."

I stomped to my room to find a Sharpie.

"Hold out your hand, then." I wrote the code on her palm. Stubborn girl.

I was closing the locker door to head for the showers when my phone burped a text. For a second, I was excited, thinking it might be Red. But there was no way she'd be texting me. Since I didn't have her number, she didn't have mine.

> Sandra Bodelli: Hey, handsome. Want to come over?
> My roommate won't be here tonight.

I frowned. "Who's Sandra Bodelli?"

Justin sneaked behind me to look at my phone. "Damn. You're the man, Cal. Remember the girl from engineering who came to practice last week?"

I looked at him blankly.

He shook his head. "How can you forget? She put her number in your phone. Blond, big eyes"—he cupped his chest with his hands—"beautiful ass...ets?"

I shrugged. "I'll take it."

Justin roared like a maniac. I ignored him and texted Sandra that I'd meet her in an hour.

I'd forget Red tonight.

Slightly drunk and running on fumes, I stumbled back home at two in the morning. It was dark, but I didn't bother turning on the lights as I stripped out of my clothes in the living room.

Opening the fridge, I grabbed a carton of orange juice and—because I heard my mom's voice in my head telling me not to drink from the carton—grabbed a glass from the cupboard and poured. I chugged three glasses and let out a loud burp.

Ready to pass out, I was heading to my bedroom when a sharp pain hit my back.

"Oww! What the fuck?"

The lights turned on, blinding me as I crumpled to the floor in pain.

"Good *God!*" Red yelped, covering her eyes. "You're naked!"

"What the hell do you think you're doing?" I yelled, shooting her a murderous look. She was gripping my baseball bat, her eyes wild and round as saucers.

I knew it. She was a murderer, an assassin hired by some psycho to kill me.

"I'm so sorry! I thought you were a thief!" she yelled back.

A thief. In my own home?

She'd only hit my back, but everything hurt. My head, back, arms, legs. Moaning, I lay on my stomach on the cold floor.

"You better put that baseball bat down, or I swear I will paddle your ass black and blue," I threatened.

She must not have taken my threat seriously because I heard her move around. A moment later, a cloth landed on my bare ass. I was sure I'd find the humor in this once my body stopped hurting.

I felt her kneel beside me, her breath on my neck. "I'm sorry, Caleb. I really thought... Hey, are you okay?"

When she placed her hand on my shoulder, I flinched—not because her touch repelled me, but because it felt so damn good. She quickly withdrew her hand.

"Do I *look* okay?" My voice sounded harsher than I meant it to. "Why don't you just shoot me and get it over with?"

I could feel her glare drilling a hole in my head. "If you'd turned the lights on like a normal person, I wouldn't have hit you."

I had enough strength to lift my head and frown at her, but when I saw what she was wearing, I forgot my mad. She had on an oversize white T-shirt with a picture of a fat, orange cat drinking a margarita.

"Where'd you get the fat cat?" I couldn't help but grin.

She blinked. "What?"

"I don't think I own that shirt." I paused. "Do I?"

"You'd probably gain some respect from me if you did, but no. I stowed my stuff in my campus locker and went there to get it while you were out today."

Something must have been wrong with me because Sandra hadn't turned me on in her lingerie, but Red's shapeless shirt did. Or maybe it was just Red. I'd had to make up a lame excuse so I could leave Sandra and ended up spending the night drinking with Cameron instead.

"Why are you smiling now?" she demanded. "I swear there's something wrong with your head."

Was I smiling? I didn't even notice. Resting my cheek on the floor, I closed my eyes and breathed in her scent. I could smell the strawberry shampoo she'd used.

I decided strawberries were my favorite fruit from now on. Yeah, I was drunk. So what?

She was still kneeling beside me, close enough for me to touch. I wanted to flip over and pull her on top of me. Something told me that would get me a kick in the balls, so I stayed where I was, content to just breathe in her scent.

"I'm sorry, Caleb," she murmured after a while.

My God. This girl would be the death of me. One moment she was snarling like a wounded tiger, and the next she was as soft and sweet as a kitten.

"It's okay, Red. I think I have a few more limbs left for you to abuse. But just no more tonight, all right?"

I wiggled my fingers and feet for effect, but she didn't react.

Pulling her legs to her chest, she rested her cheek on top of her knees, and a lock of dark hair fell across her face. I had the strongest urge to tuck it behind her ear.

"Why call me Red? If you haven't noticed, my hair is dark."

My eyelids felt heavy, and I was about to close them when I noticed her toenails. She'd painted them a sexy red. And she wondered why I called her Red.

"You were wearing that hot red dress last night. And your lips. Your lips made me think of... I don't think you'd care to hear my thoughts about that."

Ignoring my comment, she got up from the floor.

"It's late. Do you need help getting to your room?" It sounded like she wanted me to say no.

"You know I'm naked, right?" I looked up at her. She was glaring at me. "This towel you covered my ass with isn't big enough to cover what's on my front."

What the hell did I just say? I expected her to stomp off, but she surprised me by laughing instead. It was a big, bold laugh so unguarded that it made me smile. I wanted her to keep laughing, but I was too exhausted to think of anything else to say.

"I can always get you a body bag," she offered. I could hear the smile in her voice.

"You're so creepy." I chuckled.

"Not as creepy as you."

I closed my eyes, grinning like a fool. "Are you flirting with me now, Red?"

If she replied, I missed it because the next thing I knew, I was waking up to the smell of bacon. I was still on the floor, but she had placed a pillow under my head and a blanket over me.

Groggy, I sat up and noticed my clothes weren't scattered on the floor anymore. She must have picked them up while I was asleep. My body still ached. Sleeping on the floor probably didn't help. I stood up and wrapped the blanket around my waist—for her sake—and headed to the kitchen. I stopped short in the hallway when I spotted her in front of the stove.

Warmth filled my chest. She was cooking breakfast.

For me.

I had to remind myself that she was just holding up her end of the bargain. Still, it made me happy.

I leaned against the wall, enjoying the view. There was something sweet and cozy about watching a girl cook breakfast for me. The smells, the sounds…the girl.

She'd tied her hair in a messy knot on top of her head, and a few tendrils had escaped, curling at the delicate line of her neck. The grace and fluidity of her movements reminded me that she was a fantastic dancer.

"Hey there, stranger," I greeted her as she turned around.

She squealed in surprise and almost dropped the plate.

"Are you always so jumpy in the morning?" I asked.

She gave me a halfhearted smile. I figured there was more to it than she was letting on—she had attacked me with a baseball bat last night—but I let it go. For now.

"Why don't you get dressed? Then you can eat your breakfast," she suggested.

Tongue tucked firmly in my cheek, I said, "You mean get undressed and eat you for breakfast?"

Sometimes I wondered if my mother had dropped me when I was a child. Even *I* thought my mouth needed to be soaped because of the things that came out of it. Red must have been getting used to me because she only shook her head.

I padded to my bedroom, brushed my teeth, and put on jeans.

By the time I headed back to the kitchen, she had a plate of bacon and another of eggs balanced on one arm. How the hell did she do that?

Watching her expertly put the plates on the counter, I took a seat.

"Three out of four shelves in your fridge are stocked with cartons of orange juice," she observed, her brows raised, curious.

"Yeah. Can you tell I hate the stuff?" I picked up my fork and watched her walk to the cupboard and pull out a glass. "Where'd you learn to cook?" I asked.

She took her time as she opened the fridge and poured orange juice in the glass before turning around to answer me. "My mom had three jobs when I was growing up, so I was by myself a lot. I had to learn how to cook or eat peanut butter and toast for the rest of my life."

I paused, thinking. "You like peanut butter?"

Something about her smile triggered a faint memory, but it was gone before I could catch it.

"It's my favorite," she answered.

"Okay, I'll get some, then."

"You don't have to," she said quickly.

"I know." And because I knew she'd argue if I said grass was green, I changed the subject. "Hey, I have an idea of how we can make this meal fun."

She gave me a dry look as she placed the glass of orange juice beside my plate and moved behind the breakfast bar. Away from my reach.

"You know those sexy French maid outfits?" I continued,

scooping eggs, bacon, and toast onto my plate. "Small black skirt, white apron, lacy headband? Of course you'd have to have the white stockings and high heels too. Oui, Monsieur Lockhart, I'll get that for you. Oui, Monsieur Lockhart, you look fantastique today. Fantastique."

"I have a question for you," she started, standing in front of me with her hands on her hips. "What exactly do you want to do *if* you grow up?"

With that, she turned and left.

What the hell did I do now? Bummed, I put my fork down. Leaning back in the chair, I rubbed my face.

I wanted her to eat breakfast with me.

I wanted her company.

What the hell was happening to me?

I felt like a dog begging for attention.

I was Caleb Lockhart. I never begged for a girl's attention. They were the ones who flocked around me, wanting my company.

I realized that I had been spoiled, and that this girl was very, very different.

Looked like I got my wish after all.

Veronica

My heart was pounding by the time I locked the bedroom door behind me. Still gripping the doorknob, I leaned my forehead against the wood and closed my eyes.

Did Caleb have to walk around half-naked all the time?

The guy was a walking poster boy. It was hard to pretend he didn't affect me. Sooner or later he'd see right through my stoic facade.

Caleb moved with relaxed self-confidence, too aware of his effect on the female population and *very* comfortable with it. He was exactly the type of guy I stayed away from.

Wasn't it ironic that I was living under the same roof with him now?

Pushing away from the door, I glanced at my watch. The campus library should be open. I needed to use the computer there to apply for jobs online and print copies of my résumé so I could bring them to businesses downtown. I had done this a few times before—to no avail—but I had to keep trying.

Esther Falls is one of the biggest cities in Manitoba, with a population of six hundred thousand. But the economy had not recovered fully after the recession. Now more than ever, it was hard to find a job, especially one that wouldn't conflict with my classes. I didn't know if I could even afford to finish my courses now.

Maybe it was time to move to a different province where jobs were more plentiful, but I loved being surrounded by the lakes of Manitoba. I appreciated the friendliness of the locals, the diversity of cultures and social practices. Besides, it wasn't like I could afford to move again.

I wondered where I'd be if Caleb hadn't offered me his spare bedroom. I owed him, and I'd find a way to pay him back somehow.

Gathering my books, I opened the drawer on my bedside table to store them and nearly shrieked. The drawer was brimming with condoms!

Good God. Was this room where Lockhart slept with his groupies? I could only hope that he changed the sheets. What if he didn't? Stripping the sheets, I decided to wash them later. Maybe sanitize the whole room too.

I took a shower and got ready for the day. I was double-checking everything in my bag as I left my room when I crashed into a very solid, wet body.

"Ow!" I cried out, rubbing my forehead.

"Hey, Red."

I looked up and was rendered speechless.

Caleb was shirtless again, his unbelievable chest gleaming with sweat. His hands held the ends of a white towel around his neck. There were small bandages on his fingers, and I could see calluses on his hands.

"Going somewhere?" he asked. His green eyes twinkled like he was up to no good.

I cleared my throat and nodded, refusing to look below his neck. "Work."

"Ah. I see." He paused. "Always so serious."

The heat emanating from his body was beginning to bother me. A lot. The way his vibrant green eyes studied me wasn't helping either. I took a step back.

There was a naughty gleam in his eyes as he asked, "Wanna see something?"

I narrowed my eyes suspiciously. "Not really."

His smile widened before he shamelessly stretched his impressive biceps. The lines and curves on his arms were tight, his skin tan and healthy.

"Watch this." With a wolfish grin, he turned to his side so that I could get a view of his butt. It was noticeably round and firm and... This was getting out of hand.

"Note the butt pop." He winked. "I'm popping it, popping it just for you. Keep your eyes on me. I haven't shown you the best part yet."

He turned and started moving the muscles on his chest. It looked like little bugs were twitching under his skin. It was creepy. I started laughing so hard that I had to wrap my arms around my stomach. This boy was insane.

"What do you think, girl? I got it good, huh? I got it really good."

I shook my head. "The only thing going good for you is that no one has picked you up for the zoo. Your cage is waiting. You'll be able to showcase yourself among your fellow apes there."

He batted his eyelashes. "You'd pay to see me. Admit it. Hey, Red?" His face turned serious as he asked in a low, deep voice, "Want a strip dance?"

We both jumped when we heard the buzz from the intercom.

Rubbing his face with his hand, he muttered, "Damn. I forgot I'm supposed to go to a charity event with my mother today. Can you hide in your bedroom for a few minutes? Be really, really quiet."

"Scared of Mommy?"

"Hell yeah. It might be awkward to explain why you're staying here with me. Just give me a few minutes. Half an hour tops, then you can go."

If his mom was going to have a problem with me staying here, then I'd better find another place as soon as possible. I needed to find a job today.

I let out a frustrated sigh. "I need to leave, Caleb. I have a lot of things to do today. I can tell her I'm housekeeping."

"No! You don't even have a broom with you. Trust me. I'll get rid of her quickly, and you'll be on your way. Okay?"

"Fine." I headed back to my room.

I stayed close to the door, listening to the sounds outside the bedroom. I heard the soft voice of an older woman, followed by Caleb's deeper tones. Twenty minutes later, there was a gentle rap on the door.

Cautious, I stayed where I was and waited. The door slowly opened an inch. "Red?"

I stood right behind the door, still out of view. "I'm here," I said.

"I have to go. So…I'll see you tonight?"

We stood on either side of the door, whispering like kids sharing secrets.

"Sure," I answered.

"Are you going to miss me?"

I paused. "Sure, Caleb."

He cleared his throat. "Later, Red," he said softly as he closed the door.

"Later, Caleb," I whispered to no one.

CHAPTER

four

Veronica

I SPENT THE REST OF MY MORNING AT THE SCHOOL LIBRARY, USING their computer to apply for jobs online, print my résumé, and make a list of businesses that were hiring.

Armed with a stack of résumés, I went to every business on my list. When that didn't yield anything promising, I felt desperate enough to submit my résumé to everyone else.

It had been four hours of nonstop walking, filling out forms, and repeatedly hearing "I'm sorry, we're not hiring" and "We'll give you a call." I was exhausted, discouraged, and starving.

The pancakes I'd had for breakfast had been digested long ago. I knew I should eat something, but I didn't want to waste the money I had left on food. I could wait until I got back to Caleb's apartment to eat.

I let out a sigh, almost tripping when the sole of my shoe started to fall off.

Overwhelmed, I stared at the gaping space between the upper and now-separating sole of my sneaker. My throat felt thick, and I had an intense urge to scream at the joke that was my life.

It would be laughable if an old, worn-out shoe was the last straw that finally broke me.

When Mom was alive, we barely scraped by with our two incomes. When her condition got worse and she had to quit her job, I had to take out a credit line on top of my school loans to keep a roof over our heads.

Eventually, she had to stay in the hospital, and I rented a bed space in a house with five other people to save money. *Safe* was a foreign concept in that house. I started carrying a pocketknife and kept my valuables in my school locker. When Mom passed away, I saved as much as I could and left the small town where we'd lived for over ten years. I had been commuting into Esther Falls for both my jobs, so moving there made sense. I rented an apartment close to the university, where I was completing a two-year program in culinary arts.

The studio apartment was as small as a postage stamp, the furniture old and secondhand, and the surrounding neighborhood was rough. But it was mine.

I had worked hard to pay for everything in it. I had privacy. I didn't need to share the bathroom with anyone, didn't need to clean up someone else's mess, didn't need to worry every night that someone would steal my things or…something worse.

All that was gone now.

Due to bankruptcy, the dance studio where I'd worked since high school had closed down without warning, leaving me broke. I also had a part-time job as a server at a small restaurant, but there was no way my hours there could cover my bills, and I fell behind. When my landlord kicked me out for failing to pay two months of rent, something inside me broke.

Then I met Caleb, and here I was.

When things became too rough to handle, Mom always said something to cheer us both up. I remembered the feel of her weak hands squeezing mine as she wasted away in that hospital bed. "Everything that happens in your life is to prepare you, Veronica," she'd said. "Metal has to go through fire to melt and be turned into a sword. Be strong because this is just a test. You are being melted, being molded into a stronger person. This burning will pass, and you will find rest. Don't give up, honey."

Closing my eyes and taking deep breaths, I composed myself. Life had taught me that it didn't wait for anyone. I had to move on. When I opened my eyes, I was ready to tackle the rest of the day, broken shoe be damned.

It was late when I arrived at Caleb's apartment. I was exhausted, but I couldn't help the grin that spread across my face. I might not have gotten a job offer, but I'd gotten my résumé into as many hands as possible. It had been a very productive day.

Opening the fridge, I wondered how fast I could make Caleb's dinner so I could slip into my bedroom before he returned home—but the fridge was as empty as my bank account.

I groaned in defeat when I heard the front door open. But when I heard heavy footsteps coming from the living room, I reached for my pocketknife in case it wasn't Caleb. I'd already made one mistake, but still—better safe than sorry.

"Red?"

I let out a sigh of relief when I heard Caleb's voice. He was sprawled on the couch, remote control in hand as he turned on the TV. His black leather shoes and dinner jacket decorated the floor. Discarding his clothes there seemed to be a habit.

I stood behind him, admiring the way the bronze in his hair glinted in the light.

"What's for dinner?" he asked, propping his feet on the coffee table.

"I just got back. I'll make you something now if you want."

He looked over his shoulder at me. If my heart tripped—which it totally didn't—it was a normal and healthy reaction to seeing a gorgeous face. It didn't mean anything.

"Are you trying to butt out of our bargain already?" he asked, turning back to the TV.

Insulted, I put my hands on my hips, glaring at him. "Unless you want orange juice soup with Pop-Tart croutons, you need to go to the store. We don't have any groceries."

He rested his head on the couch headrest and arched up and over so that he was looking at me upside down. "You're giving me a neck injury. Why don't you come around so we can talk like normal human beings?"

I narrowed my eyes at him.

He sighed. In a smooth move, he straightened, turned, then climbed to sit on top of the couch. He playfully studied me. "I'm bored," he stated.

I raised my eyebrows. Did he expect me to entertain him? "And?"

"You owe me dinner."

"I told you—"

A grin stretched across his face as he loosened his red tie. "You can pay me another way."

My jaw fell open.

He laughed. "Why is your mind always in the gutter?"

I blinked once. Twice. *My* mind was always in the gutter?

He pushed off the couch, put his shoes back on, grabbed his keys and helmet from the coffee table, and walked past me. I thought he was going to leave when I felt his hand circle around my wrist, dragging me out the door with him.

"Oh for God's sake, where are you taking me?"

God, he was tall. For every step he took, I had to take two to keep up.

He pressed the elevator button. "For a ride."

"A *ride*?"

He started laughing as he pulled me inside the elevator, pressed the Down button, and watched the door close. "I've never met a girl who twisted my words as much as you do. You have a filthy mind, Red. *Filthy*."

"What the… A filthy mind!" I sputtered.

When the elevator door opened, he dragged me into the basement parking garage.

"A ride." He clucked his tongue. "On my bike."

I pulled my wrist from his hold, rubbing my hand against my jeans. His skin was hot and made me feel strange things.

He stopped and glanced back at me. "Problem?"

"It's Sunday night. Don't you have class tomorrow?"

"So?" He shrugged a shoulder. "I'm in college, not high school. I can skip class if I want."

"Of course you can. You're rich. You don't have to work for anything."

His eyes darkened, and he shoved his hands in his pockets, giving me a long look. "Do you like to be judged for being poor? You think having money saves me from pain?"

Chastised, I fell silent. When I opened my mouth to apologize, he cut me off. "You coming or not?"

I nodded, feeling guilty, and followed behind.

When he stopped in front of a sleek black machine, I stared at him in disbelief. It looked like it ate kids for breakfast.

"Ever ride a bike before?" he asked, tossing his black helmet from hand to hand like a basketball.

I took a step back. "I'm not riding that monster."

His laugh was low and sexy. He grabbed my wrist again and pulled me close—closer than was necessary.

"I don't know," he whispered, his thumb stroking my palm in lazy circles. "I have a feeling you're going to like it."

My breath hitched, and he chuckled when I pulled away.

"N-no. I'd like to keep my limbs intact, thank you very much."

His eyes danced at me playfully. "Yeah? Where's the fun in that? Rule number one," he said, gently placing the helmet on my head, "safety first." He fastened the straps tightly under my chin.

"Rule number two," he continued, flipping the visor down. I felt slightly claustrophobic so I flipped it back up. "When I'm making a turn, lean your body toward the turn. Never the opposite way. Got it?"

"Sure."

He smiled down at me, staring for a moment. I wanted to bottle the color of his vibrant green eyes. Realizing I was staring, I shook the thought from my mind and snapped, "What?"

He shrugged, then swung his long leg to straddle his bike. "Hop on."

When I didn't, he turned his head, eyebrows raised and eyes glinting with challenge. At that moment, he looked like a gorgeous devil who'd take my soul to hell—and enjoy every minute of it. "You scared?"

My skin prickled with irritation. It would take more than a pretty boy on a big-ass motorcycle to scare me. I'd prove him wrong. I huffed and climbed on the bike, grabbing the sides of my seat.

"Where's *your* helmet?" I demanded.

"Only have one," he replied. He was so close—close enough for me to catch his masculine scent. "Nobody rides this bike but me. You're the first passenger."

He turned the engine on, revving it a few times. The bike vibrated angrily.

"Forgot to tell you the last rule," he said conversationally, looking over his shoulder. I could hear the mischief in his tone.

"I'm sure you're going to tell me."

He grinned. "Hold on to me. Really, really tight."

"No, thanks."

"Suit yourself."

I cried out as the bike zoomed forward, and my arms automatically went around him. I could feel his shoulders and hard stomach shaking with laughter.

He *so* did that on purpose! Fine, he won this round.

I vowed the next one would be mine, as we exited the garage with a roar.

I didn't like the bike. It was noisy and dangerous. But as we streaked down the road, and the wind whipped cool and damp on my skin, I felt…

Freedom.

I closed my eyes and for a moment, just a moment, allowed myself to enjoy the thrill of it.

My heart climbed into my throat when he zigzagged through curves and punched around street corners. I remembered what he'd told me and leaned to the left or right when he did, my arms tightening around him even more.

"Where are we going?" I yelled.

"Flying."

"What?"

"You'll see," he said simply.

We stopped talking after that. I lost track of time and slowly forgot about my worries and the threats of life hanging over my head. I watched the sun as it dipped low in the azure sky and birds glided in the wind above.

As we neared an old, rusted railroad bridge, Caleb stopped the bike at an empty lot. A sign that said ROAD CLOSED/ROUTE

BARRÉE in big, bold letters was bolted to one of the beams. Vines clung and twisted around the beams, so thickly the steel barely peeked through.

There were groups of people in various states of undress everywhere—girls in their underwear or bikinis, some wrapped in blankets or scarves and guys mostly in their shorts or boxers. The weather had warmed up considerably tonight, but it was still a little chilly, and the water must be cold, but everyone seemed to be having fun. They were shouting cheers and howling with laughter. I smelled the sweet-pungent scent of smoke and burned meat and noticed a crowd gathered around a barbecue and a big bonfire on the uneven hill sloping below the bridge. Makeshift tables were set up here and there.

Suddenly, I realized I was plastered to Caleb's back, my chin resting on his shoulder. I quickly moved back. His body tensed as if he knew why I needed distance from him.

And then I saw two guys shouting at each other on the bridge. When the bigger of the two pushed the smaller one, his arms flailed like helicopter blades before the bigger guy shoved him against the railing. The smaller guy lost his balance and fell over it.

Good God!

"No!" I screamed in horror.

My heart fell to my stomach as I heard a splash. I jumped from the bike, ran, and gripped the railing, gathering the courage to look down. A head broke the surface of the dark water, followed by a whoop of victory.

I blinked, realizing that this was a party where pushing people off a bridge was considered normal, and that the bridge wasn't as high above the lake as I'd thought. The guy was already climbing out of the water, up the hill, and back to the bridge where he would probably jump off again. I could feel the heat climbing up my cheeks as I heard laughter around me. I'd never seen people do this kind of thing before. What had I gotten myself into? I turned around slowly, embarrassed.

Why hadn't Caleb told me? What a jerk!

He swaggered toward me, mischief lighting his eyes. "I'm sorry, Red. I should've told you."

He didn't look sorry at all. I wanted to slap the smile off his face. I glared at him instead.

"What?" He chuckled.

His dress shirt was already unbuttoned, and he shrugged it off, dropping it carelessly to the pavement. I'd seen him shirtless before, but that didn't matter. I couldn't help but look and appreciate.

His body was a work of art. Long and lean and tan. His arm muscles flexed as he reached for his belt buckle, and then...I turned my eyes away.

"First time a girl's turned away when I'm removing my pants."

I blushed harder. "Really? I didn't know there was anything interesting down there to see."

When he didn't respond, I looked up. His smile was naughty as he said, "Take a good look then."

Oh, he was maddening! Provoking, definitely. Annoying, absolutely. That was all. There was no way I found him interesting. Not at all.

But I couldn't keep my eyes away as I watched him jump on the railing with a smooth motion, his balance impeccable as he turned around and faced me, wearing his boxers. A daredevil grin appeared on his lips, and his eyes gleamed with cockiness as they watched me. Eyes still on me, he spread his arms wide and let himself fall. I heard him yell before he hit the water.

Pulse racing with excitement, I gripped the railing, searching for him. When he resurfaced, I let out a sigh of relief.

"Are you Caleb's flavor of the month?"

Puzzled, I looked at the girl standing beside me. She was beautiful, with blond hair and a curvy body showcased in an infant-sized orange bikini. Her eyes were big and set wide apart, reminding me of an alien. The look she gave me was unfriendly.

"No," I said stiffly.

She raised an eyebrow. "Why are you with him, then?"

"Babysitting," I replied, turning from her and deciding to ignore her.

She scoffed and walked away.

I had to be careful not to hang around Caleb if I wanted to be left in peace. Clearly, the most popular guy on campus came with a pack of rabid female hyenas who wouldn't think twice about clawing out the eyes of their competition. Which I most definitely was not.

"Red!"

I spun around and watched Caleb jog toward me. His wet hair was plastered to his forehead. Water trickled down his lithe body. Jeez, could he turn it off for a minute?

"Your turn," he panted, stopping in front of me. He bent forward and rested his palms on his knees, breathing hard.

I was too busy ogling him to process his words, and it took a moment to realize what he'd said.

"Nuh-uh. Unlike you, I'm not suicidal."

"What happened to the girl I met at the club?"

"That wasn't me."

Deliberately, he straightened his body inch by gorgeous inch until he stood in all his poster boy glory.

"Come on, Red. Live a little. Or are you scared and prefer to stay in your shell?"

When I just looked at him coolly, he shook his head, shooting me a disappointed look before he turned his back, dismissing me.

Hot—I felt hot with anger. How dare he! Spoiled rich brat. Irresponsible, reckless, suicidal maniac!

I was tough. He didn't know me. I toed off my sneakers and took off my shirt, ignoring the surprised whoas and catcalls around me.

Let them look! I knew I looked good. Good enough that I'd had a short modeling stint—until the photographer asked me to pose naked. I ran out of there faster than he could say *strip*.

Caleb turned, his eyes widening in surprise. I looked at him directly, *defiantly*, as I unbuttoned my jeans and wiggled out of them. I was wearing my best underwear—a matching lacy red bra and panties. They weren't exactly new, but they still looked damn sexy. The next thing I knew, I was climbing on top of the railing, and seconds later, I was up in the air.

"Wait!" I heard him call out.

But he was too late.

God help me, I'm going to die, I thought darkly as I felt the cold wind slap my face. While I was suspended in the air, the moment felt endless. I felt horror and shock when my body hit the freezing water. Gravity pulled me down, down, down... *Where the hell is the bottom?*

Panicking, I fought my way up. When I reached the surface, I gulped in blessed sweet air.

I did it! I freaking did it!

All of a sudden, I felt hands grip my shoulders, shaking me.

"Are you crazy?"

Kicking my legs to stay afloat, I blinked the water out of my eyes and saw Caleb's face wild with incredulity.

"Yes!" I shouted.

I felt euphoric, exhilarated. My chest felt full, like it was about to burst.

"Again!" I yelled.

He laughed, the kind of laugh that was carefree and reckless, and I felt...happy. It took me a moment to recognize the feeling. It had been so long since I'd felt it.

In one night, this boy had brought me out of the shadows and into the bright light.

Dangerous. He was dangerous.

"Does anything hurt?" he asked. He stroked my arms with his palms, up and down, up and down, gently, slowly, until tingles zipped down my arms. They shot straight to my stomach, bursting into butterflies. It was the way he looked at me, I realized.

The way he held me. Caught in the moment, I could only shake my head.

"What a wild girl you are, Red."

Water trickled down his forehead, sliding down his nose to his top lip. His tongue slipped out to taste it. "Show me more."

I shivered, but surely only because I was getting cold.

I could admit to myself that Caleb excited me. He was like a trip to the jungle: mysterious, adventurous, and dangerous... uncharted territory. If I wasn't careful, I could get lost and never find my way out again.

We climbed up to the bridge for another round, and another, and another until I lost count of how many times Caleb and I jumped off. He never left my side.

He was doing somersaults and other crazy moves that had my heart leaping in my chest. When I resurfaced one last time, I expected him to swim beside me, but he was nowhere in sight. I went down again, opening my eyes underwater to search for him, but it was too dark.

"Caleb?"

Tiny prickles of fear climbed up my spine. I went under again, searching.

Nothing.

The scream was trapped in my throat as I felt something grab my waist and pull me further under. I twisted around and found Caleb laughing, water bubbles escaping his mouth. My eyes narrowed as he swam away.

Oh, it's on! I surfaced, then raced after him, intending to dunk him, but instead of swimming away, he turned around.

I squeaked, swimming away from him as fast as I could, but he was faster. I felt his hand grab for me under the water, but instead of my leg, his fingers grasped the fabric of my panties, then moved up as he cupped my hips with both palms and dragged me underwater before he swam away. I was about to chase after him again when I felt the band on my panties snap apart. *What the hell?* My eyes widened in shock as I felt the band break and the material float away from my hips.

Oh God.

My hands automatically covered my front and back, trying to pull the pieces of the panties back in place. The fabric was thin lace and not exactly brand new. It had just torn apart when Caleb had grabbed it. Now I was running out of air and had to resurface.

Oh God, oh God, oh God.

I broke the surface and spotted Caleb ten feet away. If he pulled me underwater again, he would see...

"Caleb!"

My alarmed tone caught his attention. He paused, his eyes scanning around me. "What's wrong? Are you hurt?"

I tightened my grip on the torn garment, treading water as he swam closer.

Rubbing the water from his eyes, he studied my face with concern. "Red?"

I bit my lip. "Could you...could you get my jeans?"

He frowned. "Okay?"

"Right now."

He looked at me like I had sprung another head. "Right now?"

"Right now," I said through gritted teeth.

"Why?"

"Please." My face burned. "Just get them."

He narrowed his eyes. "What are you not telling me?"

I wanted to scream with frustration. Why couldn't he just get them?

"I'm not moving until you tell me why," he insisted.

I groaned, pressing the heel of my hand to my forehead—but when I felt the material floating away again, I quickly held it down.

He wasn't going to budge. I had to tell him now…

"My…panties."

His eyes automatically shot down to the water.

"Don't look!" I yelled.

A wolfish smile spread on his lips, a twinkle in his green eyes. "What about your panties?" he drawled.

I cleared my throat. "The band tore apart."

"Huh?"

"The band holding it all together, it…" I closed my eyes, breathing for a moment before opening them again.

"Tore apart?" he provided.

I wondered what he would say if he knew he'd caused the band to break. He would never stop teasing me.

"Maybe you need help buying…panties next time. From an expert." He winked.

I glared at him.

"Did you tear them apart…on purpose?" he prodded.

I clenched my teeth. He was not going to let it go.

"You did it, you big jerk! When you dragged me down earlier…"

His grin reminded me of the Cheshire cat in *Alice in Wonderland*. I glared at him, daring him to say something.

"Just. Get. My. Jeans," I grated out.

His eyes were still gleaming, which made me nervous. What was he thinking?

"If I get them," he said casually, as if he were talking about the weather, "what do I get for it?"

"*What?*"

He chuckled, low and sexy. He reached for a lock of my hair, but I jerked back, moving away from him, kicking underwater while holding my fragmented panties. He only gave me a knowing grin and leaned into a backstroke, leisurely floating around me, circling me, like a shark sniffing prey. "I think you heard me."

"Caleb," I warned, but suddenly I was feeling giddy.

"So what will it be?"

"If you don't get my jeans right now, I will… I will…" I bit my lip, trying to think of a clever threat. But it was impossible to use my brain cells when I was almost naked, and Caleb Lockhart was looking at me like he wanted to eat me in one bite. "Poison your orange juice!" I finished lamely.

He laughed. I froze in horror as his hands drifted under the water.

"What the hell are you doing?"

"You're going to owe me for this one, Red." His hands resurfaced, and he handed me his dripping boxers.

"Are you freaking kidding me? You're not going up there naked, are you?"

He laughed harder.

"I'm serious!"

"It's not your lucky night, Red. I wore boxers *and* briefs today. You know, for support." He winked. "Usually it's just boxers. That's for future reference."

I exhaled loudly as I grabbed the boxers from him and tried tugging them on, but I discovered it wasn't easy to put on clothing underwater. Caleb stared at me with a foolish grin, enjoying the show.

I felt so giddy. All the things that I'd done tonight, what I had let myself be tonight... I'd never done anything so reckless. I'd never had so much fun in my entire life.

"Hungry?" he asked.

I nodded as we both got out of the water. He playfully pulled a lock of my hair as we climbed up to the bridge again. He was just wearing briefs, but he walked with confidence, comfortable in his own skin. I gulped as I caught sight of his thick, muscled legs.

"They're grilling hamburgers on the other side of the bridge. Wanna get some?"

I nodded again.

He grinned. "Great. Give me a minute, will you?"

He jogged away, and when he came back, he handed me his dress shirt. I was going to ask why he didn't just grab my clothes, but the way he looked at me made me close my mouth.

"Don't want you getting cold," he murmured, his voice rough as he watched me put on his dress shirt.

I blushed, feeling self-conscious.

"It needs something," he whispered.

My breath caught as he stepped closer, his eyes locked on mine. Slowly, his hand reached for the collar around my neck, and when his finger brushed my skin, I shivered.

"I need to button this," he explained softly.

He didn't take his gaze off mine as he held the sides of his shirt together and leisurely closed the top button.

"And this." He continued to speak softly, reaching for the second button.

My head swam. What the hell was he doing to me? I bit my lip and stepped back.

"I can do it," I breathed.

His smile was wolfish. "Sure, Red."

After I'd finished buttoning the shirt, Caleb pulled me to the barbecue site, refusing to let me change into my jeans.

I didn't mind a crowd, but I'd rather not socialize unless I had to. Trouble came when I mixed with people, and I didn't need trouble in my life, especially now.

He got me a hamburger, and I ate it quietly while we mingled with everyone—*well*, while he mingled. Everyone flocked around him. I realized it wasn't just his perfect looks or his popularity that made people want to be around him—it was his charisma. He was so…genuine.

Caleb was like the sun. He was so warm, so big and bright that you couldn't help but come closer. But what would happen if I got too close?

"Caleb," a female voice purred.

I turned to see the blond girl who'd reminded me of an alien sashay toward Caleb.

"Daidara."

Was that what they named them on their planet nowadays? The familiar way Caleb smiled at her made my stomach roil. It was obvious they had slept together.

So what? Caleb was a womanizer. It shouldn't surprise me. But my heart suddenly felt heavy, and I wanted to go home. I climbed back up to the bridge to look for my clothes, but I couldn't find them anywhere, so I went to where Caleb had parked his motorcycle. I'd just wait for him there until he was ready to leave.

A number of vehicles were parked nearby, and people were milling around them. Across from me was a group of college guys leaning against a blue truck. They laughed among themselves, but one of them caught my attention.

He didn't join in their laughter, strumming a song on his guitar instead. His head was bowed low, caught in the music. Then he looked up, his head turning in my direction.

It was too dark to see his face clearly, but I could tell he was looking at me. Something about him compelled me to look back. He tilted his head to the side, as if waiting for me to say something. I turned my eyes away.

I crossed my arms, feeling a little cold and wishing Caleb would finish up.

"Looks like you need this," a raspy masculine voice said from behind me.

I turned around and blinked at the heart-stopping face. It was the guy with the guitar. His features were sharp and beautiful, and his smile was crooked as he casually reached for my hand, turning it palm up and placing a blue towel there.

Someone shouted, and he looked over his shoulder. He shouted back before facing me again. "I'll see you around, Angel Face," he said. Then he jogged back to his friends, his guitar slung behind his shoulder.

That was how Caleb found me. He frowned as he turned to look at the guy who had given me the towel. When he turned to face me, his eyes were cold.

"Cover up, will you?" he muttered.

"What the hell is wrong with you?"

He shrugged, grabbing the towel from my hands and handing me my clothes. I put them on silently. Caleb walked around me, and I had a feeling he was blocking the guys from looking at me while I got dressed.

"Let's go," he said bluntly.

He swung onto his bike, looking dangerous. He wasn't smiling anymore. My good mood evaporated.

I climbed on the bike behind him, awkwardly wrapping my arms around him. He tensed when I touched him, and I quickly pulled away, stung by his reaction.

He stopped me, holding both my arms and wrapping them around his torso. When I felt the heat from his back, I inhaled sharply. I fought the urge to get as far away from him as possible.

The ride was quiet this time. When we got back to his building and rode the elevator together, it was awkwardly quiet. I could feel him thinking. What if he changed his mind and wanted to kick me out now? I didn't care. I'd leave in a heartbeat. I would live on the streets if need be, or in a shelter. Anywhere.

He entered the code to his apartment. When the alarm

beeped green, he opened the door for me, but I didn't step inside. Throwing a glance at the elevator, I debated whether I should make a run for it.

"Red."

My breath caught at the look in his eyes. The green surrounding his pupils had deepened, darkened. He stood close enough for me to touch, but he was the one who reached out and tucked a strand of my hair behind my ear.

"Come inside," he whispered. "Please."

Like a snake mesmerized by a charmer, I stepped inside, watching as Caleb closed the door behind him.

I could feel his eyes on me, hear his soft breathing—and the loud beating of my heart. When I lifted my eyes to his, I gasped at the intensity I saw there.

"Thank you," he whispered.

"For what?" I whispered back.

A soft, secret smile appeared on his lips. "For showing me something different tonight."

With that, he walked away.

CHAPTER

five

Veronica

I was determined that Caleb and I wouldn't see each other the next morning, so I woke up earlier than usual. No one had ever occupied my thoughts as much as he had last night.

"Thank you for showing me something different tonight."

What had he meant by that? Did he mean I was different from all the girls he dated? But he was a pro at this. It must be a line he used to make girls fall for him.

I shouldn't fall for his tricks so easily. Last night I had decided to limit our interactions. I didn't want him to find out that we attended the same school. The less he knew about me, the better.

I stifled a yawn as I cooked the rest of the eggs I'd found in the fridge.

It was common courtesy to inform him of my schedule, rather than coming and going whenever I wanted. So I'd started leaving sticky notes on the fridge for him. Peeling off a note, I wrote:

Caleb,

Made some eggs for breakfast. We have to get groceries later. I'll be back after 5.

Veronica

Caleb's apartment was in the ritzy part of town where there were no bus stops, so I had to walk twenty minutes to reach the closest one. Even then, the bus ride to school took an hour. If I had a car, it would only take half an hour to drive to school.

Summer break was just around the corner. I felt my spirits rise. I could work more hours and earn enough money so I could rent my own apartment and pay back Caleb. I knew he didn't want or need my money, but it was a point of pride for me to repay him eventually.

My classes were long and boring, and I found myself thinking about him. I pinched myself hard to stop. This was crazy. I had to pull myself together.

It was 5:20 p.m. by the time I returned to his apartment building. I was waiting for the elevator door to open when I felt someone standing beside me. I knew right away it was him. His presence demanded to be acknowledged.

Looking up, I caught him watching me with amused eyes and his usual smile.

"Hi," he said.

"Hi." I trained my eyes on the elevator door.

I could still feel his eyes on me.

The elevator doors opened. I stepped forward.

"Wait."

I turned. Why was my heart beating so fast?

"Want to go get those groceries now?"

No. I don't want to spend more time with you. I don't want you to look at me with those intense green eyes.

Instead I said, "Sure."

"Got my car back from the shop." He beamed as we walked past the concierge. "Parked out front."

That explained why he was taking the elevators at the main entrance. He usually entered from the basement garage.

I noticed what he was wearing now: a gray beanie, a dark-blue henley, black jeans, and black boots. He walked ahead so he could open the car door on the passenger side for me, and then I saw the print on the back of his shirt that read *I Was Born Ready.*

What a perfect description of him. I suppressed a smile as he closed my door and walked to the driver's side of the car.

After getting in, he started the car and pulled onto the street. He was quiet as he drove. And I wondered if he felt the charge in the air that came from being in such close proximity. Because I felt it, skimming my skin, teasing my senses.

Did it matter? It wasn't like I was going to act on it… I wasn't even slightly curious. Nope, not curious at all.

Liar, liar, pants on fire.

He swung the car into a parking space in front of the grocery store. I got out as fast as I could, heading straight to get a shopping cart. I fumbled as I tried to slip the dollar coin into the slot to release the lock on the shopping cart. The coin fell to the ground.

"So," he began, bending down to pick it up. His pants tightened around his legs...and around a very, very sexy butt. I quickly looked away before he caught me ogling him.

"What should we get?" he asked, inserting the coin himself. He pulled the cart free and proceeded to the store entrance.

I shrugged. "What do you like to eat?"

"Hamburger, fries, steak, pasta, seafood? And..."

I glanced at him when he didn't continue. He had a secretive smile on his lips.

What the hell was he thinking now?

"And?" I prompted.

"You," he replied. I could hear the smile in his voice.

I rolled my eyes.

Yeah, right. Me and possibly the whole blond population, I thought darkly.

The seafood section was closest, so I told him to head there first.

"Look at these poor creatures," he said, his voice as excited as a child's.

I glanced over and saw him pointing at a bunch of huge crabs in a tank.

"I think that one is staring at you," he teased.

I chuckled. "Which one?" I asked, unable to resist sharing his good mood.

"That one." He pointed at the biggest crab, its eyes poking out of its head. "Looks like that guy from *Star Trek*."

I snorted.

"Damn. I remember wanting one for a pet when I was four," he continued, leaning over the top of the aquarium. His nose scrunched up. "How do you even cook them?"

"You boil them alive," I answered.

His eyes rounded. "What the hell? That is just *so* wrong."

He looked so horrified—and so cute—that I wanted to laugh.

"Yep. That, or you can freeze them alive," I added.

"You're kidding."

I shook my head no.

"That is so not the way I want to die."

I pressed my lips together to keep from laughing as I took in his expression. He looked so serious.

Grabbing a package of shrimp from the freezer, I placed it in the cart. Caleb was still standing in front of the aquarium, now with a huge grin on his face. I walked over to stand beside him, curious to know what he found so amusing. I bit my lip as I saw one crab climb on top of another, their pincers joined together so I couldn't even tell which pincer belonged to which crab.

"These are some kinky crabs." Caleb laughed. "They're doing it in front of us. Look! Exhibitionists, the lot of them."

I tapped his shoulder. "Come on, pervert, or we're never going to get out of here."

I told him to pick whatever he wanted, and I'd come up with a way to cook it. He pulled stuff off shelves randomly and filled our cart.

"Get whatever you want," he said, generous as ever. He pushed the cart into the cookies and chips aisle.

Out of the corner of my eye, I spotted a box of chocolate cupcakes with peanut butter frosting topped with glittery sprinkles that looked like they would melt in my mouth. I let out a sigh and continued walking past.

"Wait. I want some cupcakes," Caleb announced, grabbing the box I was just eyeing.

I doubted he really wanted them. A guy that cut and lean didn't eat sweets. He definitely saw me eyeing those cupcakes. Why was he being so nice? I was supposed to *not* like him. But he was just so…thoughtful.

An older woman wearing the store's uniform was giving out samples of food. "Want to try some?" she asked.

"Sure, ma'am. Thank you." Caleb politely reached for the small cookie in a cupcake wrapper she was holding out for him. "I'll grab one for the lady, as well," he added, motioning toward me.

The older woman smiled and asked me, "Chocolate, vanilla, or peanut butter?"

"She'll want the peanut butter," Caleb replied before I could. "It's her favorite."

I looked at him for a moment, surprised that he'd remembered. When I caught him looking back at me with a grin, I looked away.

I was just reaching for the cookie when he fished it out of the wrapper. My lips parted in surprise. He placed the treat in my open mouth, his thumb briefly making contact with my tongue. His index finger lingered on my bottom lip, rubbing it gently. His eyes became hooded as they watched me. They looked...hungry.

"Sorry, just some cream on your lip there," he said, not sounding sorry at all.

I felt hot. I knew I was blushing. Embarrassed, I spun around and walked away.

By the time we were at the cashier, our cart was overflowing. *This could feed a family of twenty*, I thought. I turned away and hummed to myself when the cashier told him how much the bill was. I was scared to hear it.

By the time we hauled everything into his apartment, I was exhausted. Just looking at the number of bags on the counter made me shudder. There were even bags on the floor. Together, we worked to get everything put away.

My heart beat faster every time I caught him looking at me. Or when he accidentally grazed his hand against mine. We were both exhausted and hungry by the time we finished, so he ended up ordering pizza.

Something about the way he looked at me pulled at my heart. I didn't like it. All of a sudden, I felt exposed and vulnerable. When the pizza came, I grabbed a slice and went back to my room.

I crossed my legs and sat on the floor beside my bed. Chewing my pizza, I tried to calm the knots in my stomach. I couldn't let a boy into my life, so I decided to avoid Caleb after that. I made sure we never saw each other in the mornings or between the time I got home from my classes and left for my evening shift at the restaurant.

It was spring and the trees were lush, the grass fresh and green, and the flowers colorful and fragrant. I sat on the grass beside the building where my next class would be, appreciating the clear sky and the cool breeze that teased my skin. I heard the whiz of a dragonfly's wings as it passed, landing on a red tulip. Through the windows in front of me, I watched as students walked with urgency, carrying their huge backpacks. Someone had left an eraser on the bench, and I picked it up, rolling it around my fingers.

He calls me Red all the time. I don't think I've heard him say my name even once.

The more I told myself not to think about him, the more I did. So I thought of the way his green eyes crinkled at the corners and how they twinkled every time he laughed or said something funny or inappropriate. The way he looked at me—so *focused* on me, as if he was remembering everything. The warmth of his palm and the way his long fingers had curled around mine when we were at the lake.

I hated myself for thinking about him so much. Other than a word or two, it had been days since we last spoke. He hadn't sought me out. Wasn't that a big indication that I was just another pastime to him? He'd been bored that night we went to the lake, and I was conveniently there. I meant nothing to him.

I wished I could rub him out of my mind with the eraser. Frustrated, I flung it in the air—and froze when I heard a familiar laugh. The eraser fell to the ground as I spotted Caleb and his group of friends walking in my direction. He tipped his head back and laughed.

I drew in a sharp breath, stood, and half ran in the opposite direction. Did he see me? Maybe he didn't. It happened too fast.

At the end of my shift on Saturday, my boss told me I wouldn't be getting any hours at the restaurant the next weekend. Life seemed bleaker.

The next day, I felt more desperate and determined to find another job. I needed to widen my job search, which would take the whole day. I woke up early and started to make Caleb's breakfast and lunch, because I was expecting to return late that night.

I was just placing his plate in the food warmer when I heard footsteps behind me. My heart pounded in panic.

"Why are you avoiding me?" Caleb asked, straight as you please.

I nearly dropped the plate. He stood before me, wearing only gray sweatpants and a towel around his neck. Sweat glistened on his forehead, on his impressive chest, and down to his hard stomach where a light trail of dark hair disappeared below his waistband. He'd obviously just finished a workout. I noticed a couple of Band-Aids on his fingers again and a long scratch on his forearm. He seemed to need to be constantly busy. All through the week I'd heard him hammering on something, even retiling his bathroom. I was surprised he knew how to do that stuff—not that it mattered.

I cleared my throat. "I... I'm not avoiding you."

He tilted his head, studying me. I stood my ground, even though I wanted to squirm.

Why did he have to look so good?

"I never pegged you for a liar," he said.

Anger flared in my chest. And then I realized he was right. I *was* lying—but I wasn't going to admit that.

"Did you need something?" I asked, irritated.

He rubbed his hand across his face. "Yes."

He walked toward me slowly, his intense green eyes locking on mine. I stood frozen, unable to move, unable to breathe. Something in the air was so thick I could almost touch it.

Desire.

I had never felt this with any other guy. Why did it have to be Caleb? He stopped a foot away, his hands in his pockets as his eyes held mine captive.

"I need you to stop," he whispered.

"Stop?"

"Whatever you're doing to me."

I swallowed the lump in my throat.

He narrowed his eyes. They were gleaming with anger. "I need to get you out of my mind."

I bit my lip, balling my hands into fists. I could say the same to him, but I didn't. I was silent, waiting. And then his eyes softened. He stepped closer. His hand reached for my hair, and he tucked a lock behind my ear.

"You're something else, Red. I won't be able to pull away next time," he said before he walked away.

It sounded like a promise.

CHAPTER

Caleb

Wet dreams were a thing of the past for me.

Or so I thought.

Lifting the blanket, I took a peek and let out a frustrated groan as I plopped back down in bed.

What was she doing to me?

Resigned, I closed my eyes. An image flashed in my head of Red in that red lacy underwear as she jumped off the bridge with me.

And then Red *without* it…

I felt myself twitch.

"Damn."

This was pretty pathetic.

The cold shower didn't help. I had three hours before my class started, so I pounded an hour on the treadmill and another on weights. By the time I drove to school, I felt a little more relaxed.

Music blasted from my earphones as I headed to class. I was a little early, but that was nothing new. I'd normally hang with the guys—have a few laughs, bullshit about sexual conquests, or rag one another about anything—but I wasn't in the mood for that today.

Dumping my backpack on the classroom floor, I sprawled in my seat, pulling my hoodie over my face to cover my eyes and discourage anyone who wanted to chat.

Why was she avoiding me like I had leprosy? The last time I saw her was a few days before, after I told her I wouldn't be able to pull away next time. It was the truth. I liked her.

I wanted her.

She was different. She did something to me. I hadn't figured out yet what that was.

I'd like to think I knew all types of girls. Red appeared to be cool and collected, but I could feel her fire burning just below the surface. There had been a few moments when I'd pushed the right buttons so that her cool and collected exterior disappeared and that low-burning fire bloomed into a red blaze.

She was a hellcat, her eyes glinting with anticipation every time I threw a challenge at her. But she wouldn't let herself give in, holding on to her control like a lifeline.

Life had dealt her a bad hand, made her homeless and broke. She'd put up layers to protect herself.

I wanted to be the one to peel those layers one by one and find the real woman beneath.

When I felt smooth hands pull my hoodie back, I opened my eyes.

"Hi, Caleb."

Lily's blue eyes blinked at me, her soft pink lips curving into a smile. She was gorgeous, no doubt. A lock of her silky blond hair fell on the side of her face. Any hot-blooded male would want to touch.

So what the hell did it say about me that I didn't?

What the hell was wrong with me?

"Hey, Lil."

She angled her head to the side, looking at me expectantly.

I waited a beat.

Another lock of hair fell and bounced next to the other one.

How the hell did she do that? Did she have magic powers to control all that hair?

Her irritated sigh was nearly inaudible as she finally flicked her hair over her shoulder, tucking it behind her ear. She was disappointed that I hadn't done it for her, her eyes narrowing briefly at my face. Then she smiled sweetly again.

"Beatrice-Rose told me you attended the charity event with your mother last week. I'm sorry I missed you."

I shrugged, gave her a smile. "There's always next time."

She chewed on her bottom lip, her pink tongue darting out to wet it. "Why don't I make it up to you? Dinner?"

I was going to politely decline when an image of Red flashed in my mind again.

From the first moment I saw Red dance, I knew that I would have a hard time resisting her. Not that she tried to get my attention. If anything, she stayed away from me.

A sweet, honest compliment; a lingering, adoring look. A

smile that hinted of secret pleasures to come; a fleeting, intimate touch to the back of her hand, her shoulder, or the small of her back. In my experience, these things always, always worked on girls.

They didn't even penetrate the thick shield surrounding Red. I practically had to beg her to give me attention. But she'd only flicked me off like dirt from her sleeve, dusting her hands off for good measure.

It was humbling.

It was always a given that the girl I liked felt the same way. With Red, I felt unsure for the first time. It was messed up.

Maybe a night out with Lily was just what I needed. Maybe I needed to get back to my routine, back to my life before Red. Maybe then I would stop thinking about her.

"Sounds good. I'll call you, Lil."

She leaned close and kissed my cheek. "Can't wait."

But I didn't call Lily.

Instead, I holed up in my room, flipping the sticky note Red had left on the fridge in my fingers. I stared at the ceiling as Radiohead crooned low in my ears about a creep, a weirdo, and what the hell was he doing here.

When I heard a noise, I pulled out my earbuds. Footsteps—I knew it was Red. She always walked quietly, warily, as if she was scared to make a sound. A few seconds later, I heard a door close. I quickly glanced at the clock and noted it was 7:00 p.m.

I jumped off my bed. I'd knock on her door, ask if she wanted to take another ride with me. But when I reached her door, my fist inches away from knocking, I stopped. Took a deep breath.

I knew Red was attracted to me. I could see the way her eyes lingered on me, the way she resisted smiling back. She was fighting it, and the last thing I wanted was to force myself on someone. So I retreated back to my room.

When my phone burped a text, it was from Lily.

LILY: Is it next time yet?

I blew out a breath and stared at my phone screen for a minute, debating whether I should go out with Lily or not. Red's sticky note was on my bedside table, mocking me.

Fine. I'd forget Red tonight.

Lily was just my type. She was blond, blue-eyed, and sweet. I took her out to dinner. She laughed at all my jokes, agreed to everything I suggested, even asked me to come to her place after our date.

But when I walked her to her door, I politely declined her invitation to go inside, bid her good night, and left.

It wasn't fair to her that I was thinking of a different girl.

How was it even possible to be obsessed with someone I'd just met?

Ridiculous.

With my temper simmering, I stepped on the gas and drove past the speed limit on the highway. Through the open window, the wind whipped my hair and slapped my face, taunting me.

When I reached the city, I pulled off the highway and parked my car in front of a twenty-four-hour store. I bought a big tub of peanut butter.

I remembered how her eyes had shone with delight when she spotted it at the grocery store.

I was so whipped.

By the time I got home, the lights were all off except for the one in the living room. I couldn't help laughing as I recalled that time she'd hit me with a baseball bat.

It was already past ten. She was probably sleeping. I tiptoed to her door and was crouching to place the tub of peanut butter on the floor when the door suddenly swung open.

I froze.

"You're back already," she said. Her voice was low, breathless.

Was she waiting for me?

I looked up, my breath hitching at the sight of her. Dark, catlike eyes stared at me. Suddenly it didn't feel so ridiculous to be obsessed with someone I'd just met.

I cleared my throat. "Yeah." I swiftly picked up the tub of peanut butter and hid it behind my back.

Had she seen it?

"Did you have dinner yet?" she asked.

I had, but if I told her that, she'd just go back in her room and ignore me.

"No."

"Are you hungry, then?"

"Always."

Her lips twitched into a small smile, but it was gone as fast as it appeared. "Is that for me?"

Tongue in cheek, I said, "Is what for you?"

Her eyes warmed with laughter. "That peanut butter you're hiding behind you."

Busted.

"Let's make a deal. I'll give it to you after you fix me something to eat."

She nodded, and a lock of hair fell on the side of her face. My hand moved automatically, as if it had a mind of its own, and tucked the hair behind her ear.

It was irresistible.

She was irresistible.

A pretty blush appeared on her cheeks. "Pancakes?"

I nodded, feeling myself grin for the first time in days. "Pancakes."

CHAPTER

seven

Veronica

I DOUBLED MY DETERMINATION TO FIND A JOB THE NEXT DAY. I felt threatened by the unfamiliar emotions Caleb could bring out in me, at how quickly I forgot all the precautions I put in place when he was near. I had to find a good-paying job and move out of his place, be on my own again.

By the third hour of job hunting, I glanced at my list, noting only one name left that wasn't crossed out.

Hawthorne Auto Repair Shop—cashier/clerk. Apply in person. Salary to be negotiated.

Hawthorne Auto Repair Shop was on the opposite side of town from Caleb's place, but that didn't stop me. I boarded the bus and hoped for the best.

The garage was located on a big lot, a long, rectangular building freshly painted in metal gray with dark-blue trim. A smaller building with a slanted roof was attached to the left side. Cars were neatly parked side by side in rows of three.

The whirring of machinery, metal grinding against metal, and the heavy scent of diesel greeted me as I entered the garage. A young guy in a blue mechanic's uniform was talking on his cell phone, his face youthful and stained with grease. He signaled for me to wait and jogged toward me.

"Can I help you?" he asked. The name tag on his uniform said DYLAN.

"I'm here to submit my résumé for the cashier/clerk position."

"Hallelujah!" His face broke into a wide grin. "I'm Dylan, and the office is just over there." He pointed to the door on his left. "I'd walk you over, but I just need to finish this." He nodded at his phone.

Encouraged by his reaction, I smiled, then headed in the direction he had indicated.

I entered the office and saw a tall, slim-as-a-rose brunette standing behind the counter and cash register, her eyes narrowed into slits as she listened to a man I assumed was a customer. Her eyes shifted to me for a moment when the bell on the door jingled as it closed.

"Do you think I'm the one who puts these taxes on our customers' bills? If I did, I'd add an asshole tax just before the idiot tax. Especially for *some* people," she said in a no-nonsense tone, one perfect eyebrow arched.

She flipped her stylishly cut hair behind her shoulder.

"Not saying it's you, but if you don't pay for our service, you don't get your car. Just try it," she warned, her eyes gleaming with challenge when the customer reached for the keys on the counter. "Try driving that car out of this lot without paying your bill, *plus* taxes. I assure you, *sir*, you might get away from me but not from the cops."

I bit my lip, wondering if I should turn around and leave, come back at a better time.

Her eyes flicked back to mine, and she gave me a quick wink.

I decided to wait and looked around the office. Facing the counter, there were two desks crowded with paperwork and paraphernalia. Shelves displaying car parts lined the walls, some behind glass. On the far end of the room was a glass door leading to the outside. The argument continued, but I noticed that the customer ended up paying his bill, *plus* taxes. Eventually he grabbed his keys and brushed past me on his way out.

And, in my opinion, barely kept his life.

"Bastard," the brunette muttered under her breath. "Be gone, negative energy. Whew. Hello there, gorgeous. Here to pick up your car?"

She was absolutely unapologetic, her hazel eyes clear and direct as they focused on me. And I just had to grin. I liked her already.

I couldn't help but admire the long, green Bohemian dress she was wearing. She had a small beauty mark on the side of her upper lip. She was of mixed race, possibly Asian and Caucasian. Behind her chic glasses, her hazel eyes slanted beautifully upward.

I shook my head. "Sorry, no. I'm here to hand in my résumé, if the cashier position is still open. I saw the ad online."

Her brows knit in confusion. "What ad?"

She reached for my résumé, her eyes skimming it.

"I'm Veronica Strafford," I said.

"Kara Hawthorne. Sweetie, I think you got the wrong shop—"

"Hey, Kar!"

We both turned at the voice. Dylan opened the office's back door, poking his head inside. Sounds from the garage filtered through, loud but not deafening.

"Dad told me to post an ad on the internet for a part-time cashier to help you around here. You're welcome." His eyes shifted, and he grinned when he saw me. Then he winked.

"Will you stop winking? You look like you're having an epileptic attack. And why did Dad ask *you* and not me?" She sounded insulted.

He rolled his eyes. "Chill, chill. This is exactly why Dad asked me. You've been a raging psycho lately, and you need help." He winked at me again.

I pressed my lips together to keep from laughing. It seemed such normal banter between brother and sister.

"Go to hell." Kara turned her attention to me. "Sorry about that moron. We don't let him out of his cage much."

I smiled.

"I heard that!" Dylan piped up as he disappeared behind the closed door.

Kara waved her hand dismissively. "Okay, let's take a look again," she said, scanning my résumé. "Can you give me three references?"

"Absolutely." I handed her a piece of paper with my references.

"Give me a second while I check these out," she informed me, already heading to the back office for the phone.

When she came back a few minutes later, there was a radiant

smile on her face. "I got ahold of two out of three of your references. Before anything else, I have a few questions I need to ask you now."

"Okay."

"Do you wear fur?"

"No."

"Real leather?"

My mouth twitched. "No."

"Good. I'm an animal lover. Are you vegan or vegetarian?"

"Um…no."

"That's too bad." She let out a sigh before grinning. "You're hired. Care to start today?"

My heart did a quick dance in my chest, and I felt a grin stretch across my lips, mirroring hers.

"I'd love to."

"Call me Kar, then. And since I'm probably going to boss the hell out of you at work, want to have lunch with me now and we can discuss the rest?"

I nodded.

"There's a vegetarian restaurant down the street. Okay with you?"

"Sounds perfect."

She grabbed her purse and keys from a drawer in her desk, flipped the sign on the door saying that she'd be back in an hour, and locked the office behind us.

Now that I'd found a job, I allowed myself to buy a meal to celebrate, but just this one time. I needed every cent to pay off my loans.

Over fries, mushroom burgers, and milk shakes, we discussed my hourly rate, my responsibilities, and her expectations.

I didn't warm up to anyone easily, but I couldn't help it with Kara. She was in college and attending the same university. We just hadn't met until today. Some people might find her bluntness intimidating, but I really appreciated her no-bullshit attitude.

We were laughing over her methods of dealing with difficult customers when she stopped mid-sentence, staring at something over my shoulder. Her eyes widened in shock, then flashed with hurt, before her shields went up.

"My ex. My ex from hell. He's here, and he's with someone. Don't look!"

But I already had. Kara snarled in dismay, glaring at me. I chuckled at her expression.

A dark-haired guy was seated three tables away, his eyes a startling blue as they drank in Kara's face. They quickly shifted to me for a second before they went back to Kara.

"He's staring at you," I said when I finally turned back to her.

"Fuck him. I hate him. I hope he's burned alive, flayed alive. *Boiled* alive."

"You're scary."

She glared at me. "And you suck. He totally saw you checking him out, and now he knows I'm talking about him. His ego is big enough without our help—trust me." Her eyes narrowed, then gleamed. "Let me deflate it a little. Let's go," she commanded, already rising from her seat.

I looked at my burger longingly—wondering if I'd have time

to ask the hostess to box it—but one glance at Kara told me that wasn't going to happen. She was a woman on a mission.

She stopped beside her ex's table.

"Hello, Cameron," Kara greeted him. She fluttered her eyelashes at him, her voice full of sass. "How are the drugs working, honey?"

Cameron, who was taking a sip of his drink, choked at Kara's question.

His date looked up at Kara, confused. "Drugs?"

"Oh, I'm sorry. Didn't you know?" Kara's voice dripped with fake sympathy. "He needs drugs to get *it* up. It's going to be a very short, very *soft* ride for you, sweetie. Ta-ta for now!" She flicked her fingers in a wave of goodbye and hurried to the exit.

"Goddamn it, Kara!"

I startled as I heard Cameron speak. He rose, sliding out from his seat and racing past me after Kara. "Kar! Get back here!"

By the time I caught up to them outside, I was surprised at the sight before me. Cameron was gripping her arms, his lips on hers. I watched as she kneed him in the balls and he crumpled to the ground, his face twisting in agony.

"Kara, you—" Cameron wheezed.

She kicked him in the stomach before he could finish.

"What the hell, Kar?" I yelled, pulling her back from the poor guy.

She sneered down at him. "Don't you ever, *ever* touch me again with those filthy phalanges, you motherfucking dickless baboon!"

CHAPTER

eight

Veronica

By the time I got home, it was late. I stepped off the elevator and walked to Caleb's apartment door, entering the code on the keypad. The door made a muted beeping noise before the locks clicked open. The lights were on, and I could detect a faint smell of burned toast. Caleb must be home.

I felt guilty for not cooking dinner. I had planned on getting home earlier to make something for Caleb to eat, but I'd spent more time with Kara than I'd planned. I made a mental note to give my resignation to my other part-time job since Kara offered more hours and pay.

"Caleb?" I called out, covering my eyes with my hand and opening just a slit between my fingers so I could see where I was going. Better safe than sorry. He had a habit of walking around naked in his home. I could still remember—

I shook my head to clear my thoughts and tried to assassinate the feeling of excited anticipation at seeing him again.

I found him in the kitchen, standing in front of the open fridge, drinking a glass of orange juice. He wore a crisp black suit and tie, his bronze hair slicked back to frame his gorgeous face.

The suit caught me off guard. He looked so good that he seemed unreal. Had he gone to another charity event with his mother?

I just stood there, immobilized, unable to pry my gaze away. His green eyes widened slightly when he saw me. He closed the fridge and placed the glass on the counter. Slowly, he lifted his head. Our eyes met.

Silence.

Embarrassed, I broke our gaze, but my eyes couldn't help dragging to his lips. They were rosy, irresistible, and probably cold from drinking his favorite juice.

His tongue quickly darted out to lick the juice on his lips. That was too much. The butterflies were in my stomach now, wreaking havoc with my emotions.

"Hi, Red. Like what you see?" His voice was huskier than normal.

Oh God.

The tub of peanut butter last night almost made me succumb to his charms again. *Almost.* I barely looked at him and answered his questions with one-word answers, planning to make his pancakes as fast as I could, then run back to my room. Other than our encounter last night, I'd been away from him for a long time, and I felt overwhelmed now that his full attention was on me. I blushed, forcing myself to look away from him. Where was my tongue? My brain? I couldn't let him take the upper hand.

"I see," he said quietly, his voice deepening. "Are you just going to pretend I'm not turning you on right now?"

Oh God. Oh God. Oh God.

I watched him walk slowly toward me, his hooded eyes intense on my face. He stopped a few inches away. I could smell the faint scent of his cologne, feel the warmth emanating from his body.

"I told you I wouldn't be able to pull away next time," he whispered.

In one swift move, he had me pinned against the wall. His green eyes bored into mine, then flicked down to my mouth, lingering there.

"I should leave you alone, but I can't." My eyes closed as his fingers traced a line on my cheek, down to the hollow of my throat where my pulse was beating wildly.

"I'm greedy." His head dipped to my neck, and I gasped as his soft lips lightly brushed the sensitive area below my ear. "And I want more."

"Caleb." His name came out in a breathy whisper. I felt intoxicated. Mesmerized.

"Just a taste." He inhaled deeply. My head fell back to grant him more access. "You smell so good."

I fisted my hands by my sides to prevent myself from touching him.

His hands stroked down my body, gentle and teasing, until they gripped my hips. "Kiss me," he coaxed, sucking my bottom lip, then licking and biting lightly.

My knees felt weak. His arm snaked around my waist, pulling

me against his body as his other hand slipped up and secured the back of my neck. His lips became hard and demanding, challenging me to kiss him back.

My lips parted as he clutched a fistful of my hair, hungrily taking my mouth. His kiss turned insatiable, almost desperate.

I knew he was capable of this. I was prepared for it. What I wasn't prepared for was my reaction. I believed that I could resist him, that I was strong enough not to give in. I was wrong— so wrong. Because this, I realized as his mouth seduced me, was surrender.

I felt his hunger, and I realized that same hunger was mirrored inside me and had been building for a while now. Almost as desperate as he was, I kissed him back.

The world became hazy. I only felt. And then I heard a moan. The sound had come from me.

"No!" I protested against his lips. My palms flattened against his chest to push him away, but he held on, stroking my arms gently, persuasively.

He exhaled slowly, and I heard him swallow as he rested his forehead against mine. I could feel his breath, smell the masculine scent of him.

"Red—"

"Don't."

I ran to my room and closed the door behind me. I had to get out of here soon. There was no way I could stay in his apartment. Caleb disarmed me, made me weak.

My hands shook as I touched my lips. I had never been kissed like that in my whole life.

Was it supposed to feel like I'd been branded?

I had never believed what they said about Caleb Lockhart on campus. They said he could kiss a dead fish to life.

Now, I believed.

Determined not to see Caleb the next morning, I woke up early to cook his breakfast, posted a note on the fridge, and rushed to leave for school.

I didn't want to face him after what had happened last night. It shouldn't happen again. Wouldn't happen again. If I gave in, I'd just be *some* girl in his book, another notch in his bedpost. I didn't want him to think of me that way.

Wait—why did I suddenly care what he thought about me?

I didn't. Really.

The weather matched my mood with its ominous dark clouds as I walked the hallways to my second class. It looked like it was going to rain, and it had been unusually chilly this morning when I left the apartment. I couldn't wait for this day to end. I glanced at my watch and noted that I still had a few minutes before my next class started.

"Red!"

Oh God, *no*.

Only one person called me that. I walked faster, ignoring him, hoping he'd give up and leave me alone. I felt safer when I reached the lecture hall, squeezing myself into the only available seat in the second row.

"Lockhart, my man!" the guy behind me yelled.

My head whipped around so fast I felt dizzy.

Caleb was standing at the door, looking fresh and gorgeous in dark jeans and a gray sweater, sleeves rolled up exposing his forearms. His gaze was searching.

"What the hell are you doing here?" the guy asked. "You're not in this class."

That's right! He shouldn't be here. Isn't there a rule that prohibits students from sitting in a class they're not enrolled in?

"I definitely am today," Caleb replied. His smile reached his ears when he spotted me. I whipped my eyes to the front, sending a silent prayer of gratitude that all the seats in my row were taken.

"See something I like," he added.

I could hear the grin in his voice. I gritted my teeth. What was taking the professor so long? He should've been here by now.

"Veronica Strafford," a quiet male voice whispered behind me.

I turned my head to check who it was. A classmate I'd never talked to flashed an amused smile as he handed me a folded piece of paper. I looked at it dumbly.

The guy's black bangs covered one dark eye, while the other one gazed at me intently. "For you," he said, shoving the paper in my hand when I didn't reach for it.

My eyes shifted to Caleb. He was sitting two rows behind me, watching with laughter in his eyes. I turned to face the front again, crumpling the paper in my hand. When I felt a nudge on my back, I turned around and glared. It was the same guy again.

"He said read it, or he will exchange seats with the guy beside you."

I clenched my teeth. I wanted to throw his note in his face, but I didn't want to make a spectacle. I opened the note.

I'm NOT sorry I kissed you last night.

Caleb

I crushed the paper in my hand again, anger flaring in my chest.

"What did you give her?" I heard another male voice behind me. A different one this time. Good Lord, were *all* of Caleb's teammates in this class? "A note? What's on it?"

I was about to tear it up when someone plucked it out of my hands.

"Amos, you asshole! Come back here!" Caleb yelled, but he was laughing.

I watched in horror as Amos jumped on the stage, clearing his throat to get everyone's attention.

"Passing notes in class like you're in high school, eh?" He raised his brows, turning his gaze on me and grinning. "And you are?"

"Veronica Strafford!" someone yelled.

Why couldn't I move? Or say something? I knew I had to do something, but I was paralyzed. It was like watching a train wreck happen in front of me.

"Let's see then, Veronica… What do we have here?" he continued.

All the blood drained from my face as I watched him open the note, exaggerating every movement. His eyes widened before his voice boomed out to the entire class, "'I'm not sorry I kissed you last night. Caleb.'"

I wanted to curl up and die.

The whole class erupted in a buzz. I could feel eyes darting toward me like bullets. What possessed this guy to read that note in front of the class?

"That should be enough entertainment for you today, kids!"

I glared at Caleb. He was smirking, completely unrepentant. I wanted to kick him in the balls and wipe that smirk off his face.

I didn't even wait for the professor. I just ran out of there.

"Red, wait!"

I whipped around, ready to cut him to pieces. "You have two strikes already," I hissed, balling my hands into fists to keep from punching his face.

His smile disappeared. "Does that mean I only have one more left?"

I scoffed and whipped around, making sure my long hair struck his irritatingly gorgeous face.

"Ouch. That hurt."

Good! But that didn't give me any satisfaction. I was so embarrassed, so mad…

I kept walking. I knew he was following me, because I could hear his footsteps trying to catch up. I walked faster, almost running, and threw a glare over my shoulder.

"Red, no!"

And just as I turned, my face slammed into the glass door.

My head spun as my face throbbed. Livid now and mortified

beyond belief, I closed my eyes, taking deep breaths. I knew people were staring and laughing at me. I could hear them.

Nobody's fault but mine.

"Leave me alone!" I fumed.

I wrenched the doors open, hoping one would slam back in his face. I just wanted to hide somewhere.

"Are you okay?" he asked.

I gritted my teeth, ignoring him.

"Red, what's wrong?"

I stopped in my tracks and shot him an incredulous look. "Are you serious?"

He looked startled by my anger. I was bristling.

"Are you really that mad?" he asked quietly, his eyes gentle as they studied my face.

I hesitated for a few seconds, processing the emotions churning in my stomach. "I don't like being cornered," I said finally. "I don't like catering to a self-indulgent child. And most of all, I don't like being forced to do something I don't like."

His eyes widened in shock before they turned flat and cold.

"Got it," he said in a clipped tone before he turned and strode away.

In the two weeks that followed, we avoided each other.

I woke up early and cooked his meals, storing his dinner in the fridge and leaving a note for him to heat it up.

I attended my classes diligently and took the bus to work after. If I didn't go to the library after work, I hung out with

Kara. I avoided coming home early every day just in case Caleb decided to seek me out. But he never did. There was an emptiness in my chest that I couldn't understand, but I ignored it. I just had to.

I felt like a trespasser, an unwanted boarder in his home. Every day I told myself to pack up what little I had and leave. But where would I go?

I wanted to ask Kara if she was willing to rent me a room in her apartment, but it seemed like an intrusion to even bring it up. I didn't want to impose. I might spend almost every day with her, but we'd only known each other a few weeks.

If Caleb said or implied that he didn't want me living at his place anymore, I would have left quickly. But he never did.

On rare occasions when I saw him at the apartment, he always gave me a polite nod. I always nodded back and walked away quickly before he could say anything. Not that he tried.

I just had to finish this semester, and then I'd leave his place. I would have enough saved up by then to rent a small apartment. I even got a side job checking test papers for Professor Phillips. Usually these kinds of jobs made me happy, since they meant extra cash, but this time it didn't. Nothing did.

Caleb had pierced my bubble, and I was angry at him for it, but angrier at myself for allowing it. But if I was honest with myself, I knew that what was really bothering me most was that I missed him.

It was ridiculous. How could I miss someone I'd spent so little time with? How could someone I barely knew affect me this deeply? It was weak, and I couldn't afford any weakness right now.

My mood became darker every day. Soon the only thing that cheered me up was the time I spent with Kara.

I was already at the office, folding invoices at my desk and meticulously placing them in envelopes to mail out, when the bell on the door jingled.

I looked up as Kara sashayed in, hips swaying, gold bracelets tinkling. It was Sunday, and I knew she'd attended Mass with her dad and Dylan. She always volunteered for cleanup right after, but her makeup was still perfect, and there wasn't a wrinkle on her clothes. I felt underdressed in my shirt and jeans.

"How was church?" I asked.

"I'm still a sinner. Why do you think I go every Sunday?" She placed her purse on top of her desk. "What do you think of this top? Does it make my boobs pass for at least a B cup?"

"Yes, they look superb. What's with you and your obsession with your boobs?"

She sighed dramatically. "Hey, hey, hey. Not all of us are blessed with huge, round tits like yours, so stop being a bitch about it." She wagged her finger at me. "Mine are more like mosquito bites so I'll talk about them all I want."

She took a sip from her smoothie, shivering in disgust. "Ugh. I know this is healthy, but I swear the smoothie bar down the street doesn't add anything besides roots and dirt. Is it supposed to taste like shit that has been sitting on the lawn for ten days?"

I winced when she took another sip. It looked very green. "Maybe you'll start mooing in a minute," I suggested.

Her eyes narrowed at me. "What's up with you? You've been moping around like you've swallowed the wrong dick."

I sighed again, opening and closing the cap on my coconut juice. When I looked up, Kara was eyeing my drink with undisguised longing.

"Know what?" Kara said. "I'll trade you. Here." She snatched my drink from my hand, replacing it with hers. "*You* need this. Since you look like you swallowed the wrong—"

I held up a hand. "Can we stop talking about body parts, please?"

"Well." She took a sip from *my* drink. "What's up?"

It had been a long time since I shared anything about myself. Forced to be an adult after my dad left us, I sometimes felt more like ninety than my actual twenty-one.

It felt weird to even consider confiding in someone, but I found myself telling Kara about Caleb.

"You're staying at his place?" Her mouth hung open. "He's gorgeous as hell, but he's a horndog. You know that, right?"

Suddenly it was like my mouth couldn't be stopped. Everything spilled. When I told her about the kiss, her eyes bugged out. I told her how determined I was to look for an apartment, a room, anything cheap to rent to get away from Caleb.

She shook her head. "Did you know he's Cameron's best friend?" She clucked her tongue, frowning at me. "Why didn't you tell me about this before, you moron? You know you have to stay with me from now on, right?"

Shocked, I could only stare at her. "What?" I managed.

"Well, why not?"

"You barely know me. I've only been working here a few weeks."

Her smile was wide. "I've spent enough days with you to know you're not a serial killer. Plus, I love you already, bitch."

My chest tightened painfully. I wanted to hug her, but I just smiled. "Love you too, asshole."

CHAPTER
nine

Veronica

As soon as I entered Caleb's apartment, I noticed the quiet. If Caleb came home early, I'd usually hear him moving around, followed by the smell of burned toast lingering in the air. He always cranked the toaster dial higher than necessary when he wasn't paying attention. But there was no scent of food as I headed to the kitchen. I wanted to tell him that I was moving out tomorrow before I started packing my things.

A movement on the balcony had me reaching automatically for my pocketknife. There was little moonlight, and I strained my eyes to see who it was.

Opening the french doors, I stepped out into the night air.

Caleb was sitting in the dark, elbows on his knees, head lowered like he was grieving.

I knew something had happened. Something bad.

I'd never seen him so subdued, so alone.

"Caleb?"

The only acknowledgment he gave me was a slight movement of his head.

Slowly, I approached him. This was the first time I'd willingly sought him out after weeks of avoiding him. My eyes adjusted to the darkness, and I could see him clearly now. I hadn't seen his face up close in so long that the sight of it hit me like a punch. Even in sadness, he was strikingly handsome, and I couldn't help admiring his beauty.

"Do you want to be alone?" I asked softly.

It was a moment before he responded. "No."

Other than the bench he was sitting on, the balcony was empty. It was clear he didn't usually spend much time out here. I sat beside him quietly, waiting for him to give me a sign, anything, so I'd know what to do.

"My parents are getting a divorce," he said after a while. His voice was detached, as if he'd just asked me to pass the salt.

There was nothing I could say to make it better. Slowly, I reached for Caleb's hand, holding it in mine. If I could give him anything, it was my presence at this moment. His hand was as cold as mine was warm, as big as mine was small. I used both my hands to rub warmth into his hand. I glanced at his face. I could see how sadness was pulling down the corners of his eyes. His jaw was tight, his lips pulled back in a disapproving curve.

"I was expecting it. For a long while now, actually." He whispered so softly that I had to lean toward him to hear.

"He had other women. He cheated on my mother so many times, but she stuck by him. She didn't believe in divorce. She was crying when I saw her today. I could barely get her out of bed to eat something."

His hand fisted in a tight ball as his anger surfaced. I knew he was barely holding it back.

"I fucking hate him. I want to kill him."

"You could," I replied softly. "But what purpose would that serve? I've always wondered why life chooses certain people to punish."

I felt his green eyes on me, but I looked out into the night.

"No matter how much you want to protect the people you love, Caleb, you can't. You can only be there for them. You can't choose their path because it is theirs alone. It's their fight, not yours."

There were no stars in the sky. The city was too bright, with its skyscrapers and gaudy blinking neon signs obliterating their light.

I took a deep breath and continued. "I've learned to accept that it's not my fault when bad things happen to me or to the people I love. It's just the way life is. It's not fair. If you're one of the unlucky ones, then fight. Be stronger. Be stronger because you have no choice. Be stronger than you are right now because if you're not, life will swallow you up and spit you out. And then you'll die with a broken heart."

Just like my mom.

I knew I sounded cynical, but life had made me tough. When I shifted my eyes to his face, he was watching me. Even in the dark, his eyes looked fierce as they searched mine.

"Stop brooding, Caleb. Fight back." I smiled at him, squeezing his hand. "Give me back your smiles because there is something wrong with the universe without them."

His eyes flashed with surprise, and I blushed, not having meant to tell him that. But it seemed like the night for confessions in the dark.

The truth was that I missed him. I felt the loss of his presence more evidently now that he was in front of me. It was harder to deny the truth, impossible even, when his complete attention was on me.

He smiled.

I rose from the seat, smiling back at him. "Pancakes?" I asked.

His eyes were tender as he looked at me. He unfolded his long body from the seat and stood facing me.

I held my breath, looking up at him as he stood close.

"Thank you, Red," he whispered warmly. His voice felt like a caress.

I nodded. My chest felt tight, and I had no idea what my face was showing so I turned away, walking to the kitchen.

There was a hitch in my stride when I felt his hand reach for mine, interlacing my fingers with his. I looked down at our joined hands, my heart stuttering at the feel of his skin. I shifted my eyes to his, and he was smiling. His eyes soft and vulnerable.

"Don't let go of my hand, Red," he said as he walked us out of the apartment.

"What about pancakes?" I asked, confused.

"Pancakes means holding your hand and walking on the beach right now."

There was another stutter in my heart, this time stronger.

He looked over his shoulder at me when I didn't respond and

grinned as we rode the elevator to the basement garage. Before I could reach for the car door, he was there, opening it for me.

"Ready?" he asked as we fastened our seat belts. The twinkle in his eyes was back.

"Ready," I answered.

Without hesitation, he reached for my hand again and rested our intertwined hands on the middle console.

The beach was a good half-hour drive from Caleb's place. We drove there with our windows open, the wind blowing my long hair. It was dark, the roads free of traffic.

I felt excited, energized, and at the same time Caleb's hand in mine calmed my anxious mind.

He threw me a glance, his thumb stroking my palm.

"I'm glad you're here with me, Red."

I swallowed the lump in my throat. No one had said that to me before. I turned my gaze out the window so he wouldn't see how much his words had affected me.

Tonight I was seeing a side of Caleb I hadn't encountered before. I didn't know what to think of it, or maybe I did but refused to think about it.

All I knew was that I liked this boy as I had never liked anyone before.

He parked his car in front of the lakeside shops that had already closed for the night. We took off our shoes, then walked on the beach, the white sand cool as our feet dug into it.

The wind was a little chilly, and I wrapped my arms around my middle to ward off the cold. Out of the corner of my eye, I saw Caleb shrug out of his jacket.

"Here," he said, placing it on my shoulders.

"What about you?"

"Just hold my hand. You warm me up."

But he was the one who warmed me up inside as his hand reached for mine again, pulling me close to his side as we walked.

"I knew you were avoiding me," he began after a moment. His voice held no resentment, only understanding. That surprised me. "I knew you didn't want anything to do with me the past few weeks, but I thought about you. Actually," he corrected, his voice deepening. "I think I'm a little obsessed."

He sighed when I didn't respond as quickly as he may have expected. "I'm sorry if I made you feel like I was forcing you to do something you didn't like."

I walked beside him for a moment, listening to the sound of the waves before I answered. "I'm sorry I said that. It's not that, really... You confuse me, Caleb."

I knew he was waiting for me to say something more, to explain, but the words were stuck in my throat.

"Sometimes I think you're a very sad girl, Red."

He was more observant than I'd given him credit for. Because he was right, I realized. I had been sad for a long, long time. I had been starved for love and affection for so long that I'd forgotten what it felt like. I had refused to let anyone in, afraid to be hurt again. But this boy holding my hand was stripping me of my armor bit by bit.

It scared me.

"All I could think about was how to make you smile again. Not the fake ones you give to people to be polite. I want your real smile, where your eyes light up and your lips stretch up to your ears."

My ears were ringing. What was he trying to say?

"You confuse me," I repeated. "I-I don't know what you want."

He stopped suddenly, and I had to turn around to face him.

"Don't you?" he asked solemnly, directly.

His eyes were burning with emotion. I looked away.

Who was this boy? This intense, serious boy who looked at me as if he could see my soul.

"I-I'm not ready, Caleb."

He nodded. "That's okay. I've been waiting for you to come along for a long time now. I think I can wait some more."

"Don't you think this is too fast?"

"The thing is, I've made up my mind. And my mind says it's you. If I'd just met you today, I would still want you today, tomorrow, five days from now..." His voice trailed off, and I was scared he was going to say forever or some ridiculous thing like that.

I didn't believe in forever. Forever was for people who believed in fairy tales. And I never had.

"You're scaring me."

He let out a quiet laugh. "I know. You just have to endure it." He paused. "After all, how could you give up a handsome boy like me?"

And the usual Caleb was back.

"But you have to promise me something," I said.

"What is it?"

"Don't kiss me."

He did that thing again where he angled his head and studied me. I squirmed.

"You're afraid of my kisses." It wasn't a question. "You're afraid of how they make you feel."

I swallowed a chunk of cowardice that was lodged in my throat. Of course, he was right. How could he know what I was feeling before I realized it myself?

"Why promise something when I'd fail miserably?"

"Will you try at least?" I persisted.

"No, Red."

He looked to the water, sighed, and looked at me.

"I don't think I could keep from kissing you if I wanted to. It's not even a choice for me anymore. I need to touch you, to breathe you in. I need to see you look up at me and smile. I need to see you happy...even grumpy or angry, as long as I can see you. I crave everything about you. I crave everything about you a little too much."

I held my breath as my heart knocked wildly against my chest.

Suddenly he sat on the sand, resting his back on a broken tree trunk and tugging me down with him.

"Lie back on me."

I had about two seconds before he was pulling me down onto his lap, my back against his chest, my legs encased between his. I was drowning in Caleb.

"Just relax. I won't kiss you tonight if you really don't want me to."

Suddenly, I wanted him to kiss me again.

What was wrong with me? When he was offering it, I didn't want it, but now faced with the possibility that he wouldn't kiss me tonight, I suddenly yearned for it.

I shifted in his arms and rested my cheek on his shoulder, inhaling his scent. He stiffened.

"Don't do that if you don't want to be kissed tonight. I only have so much control before I—" He cut himself off before he could finish.

"Before you what?" I could hear the smile in my voice. Even to my ears, I sounded…happy.

Caleb couldn't resist me. Caleb, the gorgeous and charming boy that everyone wanted, couldn't resist me. *Me*, someone used to not being wanted. It seemed unreal.

His eyes narrowed. "Are you deliberately provoking me?"

I looked up and saw his serious expression. Before I could tear my gaze away, he cupped my face with his hands and forced me to look at him.

"What do you want, Red?" he whispered, his voice husky.

I opened my mouth, but nothing came out. Hadn't he figured out that I'd changed my mind and wanted him to kiss me? Was I not throwing him enough signals?

"Say it, or I won't do it," he declared, his eyes mesmerizing me into surrender.

"Kiss me, Caleb."

I didn't have to say it twice. His mouth claimed my lips. Gone were the butterfly kisses; gone were the teasing and coaxing. This was a branding. One of his hands was on my back, pushing me against him, while the other plunged into my hair, cupping my head so that he could control the kiss.

I own you, his kiss said. We kissed for a long, long time.

CHAPTER

Veronica

SEVERAL MINUTES HAD PASSED SINCE MY ALARM WENT OFF, BUT I was still in bed, thinking about last night, when I heard a soft knock on my door.

"Caleb?" I called out, alarmed.

"Can I come in?" I heard him mumble behind the door.

"No!" I sat up in bed quickly, thinking of my morning breath and rat's-nest hair. "Can you give me two minutes?"

I didn't wait for his reply but darted to the bathroom, brushing my teeth and hair hurriedly. I paused when I saw my reflection in the mirror. Something was different about me. My cheeks had color in them, and my eyes were brighter.

"Red?"

Letting out a loud breath, I opened the door. Caleb was standing there, smiling, his eyes lighting up when he saw me. Even with bed-rumpled hair and a sleep line imprinted on his left cheek, he looked gorgeous. Butterflies swirled in my stomach at the sight of him.

"Do you sleep naked? Is that why you needed two minutes?"

I blushed but retorted, "Wouldn't you like to know?"

His eyes twinkled and easily expressed what he was thinking. "Can I come in?"

He raised his arms, and I noticed he was carrying a tray of food. There were a plate of deformed pancakes, butter and syrup on the side, a bowl of cut-up strawberries, a steaming cup of green tea, and a glass of orange juice. And a rose was lying on the side.

My eyes flicked up to his when he cleared his throat. I realized I had been staring at the tray for a while, with my heart floating giddily around my ribs.

"I made you pancakes since we didn't make them last night," he explained.

Was he blushing?

"But I'm sorry I kind of messed them up a bit."

He looked so adorable, so sweet. I had an inexplicable urge to kiss him and to scream my heart out, but I held it all in.

"Come in," I choked out.

He looked at me knowingly and smiled. "Breathe, Red. It will pass."

He'd never been in my room before, not since I moved in. I gazed around me, wondering what he thought of it now that I had settled in. Like the rest of his place, it was designed in a modern industrial style, with light-gray concrete walls, gorgeous exposed beams on the tall ceiling, and hardwood floors. The huge bed dominated the room, the dark-blue duvet haphazardly thrown on the floor when I rushed to the bathroom. My books were neatly stacked on the nightstand, my backpack on the floor. A wide window encompassed the whole wall to my right, with a round, white table with curved legs and two high-backed chairs tucked beside it. The room had always seemed spacious, but as I watched him walk to the sitting area, it suddenly felt small.

He set the tray on the table. "Come on, let's eat." He waved me over. When he drew back the curtains, sunlight rushed in, and the view of the city below made everything perfect.

No, I realized, Caleb made it perfect. Even if we were in a windowless basement, his presence would make it better.

It would be so easy to give in to him, to let myself fall for him, but what would happen when he got tired of me? Where would I be?

These emotions I felt for him were getting stronger and made me feel I was on unstable ground. That made me weary, defensive. But most of all, it made me feel vulnerable. I took a step back.

"Caleb, I don't have time to sit down and eat. My bus leaves in an hour."

"I'm driving you to school from now on."

"You can't do that."

"Yes, I can."

I glared at him. "No, you can't."

"I can and I will," he countered stubbornly.

I placed my hands on my hips. "Why are you bossing me around?"

He let out a sigh. "Can't we just eat in peace? I made these for you. I really, really worked hard because…I wanted to make you smile this morning."

I felt myself softening. He hated cooking, but he'd done it for me. He motioned to the chair he'd pulled out. When I was seated, he positioned the other chair so that we were sitting beside each other.

"Where did you get the rose?" My mouth wanted to twitch into a smile so I bit my lip.

He looked at me from beneath his lashes. "I snatched one in the lobby downstairs. They won't miss it."

I nodded pensively, biting my lip harder. "Thank you for the pancakes."

"You're very welcome."

He motioned to the tray of food nervously.

Since the pancakes were pretty much cut in different sizes, I grabbed my fork, stabbed a piece, and put it in my mouth. I chewed slowly.

CRUNCH.

"Um," I mumbled, trying to politely spit out the pieces of eggshell.

Caleb hung his head, handing me a napkin.

"I'm sorry, Red. I've never cooked pancakes before. Just wanted to make some for you." There was a mix of mortification and sadness in his voice.

Ah, dammit all to hell and back.

Grabbing his face, I planted a kiss on his lips. We both froze.

One, one thousand. Two, one thousand. Three, one thousand…

I tried to pull away, but his big hands held my face, keeping me still. Then his lips began to move.

His kiss wasn't as I remembered it.

It was better.

Soft lips, gentle bites, tease, tease, tease.

"You taste so good. Better," he corrected. His voice was deep and husky. "Are you my girlfriend now, Red?"

His hands still held my face so that I was exposed and vulnerable to his gaze. I looked away.

"No," I replied.

His hands fell away. "What, then?" he demanded.

Panic was climbing fast in my chest. I felt suffocated. Why couldn't he leave it alone?

He wanted too much. Too fast.

"Nothing," I told him, leaning away. "We're friends."

"I'm not your friend. Friends don't want each other like I want you." His tone was hard, confrontational.

I stood up, stepping out of reach. "I'm not ready to discuss this."

"Fine," he barked, rising. "If that's the way you want it, but I don't want you kissing anyone but *me*."

His tone was commanding and possessive. I didn't like it at all.

"Hey, buddy, listen up!" I snapped, drilling a finger into his chest. "Just because I kissed you last night doesn't mean you can tell me what to do!" His chest was rock hard. "Do it again, I dare you, and I'm out."

His teeth were clenched, his jaw hard.

"This!" I exploded, gesturing between us. "This is what happens with kissing. It complicates things!"

"No," he said sadly, scrubbing his face with his hand. "It doesn't. Exclusivity. Is it too much to ask? Are you with someone else? Is that why?"

It was faint, but I detected hurt in his voice. My anger faded.

"No, Caleb." I looked him in the eye so he could see my honesty. "I'm not with someone else. But I'm not with you either."

"Yes, you are," he insisted.

"No, I'm not."

"What do you call what happened last night, then?" he challenged.

I kept my mouth shut.

"I kissed you. And," he added, "you kissed me back."

I gritted my teeth.

"You kissed me just a couple minutes ago," he pointed out. "Do you need a reminder?"

His tone wasn't playful anymore. It was serious and territorial.

"I am not your property," I informed him, balling my fists.

He was in front of me in a flash. Close, oh, so close. "You drive me crazy," he whispered roughly.

His breath fanned my face. "Crazy," he repeated before he lowered his head. He kissed my bottom lip lightly, biting and pulling at it until I gasped.

I closed my eyes, wanting more. I could feel myself leaning closer to him, wanting to pull him to me, wishing he would—and then he did. Pleasure and desire flowed through my system as he continued to kiss me.

"What do you want, Red?" he murmured.

His tongue traced the seam of my lips, and a moan escaped from my throat.

"The way you kiss me tells me you want me. And not just as friends."

Torn, I pushed away from him. He was too much. I turned away, ready to walk out. He grabbed my arm firmly, then let go as I faced him again.

"Please, don't run away," he said softly. "I don't think I can be your friend. If you just want to be friends, then I want nothing from you."

My heart was beating too loud, too fast.

His eyes blazed. "I want too much from you to just be your friend."

All or nothing? It was an ultimatum. Panic was budding in my chest again.

I don't want to lose you yet, Caleb.

"Don't ask this of me. You want too much. It's all so fast," I blurted out.

He closed his eyes, lowering his head and gripping the back of his neck with both his hands as he sat on the chair.

"I'm sorry. You're right," he said softly. When he looked up, his eyes were solemn. "I don't know what the hell I'm doing. I know I'm handling it all wrong, but I can't seem to stop. I just want it all with you. Everything. And I'm clueless how…" he finished helplessly, his hands falling to his lap.

My heart felt heavy. Why did I feel like I wanted to gather him in my arms and take away his pain?

I was falling, falling…and there was no safety net. He was asking me to risk everything.

I swallowed. "Can we take it slow?"

He took a deep breath, nodding. "Let's do that. How about you get ready, and I'll drive us both to school?" He smiled adorably. "If that's okay?"

I sighed. "Okay."

I realized he'd gotten what he wanted in the end.

CHAPTER
eleven

Veronica

"SO YOU MADE ME CLEAN MY APARTMENT LAST NIGHT FOR NOTHING?"

Kara glared daggers at me as she parked in front of the strip mall. There were only a few cars in the parking lot, but Kara insisted on taking the spot farthest from the yoga studio.

"Caleb needs a friend right now," I said lamely as soon as we got out of the car and started walking.

She slurped an extra-large strawberry milk shake through two yellow straws. She was lactose intolerant, but that didn't seem to deter her.

"Kar, you're not supposed to eat or drink anything substantial before we go to yoga class. And is that made of soy milk?"

She snarled at me, defensive. "I'm allowed to drink real milk. I'm a lacto-vegetarian. Not vegan. There is a huge difference. Besides, my stomach is made of steel. Steel, baby." She patted her belly.

"Uh-huh."

We were on our way to a hot yoga class. Kara had insisted we go together to strengthen her decision on starting her life over without "that asshole Cameron," as she put it. She said she needed to try new things, meet new people, and move on.

I figured it would be more beneficial if she stopped talking about him, but what are friends for if not to support each other's idiosyncrasies? Or, in her case, addiction.

When we reached the entrance to the studio, Kara leaned against the glass wall beside the front door, busily drinking her milk shake. I stood next to her, looking around.

It was drizzling a little, and the temperature had dropped to jacket weather. Spring was stubbornly holding on to the tiara and refusing to pass it to summer. A few brave locals had moved on from sweaters and pants to shorts and spaghetti straps.

"So, how much did you actually clean?" I asked.

She looked away. "I changed the sheets on the bed."

"That it?" I grinned.

"Uh-huh." She pinched my cheek. "So his parents are divorcing, huh?" she asked.

My smile disappeared. "Yes, but don't tell anyone."

"Who am I going to tell? Oprah? Seriously." She rolled her eyes. "Some kids take it harder than others when their parents divorce, I guess."

I frowned but didn't comment.

"Anyway, that's why you make sure you date a lot before settling, because you know what? I've only dated and slept with that asshole."

"Cameron?"

"No, Brad fucking Pitt, Ver."

"Yeah? How much did he pay you after?" I deadpanned.

Her laugh was big and boisterous, and I had to join in. Then she turned serious.

"I feel dry," she said, sighing. "Am I supposed to feel dry? Like the Bahara Desert."

"You mean the Sahara," I corrected.

She flicked her fingers at me. "You know I was blond in my past life, right? That's my excuse, and I'm sticking to it. I don't have shit for brains, but man, you're up there with NASA."

I laughed, shaking my head.

She slurped the last of her milk shake and did a free throw into the garbage can. The cup bounced on the rim and fell to the ground, spilling its contents like pink vomit.

"Shit!" she hissed.

"That's littering. You'd better pick that up," I said when she started to walk away.

But before she could respond, someone else snatched the cup off the ground.

"I don't want anyone getting fined for littering," a male voice said, laughing. "Hi."

He was tall, with a military haircut that emphasized his strong facial structure. Deep-brown eyes crinkled at the corners as he smiled. A shadow of beard covered his square jaw, making him look very masculine, and tattoos decorated both his muscled and toned brown arms. It was obvious he went to the gym—there was one next door to the yoga studio. He wore a black muscle shirt that showed all of the dark, intricate tats, and there were a lot of them.

"Hi," Kara choked out.

"I'm Theo."

"Kara."

I spotted a tongue ring when he spoke. I glanced at Kara and almost laughed at the expression on her face. Her mouth was slightly open in awe, her big hazel eyes rounding.

Theo looked at Kara curiously as he dropped the milk shake in the garbage. I elbowed her inconspicuously. She blinked several times before she started to wake up, but it was too late. A car had stopped in front of us, and Theo was already waving goodbye and sliding into the car.

"Shit, Ver. I think I found the guy who's gonna pop my cherry."

I laughed. "Memo for you, Kar. Your cherry has already been popped."

"Pop my second cherry?"

"Unless you sprouted another vagina, I don't think you have a second cherry." Kara didn't respond, staring at the car as it drove away. "Let's go. Yoga releases tension, which you *really* need right now."

"Pizza can do that, too, girlfriend. Or getting laid."

I smirked, grabbed her hand, and dragged her inside the building.

When we entered the yoga class, the heat felt like a slap in the face. The hot air encased every part of my body like a bodysuit. We were about ten minutes into the class when I threw a glance at Kara. She looked green. *Uh-oh.*

"Kar," I hissed. "Are you okay?"

We weren't allowed to talk, but she looked ready to pass out.

She shook her head, whimpering, "Can we leave?"

We weren't allowed to leave either. The instructor wanted us to lie down and get our breath back if we felt dizzy. *Screw it.*

"Let's go, Kar."

Sympathetic eyes darted our way as I helped her up. The instructor came to check on us, but Kara told her she was fine. In the hallway, the rush of air-conditioning greeted us like a taste of ambrosia.

"Fuck, yes!" Kara said breathlessly, disentangling herself from my arms and dumping her limp, sweaty carcass on the floor, spread-eagle. "It smelled like old vagina in there. Someone farted while doing those exorcist dance moves. I swear, if you pull me back in there, I'm going to slap you to kingdom come, my friend. Right down to purgatory."

Kara had never done yoga before, and the expression on her face cracked me up. Loud peals of laughter echoed in the hallway.

When the instructor opened the classroom door and reprimanded us with a glare, I pulled Kara up and we stumbled to the lockers.

Pictures of Buddha and Asian gardens hung on the orange walls. Three bathroom stalls were installed on the right half of the room and the lockers on the left.

"I told you not to drink that milk shake, Kar."

She groaned and went straight to a bathroom stall. "Why do I have to be lactose intolerant? Why? *Why?*" she lamented, slamming the door. "Why the fuck don't people flush the toilet? Do they think I enjoy looking at their crap? Enjoy smelling it? Fucking flush the toilet already!" she growled.

I heard a toilet flush.

"I think you're right. You need to get laid."

"I'm gonna find that god we saw earlier. Just watch me. He is hot enough to compete with that asshole Cameron. He even has a tongue ring. Did you know Cameron has one too? And I don't know if you've figured this out or not, but our names are kinda similar—Cam/Kara/Kar, it's like karma. Isn't that sweet as fuck?"

Here we go again.

CHAPTER

twelve

Caleb

THE LAST THING I THOUGHT I WOULD EVER BE WAS A CLINGY boyfriend.

I dated girls, I hung out with girls, I slept with girls—but that was about it. There was never anyone I was even close to being serious with, and I was fine with that.

Ignorance is bliss and all that crap.

Why did Red make me want more?

I'd finally convinced her to let me drive her to school. Barely. She didn't give an inch. If she did, she made me work for it. Some mornings I'd find her gone, so I made sure to wake up earlier than usual.

I used to hate waking up early, but now I liked it because there was something to look forward to.

I glanced at her as I drove us to school. I could only see her beautiful profile: the catlike slant of her eye, the slash of her cheekbone, the fullness of her bottom lip, her dark hair whipping in the wind from the open window. And my heart ached a little.

What is it about this girl?

Red tore my world apart, brick by brick, and revealed something more. Something inside me I had long forgotten. Something I yearned for.

"What are you doing after class tonight?" I asked. "And don't say work because I know it's your night off."

When she didn't respond, I threw her a glance. She was biting her lip, looking indecisive. Her hand was tightly wrapped around her seat belt. I spotted a small cut on the skin of one of her knuckles. I had noticed her skin was sensitive and easily bruised.

My chest tightened.

I wanted to shield this girl.

More than anything in my life.

But why? Why her? Why now?

Was it because she was the most beautiful thing I've ever seen? Was it because she was the first girl to turn me down? Was it because she was a challenge?

I'd seen her wake up early every day, go to school and work, and even though exhausted after a full day, she'd make sure I had something to eat. The light would be on in her room late at night, and I knew she was studying. Through her door, I could hear the soft background music she played, hear her muffled voice as she memorized her notes, but what I never heard was a complaint. Not even once.

She worked hard without expecting much in return, and when she received more than she expected, she was distrustful. It was like watching someone at war with the world every day. And maybe she was. Maybe that was why she'd set her defenses so high, never dropping them for even a moment. Maybe she didn't even know how to let them down anymore.

She was like a puzzle that was missing a few pieces. Maybe I'd carve my own pieces to complete her.

I was treading dangerous waters, and I was clueless how a real relationship worked, but I was never one to give up easily when I really wanted something. And I wanted a relationship with this girl.

She didn't want to commit to me. She wanted it slow, so we'd take it slow.

"I'm studying for exams tonight," she finally answered me.

"What exams?"

I could feel her dark eyes boring into me, and I was reminded of her forceful personality. Sometimes I wanted to protect this girl so much that I forgot how strong she really was. "What's this about?"

She sounded distrustful. It wasn't like I planned on eating her tonight.

Well, not yet.

"We have a basketball game tonight. Wanna watch me play?" She hadn't seen me play before, and I wanted to show off. "They're also setting up a drive-in theater in the campus parking lot. Come with me," I said, my eyes shifting from the road to her.

"I don't know, Caleb…"

She was already giving in. I could hear it in her voice. I gave her a goofy grin. Her mouth twitched. My girl rarely smiled, but when she did, I felt like Superman.

"Don't you want to show off your boyfriend to the world? Everyone wants my attention, but you get all of it, Red."

She snorted.

"What a prize you are," she said sarcastically. "And you're not my boyfriend."

People tended to misinterpret me. Just because I was a guy who smiled a lot, that didn't mean I took everything in stride. I get hurt easily. I'm just really good at hiding my feelings with flippancy.

What she'd just said… That hurt. I didn't know if she meant it or if she was joking. She must have noticed my change of mood because she turned toward me and studied my face.

"I'm sorry. I was just joking," she said quietly, her voice apologetic, her eyes beseeching.

How could I be mad at her when she was so sweet? I wasn't mad anymore, but I wanted her to work for my forgiveness. I always worked harder when it came to her, and I wanted her to do the same for me. I wanted to feel like I was worth it to her.

"Caleb?"

I gave her a small nod, my expression neutral. I couldn't wait to see what she would do next.

She gently touched my arm, and I felt a jolt when her skin touched mine. She must have felt it too because she pulled her hand away.

"All right, I'm going to your practice, but only if Kara goes with me."

"Kara?" I raised my brows. *Cameron's* Kara?

Red explained how she had met Kara at work, and how they'd bonded and were close friends now. I felt pathetic because I was a little jealous.

I knew Kara through Cameron. When they broke up, Cameron refused to talk about her. Even now, he couldn't say her name.

"So you're coming?" I sent her a goofy grin. Her mouth twitched into a smile. I did a fist pump and yelled at the top of my lungs, "*Go, Caleb. Go, Caleb, go! Go, Caleb. Go, Caleb, go! Aaaaah! CALEB!*"

I would have danced if I wasn't driving. I had her laughing after my cheer.

I felt like I was flying.

After I parked the car, I climbed out quickly to open her door, but she beat me to it. She started walking away from me like I had leprosy.

"I'll see you later," she said over her shoulder. "If Kar agrees, okay?"

She didn't wait for my answer and opened the entrance to the classroom building. It nearly hit my face as it started to swing closed.

"Wait." I jogged to catch up to her. I noticed her looking around warily. Was she hiding from someone?

A few students were lounging in the corridors, some in front of their lockers, grabbing and storing books, checking their phones, and others in groups chatting. No one was paying attention to us. What was she worried about?

"I'd like to walk you to your class," I said.

"No!"

I frowned. "Why not?" Even to my ears I sounded like a petulant child.

"Caleb, I'll see you later, okay?" Her voice was firm as she waved goodbye and walked away as fast as she could.

Why did I feel like she didn't want to be seen with me? Was she ashamed of me?

Me—Caleb Lockhart, MVP and most prized catch on campus—shot down by an antagonistic girl.

I knew girls loved to talk about their feelings. Red was the only girl I knew who didn't. Something must have happened to her to make her wary. Maybe an ex-boyfriend? Just the thought of her having an ex-boyfriend made me want to kill someone.

I'd never been possessive of anyone or anything. I wasn't a possessive person. Was I?

If not, why did I want to punch that guy's face when I saw him checking her out as she passed him? I gave him a hard glare so he'd get the message.

Shit, I was definitely possessive of her. First time *that's* happened.

It wasn't like she encouraged me. Far from it. But here I was chasing after her, feeling like a desperate, jealous, insane person. This was getting *so* messed up.

"Red!" I yelled down the hallway.

She turned to look at me, horrified, and then she started half jogging and half walking away from me. I caught up to her easily.

"Why don't you want to be seen with me? Are you ashamed of me?" I asked incredulously. I couldn't, for the life of me, understand her.

And I must have been screwed up in the head, but I loved that. I loved that I couldn't figure her out, that she was giving me a hard time.

"Everyone is looking!" She gritted her teeth.

"So?"

"So!"

I snatched her backpack from her, wrapped my hand around her arm to keep her from walking away, and scooped her off her feet.

"Everyone!" I yelled in the hallway. "She's mine. If you touch even a hair on her head, I will hunt you down. Now spread the word far and wide."

I heard people laugh and cheer. Someone yelled, "You're the man, Lockhart!"

Red's eyes were as big as saucers, and her mouth was open in horror.

"What did you do?" she moaned, covering her face with her hands.

"I'm protecting you."

"Bullshit. You were staking your territory, and I told you how I feel about that."

I loved it when her eyes blazed.

"You're mine. Face it." I put her down.

She eyed me for a moment, still looking like she wanted to kill me, before blowing out a breath and turning away.

I watched her walk away from me.

Would she turn around and look at me?

Was I just kidding myself that there was something more here? Maybe it was all one-sided. Maybe she didn't feel the same way I did. Maybe I was fooling myself.

I waited. Waited. I wasn't asking for a whole bucket of water. Just a drop. Just a drop was more than enough. Just one look.

Turn around and look at me.

But she didn't.

I was about to turn away, feeling a heaviness in my chest, when I saw her stop. She just stood there a second, two, three.

And then she turned, just a little so that I saw her glance at me. There was a small smile playing on her lips before she disappeared down the corridor.

I think my grin almost broke my face.

God, I wanted her. I wanted her like I'd never wanted anything before in my life.

I yearned to be a part of her world. I wanted to be hers.

And after that glance, after that small smile from her, it looked like there would be more. Definitely more. *Man, I'm in trouble.* It wouldn't be easy, and I knew the ride would be rough, but that was okay.

She was worth it. I just knew it.

CHAPTER

thirteen

Veronica

"FIVE BUCKS SAYS SOMEONE WILL CHANGE THAT BORING-ASS MOVIE we're supposed to watch to porn." Kara took a sip from her milk shake.

I choked on my drink, shaking my head. I really hoped she was wrong.

The school grounds were illuminated by three tower spotlights, blinding anyone who looked directly at them. More than half of the parking lot was already filled with parked cars. Alcohol wasn't allowed, but I'd seen empty beer bottles scattered on the ground.

"I'm sorry I made you postpone your visit to the nursing home, Kar."

Her grandma had lived in a nursing home for years and had passed away, but Kara continued to visit there. She acted rough and tough, but inside she was a soft teddy bear.

She shrugged. "I'll bring them some damn whiskey next week, and they'll love me again," she replied.

"I'll throw in some gin. I owe you."

"You owe me your firstborn."

"Thanks, really," I said, then looked at her more closely. "Why is your face shiny?"

Her brows drew together. "Are you for real? This is what you would call a highlighter. I'm a princess. I glitter. I sparkle. I rule over the land."

"The land of glitter."

"Exactly. Now you're learning. Where are you going?"

I stopped in my tracks. "Don't they practice at the North Gym?"

She shook her head and steered me in the other direction. "Unless it changed, it's always been at the South Gym. Trust me." Her voice turned cold. "I know."

I felt guilty. I knew it would be hard for her to see Cameron again.

"Kar—"

"I'm absolutely fine. I'm made of steel," she said with confidence. She paused at the entrance and took a deep breath. "Steel, baby."

As Kara opened the gym doors, I heard the sharp sound of a whistle, shoes squeaking against the floor, and a lot of yelling. Only a few people were watching—mostly girls, which was not surprising since the sun was setting and most of the students were probably at the drive-in theater. We sat in the middle row of the bleachers near the exit.

I heard Kara take another deep breath as her eyes darted to

the court. A look of pain flitted over her face, but she masked it quickly. I followed her line of sight and spotted Cameron passing the ball to...Caleb.

I felt a huge smile on my face. Caleb was wearing a red jersey, with *LOCKHART* and a number 7 printed on the back. He caught the ball in his big hands, raised his arms, and expertly threw it into the basket. The girls on the sidelines cheered.

Caleb raised his head to look at the wall clock and then glanced toward the front entrance. Someone yelled at him to get his attention back to the game. He was distracted. I felt a pinch in my heart.

Was he waiting for me?

Oh, Caleb, what am I going to do with you?

The squeeze in my heart was getting uncomfortable. I took a deep breath.

No one had ever paid attention to me like Caleb did, and no one had affected me this much, no one I really wanted. It flattered me and made me feel very special because he could have gotten any girl he wanted, but he chose me.

I liked him. A lot. I was so very, very close to giving in. Could I do it? Could I trust him?

My fear of getting hurt was stronger than my like for him. I barely knew him. What if he only liked me because I was a challenge, and once I gave in, he would spit me out faster than I could blink? How much of myself was I willing to lose?

Nothing, I thought. I had no plans of giving up any part of myself. I didn't want to be like my mother. This boy would break my heart.

My mother and father were married for three years before they adopted me. They couldn't have kids and my father really wanted children, so they got me. We were happy until I turned five, when my father lost his job and started gambling and drinking and whoring.

I remembered waking up in the middle of the night as he stumbled into our small studio apartment drunk as a skunk, throwing things around, blaming me for losing his job, for not having kids, for starting the bad luck that he couldn't shake since they adopted me.

I was five. I didn't understand back then. All I knew was that this man—who I'd thought was my father, who had loved me like his daughter and bounced me on his lap and carried me on his shoulders—terrified me now.

He burst in my room, mad as a bull, banging the door against the wall. I thought he was going to kill me. Petrified, I huddled in my blanket in the corner of my room. He was about to smack me in the head when my mother yelled for him to stop.

He turned on her instead and started slapping her.

I hated him with a passion. This man, the only man I loved, broke my heart into pieces. My heart had never been whole after that night.

He left us for a while, but he kept coming back and my mother just…accepted him. I didn't understand it. She was a strong woman, and yet when this man came in her life, she lost her self-respect and pride, allowing him to abuse her time and time again. I loved my mother very much, but I think I resented her a little for it.

From then on, I swore never to be like her. I would not let myself fall in love with someone and lose myself. I may have serious issues, but I wasn't interested in anyone fixing me.

Even when she was dying, she called out his name. He never showed up.

Caleb is different, my subconscious argued. *Caleb is not like your father.*

He was sweet and kind, funny and immature sometimes, but he was always there if I needed help. No matter how hard I pushed him away, he just kept coming back for more. He had to be masochistic.

Our eyes met.

I wasn't being completely honest with myself, because at that moment, when his face broke into a grin as he waved at me, I felt like he had me in the palm of his hand.

I took a deep breath. Everything was okay. I liked him, and I had already admitted that to myself. I could pull away whenever I wanted to. I would not let myself fall for him. My self-preservation was stronger than anything else.

The coach called a time-out. Caleb's smile was from ear to ear as he sauntered toward me like he'd already won the game and I was his prize. I couldn't help smiling back. Several girls approached him and tried to engage him in conversation. He just gave them a polite smile, shook his head, and continued over to me.

It's me he wants.

He climbed the bleachers, his gaze never leaving mine.

"Hey, Red," he whispered when he reached me, his eyes dancing happily. "You're here."

He sat beside me, gently pulling a lock of my hair.

"Hey, Kar, nice to see you again." He leaned forward to address her. "I didn't know you were friends with my girl until she told me today."

My girl?

I frowned at him. His smile only widened.

"She didn't tell you she works for me now?" Kara asked.

"No," he replied, his smile fading a little. "She didn't. She doesn't tell me a lot of things."

He pulled another lock of my hair. I reached out and pulled his. He only grinned and leaned down so I could get a better grip. I rolled my eyes.

Kara laughed, but it sounded forced. "Keep working on her. Maybe she'll give you an inch in a few years, eh?"

Her eyes shifted to the court, and she placed her hand on her chest as if in great pain, squeezing her fingers together. I followed her gaze and saw a girl flirting with Cameron.

"I need to fucking breathe. Be right back," Kara said, her words tripping over each other.

"Kar—"

"I'm fine. I'll be right back," she told me, then leaned close. "Don't be a moron. He really, really likes you," she whispered in my ear before she climbed down the bleachers.

I watched her walk away for a few seconds.

"Is she all right?" Caleb asked, concerned. He reached for my face, then tucked an errant strand of hair behind my ear. He really liked doing that.

"I'm not sure."

He sighed. "Is it Cameron?"

I nodded.

"Cameron doesn't talk about it, but I know he isn't all right either. His phone background is her picture."

My eyes widened in surprise. "Really?"

He nodded, smiling. "Red?"

I looked at him curiously. "Yes?"

"Wanna make out in my car after practice? At the movies?"

I had no idea how he could make me blush so easily. He really loved catching me off guard. It was dangerous to be alone with him, even more dangerous when his attention was solely on me. To distract myself, I looked around and noticed several pairs of eyes giving me measuring looks.

"I think your girlfriends are annoyed with me for monopolizing all your attention." I motioned with my chin to the girls standing on the sideline. He didn't even look.

"Is anyone bothering you?"

I shook my head. "No, and if there is someone bothering me, I can take care of myself."

"Regardless," he insisted. He reached for my hand, his thumb absently making circles on my palm. I shivered at the contact. "Will you tell me if anyone starts bothering you? I'll protect you."

My throat felt tight, so I just nodded. No one had ever said that to me before. Not the way he did. Like he meant it.

"I have to go back to practice," he said when the coach whistled. "I want to impress my girl. My *only* girl."

Before I could tell him I wasn't his girl, he was already back on the court. He was good—really, really good. No wonder he was the most valuable player on the team.

I was so engrossed in watching Caleb that, before I knew it, practice was ending. Caleb motioned to the locker room, indicating he was going to get changed.

I looked around and realized Kara hadn't been back in a long while. Worried, I got up to find her. I checked the washroom, but all the stalls were empty.

She must have left. I instantly felt guilty. She probably couldn't stand seeing Cameron around other girls. I left the washroom and pulled out my phone to text her just as two girls went in. I thought I heard Kara's name.

"Cameron is with that Flat Board again. I thought they broke up. What's he doing with her?"

"Maybe they got back together," the other girl answered. "She looked pretty shaken up."

My steps faltered, eyes widening in anger at what I was hearing.

"That Kara needs to stay in her lane. She keeps throwing herself at him."

"I don't know. He looked like he wasn't over her."

"Please. She's a ho ba—"

I couldn't take another word. I was ready to go to war when Caleb suddenly grabbed my arm. He shook his head. I gritted my teeth, fighting the urge to scratch out that girl's eyes.

"I just got a text from Cameron," he said. "He's with Kara."

"What?" I was shocked. Kara wouldn't even talk to Cameron, let alone leave with him. "I have to find her. Why would she be with him?"

"I know they're not on good terms right now, but trust me, Cameron won't let anything bad happen to her. You can talk to her later, give her a call."

I nodded, worried. He squeezed my hand, and I looked up into his eyes.

"I wish someday you'd care for me that way," he whispered. "More."

I held my breath.

"I wish you'd…" He cut himself off, shook his head, and straightened. "Still up for the movie? It's starting soon."

"Actually, Caleb, I had a long day," I admitted. "Maybe we should just go back to your apartment."

He gave me a silent nod. I could see in his face that he was exhausted too. I'd also seen him rotate his left shoulder a few times, massaging it with his hand.

Besides…a date with Caleb Lockhart in an enclosed space would fall on the girlfriend-boyfriend list of things to do, wouldn't it?

"What do you want to eat?" I asked, changing the subject.

I had made chicken potpie for dinner, but if he wanted something else, I'd cook it. When he didn't respond, I looked at him. The gleam in his eyes was telling.

"Do you really want to know?" he asked, his voice heavy with meaning. "I don't think you're ready."

My heart began to pound.

He stared at my lips before his eyes flicked up to mine. "Or are you?"

I held my breath. He was too much to handle.

"Pancakes," I choked out.

Whenever we said *pancakes*, we never really cooked or had pancakes. It was our code word for *Let's get away from here and do something else together.*

He laced his fingers with mine. "Pancakes it is."

CHAPTER

fourteen

Veronica

"SHUT THE FUCK UP, BIRDS!"

I stood on the sidewalk outside Kara's apartment, gawking at her as she yelled and glared at the birds perched on a tree and happily singing.

After Caleb's practice, he and I had skipped the drive-in theater and had just arrived at his apartment when his phone rang. It was Cameron asking if he could come over. I had a feeling something bad had happened between him and Kara so I hurried out, declining Caleb's insistent offer that he'd drive me, and took the bus to check on Kara.

She sat on a white bench, half hidden by one of the two columns lining her porch and the big pots of blue and hot-pink flowers hanging from the ceiling. Suddenly, she jumped up and went inside her apartment, and just as suddenly came out with a spade in her hand and started stabbing the left column like a madwoman.

"I hate you! I hate you. I hate you."

"Uh, Kar?"

She turned at the sound of my voice, her hands going limp at her sides. She lowered her head, and I was afraid she was crying.

"Are you okay?" I asked, walking to her cautiously.

I glanced at the column, wondering what had upset her about it. There was writing on it, but it was unrecognizable now.

She let out a heavy sigh. When she looked up, her eyes were bright but dry. "I'm really glad you came," she mumbled. She walked the few steps to me and squished me in a hug.

When I felt wetness on my shoulder, I wrapped my arms around her awkwardly.

My heart felt heavy. This was a familiar scene to me. Most of my life, I'd seen my mom crying and locking herself in her bedroom for days after my dad left. Unlike my mom, who rejected any kind of touch, Kara clung to me.

"You're such a pathetic hugger." She sniffed again. "Hug me like you mean it, jerkface."

I choked on a laugh, hugging her tighter. "Wanna talk about it? I brought ice cream."

"Cookies and cream?" she asked.

"Yes."

"Come on in," she said.

I followed her inside. Her apartment was as interesting as her personality. Wide windows were covered with pale-blue lace curtains. The walls, painted a creamy white, boasted postcards from different countries. One wall was solely dedicated to photographs of her family and friends. Kara was a family-oriented person, whether she liked to admit it or not.

Jeweled lamps stood on white high tables with curved legs. There was a couch the shape of a woman's lips in the living room, flanked by two high-back French chairs that surprisingly looked great with the couch. Elegant throw pillows in royal blue sat on them. In the middle was a round coffee table with a messy collection of empty beer cans, an open jar of Nutella with a spoon in it, and crumpled tissues scattered everywhere. Her TV was on, and *Gone with the Wind* was playing on the screen.

"I see you've been busy," I commented, dropping onto one of the chairs.

Kara sprawled on the couch and stared at the ceiling.

"What happened, Kar?"

"He drove me back to his place," she answered after a moment. I could hear the pain in her voice. "Nothing happened. Nothing at all. So why does that hurt more?"

"Kar…"

She covered her eyes with her arm. "Could you grab us some beers from the fridge, Ver?"

"Sure."

In the kitchen, my hand froze on the fridge door handle when I spotted a picture held by a magnet on the door. Kara was sitting on Cameron's lap, her arms around his neck, glasses askew, smiling like a loon at the camera. Cameron's arms caged her body, and he bit her chin playfully. His eyes were closed, oblivious that someone was taking their picture.

They looked very happy.

I closed my eyes, silently sympathizing with her. This was one of the reasons why I didn't want a relationship.

Relationships were complicated. They twisted you up inside until you were no longer yourself and pushed you to do stupid things you'd promised yourself you'd never do. Ridiculous.

I placed the ice cream in the freezer, grabbed two cans of beer, and padded back to the living room. Kara scooted upright on the couch when she saw me and reached for the beer I handed her.

She popped it open, and the cracking sound made me cringe as I sat on the chair beside her.

I counted five empty cans on the coffee table. Studying her face, I noticed she didn't even look slightly drunk, her hold on the can steady. Her eyes were puffy from crying, and her nose was red.

I took a sip of my beer, then placed it on the table. I waited for her to open up, but she didn't. She just kept sipping her beer, her eyes transfixed on the TV screen. Suddenly, I heard her sob.

"He used to do that to me, that asshole. Just like Rhett Butler with Scarlett." She took a long sip from her beer, then wiped her cheeks with the backs of her hands.

I glanced at the screen. "What, give you horse rides?"

"No, Sherlock." She sat up straight. "See right through me. That asshole can see right through me." There was a gleam in her eye as she rose from the couch and walked to her bedroom with purpose. I followed.

"So then maybe I should be unpredictable, huh?" she continued, opening her closet, which was bursting with clothes. She pushed hangers aside, pulled out a dress, and walked to the mirror. "I'm done being pathetic," she declared, plastering a tight hot-pink dress to her front. "I may have no tits, but I'm a strong, independent, confident woman."

"Okay, but what's the connection between having no tits and being a strong, independent, confident woman?"

"Just saying," she huffed. "I may be a plain Jane by society's standards, but beauty fades. The strength of your character doesn't. And mine is as strong as the wind, baby. As strong as the wind."

She went back to her closet, pulling out another dress. This time, it was a strappy black number.

"What are you doing?" I asked, curious.

"There's a party at a friend's house today. Please go with me."

I shut my eyes as she pulled her shirt up and off. I let out a sigh. I didn't want to go to a party, but she seemed to need it. I opened one eye. "You done?"

"Yep. You'll have fun." All dressed now, she went to her vanity table. "I'll find you someone, and you guys can, I don't know, watch bacteria grow or something."

I grabbed one of the smaller pillows from her bed and threw it at her. "Kiss my fat ass."

She dodged, and the pillow landed at her feet. "Once you kiss my flat ass." She winked. "I should have a dress for you somewhere in my closet. Take your pick."

I wasn't dressed to party, but it didn't matter. Besides, there was absolutely no way I'd fit in her clothes, and we both knew it. She was tall and slim, and I was short and curvy.

"I'm good, Kar, thanks." I picked up the pillow from the floor and tossed it back on her bed. "I hope you're wearing panties in that excuse for a dress because I'd hate to see your cooch, but you look gorgeous." The short, black dress made her long legs look even longer.

"I'll look more gorgeous once I'm done with my makeup. Want me to do your face?"

"I'm fine, thanks."

"Do me a favor and put on some lipstick, please."

I frowned when she handed me tubes of lipstick and mascara. I put the mascara back in her case.

"What happened today, Kar?"

She shrugged, but it was obvious she was pretending it didn't matter. "I just want to have fun tonight," she replied, expertly putting in her contact lenses.

I nodded. I found that the more I nagged her, the more she closed up. She'd tell me what was bothering her in her own time.

"How is it," she began, angrily digging the hairbrush against her skull, "that he's got more dick in his personality than what's snuggling in his underwear?" Then she blinked. "Actually, that's not true. Cameron's—"

"Stop!" I covered my ears. "I really don't want to hear this!"

She snorted. "Bitch, please. As if you haven't."

I met her eyes in the mirror.

Her eyes rounded in disbelief. "Ver?"

I pursed my lips, shook my head. "I'm a virgin," I confessed.

"What? How…?" She blinked, her jaw dropping. "Virgin… like the Virgin Mary?"

I took a healthy swig of beer. I don't even like beer.

She whistled. "Damn. That's good. I'm proud of you. Really, really impressed. But how is it you haven't boned Lockhart yet?"

"Kar!"

"I mean, how can you resist him? And don't tell me he hasn't tried to get you in bed. That guy's a walking hard-on. Or you just really don't want to?"

"It's not like that."

She paused in applying her mascara, mouth slightly open, eyes directed at me, waiting for me to explain.

"I'm not waiting till after marriage or anything like that, but giving myself to someone… It's a big deal for me. I want it to mean something. It means…"

Everything, I realized. When I decided to give myself to someone, it would mean everything to me.

"I get that. I really do," Kara said, her expression grave.

"Besides, Caleb isn't known for his celibacy," I reasoned. It bothered me more than it should.

"Has he slept with anyone else since he met you?"

The thought of him sleeping with someone else left a bitter taste in my mouth. "I don't know," I replied.

Kara narrowed her eyes, a naughty gleam in them. "It's frustrating to be in love with someone who's slept with everyone, isn't it?" I knew she was talking about Cameron. "Maybe he needs some competition. Hot-guys buffet at the party, my friend." She winked at me, fluffing her hair. "Let's go be bad, BFF."

CHAPTER
fifteen

Veronica

KARA RANG THE BELL TEN TIMES, AS IF SOMEONE COULD HEAR her from the other side of the door where the party was in full swing. When that didn't get a response, she jiggled the doorknob.

"Who locks the door at a house party?" She glared at the still-closed door and started banging with her open palms.

"Uh, Kar, we can just go in the back," I suggested.

She kept on banging—with her fists this time. "Open up, you motherfuckers, or I'll—!"

The door suddenly opened, and a tall, muscular guy stepped out. His warm-brown eyes lit up with surprise and pleasure when they spotted Kara. I recognized him right away from the tattoos on his arms. It was the guy from the gym.

He said something to her, but the deafening blast of music coming from inside made it impossible to hear him. Sending her an apologetic look, he stepped forward and closed the door behind him, muffling the noise.

"Hello again," he said, looking a little flushed.

Kara was tall but had to tilt her head to look up at the guy. I was standing behind her and couldn't see her face, but I knew she was probably staring at him again, slack-jawed. "Hi! Theo, right?"

She was using her fake sweet voice. I smirked.

He nodded. "Yes, I'm Theo. We met in front of the studio when you were, um...ah...littering?" he asked shyly. A dimple appeared on his cheek. He looked boyish, despite his huge build, and happy that she remembered him. "It's nice to see you again, Kara."

"I know. I actually can't believe you're in front of me again." I could hear the grin in her voice. "My friend lurking behind me is Ver."

His eyes widened in surprise as he noticed me. "Hi," he said, smiling sheepishly. I smiled back.

"So," Kara started, "can we join the party?"

"Of course!" He flushed again. "Please come in."

There was something adorable and sweet about Theo, a big guy who blushed and seemed out of sorts when Kara flirted with him.

Music bombarded my ears when he opened the door. He gestured for us to enter first. Inside, warm bodies were packed close together, rubbing and dancing. The smells of beer and sweat and various perfumes permeated the air. Kara's eyes sparkled, the anger and sadness from earlier fading as she took in the surroundings.

"Kar, I'm going to grab a drink. Have fun, but behave," I added, waving her to the dance floor.

She grinned at me, looking grateful. She blew me a kiss, mouthing *I love you* before turning to grab Theo's hand. "Dance with me, Theo."

I watched for a moment as she pulled him into the mass of writhing bodies on the dance floor, swishing her hips to the beat of the music, dancing around him. He looked adorably awkward as he just stood stock-still, not dancing and blushing the whole time.

Kara might flirt with Theo, but I knew that was all she would do. In her mind, she wanted to remain loyal to Cameron, to someone who had broken her heart. I knew she was still in love with Cameron, and watching her now, I realized how much that love was hurting her.

Wasn't love supposed to feel good? Make you feel all warm and protected? Then why did it hurt so much?

Feeling thirsty, I went to the kitchen to search the fridge for a drink. It was nearly empty, only a few bottles of beer remaining, along with a small bottle of orange juice—as if it had been waiting for me, reminding me of someone I was trying hard not to think about.

I reached for the orange juice anyway, twisting the cap and feeling a smile on my face as I took a long drink. By the time I went back to the living room, I couldn't see Kara and Theo anymore. I was about to search for them, just to make sure I knew where she was and that she was safe, when the music suddenly stopped playing. The sharp echo of the microphone stabbed my ears.

The crowd was cheering instead of complaining, and I automatically searched for the reason. There, on a makeshift stage beside the huge speakers, a band was getting ready to play.

The dim lighting made it hard to see clearly, but there was something vaguely familiar about the vocalist. He picked up his guitar with ease and familiarity, as if he had done it a thousand times before, and folded his long legs as he sat on a stool.

He looked down for a moment to adjust his guitar, his wavy hair sliding silkily over his forehead, hiding his face. He raked his fingers impatiently through his hair, rising from his seat and setting his guitar down to search his pockets. He laughed lightly at himself when he found an elastic band in his pocket and quickly gathered his hair in a bun. I could hear his fangirls sighing.

"I hope everyone is having a great time. Thank you for letting us play for you tonight," he said. He had a faint accent I couldn't identify. French, maybe?

The crowd went wild at the first note from his guitar. Girls screamed, *Damon! Damon!*

His voice was deep, almost raspy. I found a spot near the staircase and leaned against the wall, drinking my orange juice as I listened.

A couple of girls lifted their shirts and flashed him. I wanted to march in front of them and pull their shirts down. He looked down, smiling and seemingly embarrassed as he continued singing.

A movement in my peripheral vision made me look up, and I thought I saw Kara and Theo walk into the kitchen. What were they up to?

I stayed where I was, enjoying a few songs to give them

privacy. When the band called for a quick break, I decided to look for Kara in the kitchen, but I only saw a guy on the floor, passed out drunk. Where was she?

Deciding to get another drink, I opened the fridge and found it empty. I sighed loudly and leaned against the counter, crossing my arms and feeling out of place.

What was Caleb doing now?

Stop! Stop thinking about him!

I'd made him chicken potpie for dinner, but Cameron had phoned before we could eat, and then I'd left to check on Kara. Did Caleb eat already?

Stop it!

I miss him.

No! You do not miss him.

If he were here right now, he'd probably do something ridiculous like sing onstage with the band or do cartwheels in the middle of the dance floor. He was so silly. And sweet. And so attractive. So…appealing.

I closed my eyes, imagining the way his eyes looked at my lips, how with just one look I knew what he was thinking…

I looked up when I heard someone clear their throat. It was the lead vocalist from the band, the one who looked familiar. He was leaning against the doorjamb, arms crossed, almost like he had been there for a while, watching me with an amused smile. I narrowed my eyes at him.

"Hey, Angel Face. I—"

A group of guys suddenly grabbed him, each guy holding one of his arms or legs. I moved away as they carried him toward the back of the house, laughing raucously. A few moments later, I heard a loud splash, followed by "You assholes!" They must have thrown him into the pool.

I grinned in spite of myself. That was definitely something Caleb would do. Why was I always thinking about him? Frowning, I shook my head. This was not good. I needed fresh air to clear my head.

Stepping out to the backyard, I walked to the garden and stopped when I heard Kara's voice. I found her and Theo sitting on a stone bench, surrounded by high, thick shrubs that almost hid them from view. They were facing each other, leaning close to each other. I spun around with every intention of leaving them alone when I heard angry footsteps.

"Theodore, we're running out of beer!"

Kara and Theo pulled away from each other. A girl stood a few feet away from me and was glaring daggers at them.

She was stunning. Her hair was pixie-cut and dyed a shocking blue—like the skin color of a Smurf. Her face was heart-shaped, cheekbones high and sharp. But what fascinated me more than her hair were her eyes. They were two different colors. One was a vivid blue, and the other was dark brown.

She was petite, but she had the body of an Amazon. She dressed her luscious curves in a black shirt that said *Bow to me, you useless mortals* and white-washed jeans that were ripped at the knees. She finished the look with black combat boots.

This girl screamed balls-kicker.

"Dude, I'm busy. Can't you get your brother to get some?" Theo grumbled.

"No. He's busy exchanging spit and germs and God-knows-what with that walking STD over there."

I choked on a laugh.

Theo blushed. "Language, dude."

"I am not your dude!"

The girl looked like she was going to stamp her foot.

"I'm sorry, Kara," he apologized.

Kara looked like she was on the verge of laughter. "It's all right," she replied as she stood. "I'll see you around, then?"

I headed back inside to let them finish their conversation in private. When Kara found me, she was grinning.

"So, we have a plan," she started, hooking her arm through mine.

"We do?"

"You and I are going to ride in Theo's car to get some beer at the store. He's meeting us at the front with his girl buddy. Let's go!"

I frowned. "He's a stranger, Kar." I knew Theo looked like a sweet guy, but looks could be deceiving. "What if he ends up being one of those sex-slave traders and sells us to the mob? Haven't you seen that movie with Liam Neeson where his daughter gets kidnapped and sold into sex slavery?"

Kara barked out a laugh. "Then I'd chop his balls off. Let your hair down just this one night for me! I'm brokenhearted, and I haven't been banged in…" She muttered something under her breath. I heard the words *months*, *days*, and *hours*. "But who's counting?"

"You drive me crazy."

She winked. "You love me."

She dragged me to the front of the house, where Theo pulled up in a sleek, black 1967 Chevy Impala. Kara sat in the passenger seat, while I climbed in beside the blue-haired girl in the back.

"I don't know why I have to sit here, Theo." She pouted, her voice dripping with annoyance. "I always ride beside you."

"Be nice, Beth." Theo glanced at Kara and back at me apologetically. "I'm sorry. She forgot to take her polite pills today. She's Beth, by the way. Beth, this is Kara and Ver."

"Hi, Beth." I smiled at her. She smiled back.

Kara turned in her seat. "You can call me Kar."

Beth rolled her eyes at Kara. Suddenly, the tune of "Baby Got Back" filled the car. It was Beth's phone ringing. She frowned at it before she answered. "Hello! The number you dialed is busy finding fucks to give. Please try again later."

I laughed. I liked this girl.

CHAPTER
sixteen

Veronica

"So, Kara," Theo started, "what's your story?"

Beth rolled her eyes again and let out an exasperated sigh. "He's always like this. Watch out. Theo could fish out a priest's secrets. Before you know it, you'll find yourself telling Theo all your dirtiest deeds." She smirked.

"Is that true?" Kara asked, her voice flirty.

I was glad that Kara was having fun, or else she was trying hard not to be sad. Beside me, Beth squirmed in her seat. She seemed itchy, like she wanted to pounce between Theo and Kara to separate them. I bit back a laugh. The girl was nuts about Theo. That, or she was overly protective of him.

Were they siblings? It didn't seem like it when I computed the way she looked at him. She looked at him like...Caleb looked at me.

I sighed. Caleb thoughts weren't allowed tonight. I tuned out for a moment until I heard Beth's annoyed voice cut in.

"So you're using Theo as a rebound because you broke up with your ex?" Beth demanded all of a sudden. Her hand went to Theo's shoulder protectively.

"Beth," Theo warned.

Kara chuckled. "Relax. Theo is a nice guy, and I only fall for the bad guys. He's all yours, girl."

Theo groaned at the same time Beth said, "Good." Then she added, "I'm not always a bitch. I sleep sometimes too, you know. Like a normal human being."

The tension disappeared. Kara and I laughed, and Theo snorted.

"Theo's a softie. People take advantage of him all the time because he's such a nice guy. He needs me to protect him."

"I'd like to think I'm the one protecting you, since I'm older." He flashed her a grin.

"Look," Beth said, flicking Theo's ear. "Tell me I'm right or tell me you're wrong, Theo. Take your pick."

Kara and I kept quiet, enjoying their banter for a while. They were like an old married couple.

Theo parked in front of the liquor store and asked us to stay in the car and wait for him.

"See how he can make you do things for him?" Beth ranted. "I mean, what kind of girl in this day and age would just accept a guy ordering her around like that? It's a talent, I'm telling you! He's so irritating." Her face mirrored her displeasure, but her eyes told a different story as they followed Theo's form until he disappeared inside the store.

Kara and I shared a knowing look. Beth scooted between the

front seats so she could switch the radio station. She settled on indie rock before sitting back in her seat.

"I think it's because he's a very nice guy," I offered. "He doesn't *tell* you what to do; he *asks* in his own sweet way. I like your Theo."

Beth shifted in her seat, smiling. She seemed satisfied when I said *your* Theo.

"So, Kar." Beth started. When Kara didn't answer, Beth called her again. Finally, Beth reached forward and tapped Kara on the shoulder.

"Yeah? Sorry." Kara sighed, raking her fingers through her hair. She sounded tired.

Beth whistled. "You got it bad for the ex, girl."

She scooted closer to Kara. Now that she was sure Kara wasn't moving in on Theo, Beth was warming up to her. "If he doesn't give a fuck about you, why do you still love him?"

Kara looked at her seriously. "Would you keep loving Theo if he didn't feel the same way about you?"

Before Beth could say anything else, Theo came back, smiling and holding beer. A lot of beer. Beth scooted between the front seats again. She pulled the keys from the ignition, rolled down the window, and passed them to Theo's outstretched hand. He walked back to open the trunk and put the beer in, then got in and started the car. They seemed to have a routine. It was so cute to watch.

We were a block away from the liquor store when the car shuddered to a stop.

Theo groaned. "Man," he moaned, resting his head on the steering wheel. "I'm so sorry."

"I told you to sell this piece of shite, Tee. What is it this time?"

"It's just the battery. I need a boost."

"My dad owns a car repair shop," Kara offered. "You can bring it in, and I'll give you a discount."

Theo looked at her gratefully. His smile was embarrassed.

Beth tossed a set of keys to Theo. "Grab my car so you can give it a boost." She turned toward us to explain. "I live just a couple blocks away. He can run it. Go, Tee."

Theo stepped out of the car and hesitated before closing the door. "I don't want to leave you girls alone here. It's late."

"This is not the time for that caveman crap, Theo," Beth chided. "I'm hungry, and I have to pee. Go!" She made a shooing motion with her hand.

Theo looked worriedly at us, and I gave him a smile so he knew I was okay with it.

"Lock your doors, and keep your phones with you. Dial 911—"

Beth reached for the handle and closed the car door in his face. Theo just shook his head, waved, and left.

"He is such an old-fashioned nerd." Beth huffed. "He thinks guys should take care of everything. It's stupid."

"I think it's sweet," I said, smiling at her.

She pouted. The car was parked under a streetlamp, and its light created a halo around Beth. With her blue hair, she looked supernatural, like a sea fairy.

"You're so in love with him," Kara commented, turning to stare at her.

"What?"

"You heard me. Does he know?"

Beth was silent for a moment before she answered. "No. Yes. I don't know."

I could tell she was debating whether she should trust us or not. I guessed she'd decided to trust us, since after a minute she said, "He's pretty dense, and I don't want to tell him. It's going to…ruin what we have, you know?"

She cracked her knuckles and turned to Kara. "So what happened to you and your ex?"

I glanced at Kara, worried. She looked pale and subdued.

"I was going to wait until Ver and I were alone, but I think we can welcome an ugly face like you into our little group. What do you think, Ver?"

I chuckled. "Sure. One with pretty blue hair, preferably."

Beth beamed at me, then suggested, "Well, if we're listening to this drama queen here, let's go outside for some fresh air. Sit on the hood and drink beer? No one is around."

We all agreed. We lounged on the hood of Theo's car, Kara and I flanking Beth. They were drinking beer, but I declined. I didn't want to get drunk when Kara needed me sober.

"So, what's up?" Beth started.

Kara pulled her long legs to her chest, wrapping her arms around them and resting her forehead on her knees. "Ver brought me to watch her boyfriend's basketball practice today—"

"He's not my boyfriend."

"—and my ex was there. I wasn't feeling well so I left. Cameron saw me and eventually found me. He brought me to his place." She shrugged. "Nothing happened. End of story."

Beth nudged Kara and told her to stretch out her legs. She settled her head on my lap and draped her feet over Kara's legs. I couldn't help but smile at the way Beth *fit* with us, how at ease she was with us. "Come on. You gotta give me more than that."

"There was no closure between us when we broke up," Kara said. "We were happy, and then one day he just…changed."

When Kara didn't continue, I glanced at her. Tears were flowing down her cheeks, but she wasn't blinking. I wondered if she was even aware she was crying.

"Kar?"

"I gave so much to that boy. I can't possibly give anything anymore. That's what I thought before he brought me back to his place, you know? That I was done. There was nothing more I could give before I went mental," she sobbed, taking a long drink from her beer.

"But when I was there, I realized that I could still give him more of me. If that's what he needed to come back to me. I'm such a pathetic loser."

"No, Kar," I said.

She shook her head. "I just need you to listen for now, okay?" she said, looking at me and Beth.

Beth and I nodded, helpless.

"Today at basketball practice, I knew he was going to be there. I knew it, but I still went because…because I'm a hypocrite. I say I don't want to see him, but I'm lying. Because I still…I still love him. I know he still loves me, and I don't understand what's stopping him from being with me. I feel like he's putting a barrier between us, and I can't fucking climb over it."

I understood what she was saying. I had placed barriers between me and Caleb, but I was scared he was finding ways to climb over them. I shook my head. Why was I thinking of Caleb? This was Kar's night.

"You know there are different kinds of kisses from Cameron." She sighed deeply. "His public kisses are just small nips here and there. There are the possessive kisses where he uses a little tongue. And then there's *the* kiss where you know he won't stop until you get what you both want, you know? And that's normally when we end up in bed. All those times when he gave me *the* kiss, never once did he not make love to me. Never. But tonight, he stopped." She started crying again. "He *stopped*, Ver, and I don't fucking know *why*." She was sobbing uncontrollably now, gut-wrenching cries that tore my heart.

Beth sat up, sensing that Kara needed me. She gave me space and slid off the car hood so I could scoot over and gather Kar in my arms. She curled herself to me, seeking comfort. Beth rubbed her back.

I had never seen Kara Hawthorne break down like this. She appeared so strong that I hadn't even thought it possible.

"We don't need to confess if we murder someone, you know," Beth said. "I know a lot of good places to hide a dead body. Just saying."

Kara looked at Beth like she'd sprouted another head, and then we all burst out laughing.

Kara rubbed her cheeks with her hands. "Dammit, I'm pathetic, aren't I?"

I nodded. "Yes, you are."

"Jeez—"

I held up a hand to stop her. "Listen. Do you want to know what I think or not?"

She stopped and turned to me. "Of course I do. Hit me."

"Making someone the center of your universe is not healthy, and I think you've done that with Cameron. You've lost your friends because you'd rather be with him, and you've lost the old you, right?" I gave her a sympathetic look. I knew this because I'd watched it happen with my mom.

"You know when people say 'You complete me'?" I continued. "I don't believe in that. How do you complete someone when you've lost yourself in loving them? How do you find yourself? You have to learn to be strong without him, so when one of you is weak, you're not stuck in the same hole of weakness together. That's what will destroy you. You can't be weak together."

I glanced at Kara. Her eyes were closed, and tears ran down her cheeks. I reached for her hand, lending her comfort and strength from my touch.

"Wallowing in the past is not healthy," I said. "If you were so great together, why aren't you together now? Maybe you'll be back together in the future, maybe you won't. People tend to only remember the good memories, but that's not right. You have to remember the bad memories too."

After a few moments, Kara threw herself at me, her arms in a tight bear hug. "I love you, Ver. Thank you."

"Ah! I love you too, Ver." Beth threw herself at us. "You're like the female version of Dr. Phil."

"Group hug," Kara mumbled on my shoulder.

"Is your drama having a commercial soon? I need to pee," Beth moaned.

Right on cue, Theo showed up in a Toyota, waving at us.

"Here comes mine," Beth whispered.

CHAPTER

seventeen

Veronica

AFTER THEO BOOSTED HIS CAR, BETH TOLD HIM TO GO BACK TO
the party without us. It took a bit of convincing for Theo to
leave since he wanted to make sure we got home safe. That guy
was fiercely sweet and thoughtful. No wonder Beth was in love
with him.

Since Kara and Beth were both drunk, I was the designated
driver.

"Where do you guys want to go?" I asked, putting on my
seat belt.

Kara was almost passed out in the backseat, her head drooping
to her chest. I had made sure she had her seat belt on.

"Should we just go back to Kar's?" I prompted.

Beth was busy scavenging for something in the glove box.
"Aha! I knew it was here somewhere," she crowed in victory,
holding a small tube in her hand.

"What? What is that?"

"Superglue!" she squealed excitedly.

"Uh-huh. You're definitely drunk, aren't you? I should take you guys home."

"No! Ver, believe me when I tell you this is definitely *not* drunk. If I were, you wouldn't have to ask me."

"Okay."

"Now, where does that Cameron live?"

"Why?" I narrowed my eyes in suspicion. I could see the wheels turning in her scheming mind.

"Because we are going to give Kar here a little revenge."

Kara piped in, "Revenge?" She sounded sleepy but interested.

"I have this magical glue, and we just need to put this in the keyhole of your ex's front door. He won't be able to get in unless he kicks the door down or changes the locks."

"Oh shit, yes!" Kara shouted. "Yes, please! Let's do it!"

"Kara—"

"Ver, please? I really need this."

I sighed. These two were going to get in a lot of trouble if left unattended. I was about to refuse when an image of Kara crying appeared in my mind. "Fine."

They cheered happily, clapping and bouncing in their seats like little girls.

"I'll tell you where to go. Now drive, baby, drive!" Kara cheered.

It was past midnight, and the streets were uncannily quiet. The streetlights cast an eerie glow on the road where the trees stood like sentries. The windows of the car were rolled down, and the air caressed my face and hair like a lover's touch. I shivered. It was getting chilly, and I needed to pee.

"Don't park in front of his house, okay?" Beth whispered eagerly.

I parked five houses down from Cameron's house. Were we really doing this?

"We could get arrested for this," I warned.

"It would be worth it!" Kara snapped off her seat belt and scooted forward, lodging herself between the front seats.

"Why don't you look for dog shit and put that in his mailbox too?" I suggested sarcastically.

"Shit, Ver," Kara exclaimed. "I always knew you were a smart cookie."

"Oh God," I groaned. I didn't think she would take me seriously. I should have known better.

"Damn right," Beth agreed, patting my shoulder. "That was a Shakespeare moment right there. Wait, no. I meant Einstein. Einstein moment. Genius, Ver. You are now officially a goddess in my two fucked-up eyes."

I laughed. We all got out of the car and linked arms as we walked, both girls flanking me since I was the sober, steady one.

"You lookin' for dog shit there, Beth?" Kara asked. "Keep your fucked-up eyes open."

"My fucked-up eyes can't get wider than this, baby. I am looking for shit. My eyes are a shit telescope. I can spot shit a mile away."

We were giggling, the sound ringing harshly in the quiet. Suddenly, Kara wrenched her arm away. She was half walking, half running like a penguin, her legs comically squeezed together. She crouched between two cars, spreading her skirt. And then...

"Kar! Are you taking a piss on the road?" Beth asked right before she started laughing maniacally. "She's pissing on the road!" She guffawed, pointing at still-crouching Kara.

"Hey, guys, do you have any toilet paper with you?" Kara grinned like a lunatic.

We were making such a ruckus that it took a minute for me to realize something was wrong. Something didn't sound *nice*. The hair on the back of my neck pricked up as I slowly, painfully turned around.

Oh, my freaking corpse in a casket, there was an angry dog a few feet away, growling and glaring at us like we were his next meal.

"Ah, guys," I whispered quietly, shaking in my shoes.

"I see it," Beth hissed. "You guys climb on top of the cars. That fucker can't climb."

"Kara, get the hell up!" I hissed as I slowly followed Beth and jumped on top of a car.

Kara was still squatting, now frozen in fear.

"Kar, wake the *fuck* up and climb on the car!" I yelled loudly now, unable to keep myself from cursing.

But she wasn't listening. I screamed in horror as she jumped up and ran up the street. The huge dog sped past us, barking and growling like a sinister monster from hell after Kara's feet or legs or hands...or soul.

I jumped off the car and ran as fast as I could to stop the canine from eating Kara. How the hell I was going to do that,

I had no clue. I looked around, searching for a weapon, and spotted an orange toy truck on someone's front lawn. I made a run for it, grabbed it, and ran as fast as I could to catch up to them. My heart lodged in my throat when I saw Kara jump over a fence, her foot getting caught between the slats. She landed face-first on the grass on the other side of the fence.

"Kar!" I shouted.

The dog kept barking and growling for a few moments before it finally gave up and ran away. My knees felt like overcooked noodles, and I fell to the ground. I heard Kara let out a whoop, still facedown in the grass. When I spotted the orange toy truck in my hand, I started laughing like a lunatic.

"Let's go get hammered tonight, bitches!" Beth yelled behind me.

Kara sat up, her hair sticking to her face, her shoulders shaking with laughter.

I laughed harder.

Caleb

"You look like shit."

"I feel like shit," Cameron replied, collapsing on the couch.

He looked gaunt, like he hadn't eaten in a week. His clothes were rumpled, his hair a mess, his eyes red. Cameron had phoned me half an hour ago, sounding panicked—and in pain. At first I thought someone had died because he kept saying, "She's gone. Fucking gone."

It took me a minute to realize he was talking about Kara. He ended the conversation with "I'm coming over. I need to get the hell away from this place."

So I told Red what was up, and she raced out the door to comfort her BFF. Not that I was jealous. I wasn't.

Maybe a little.

I just...wanted to spend more time with her. But Cameron needed me, and Kara needed Red. And of course, as always, she had refused my offer to give her a ride.

"She did that to you?" I pointed at my cheek. His was starting to swell.

He cupped his jaw, wincing. "Yeah, damn near fainted."

I wasn't sure if he was joking or not. I grabbed an ice pack from the freezer and tossed it to him. "She's got a mean right hook."

He caught it easily, then lay down on the couch while he placed it on his cheek. "I should know. I taught her how."

"Sorry, man. Want to talk about it?" I asked as I took a seat across from him.

"No. Just need a place to crash. Everything in my apartment reminds me of her. She's everywhere."

Damn tight-lipped son of a gun. He would feel better if he'd just open up. I worried about him. My mother had told me what happened with his family, but Cameron never talked about it. I would probably be hurt if I didn't know that he never shared anything about himself with anyone. He was a very private person.

"You know I don't need to tell you that if-you-need-anything-I'm-here crap, right?"

He placed his arm on his forehead, covering his eyes. "Thanks, man."

If he'd come here to be left alone, he should have gone somewhere else, because I wasn't going to give up that easily. "Want some beer?"

"Yeah."

So we drank beer, exchanged insults like we usually did, ate the chicken potpie Red had made for dinner, drank more beer, and finally passed out on the couch. I woke up in the middle of the night searching for my phone. When I finally found it stuffed between the cushions, I grabbed it and pushed the Home button.

Blinded by my phone screen's harsh light, I groaned. It took a second before I could focus and then—"Dammit!"—it slipped from my hand, fell on my face, and slid to the floor.

Annoyed, I sat up and fished my phone from the floor. I had a lot of messages and missed calls. All from girls that I'd probably dated, but none from the girl I wanted.

Red had a pay-as-you-go phone, and I knew she'd only use it in a life-or-death situation. She was worried about charges so I'd tried to give her my spare phone, but with her muleheaded I-might-be-poor-but-I'm-not-a-gold-digger-so-I'm-just-going-to-despise-everything-you-give-me attitude, she'd thrown it back in my face.

Restless, I went to the kitchen to grab a glass of orange juice, but I remembered Red had been there a couple hours ago. I was getting irritated with myself for constantly thinking about her, and I just wanted to forget her for a minute. I went back to the living room where Cameron was thankfully passed out, sat on the couch, and checked my phone again. Still nothing.

I was obsessed. When was the last time I checked my phone for a call or text from a girl? Ah, yeah, that would be never.

I didn't know why I bothered comparing my experiences with other girls. So far nothing with Red had been predictable.

I felt like old, forgotten clothing, and all I wanted was to be her favorite shirt again.

I was walking around the house like a ghost, checking my phone for the hundredth time, when I passed her room. I stared at the door, willing it to open by itself. I stared at that doorknob like a scientist looking through a microscope. I knew this was bordering on creepy, but I never said I wasn't creepy. I reached for the doorknob, paused to take another breath, and opened the door a crack.

A whiff of her scent sneaked out, filling my nostrils.

Strawberries.

I closed my eyes and inhaled.

Creep.

This was invasion of privacy. This was so wrong. But I was only going to take a peek, maybe hang for a few minutes. It wasn't like I was going to go through her things…no. That was psycho. I only wanted to feel close to her by being here. I opened the door another inch.

"What are you doing?"

I jumped a foot, and an unholy girlie squeal came out of my mouth that I knew I would be ashamed of for the rest of my life. If Cameron told anyone about it, I would never admit to it.

I slammed the door shut, and when I'd sort of regained my composure, I said, "You scared the shit out of me."

"Well, you've been standing there for at least five minutes. I just took a piss, and you're still here."

"Well..." I trailed off.

Cameron shrugged and went back to the couch to sleep. I let out a sigh of relief. It wasn't that I didn't want to tell him Red was living with me, but I didn't want him to know I was sneaking into her room. I didn't think he was in a state to discuss anything besides beer and basketball right now anyway. I looked at Red's door again.

Screw it. I opened it and stepped in.

Red all around. Her scent, her things, her *presence* was so strong that I felt dizzy.

Damn, did I have it bad.

I could tell she had settled in. A blanket with vibrant colors covered the bed. A brush lay on the dresser, a water bottle sat on the study desk, and her books were neatly stacked on the set of drawers beside the bed... The top drawer! Shit. I just remembered I had stacked condoms in there. A lot of condoms. I groaned in distress.

Did she think I was a man whore now? She probably thought I slept around a lot, and she would be right. But I hadn't slept with anyone since I met her, and that was a feat.

I had been having sex since I hit puberty. But Red made me want to wait. I didn't want easy anymore. I didn't want meaningless. I wanted Red.

I sat on her bed and opened the drawer. The condoms were

gone. Where had she put them? I decided to ask the next time I saw her. She would probably blush. She didn't turn pink. She turned red. It would start on her neck, and I could see it creeping up her face and ears until she looked like a ripe tomato. It was so cute. I closed the drawer and threw myself on the bed.

Surrounded—that was how I felt. Surrounded by her. My last thought before I fell asleep was that I was now officially a creep.

The next thing I knew, I was waking up with my phone ringing beside me. I hit Answer and grunted in greeting.

"Hey."

My eyes popped open. "Red?"

"Yeah." Her voice was low and breathy and *flirty*, and it caught my full attention. She sounded very much like the first time I met her at the club. When my thoughts cleared, I realized she was probably drunk.

"Where are you?" I sat up and turned on the lamp. The clock indicated it was three in the morning. I raked my fingers through my hair, wondering if she was in trouble.

"At Kar's. You wouldn't believe what happened tonight."

I heard moving around in the background, like she was in bed and trying to make herself comfortable. I let out a relieved sigh. She was safe and in bed.

"Why don't you tell me about it, baby?" I asked, wondering where the hell *baby* had come from.

She giggled. I smiled at the sound, flopping myself back on her bed.

"Baby. I like that."

"I like you this way," I said, imagining her lying in bed, her hair spread on her pillow, happy and beautiful and without a care in the world.

"What way?" she asked sleepily.

"Happy. Like you're not worried about anything right now, because you usually are."

She paused for a moment, and I thought she had fallen asleep. Then she said, "You make me happy, Caleb."

I opened my mouth to say something, but nothing came out.

"I wish…"

"Yeah?" I whispered, my heart in my throat.

"I wish you were here. I miss you kissing me," she whispered.

I cleared my throat. "Me too," I answered. "You know you won't remember any of this tomorrow."

"Yes, I will," she insisted.

"No, you won't. But I will." I sighed. "Red?"

"Yes, Caleb?"

"Don't break my heart."

CHAPTER

eighteen

Veronica

"WHO THE HELL PUT THAT ALARM CLOCK ON SPEAKER?"

I opened one eye at the sound of Kara's groggy, irate voice. It took me a second to realize why I was hearing her voice in the morning.

Last night was Caleb's basketball practice and the drive-in movie we missed. Caleb… Why did it feel like I was missing something important? I racked my brain on what else we did last night.

Drinking large amounts of alcohol, gorging on pizza, Kara vomiting her guts out on the front lawn last night…or was that Beth? Something else happened, though, and it was just at the edge of my consciousness…

"M'eyes. M'head. M'mouth," Kara lamented. "Th' hell were we thinking, partying on a school night?"

"Going-away party for my brother. He just accepted a job

in Paris." Beth moaned. I think I heard her over to my right. Maybe she was lying on the floor?

Ugh. My body felt like it was being weighed down by a big piano.

"Gonna skip classes today," Kara mumbled, sounding like she'd just covered her face with a blanket.

"No!" I heard Beth get up quickly. "Shite. I'm dizzy."

I opened one eye. "You 'kay?"

She was a blur of blue hair and…was that paint on her face? What the heck did we do last night?

"I gotta go. Theo. Theo day today. What time is it?"

"It's time to shut the fuck up and go back to sleep," Kara grumbled.

Hmm. Yes, Kara was so smart. Time to shut up and go back to sleep.

I was thankful that I was one of those rare people who didn't get hangovers. Well, I did, but not the normal hangover that included a headache, dry mouth, and vomiting. I just felt heavy.

"Damn. Where are the keys to my car, Ver? Ver!"

I groaned when I felt Beth shaking me.

"Lemme 'lone," I mumbled.

"I'm listing all the reasons in my head why I shouldn't stab you," Kara growled at Beth.

Why wouldn't they shut up? I burrowed deeper under the covers.

"I have to borrow a shirt from you, Kar," Beth insisted.

I heard a thud.

"Ow. Shit," Beth cursed.

Kara must have thrown something at her.

"You're going to be sorry," Beth warned.

Something hard hit my face. "Ow!"

"I'm so sorry, Ver! That was supposed to be for Kar!"

"Please feel free to shut the fuck up," Kara barked.

"I'm shutting the fuck up once I get my shit together. Ver, where are my fucking keys?"

Her keys? I think I left them on the living room table.

"Li'ing room, ee'think," I mumbled.

I heard her moving around, cursing and then cursing some more. "Your clothes are for five-year-olds with no tits, Kar. I can't fit into any of your shirts!"

Kara moaned. "I am surrounded by bitches with huge tits. Why can't I just have a little more, God, why? Even lemons are good enough, but I have *grapes*!"

I snorted. I heard Beth laughing. "See you later, bitches!" she yelled. The door slammed behind her, and then finally, thank God, silence. Just as I was about to fall asleep again, I heard Kara's phone ring.

"Goddamnsumbitchmothafuck!"

She groped for her phone, and I thought she was going to kill whoever was calling. I was surprised when she answered in a sweet—if groggy—voice. "Hello? Who's this? No way. How did you get my number? Oh, of course. Hold on." She turned to me, holding out her phone. "It's Caleb."

"What?" Frowning, I wiggled my arms out from under the blanket and pressed the phone to my ear.

"Hello?"

"Hey, Red."

Caleb sounded so chirpy in the morning. I could already see his sunny smile and cheerful green eyes laughing at me. His hair was probably still wet and combed back from the shower—until it dried, at which point it would be all over the place.

I smiled. "Hey, Caleb."

Kara was poking my back and making small excited noises behind me.

"Do you need a ride?"

"Huh?" I propped myself up with my elbow, flicking the hair off my face.

"You told me last night you have an exam this afternoon."

I groaned. "Dammit. I forgot."

"I'm picking you up. Be there in ten. See you soon, Red."

"Caleb—"

He hung up before I could say anything. I stared at the phone, dumbfounded.

"He's picking you up?" Kara asked.

"Yeah." I pushed my face into my pillow. "How is he going to pick me up? He doesn't even know where you live."

"He's been here before to pick up…Cameron," she said. "A long time ago." She sighed loudly, covering her face with a pillow. "I'm going back to sleep."

I looked at her for a moment and, when she didn't stir, forced myself out of bed and grabbed the biggest clothes I could find in her closet before heading to the shower. I used my fingers to brush my teeth since Kara didn't have a spare toothbrush. When I was done, I eyed her clothes dubiously. I really didn't think they would fit me.

I jumped at the knock on the bathroom door.

"Red?"

I frowned. "Caleb?"

He was here already? I didn't hear the doorbell.

"Did you break in?"

He chuckled. "Nothing too exciting. Kara wasn't too happy I woke her up." He paused. "I brought you clothes, toothbrush, and breakfast. I got you green tea too."

What was this boy doing to me? It wasn't even afternoon, and he was already giving me butterflies.

"Red?"

I cleared my throat. "Okay. Just leave them on the counter outside the door. Thank you."

"Anytime." I could imagine him winking and fought the sudden urge to see his face right away. I missed him. I could admit that now.

I missed Caleb. I missed Caleb. I missed Caleb.

Sighing, I wrapped myself in a towel and opened the door. I let out a squeak when I saw him lounging against the counter. His gaze zeroed in on my face before slowly traveling down my body, then back up again.

"What the hell, Caleb! I said leave them on the counter!"

"I did." He nodded at the counter.

"You didn't say you were going to stand there waiting for me!" I sputtered.

He looked like a naughty boy caught stealing from a cookie jar. He wore dark jeans and a gray crew-neck shirt that molded to his shoulders and biceps and showed off his muscled torso and narrow waist. He looked so good, and my heart pounded in response. And then he smiled. I was done for.

"You look really sexy, Red."

I held my breath as he walked toward me, moving in very close. I could feel the heat his body was throwing off. I gripped my towel tighter around me.

The tip of his nose brushed the back of my ear, and he inhaled. I shivered.

"You smell so good," he whispered, his voice deeper than normal. "I'm going to hang with Kara in the kitchen... See you real soon, Red."

Right. Real soon.

By the time I headed to the kitchen, I was feeling better. I heard Kara's defiant tone, and I knew she was talking about Cameron.

"Not anymore. I think I'm moving on," she spat out.

Caleb sighed. "I know he still loves you."

"It doesn't matter when he can't... Did he tell you that?"

Caleb looked indecisive, as if he was carefully weighing what to tell Kara. "No, but from the looks of him yesterday, he was in really bad shape."

She snorted. "Good." She looked down and gripped her coffee cup in her palms. "But that's not enough for me anymore, Caleb. I need more than that. I can't wait for him forever."

"I think he really needs a friend right now, but he won't let me in." He sighed. "I think you're the only one he'll let in, Kar."

She shook her head vehemently. "Look, Caleb—"

"Kar, he's *not* okay."

She closed her eyes tightly, a tear rolling down her cheek.

"Don't give up on him when he needs you most," Caleb pleaded.

Silently, I walked to Kara, laying my hand on her shoulder for comfort. When she opened her eyes and made eye contact with me, she broke down.

There was nothing I could do but stay by her side.

CHAPTER
nineteen

Caleb

"HOW WAS YOUR NIGHT?" I ASKED RED AS I DROVE US TO SCHOOL. I wondered if she would remember the conversation we'd had last night. I didn't expect her to, but I really wanted to know.

She looked at me from beneath her lashes, shaking her head. I caught the playful smile on her lips before she turned her head away and looked out the window.

This felt good. This felt like we were starting to create our own routine. That was good, right?

I was thinking of brushing up on girlfriend-boyfriend rules. Maybe I could ask Cameron, but then I remembered he sucked at relationships. Maybe my brother, Ben?

Oh, wait. He sucked too.

I racked my brain for any of my friends who had a long-term relationship, and I realized with shame that I had none. They were all like me, unless I counted Andrei, who had been with his girlfriend for two years now. But theirs was an open relationship. Screw that.

I wanted Red to be mine *only*.

I knew I was being possessive, maybe even overbearing, but...*I didn't know how to be anything else.*

I just hoped she would accept all of it—all of me.

How the mighty have fallen! I thought to myself. Caleb Lockhart, clueless on how to make a girl fall in love with him.

Love.

Wait, what?

Damn.

I shook my head. I was never one to hide my emotions. What was the point of having feelings if you couldn't admit to them, even to yourself? All I knew was that I had never felt this way before with anyone else...and it felt really good. Like something I could hold on to for a long time.

I looked at Red's hands. I missed holding her hand while I drove, but I couldn't because she was holding the coffee cup with both hands.

"Red?" I glanced at her.

She was still staring out the window, but her body was turned toward me, and I had enough common sense to know that she was paying attention to me. Body Language 101.

"Are you going to drink that tea?" I asked.

She shook her head, still not looking at me. Okay, then. I grabbed the tea from her hands and placed it in the cup holder. She turned her eyes on me, puzzled. I gave her a smile and reached for her hand, interlacing our fingers.

There.

Everything was all right in Caleb's world again. I let out a satisfied sigh.

Once we got to school, I walked her to class. I knew people were staring at us. I had a reputation on campus. I was fine with it, but I was concerned about Red. I hoped it didn't bother her.

"So, I'll meet you at the cafeteria after your exam," I said. "We'll have a bite to eat before I drive you to work." I realized what I was doing. I was telling her what to do again, so I rephrased. "If you like. We could eat anywhere. You call the shots."

"Caleb."

"Yes?"

"Thank you for..." She lifted her hands, palms up, in a helpless gesture.

My heart ached. She didn't know how to express her emotions. I wanted so badly to know what had happened, why she was this way. I guessed I needed to earn her trust first.

"You don't need to say a word," I said, meaning it.

She looked at me with bewildered eyes, as if she was trying to decide whether to believe me or not.

She said her exam would take two hours, so I decided to go to the multipurpose room to play pool or just hang with my teammates. I was waiting for my turn when I felt someone poke my back. I turned around and stared into the smiling eyes of Beatrice-Rose.

"Hey, Caleb!" she exclaimed. She tried to wrap her arms around my neck, but she was petite and ended up hugging my torso instead.

"Hey, Beatrice-Rose! How are you?" She had cut her blond hair short, and her bangs swayed softly above her pale-blue eyes. "You look great," I said, smiling back.

She pulled back, moving her hands to my biceps. Was she squeezing them? I bet she was. She liked big arms on guys.

"Oh, Caleb, be still my heart. You look gorgeous, as always."

It was good to see her again. She was a childhood friend... and then *more* than a friend on and off for years. She had taken two semesters off from school to go to Paris to... I racked my brain, trying to remember what she'd told me before she left. Ah. To find herself. Soul searching or something like that.

She pouted, shaking her head at me. "Why are you calling me Beatrice-Rose? Call me B, like you used to."

I gave her an indulgent smile. "Sure, B. So, did you find your soul in Paris?"

She paused, as if she didn't expect the question and her brain was trying to adjust to the conversation. Then she threw her head back, laughing.

"Oh, Caleb, how I've missed you! Why don't we catch up tonight? Dinner, same time and place?"

I knew I looked uncomfortable. Damn, I felt uncomfortable. How did I explain this to her? We had a past, but never a commitment. People thought she was the closest thing I had to a girlfriend, but I'd never called her that. I'd never wanted one until Red.

Beatrice-Rose had approached me a few times over the years to *hang out*, and I almost always said yes—unless I was dating a different girl. But that stopped a few years ago because I didn't want to ruin our friendship. And it sure wasn't going to happen today, tomorrow, or ever, because...

"I have a girlfriend."

She removed her hands from my arms. "Okay, Caleb. You mean you're dating someone else right now? That's fine. She'll be gone next week, yes?"

I shook my head. "No. I'm really serious with this one."

She raised an eyebrow, surprise on her face. When a girl raised an eyebrow without smiling, I knew it spelled trouble for me.

"Really, Caleb?"

I nodded.

"Wow. Let me get my breath back here." She placed her hand on her chest dramatically, then smiled at me widely. "Caleb, I am so happy for you! This is major news."

I nodded, pleased that she'd taken it well. I liked Beatrice-Rose as a person. She was always classy and poised, kind to everyone. That was why we got along really well.

"Finally found *the one*, did you? I hope she gives you a really hard time." She chuckled.

"Oh, she does, believe me. She's different, you know?"

Beatrice-Rose was quiet for a moment, her eyes studying my face. I squirmed.

"Yes, I can see that. Well, it's official, then! I have to meet her."

"I'm sure you will sometime," I confirmed.

Our families were very close. When we were kids, Beatrice-Rose, my brother, and I often spent time together on family trips or gatherings.

"We have to catch up and have some coffee soon. We're still friends, aren't we?"

I smiled at her and nodded, because whatever had happened between us before, she was right. We were still friends. "Of course."

She smiled and waved. "See you later, then."

I looked at my watch. Twenty more minutes until Red was done, but I decided to go to the cafeteria. I didn't want her sitting alone, and I wanted to get her something to eat. I bought her favorite—green tea and a cinnamon bun—and was looking for a seat when I saw her, already at a table in the back corner of the room.

"Hey, Red. I'm sorry. I thought I still had"—I checked my watch—"ten minutes before you were done. Did you wait long?"

She shook her head. "I just got here."

"How was your exam?"

Her face split into a wonderful smile that stunned me. She was so beautiful...

Damn, I'm whipped.

So, I realized, this was what made her happy. Acing her exams. Good to know.

I sat across from her, stretching my legs under the table to loosely bracket hers. I noticed she moved her legs close together, being very careful not to touch mine. She was fighting it. I grinned.

"I bought you some food," I said, pushing the tray in front of her.

She studied me again, her dark eyes looking vulnerable. This girl was so wary of love that it made my heart ache.

"You don't have to throw yourself at me. A simple thank-you will do," I quipped.

"Why are you doing this? Why do you take care of me so much?"

My Red. So alone. So lonely. I'm here now.

"I don't think you'll believe me, even if I tell you."

Her shoulders lifted in a sigh. She lowered her head, staring at her tea. She was avoiding my eyes, which was fine. That just meant I could admire her to my heart's content.

"We need to do something about Kara and Cameron," she said after a moment.

I smiled. "I agree. How about this summer? This semester is almost done. After it's over, we could go to my mom's beach house and take them with us."

"I don't know. Don't you think that's going a little overboard?" She lifted her eyes, studying my face for a few moments. "Your hair is getting long."

Okay, change of subject. My hand automatically ran through my hair. "I still look gorgeous. What, you want me to cut it?"

"No," she said a little too quickly. "I mean, do whatever you want. Why are you asking me?"

I frowned, leaning forward. "Why do you fight it so much?"

I waited for her answer, but it didn't come.

"You're fighting what you feel for me. I can feel it. Why?" I persisted.

She pulled her hands into her lap, hiding them from me. I let out a sigh.

"Let's play a game," I suggested. "How about I'll tell you

something I know about you, and then you tell me something you know about me."

That did it. I got half a smile from her.

"Shouldn't it be the other way around?"

I shook my head. "Nope. You see, I like discovering things by myself. I don't like things handed to me. I like it when I have to work hard."

She tilted her head as if trying to decipher the meaning behind my words.

Yes, I thought, *I am talking about you.*

"I'll go first then, since you look very enthusiastic about this."

She looked nervous but interested. I had her attention now.

"You don't like black olives," I said.

Her eyes narrowed. She was ever the suspicious one. I laughed.

"How do you know that?" she demanded.

Tongue in cheek, I replied, "Well…I had you investigated."

"What the—" she stammered.

I laughed. "Kidding. When we ordered pizza the other night, you picked them off. Now it's your turn."

She bit her lip. "You hate dishes in the sink, except for an empty glass. You always leave an empty glass."

My smile reached my ears. She was paying attention to me. Since she wasn't drinking her tea, I grabbed it and took a sip.

"You don't like the dark," I said. "You sleep with your lights on."

I meant to tease her, but something like fear flashed in her eyes. She was quiet for a moment, and I wondered what she was thinking. But then the cobwebs in her eyes cleared and she smirked.

"I can sleep with it off sometimes." She paused, then her nose twitched. "Your feet smell."

I choked on green tea. "Hey, only after basketball practice." I coughed. "My feet are sexy."

She wrinkled her nose, fighting a smile. "You call your mom every day just to say hi," she said.

I grinned. She probably didn't realize it, but it was my turn. I didn't say anything, though. I found that I liked it a lot when she talked about me.

"Not denying it. I'm a proud mama's boy, but just a couple times a week."

Since she wasn't eating her bun, I pinched a piece off and fed it to her. She glared at me but accepted it. She pinched off almost half of the bun and shoved it in my mouth in retaliation.

"You like girls."

I chewed fast and swallowed. "Ha! That's too easy. But wrong. I only like one girl now. And it feels like it's going to stay that way for a long, long time."

She gulped. I reached for her hand, rubbing her skin with my thumb.

"I don't know what to do with you," she said softly.

"Give me a chance," I whispered.

Be with me.

I stared into her eyes. I felt like I could drown in their depths. They held so much in them. So much pain, so much love.

"I want to tell you something," I said, still holding her hand. When she nodded, I began. "When I've told you that I haven't felt this way before, I've never been more serious in my life."

She looked at me as if she was about to say something, but then changed her mind and just kept silent. I dropped it. If she wasn't ready, then she wasn't ready. I had a lot of time to convince her. She'd learn to trust me eventually.

"Pancakes?" I asked hopefully.

She shook her head. "I have work in a few hours, Caleb. I can't."

"I'll drive you to work."

"No."

"Don't you get tired of saying no to me?"

"No."

Oh, this girl... I scooted my chair beside hers, and she looked askance at me. Wrapping my hand around her wrist, I pulled her up from her chair. She gasped as she landed on my lap.

"Caleb," she murmured. "What are you doing?"

I could feel my body responding to her, and I instantly turned hard. She smelled so good, felt so good. I closed my eyes. What. The. Hell. Was. I. Doing?

"Damn." I raked my hair with my fingers, frustrated. I was turned on, and she hadn't lifted a finger. "I'm sorry, Red. I'm just..."

Horny.

Yeah, dude, tell her. I bet that would go really smoothly.

"I want you."

Her eyes widened in realization.

Now you get it. Please, don't run away.

I felt nervous, my heart pounding, sweat on my forehead. She froze, staring at me like a deer caught in headlights.

"I want you so much it hurts. You're the only thing I think about. I'm fucking obsessed with you."

My. Mouth.

My problem sometimes was that I was too honest for my own good. I held her face between my hands. We were in the cafeteria at lunchtime, with people gaping around us. I didn't care.

"Caleb, we are in the cafe—"

"I don't care about them. They're not important. No one has ever been important to me. Until you."

She was breathing hard, like she'd just run a marathon.

"Do you trust me?" I asked.

She looked hesitant, but nodded eventually.

"All right, then. Let's get the hell away from here. We have time before your shift starts."

I grasped her waist as I rose, sliding her to standing. I grabbed her backpack and slung it over my shoulder, then reached for her hand.

"Pancakes," I said, but she didn't reply.

"Pancakes," I repeated, waiting for her to acknowledge me.

She looked up with those expressive, lovely eyes. "Pancakes," she replied.

* * *

Veronica

Caleb drove us to the beach again. This seemed to be his go-to place if he was feeling intense emotions. That was fine. I liked the beach, especially when he was with me.

He held my hand again as we drove there. It felt good. It

also made me uncomfortable because I knew it was becoming a habit, and I didn't know how to stop it—or if I wanted to.

The sun was sprawled in the clear blue sky, but there were only a few people at the beach sunbathing. I could taste the water in the air, the humidity enveloping me. With Caleb holding my hand and his green eyes looking into mine, I felt like I was in a different universe. Somewhere no problems existed. Somewhere hope and happiness lived.

He spread a blanket on the sand and pulled me down with him. He was lying on his side facing me while I was on my back. He draped his arm over my waist, pulling me closer to him. The beach seemed to have a mellowing effect on me because I let him hold me without any protest. Or maybe Caleb was growing on me.

"What's wrong, Red?"

I realized I had been staring at the sky, lost in my thoughts.

"Will you tell me what you're thinking?" His fingers reached for mine again, intertwining. Caleb had a fascination with lacing our fingers together. I liked it a lot too. Sometimes when I hadn't seen him in a while, my hand tingled, as if missing his.

Missing something was the last thing I wanted. I didn't want to yearn for anything. Yearning meant heartbreak. Every time I felt myself responding to Caleb, I stopped myself. But his strong presence and his constant *caring* were breaking down my defenses.

I constantly pushed him away, but he kept coming back. I knew he wanted to know why I was so afraid, why I kept myself at a distance.

I could feel his eyes on me and his silent plea that I open up to him. When I turned to look at him, something in his eyes had my heart skipping a beat. "Caleb…"

He didn't say anything. He didn't need to. I saw the under-standing in his eyes, the patience. And I knew even if I didn't say anything in this moment, he would be okay with that. And that somehow made it impossible for me to keep holding back.

"It's hard for me to talk about it," I started. "I need to…" I sat up, feeling the need to put some space between us. I was going to give this part of myself to him, expose my weakness to him willingly, and I needed some distance. Some sort of protec-tion. I wrapped my arms around my middle. He sat up beside me, silent, waiting.

"My dad was the only man I loved, and the only person to break my heart. I remember times when he was so attentive, so loving, but then he would change drastically. In the blink of an eye, he'd be a different person.

"He made me feel…unworthy. Always reminded me that I didn't deserve to be loved, that it was my fault his relationship with my mom fell apart. It made me feel…guilty.

"He blamed me for every bad thing that happened to him. Over and over again. I-I can still hear his voice sometimes. I usually block it, but sometimes…sometimes I feel like he's right." I shook my head, erasing the memories forcing their way into my head.

"No, Red. He couldn't have been more wrong."

I shook my head again. "It's okay. I don't really want to discuss him anymore."

"Did he…hurt you?"

I lowered my eyes, afraid to answer.

"Red?"

I looked up but didn't say anything. Caleb nodded, acknowledging that he understood I wasn't ready to talk about it, and why I was this way—guarded, stubborn, suspicious.

I wanted him to know me. But I was scared to tell him the ugly parts of my life, afraid they would scare him away. But something about Caleb made me feel that he was going to stay. So I started telling him about my mom and dad.

"I was making sandwiches after school one day, and I remember feeling very excited because my mom promised we would go to the movies. We both loved movies. That was how we bonded, you know? Movies. I wanted to watch a comedy, but she wanted a romance."

I tried to turn away from him, but Caleb stopped me, pleading with his eyes to stay with him this way. I relented.

"So I was ready, even wrapped up some sandwiches and drinks to bring. I kept them in my backpack to sneak them in. We couldn't afford the popcorn they sell at the movies, but I didn't care about that. I wanted to spend time with my mom. We were walking to the theater, and then I saw my dad. He was in a car. And I was thinking, *Why is he in a car? We don't have a car...* and then a woman got inside the car with him. And they kissed.

"My mom..." I choked. "My mom saw it, but she didn't... didn't do anything. But I saw how it hurt her. She...placed her fist on her chest, just like this," I said, imitating the way I remembered her doing it. "And closed her eyes, just taking deep breaths. I waited for her to confront my dad… But then she just smiled and told me we should get going or we'd miss the beginning of the show."

Caleb wrapped his arms around me, and I melted into him. I wasn't going to cry. He smelled so good. So familiar.

"She passed away…my mom. I was adopted. I really don't know who my biological parents are, but that doesn't matter to me anymore. All I needed was my mom. She wasn't perfect, but she tried her best. She never left him, and I didn't understand that. I still don't."

Caleb started rubbing my back, and I let out a sigh of pleasure. It felt good. It felt really good.

"I understand," he said quietly. "I don't understand why my mom didn't leave my dad either." He held my shoulders and turned me so he could look into my eyes.

"I swear when we get married, we are never going to divorce. You're it for me. Until I die. And that goes for you as well, okay?"

I stared at him in horror. My mouth opened, but nothing came out. If he was trying to distract me from my sad memories, he was succeeding.

He grinned at me and placed a finger on my chin to close my mouth.

"Breathe," he said. "Everything is going to be okay."

I sputtered, glaring at him. I started to get up, but he just wrapped me in his arms, holding me in place.

"What, you mad that I don't have a ring with me?" His green eyes danced playfully, but there was a depth there, something vulnerable begging me not to walk away.

I blinked.

"What the hell, Caleb." There were butterflies in my stomach, and I felt a little queasy.

He placed his chin on top of my head as he chuckled. "When I propose, I want to sweep you off your feet, so no, you are not getting a proposal from me today. Be patient."

Was he joking? I didn't even try to figure him out anymore. He was *definitely* joking. There was no way he could be serious about this.

I would not take him seriously.

"Haven't you figured me out yet? I'm pretty simple, Red. You're the one who thinks I'm complicated."

Silence.

"How about I tell you a story," he said.

I shook my head again, fighting a smile. "Okay."

I pulled away and looked at him, ready to listen.

"It's one of my favorite parts in *Alice in Wonderland*. Alice asks the White Rabbit, 'How long is forever?' The White Rabbit answers, 'Sometimes just one second.' This"—he kissed my lips—"this feels like forever right here." He stared into my eyes. "How can I not wish for that?"

CHAPTER

twenty

Veronica

"Wait, back the fuck up. What?" Kara's eyes were as round as saucers while she gaped at me like a fish.

It had been a few hours since Caleb dropped that bomb about getting married. I'd tried to forget about it because…surely he'd been joking? But it kept creeping into my mind, gnawing at me. Deciding to tell Kara, I waited until the end of our shift. I sat at my desk, watching her count the cash from the till.

"You heard me," I said.

Kara blinked once, twice, thrice. "He…*proposed*? You shitting me right now, Strafford?" She waved the wad of cash in her hand at me.

I laughed. "He didn't downright propose, but he implied it."

"Well, fuck."

I nodded. I didn't know how to feel about it either, even now. Part of me was horrified. Horrified that this was happening all too fast. He couldn't possibly have meant what he said. But the other part of me, the one that wanted to hope, the one that was falling—falling for Caleb, yes, that part—was trying to come out. And I was barely holding on to her leash.

"What did you tell him? Fuck. I have to count all over again now." She shook her head and placed the cash back in the till so she could give me her full attention.

"Nothing." I shrugged. "Should I have said something? How can I believe what he's saying when we've only known each other a few months, Kar? It's not possible." I glanced up at her. "Right?"

She pursed her lips. "I don't know, Ver. Did Lockhart say the big *L* word to you?"

I shook my head. "He didn't."

"Well, *psh*. And he proposed?"

"He didn't *really* propose, but—"

"Dude's horny. He's either in love with you, or he's horny," she pronounced, clucking her tongue. "Or both."

I stared at her. "What?"

"He's horny like a unicorn during mating season." Kara shrugged as if it was the most obvious problem and she had just solved it. She walked over to her desk, opened a drawer, and grabbed her compact. She started powdering her nose.

"Well…"

"Guys are sweet on you when they're horny. Cameron is… was like that. Lockhart needs to get laid."

I laughed. "Well, I don't think he's going to get it from me."

She narrowed her eyes at me. "Why do you bullshit yourself so much?"

"I... What?"

Kara rolled her eyes. "You give good advice to other people, but you can't figure out what to do with yourself. Seriously, Ver, think about it. The guy came to my house to pick you up for an exam that you forgot about and brought you clothes. He's pretty much become your manservant, and he lets you live in his apartment for free. What the hell more do you want him to do? Donate his balls for you?"

I closed my eyes. When she put it that way... I knew he liked me, but I wasn't sure how long that was going to last. Caleb might be sincere now, but nothing lasts forever.

"You think someone like Caleb couldn't possibly commit," Kara deduced, applying a layer of shocking-pink lipstick. It looked really good on her.

"You're a mind reader now too? That shade is totally your color, by the way."

She nodded. "I know, right? It's a cruelty-free lipstick, and it was on sale! I bought three in different shades. I'll show them to you later. Anyway, I have a vagina, Ver. I know this. I feel this in my soul. I get you."

Kara walked toward me and slapped the side of my head.

"Ouch!" I wasn't expecting that.

"Wake up, idiot." She flicked her fingers at me. "Fine, you don't want to have sex with him. I respect that. I really do. I bow to your superpower virginity, but give the guy a chance."

"I do want to give him a chance. Dammit!" I blew out a breath in frustration, massaging the tension in my neck. "I'm scared, that's all. I can't think when he's near. I'm in a constant battle with myself over whether to give in or not. I hate this. I don't want to be like my mom."

"Ver, you have a pussy. It's between your legs. You don't actually need to *be* one." She paused, growing serious. "The things we run away from are the ones that always come back to bite us in the ass. You feel me? You can run away, but this will come back and bite you harder. Caleb is not your father, and you aren't your mom. You're stronger than she was. Fucking deal with it!" she ranted, shaking her head at me.

Needing some space, I turned away from her piercing gaze. She was right. I was being stupid. The more I fought against the attraction I felt for Caleb, the harder it was to stay away.

Because I was in deep already, I realized. I was also deep in denial.

What the hell had happened to me? I'd kicked ass before. Why did I feel like a fake now? I felt like I was living someone else's life, like I was a spectator instead of a participant. Where was my spunk? The thing I was most scared of was becoming like my mother, and I'd tried everything not to let that happen. Little did I know I was becoming like her all along because I was afraid of facing reality.

The reality was that I really liked Caleb. Really, *really* liked Caleb.

I had a sudden urge to see him. I wanted to make sure he still felt the same way. What if all of it was a joke? My heart was pounding. No, Caleb wasn't cruel like that.

I had been running away from risks all my life. So what if he broke my heart? I was not my mom. I wouldn't be like her even if Caleb broke my heart.

I glanced at the clock. It was two minutes before closing. "Kar, can we close shop yet? I need to talk to Caleb."

"Atta girl!" she exclaimed. "Yeah, we can close now."

"Thanks, Kar. You're a lifesaver."

After closing, I boarded the bus, willing it to move faster. Caleb had basketball practice after he dropped me off at work. He wouldn't be home for a couple of hours yet. I had time to cook him a great dinner of steak and potatoes. After all, what guy didn't like steak and potatoes? He seemed to like whatever I cooked for him. The only thing I knew he wouldn't eat was mac and cheese. A nervous laugh bubbled out, and a few people stared at me. I turned my back to them until the bus arrived at my stop and let me off.

As soon as I entered Caleb's apartment, I grabbed my old MP3 player and tried to let my favorite playlist calm me. It didn't work. I was feeling anxious.

What the hell do I say to him when he comes home? What the hell do I want, anyway?

Caleb. I want Caleb.

Crap. I was hyperventilating. I'd never told a boy I liked him before. How did I start?

I was just placing his plate of food on the breakfast bar where he preferred to eat when I heard the door open. My heart pounded as I waited for him.

"Red?"

"Caleb." I sounded breathy to my ears. I cleared my throat.

Just the sight of him stunned me a little. It was obvious he'd just had a shower. His bronze hair was combed back, showcasing his gorgeous face. I nearly sighed.

"How was practice?"

He stopped midstride, his head tilted in a way that meant he was trying to figure something out.

At the moment, it was me.

"Smells wonderful here," he commented, slipping his hands into his pants pockets.

I wanted him to walk over to me, but he stayed where he was, rocking back on his heels and still studying me with those intense green eyes.

"Hungry?" I asked.

I saw his Adam's apple bob up and down. He looked nervous all of a sudden. Did I have that effect on him?

"Yes," he whispered.

I walked to him slowly. His eyes widened a little as he watched me. I stopped when I was a few inches away from him. I could feel his breath, smell the mint in it.

"I have something for you, Caleb."

I placed my hands around his neck, pulling him close to me. A small smile played on his lips. His lips… They looked so soft, so tempting. I stared at them, craving their taste, their feel against mine.

"What do you have for me, Red?"

His voice was low and raspy, green eyes hooded as they gazed down at me, his long eyelashes casting shadows on his cheeks.

"A kiss," I said breathlessly.

His hands gripped my hips possessively, pulling me closer to him. I heard his intake of breath as our hips touched and the space between us disappeared.

"I want you," he murmured before his head dipped down to claim my lips.

The soft glide of his tongue between my lips coaxed me to open up to him, and when I did, I let myself drown.

Everything blurred into sensation: the rough texture of his hands as they slipped under my shirt, his fingertips slowly drifting along the skin on my lower back, the delicious warmth from his body, the gentle bite of his teeth, the slow licks of his tongue.

It was a passionate kiss, hard and deep. It made me long for something I wasn't ready for. His hands were all over my body. My head was spinning, my heart beating too fast.

And then his phone rang.

I pulled away. We were both panting.

"Red..."

"Answer your phone, please. I need a minute."

Holy crap, what the hell was that?

He stared at me, hesitant to let me go.

"Please," I said.

I wanted to have time to get my breath back without his eyes on me. I was tripping, melting, about to fall apart.

"Hello? Beatrice-Rose?" He stiffened. "Yes, how are you? No, I can't tonight. I'm sorry. Rain check?"

Beatrice-Rose? Rain check?

He was kissing me seconds ago, and now he was planning a date with another girl?

What the *fuck*. He hadn't changed at all. He was still a man whore! Everything blurred to red. Had he been sleeping with anyone—this Beatrice-Rose—since we met? Good God. He'd practically *proposed* to me!

I wrapped my arms around my stomach as my mind thundered off like a freight train. Images of my dad cheating on my mom, my mom crying, begging him to leave his other woman, crashed through my head... Kar crying. And I just snapped. I grabbed the plate of food from the counter and stomped over to dump the food over his head as he finished the call.

He stepped away suddenly so that the food barely touched him. "What the fuck?"

The food plopped wetly onto the floor, and he stared at me in shocked silence.

"You asshole!" I screamed, backing away.

I pulled off my shoe and threw it at him. He ducked, and it missed hitting him by a few inches, which made me angrier. I grabbed my other shoe and threw it at him again. This time he caught it midair. Damned agile basketball player!

"Wha—? What did I do now?" He looked so confused, so clueless that I felt like kicking him between his legs.

"Are you kidding me?" I panted.

I wanted to pull my hair out. The balls! I couldn't believe how stupid I was. I was actually starting to believe him!

I searched for something else to throw at him, but there was nothing nearby, unless I could lift the fridge and drop it on top of his head. I snarled in frustration and turned to leave. I was leaving for good!

He grabbed my arm and whipped me around, my hands

brushing against his chest as our bodies collided. I tried to twist away, but he grabbed my other arm, immobilizing me.

His face was contorted with anger and frustration as he glared at me and growled, "I've been walking on fucking eggshells around you. I can't live like this. What do you want from me?"

I wanted to slap him, but he had my arms locked in his hands.

"Beatrice-Rose? Rain check?" I spat out. "You're making a date seconds after you kissed me?"

His eyes turned stormy. "Beatrice-Rose is a childhood friend! She left school to go to Paris and just got back. She wanted to catch up. Why do you always think the worst about me?"

I groaned. I felt like an idiot. Unless he was lying again… I narrowed my eyes at him.

"Stop being a coward, and tell me what you feel. I am done with your games, Red," he said angrily, his grip on my arms tightening.

And then his eyes turned soft. In a painful whisper he asked, "Do you want me or not?"

"I do, damn you!"

I grabbed the collar of his shirt and pulled him down for a punishing kiss. I kissed him because he put butterflies in my stomach, and I both loved and hated that feeling. I kissed him because he made me hope for something I thought was broken, something I thought I could never have. I kissed him because he was Caleb.

And because he could be *my* Caleb.

His big hands curled possessively on my shoulders before they glided down my back, pulling me against his hard body. I kissed him harder, biting his bottom lip. I heard his intake of breath, and that encouraged me to kiss him even harder. My fingers dug into his arms, taking everything he was giving me, and giving him more. Seeking out his tongue with mine, I tried to show him how I felt, since I couldn't put anything into words.

His hands slipped inside my shirt, fingers seeking the skin just below my bra. My head was spinning, and I realized I needed to catch my breath. I placed my hands on his chest, pushing him back and stepping away. We were both breathing hard, as we always did after we kissed.

"I'm sorry, Caleb. This thing we have between us…it's all so new. It's terrifying me. Every time I want to give in to you, I stop myself. You make me feel like I can be happy with you. You make me feel like I can give you…everything. My mom gave everything to my dad, and he just…he just…" I was rambling.

"Come here," Caleb said, his voice whisper soft.

I shook my head. I needed to get my feet back on the ground. I felt so unsteady.

I felt him move beside me, then touch my face so that I turned toward him. He leaned down and kissed my eyes, tasting my tears.

"You drive me batshit crazy." He kissed my forehead, my cheek, my chin.

"I know. And you drive me just as crazy…as your dinner on the floor suggests." I closed my eyes when he kissed my neck. "Caleb?"

"Hmm?"

"Wait. I want to talk."

"Shh. We have all night. We'll talk later," he whispered, kissing my shoulder. "For now, let me just kiss you."

I laughed nervously. "Okay."

He kissed everything except my lips. I was straining for his lips on mine.

"Caleb, kiss me here…"

"Where?" he murmured.

"Right here." I pointed back to my neck, but I really didn't know *exactly* where. I wanted him to kiss me everywhere. I felt hot, like my blood was boiling and my skin was on fire. His lips were soft. So, so, so soft.

"Mmm…" he purred, smelling the skin on my neck. "You smell so good, taste so good."

Then he lifted me, wrapping my legs around his waist as my arms slid around his neck. He placed me on the counter, his lips never leaving my skin. He was so very close.

"Caleb, kiss me…my lips."

He gave me a searing kiss, then pulled away. "Let me make you feel good." His hands went to caress my legs. "I want to make love with you so bad, Red. It's all I can think about."

It was as if a bucket of ice water had been dumped over my head. I grabbed his hands to stop them from doing…whatever they were going to do.

"Caleb, stop. Wait, please."

He was breathing loudly—we both were—but he stopped as soon as I asked him to.

"Caleb, I can't. I-I'm not ready."

He rested his forehead against mine again, his eyes closed.

"It's okay," he said breathlessly. "We'll take it slow."

"I mean…I don't know if I can. Caleb, I'm…"

"I'm not going to push you. This is all up to you. I promise you."

I nodded. I wondered what he would think if I told him I was still a virgin. Some guys were intimidated by the V card and would refuse to sleep with girls unless they were experienced. Other guys liked to deflower virgins. Others respected it. So…I wondered what category Caleb was in.

"I'm a virgin." There. I'd said it.

His mouth opened in shock, and he pulled back a little. "What?"

"I'm a virgin," I repeated.

His mouth closed. Opened, closed again. He blew out a breath, his hands dropping to flatten on the counter on either side of me as he looked at me.

And then his smile turned into a wolfish alpha grin. "God. You don't know how happy that made me. How proud I am of you right now. I can wait, baby."

Caleb… How did I tell him I was emotionally damaged? I didn't know how long it would take for me to trust him enough to be certain I was ready…

"What?" His smile fell when I didn't answer. "You don't—?" He paused, looked down and sighed, then looked back up at my face. His eyes were piercing. "I know you want to make love with me. I can feel it. But if you're not ready, then you're not ready. That's all there is to it."

He kissed my lips. "I won't rush you, Red," he whispered, moving closer.

I rested my cheek against his chest. His heart was beating fast.

"Besides, there are *other* things we can do," he added playfully. "I'm sorry if I scare you. I know I have no filter on my mouth, but I'm trying my best. I'm going to screw up." He paused, then said, "Contrary to popular belief, I'm not perfect."

I laughed and bit his chest. "Yeah, right."

"Ow. Feisty. I love it," he murmured, rubbing his chest where I'd bitten him.

I gasped when he said *love*.

Don't say that yet, Caleb. I'm not ready to hear it.

Say it, Caleb. I want to hear it.

I held my breath.

He looked at me like he knew what I was thinking. He smiled knowingly and whispered, "You're worth waiting for, Red. I know it."

CHAPTER

twenty-one

Veronica

A LITTLE WHILE LATER, I'D DECIDED TO CALL IT AN EARLY NIGHT
and was about to curl up with a book when I heard a knock on
my bedroom door.

"Red?"

"Come in, Caleb."

He opened the door halfway, poking his head in.

"Well, now, since you blew up like a cheetah on crack, there
went my dinner," Caleb teased, smiling charmingly. He opened
the door all the way and entered.

He'd just had a shower and was rubbing a towel to dry his hair.
He was barefoot and shirtless. A few drops of water glistened on
his chest. My eyes roamed downward to his flat stomach, and
then down to the exposed V line until it disappeared in his jeans.
He hadn't fastened the top button. My mouth felt dry.

I looked away, feeling heat creeping up my neck. I *knew* I

was blushing. And I *knew* he was grinning. He probably was half naked on purpose.

"I'm hungry," he said. But he said it in a *hungry* voice, like he wanted to eat something…and when I looked up into his eyes, I knew.

He was hungry for *me*.

Good Lord.

"Do you—" My voice sounded hoarse so I cleared my throat. "Want me to cook something for you?" My stomach growled, and I realized I was hungry too.

He blew out a breath. "I think we need to get out of here before I eat…someone."

My mouth dropped open, and I'm pretty sure my face was beet red.

He bit his lip, grinning. "Why don't we go out to eat? It's a holiday tomorrow so we can stay up late." He winked. "Wear a dress, Red."

I was so stunned by what he'd said about *eating someone* that I just nodded before he left.

In a daze, I padded to the bathroom to get ready.

I had a dilemma. The only dress I had was the red bandage dress I'd worn at the club, and he had already seen me in it.

I let out a frustrated breath. This was ridiculous. I'd had no problem wearing the same clothes before. I couldn't afford new clothes even if I wanted any.

But Caleb made me want to look beautiful for him. For once in my life, I wanted to impress a boy.

What was Caleb's type? I racked my brain, thinking of all

those times I'd seen him with a girl draped on his arm. I'd never really paid much attention to him before—his type and my type did not mix—but the times I had seen him, I did *notice* the girl was always blond.

Yeah, his usual type was blond. And my hair was black as midnight.

I stared at my image in the mirror. My dark hair fell straight as a pin to my waist. Should I curl it?

I only applied a little powder and the red lipstick that he'd named me for. My eyes were too big, my mouth too wide. Should I apply more makeup?

When I put the dress on, my boobs looked enormous. Were my hips too wide? They looked like I just gave birth. Would he think I wasn't sexy in this dress?

What was happening to me? Where had all these insecurities come from?

I shook my head. I was attractive in my own way, and I knew it. I did not need self-esteem issues bringing me down just because the most popular and gorgeous boy I'd ever met had asked me out on a date.

What did a girl *do* on a date? I knew there were rules for this, and I had no idea what they were.

I felt the panic rising.

Should I pay, or should he, or should we split the bill? What if he brought us to an expensive restaurant? In the movies, a guy sometimes forgot his wallet and then the girl ended up paying. I didn't think Caleb would stoop that low, but what if he really forgot his wallet? I had no money. Maybe we could volunteer to wash the dishes to pay for the food if that happened...

Ah. I was thinking too much again. I was just going to be myself. If Caleb had expectations, well, he'd better throw them out the window because—

Why do you always think the worst about me?

His words came back to me, and I suddenly felt sad. It wasn't really Caleb's fault. It was just how my brain worked. After what my dad had done to my mom, my default was to expect the worst of boys.

Opening up to a boy meant opening my heart and getting hurt. It meant opening up old wounds that I'd rather not think about. There was so much more that I hadn't told Caleb.

I took deep, calming breaths.

He's just a boy. You can handle him.

Handle Caleb? It felt more like he was handling me. Little flutters of panic were creeping in my chest again. I needed to stop thinking. I wanted to enjoy this night.

I was starting to hope that Caleb was different. Maybe I didn't trust him yet, but I was starting to.

I gave myself another once-over in the mirror. The red dress fit my body like a second skin, accentuating all my curves. It wasn't too short, but it showed a lot of leg, and the high heels gave the illusion that my legs were longer than they really were.

What if I fall on my face in these high heels? I groaned, disgusted with myself for all the evil thoughts in my head.

My eyes were shiny, and my cheeks had color in them— something that usually happened when Caleb was near. I looked…excited and nervous. Time to face the music. I sighed and exited my bedroom.

I held my breath when I spotted Caleb leaning against the wall across from me, waiting. He looked up, and our eyes met.

He looked dangerous silhouetted in shadow. The only light in the hallway came from the living room, highlighting the angles of his face.

His green eyes caressed me, sweeping from my hair to my toes, lingering on my eyes, my lips, lingering longer on my chest, my legs, then back up to my face again.

I felt…hot.

He wore a dark dinner jacket that fit his wide shoulders and broad back perfectly. He'd paired it with a dark-blue shirt, a skinny tie, and dark pants. His hair was combed back, and he must have used gel because the hair actually stayed in place.

What is it with Caleb in a suit? It was a huge turn-on for me. My hands tingled, itching to touch him. He looked so unreal.

"I could look at you all night," he said, his voice lower than normal.

I could have said the same to him, but words had temporarily left me.

"This is our first real date. It feels different." He stepped toward me until he was touching my face with both his hands. "This feels very real."

Butterflies. All over my stomach.

I could smell his cologne and feel his body heat. He dipped his head to kiss me gently on the side of my mouth, but he didn't pull back right away. He lingered, inhaling deeply. "God, I love the way you smell. What you do to me…"

I was shaking.

What this boy did to me I had never felt with anyone before.

Being with Caleb was like riding a roller coaster, when it started its slow, tortuous climb up, up, up, and the little jittery fingers of nervousness tickled my stomach. Then that moment when it reached the top, and I closed my eyes and held my breath for one second—knowing I was powerless to stop whatever was coming—and then I was plunging, falling, my stomach dropping to my feet, and I felt like my soul was about to detach from my body. And I laughed and screamed my lungs out until I was hoarse and my throat hurt.

And then when it was over, I wanted to do it again.

As Caleb kissed me, time stood still. His lips were soft and moist, slightly parted, teasing. I leaned up on my toes to catch more of his kiss. He smiled and licked my bottom lip and then sucked on it. I gasped, but he didn't stop. His arms came around me, pressing me against his hard body. And then he lifted his head, staring at me, out of breath.

Caleb's eyes were like deep pools of green. I could swim in them all night and not come up for air.

"My lipstick is all over your mouth now," I whispered, still breathless, wiping my lipstick off his skin with my thumb.

"Did you think your lipstick would save you from my kisses?" he teased, biting my bottom lip again. "Stain me all you want, Red."

I felt giddy. He said the craziest things, but I really wanted to believe he meant them.

He stepped back suddenly. "After you," he said gruffly, his eyes hungry again.

We would never get out of here if he kept looking at me like that. Feeling a little wobbly, I turned and walked ahead of him. I had almost reached the door when his hand caught mine.

"Wait, please. Don't walk away without my hand in yours."

I smiled, melting. "Okay, Caleb."

When we were inside his car, I asked him where we were going.

"It's a surprise. A family friend owns it. The food is spectacular, and it's private."

When he said *private*, I took that to mean expensive. I started to get nervous. Caleb's hand tightened around mine in reassurance.

How did he do that? He always knew what I was feeling.

Trees and buildings zoomed past us until Caleb parked in front of a sleek, modern building. Its walls were made of dark-red glass so I couldn't really see inside. It screamed *restaurant for the wealthy*. I looked at it dubiously. There would be rich people inside, and I did not belong there.

"Red?"

I glanced at him, panic and nervousness in my eyes.

"I'm sorry," he said. "I should have asked where you wanted to eat first."

I was about to tell him that it was all right, let's just go inside, when he shook his head and his face lit up.

"Wait." He stopped my hand just as I was about to unfasten my seat belt. "I know just the perfect date." He chuckled excitedly as he started the car.

"What? Where are we going?" I asked. He was already driving away.

"To one of my favorite places. I promise, you're going to love it. You'll see...but first, we have to make a stop."

Parking in front of a strip mall, he turned off the ignition. He gazed through the windshield for a moment, biting his lip before he turned to face me.

"Hey, Red?"

"Yes?"

"Could you give me your shoe?"

Suspicious, I narrowed my eyes at him. In response, he just grinned mischievously.

"What? Why?"

"No questions," he answered. "Please?"

The *please* got me. I pulled off a shoe and gave it to him. He looked inside before handing it back to me.

"Wait here. I'll be right back."

A few minutes later, he was back. Instead of going to the driver's side, he tapped the window on my side, raising his arms and shaking two paper bags. I rolled the window down.

"What's that?" I asked.

"Our costumes." He grinned. Not satisfied with the rolled-down window, he opened the passenger door.

He rummaged in one of the bags, pulling out a red T-shirt with a large picture of a padlock. He snapped the shirt in the air, presenting it to me like a child would: with earnest longing for my reaction.

I had no idea how he wanted me to react. Was it because the shirt was red?

He raised his brows to indicate there was more and draped the shirt over his shoulder. Reaching into the bag, he produced another red shirt. "Ta-da!" he crowed with a flourish. This one had a picture of a heart. He whipped the first one off his shoulder, holding both shirts up.

I looked at his handsome, grinning face for a moment. His cheeks were pink, his eyes twinkling. And then I started to laugh. Both shirts were red, and put together, they represented his last name: Lockhart.

"You like it?" he asked.

"Sure, Caleb." I chuckled.

Satisfied, he closed my door and jogged around the car, settling in the driver's seat.

"We'll match. I also got shorts and sneakers," he said, shaking the second bag.

I shook my head at him, smiling.

"Here's your shirt." He handed me the paper bag. "I get the lock. You get the heart. Sound good?"

When I just looked at him, he laughed again. "Red, you look drop-dead gorgeous in that dress, and I could look at you all night. But I figured instead of fancy, we'd try super casual. You game?"

I nodded, dazed by his playful grin. He started undressing, pulling off his suit jacket, removing his tie, and then unbuttoning his dress shirt. I sat there gawking. He pulled on his shirt with the lock picture. And then he started removing his pants...

"Caleb!"

He opened his pants fly, then paused to stare at me with

intense eyes, challenging me. "You can stare however long you like, Red. This body belongs to you."

"Oh God," I groaned, closing my eyes.

"Anyway…" He chuckled as I heard his clothes rustling. "It's not like we haven't seen each other in our underwear. Remember jumping off the bridge?"

God, I remembered. The image of him in his wet briefs was seared into my brain. I couldn't help it. I peeked.

He wore…boxers with yellow smiley faces.

That made me laugh again.

"Go ahead and put yours on. I won't look." His dimples winked at me.

"Yeah, right." I chortled and rolled my eyes.

His mood was so infectious, so fun and cheerful. He made me feel like it was okay to act my age, to be young and carefree, to do silly things and forget my problems. I realized Caleb liked me for who I was. I could be myself around him, and he would accept all of me.

I removed the straps of my dress, rolling it down my torso. I knew he was staring, but I acted like undressing in a car while Caleb watched was a perfectly normal thing to do.

Inside, I was a nervous wreck. I couldn't look at him.

It was too quiet inside the car. I swear he wasn't breathing. When I pulled the dress all the way down my legs and I was only wearing my bra and panties, I heard his sharp intake of breath.

"Red," he whispered. I finally glanced at him, and he looked like he wanted to… Well, he looked *hungry*. *Again*.

I gave him a haughty smile.

Where was I getting this confidence? From Caleb, I realized. He made me feel confident. He made me feel beautiful.

I put on the heart shirt and then the shorts. He let out a loud breath as I finished putting on the sneakers. I looked at him, and we both burst out laughing. We matched. As I caught my breath, I felt strangely free.

Once we were both dressed, Caleb drove us outside the city limits, passing trees and fields. He turned up the radio, singing at the top of his lungs. I laughed when he couldn't reach the high notes but kept singing anyway. Singing was obviously not one of his talents, but I gave him points for his enthusiasm.

The windows were down, the warm wind whipping our hair. When he finished belting out one last song, he simply held my hand. I didn't ask him where we were going because I felt peaceful. I felt…safe. It was a feeling that I didn't often experience. But with Caleb, I did. He took care of me, even when I wasn't exactly friendly.

I didn't realize I was staring at him until he said, "Like what you see?" There was a small smile playing on his lips.

He'd asked me this before—the first time we kissed—and I knew where that had led.

"Want me to look for a place to park and make out?" he asked, clearly remembering it too.

Yes, I do.

I couldn't believe how fast I was admitting my feelings about him to myself. I was so screwed. I shook my head and laughed. I was laughing a lot today.

A few minutes later, we entered a small town outside the city.

I hadn't been here before. The area looked like a tourist spot, with small quaint shops, local restaurants, and Victorian houses that reminded me of gingerbread and storybook gardens.

I rolled down the window, letting fresh air inside the car. It was late, but locals and tourists still milled about, shopping, eating, laughing, enjoying a lively evening with family and friends.

"I figured we'd be silly tonight," Caleb said. "Maybe pretend to be someone else."

I glanced at him, and his brows rose mischievously.

I chuckled. "All right. Who should we be?"

"Anyone," he replied, pausing. "You can be mine. If you want."

I want.

He slowed down, maneuvering among the tightly parked cars and pedestrians. It looked like a parade, with people abandoning the sidewalks and walking in groups on the road. Caleb parked as soon as he saw a spot. I couldn't wait to start our night.

When we got out of the car, people stared at us, smiling and some of them even whistling as they spotted our couple shirts. Feeling self-conscious, I glanced at Caleb.

"Couple shirts are all the rage now, Red. Let's own it, shall we?" He winked, twining his fingers with mine.

He looked so adorable, so happy that it was impossible not to share his mood.

"So, where would you like to eat first?" he asked.

Taking in our surroundings, I felt like a kid in a candy store. "Hmm. It's so hard to choose."

There was a family-owned pizzeria where I was sure they grew their own spices, an ice-cream shop where they possibly had their own cows and produced their own milk, and local restaurants boasting seafood, burgers, soups, and all kinds of delicious goodness.

"There are so many restaurants to choose from," I uttered excitedly.

He pointed at a yellow box of a place with a sign that simply said *Soup*, its paint peeling. "How about we go for soup in that restaurant over there?" he suggested. Then he pointed at the white building beside it where people sat at tables under colorful umbrellas. "And then have some pizza there. Then—will you look at that—an old-fashioned ice-cream parlor. We can walk and eat our ice cream in the park. If you're good..." His voice trailed off until I looked up at him. "I could even let you kiss me."

I smiled, willing myself not to blush. "You wish."

Soup's interior didn't look any better than its exterior. Old tables covered in red-checkered tablecloths, ancient brown seats wrapped in plastic, a beige linoleum floor, and pictures of Elvis and Madonna completed the decor. The menus on the table were sticky.

The waitress approached us. She was in her fifties, possibly sixties...I couldn't really tell. Her frizzy hair was dyed white-blond and held back by a neon-pink headband. Her name tag said Daisy. She gave us a big smile and asked what we were having as she snapped her gum noisily.

"We'll take the clam chowder, please and thank you, ma'am. My wife here is pregnant with triplets," Caleb started.

My eyes widened with shock as Caleb rubbed my tummy, leaned down, and kissed it.

"You see, she wanted to have this vacation," he continued, winking at me and giving Daisy his megawatt smile.

Daisy didn't stand a chance. She was hypnotized by the gorgeous professional pretender that was Caleb.

"And I had to work hard to save money so she could have a taste of your wonderful clam chowder," he finished, batting his eyelashes at the older woman.

Daisy beamed. "And what do you do for a living, young man?"

"I'm a stripper, ma'am."

I choked. Daisy looked at Caleb as if she thought he was out of his mind.

I suppressed my laugh and added, "We have six kids—"

"God help you!" she interrupted.

"—already. All of them twins and all boys, and now I'm pregnant with triplets. He's having a vasectomy done next week, so I wanted to enjoy all of his…manhood one last time before he gets cut," I exaggerated.

Caleb snorted.

Daisy's eyes narrowed, wondering if we were serious. "All right, you lovebirds." She grinned. "I'll get you your clam chowder before your husband gets his balls cut off," she joked, winking. She was clearly on to us.

Caleb and I burst out laughing when we were sure she was gone.

"So, Red…you want to enjoy my manhood, yeah?" Caleb wiggled his eyebrows.

I slapped his arm, laughing.

"And you want to have nine kids, is that right?" he added.

"I haven't thought about it."

He frowned.

I bit my lip. I was lying. I had dreamed of having kids once, but I was a different person then. How was I supposed to feed them? My mom and I barely had anything to eat. What if we went bankrupt and got kicked out of our house and then they got sick? The world was a dangerous, unforgiving place.

Caleb tilted his head and studied me for a moment.

"You have me. We'll raise them together," he declared. "I want to have our own basketball team."

I was saved from replying when Daisy placed our orders on the table, winked again, and left.

"I hope we don't get *E. coli* here," I commented. I sampled the soup and was pleasantly surprised by how delicious it was.

"I've been here before, when I was"—his voice trailed off while he thought—"eight? I've been back a few times. I don't think anything has changed. It may not look like much, but I promise you the food here is very good."

"You've been here before?" I asked, surprised.

He nodded, his face falling. "With my dad and Ben."

A lonely light glimmered in his eyes. "Dad grew up in a small town. He was a mechanic in a run-of-the-mill garage. That's how he met my mom," Caleb explained, reaching for my hand and rubbing his thumb on my palm.

A current sparked where his skin met mine, zinging all the way up my arm.

"My mom was a teenager at the time. She went on a trip with her friends to a cabin outside town, and on the drive back home, she met my dad. She got pregnant with my brother, Ben. They got married against the wishes of all their parents…" He shrugged. "Anyway, he was a good dad at first. During weekends, he would drive us—just me and him and Ben—to different small towns. Just visiting, he said. Exposing his sons to the side of the world that wasn't wealthy and pretentious."

He stared at our hands, intertwining our fingers and squeezing lightly.

"What happened?" I asked quietly when he didn't continue.

"I had a…baby sister."

I looked up in surprise. His eyes looked sad.

"She didn't stay with us for long." His voice shook. "The doctors said her brain didn't form properly. She died a few minutes after Mom gave birth to her."

I squeezed his hand for comfort. "Caleb."

"My mom buried herself in work. To recover—or to forget, I guess. She was often gone on business trips. And my dad… Well, he changed. I guess they grew apart. We all did. He started cheating on my mom. As if she needed more heartbreak after losing her child." He took a deep breath and released it slowly as if to calm himself. "Ben left for college shortly after."

"You were alone when you needed them most. And you were just a kid."

"I was already in high school, old enough to know better. I got in trouble a lot." He looked embarrassed, dropping his gaze to the table. I waited for him to explain. "I would lose my temper easily, picking fights all the time. I was out of control. My mom sent me to therapy, but that didn't help. I was an angry kid."

I couldn't picture him that way. "What happened?"

"Ben heard about it. He left school for a semester and came home to straighten me out. He had friends who did demolitions and flipped houses, and he dragged me along with him. I'd pour out all my anger, destroying walls with my kick-ass sledgehammer. It was better than therapy. I felt like Thor." He laughed lightly, but I could hear the lingering sadness and guilt in his voice. "I owe my brother a lot."

I remembered those first few weeks when I was living in his apartment. When we didn't talk to each other, I'd hear Caleb puttering around the house, repairing anything he could get his hands on. He'd always had bandages on his fingers and calluses on his hands.

"So did I ruin my good boy image now?" he teased.

We both knew he didn't have a good boy image to begin with, but he was trying to lighten the mood. All it did was make me sadder. I could still see the dregs of sadness in his eyes. I wanted him to know I understood his pain, that he wasn't alone, even if it pained me to talk about mine.

"My dad..." I cleared my throat. "He would often bring women in the house. I...don't know how my mom... I'm sorry, it's so ugly. I just want you to know that I understand."

He gently tugged on my hand, and I glanced up at him. "Please, Red, go on."

So we talked about parents, our childhood, and then just trivial things that made us who we were. I was learning a lot about Caleb, and everything I learned, I really, really liked.

I finished my soup and wanted to order another bowl, but

Caleb stood to pay the bill. Then he ushered me outside so we could go to the pizzeria next door.

"I'm paying for this one," I told him with as much command in my voice as I could muster.

He was shaking his head before I even finished my sentence. "A woman never pays for a date. That's something I won't budge on," he said with more command in his voice than I could have managed. "Please," he added softly.

He glanced at me, tucking a windblown lock of hair behind my ear.

I forgot that I was still hungry when he stared at me that way. The look in his eyes said that I was the most beautiful girl he had ever seen, that no one existed but the two of us. My knees felt weak, and I unconsciously leaned into him.

A group of kids ran past us, laughing and pushing at each other. And that broke the spell. Caleb cleared his throat, and I wondered if he was feeling nervous too.

He led us to the pizzeria, telling me to choose a table while he ordered for us. I was sitting under one of the umbrella tables outside when I felt a tap on my shoulder. I turned around and saw Caleb holding a humongous pizza loaded with toppings and a tray with two tall drinks.

"Hi, ah, I was wondering… I've been eating dinner by myself for quite some time now… It gets pretty lonely. Would you mind sharing this pizza with me?" He wore a polite smile, shrugging those broad shoulders.

What is he up to now?

"I'm Caleb, by the way."

Ah, so pretend we're strangers.

I chuckled, playing along. Oh, he was so fun!

"Um…" I bit my lip. "I'm not sure. I don't really eat with strangers," I teased.

But he was already taking a seat and placing the food in front of me.

"Ah. But I swear I'm not a rapist or a murderer." He winced. "That turned out bad… I mean—"

I laughed. "It's all right. Free food is good food."

"So you're not eating with me because you think I'm hot?"

I shook my head, grinning in spite of myself. Stranger or not, Caleb was Caleb.

"Tell me about yourself," he said. "What's your name?"

I shook my head. "No names."

"Mysterious girl." He clucked his tongue. He slid a plate in front of me and placed two pieces of pizza on it. "Eat."

It was fascinating the way Caleb ate—savoring each bite like it was fine French cuisine rather than local pizza. Sure, he ate like a guy, taking way-too-big bites, but at least he chewed with his mouth closed.

Perfect table manners must have been instilled in him at an early age, I realized.

"So, tell me, Mysterious Girl," he started, dabbing at his mouth with a napkin. "What makes you feel special?"

I bit my lip, thinking. Should I answer honestly?

"I guess when someone takes care of me. Giving me rides to school, buying me green tea…cooking me pancakes."

He was quiet for a moment, a smile playing on his lips as he took another bite and chewed quietly. He swallowed before asking, "Are you allergic to anything?"

"No, not really." I paused. "Are you?"

He chuckled, nodding. "Peanut butter."

My eyes widened in horror. "Oh my God, Caleb, I'm so sorry! I didn't know—" I stammered, breaking role. My favorite food was peanut butter. It was a staple for me, and it was currently sitting in his fridge.

He shook his head, laughing. "It's all right, Red. I can have it in the house. It's only a mild allergy, and only if I eat it. So don't kiss me after you eat it."

I shook my head, incredulous that he hadn't told me this before.

"So," he began. "Granny panties, boy shorts, or thong?"

And he was back. We went on asking each other questions, sometimes serious, sometimes ridiculous. He asked a lot of inappropriate questions, but in his own goofy way.

I felt full after the pizza, but Caleb insisted we try the ice cream. He bought us strawberry ice-cream cones dipped in chocolate, and we ate them as we walked in the park.

We couldn't finish them and ended up throwing them out.

It was late, but both of us were in no hurry to go home yet. He reached for my hand and dragged me down with him on the grass.

"I'm so stuffed I feel like a hippopotamus that ate an elephant." He patted his flat stomach.

I laughed, trying to picture that. How could he eat so much and still have sexy abs? "Hippos are normally herbivores," I told him. "But there have been reports of them actually eating meat. So fine, you are a hippo that ate an elephant."

"My smarty-pants Red. Your brain is so sexy, such a turn-on."

I laughed. I couldn't remember the last time I laughed this much. We grew quiet. We lay on the grass for a long time, comfortable in our silence, just holding hands and looking up at the dark, velvet sky.

Away from the city, the stars decorated the heavens, complementing the romantic radiance of the moon. The air was just beginning to cool down from the heat of the day. I smelled the grass, sharp and fresh. Wild lavender and dandelions were deemed weeds in the city, but in this place, they were special— magical even.

That was how Caleb made me feel. I was nothing but a normal girl to other people, a weed, but to Caleb I was magical and special, just like the flowers that spread with abandon on the ground.

Turning onto my side so I was facing him, I whispered, "Thank you for this night, Caleb."

He was lying on his back, but he turned his face toward me. Before he could say anything, I reached out to touch his face.

He watched me, waiting patiently.

I traced his nose with my finger, sliding down to the almost feminine shape of his lips and swirling it to the angles of his cheekbones. He closed his eyes as I slowly touched his eyebrows, a small smile flirting on his lips. When I stopped, he opened his eyes and stared at me with emotion that choked me up. I moved closer and gently kissed him.

When I pulled away, his arm snaked around me. Curling his hand around my nape, he pulled me close again.

He kissed me wildly, as if he had been craving it all day. When our lips met, relief and longing bloomed in my chest.

He moved on top of me, pressing the line of his hard body against mine, his full weight on his forearms. "Red," he whispered, sucking on my bottom lip. "My Red."

My mind emptied of everything except the feelings that Caleb's kisses elicited. I'd never thought a kiss could make me feel like I was burning and needy at the same time.

When he released my lips, he was panting. He rested his forehead against mine for a moment before rolling away and lying on the grass beside me, placing his arm over his eyes.

"Caleb?" I asked uncertainly. Did I do something wrong?

"I'm sorry." He blew out a breath. "I need…a minute." His arm dropped to his side, and he stared up at the sky, his jaw tense. "Unless you changed your mind and you're ready to make love with me, let's just stay where we are and not move for a minute, please."

My head was still spinning from his kisses, my skin tingly, but when I heard him say "make love with me," I froze.

He reached for my hand. "Don't worry," he said. "I told you I'll wait. It's just sometimes…sometimes I want you so bad that I can taste it in my mouth." He gazed at me. "Do you understand what I'm saying?"

I nodded, unable to say anything. Nobody had wanted me like this before. Not like Caleb. I watched him control his breathing until it eventually calmed down.

"Wanna come back here again sometime…with me?" he asked.

"Yes, Caleb," I answered.

"You said yes." He laughed. "Look at that. You're already falling for me."

I looked at him in shock.

He shrugged. "What? I didn't say the *L* word, so don't run screaming for the hills."

My eyes just got wider. He chuckled, pulling me tight to his side so my body was flush against his, my head resting on his chest as he rubbed my back.

"I'll wait for you, Red. We have all the time in the world." He grazed my lips with his thumb. "But when you say yes, it's going to be amazing. You're going to love it. You'll see," he promised and kissed me under the moonlight.

CHAPTER

twenty-two

Veronica

It was past midnight by the time we headed home. Tonight, something had changed between us; something had changed in me.

I wasn't exactly sure where our relationship stood now. All I knew was that I wanted to explore it more. For the first time in my life, I was willing to risk my heart.

The drive back was comfortably silent as Caleb drove one-handed, his other hand wrapped around mine. On the poorly lit country road, darkness surrounded us. It was so black that I couldn't see more than a few feet ahead of us. The clouds now covered the moon and stars we'd gazed at earlier.

Thank God for headlights.

I turned to look behind us, looking for cars or any signs of life. There were none. It was only us on the road. The trees that we passed were just a blur of shadows, the yellow lines reflecting the light back as the car lights hit them.

"This reminds me of that scene in *Jeepers Creepers*," I said, shivering from the memory.

Caleb threw me an amused glance. "You like scary movies?"

I shook my head. "No. But I keep watching them anyway."

He snickered. "We should watch scary movies together. Did you know that when you do exciting things together with someone, you associate that adrenaline feeling with that person? So…" He wiggled his eyebrows. "Scary movies are definitely a must on our to-do list."

I tried to fight my smile and failed. "Our list?"

"Yup. I have a long, long list, so you better get ready. Have you seen *Insidious*? Or *The Evil Dead*?"

I shivered again. "No. I don't think I want to talk about horror movies when it's just us on the road. I feel like someone is hovering above your car, ready to pounce on us any minute."

"I love your imagination—*shit*!"

Suddenly the car swerved to the right as a deer raced in front of us. I screamed in terror as the force threw my body against the window. I nearly banged my head.

Tires squealed against asphalt, the sound piercing my ears. The smell of burning rubber wafted into the car, choking me.

I heard Caleb let out a string of curses as the car groped for traction, careening on the rocks and dirt on the side of the road. Caleb's eyes quickly darted at me, filled with dread. I felt the blood drain from my face.

That was when I realized we could die.

My palms became moist, and sweat popped on my forehead. I had felt this before, this feeling of impending doom. That something was out to get me, and no matter what I did, I was going to die.

I watched Caleb grip the steering wheel, the veins in his arms standing out as he tried to control the vehicle. It kept on going, skidding sideways. I barely registered the dirt and dust flying around us as the car shook and rattled on the uneven terrain.

The seat belt bit through my skin, jerking me back as the car braked to a complete stop. And then silence.

I was breathing through my mouth, panting like I'd just run a mile. My whole body felt cold, and I started shaking uncontrollably, my teeth chattering.

I heard a seat belt being unfastened, and suddenly Caleb was pulling me into his lap, burying his face in my hair. I heard his loud, uneven breathing, felt the pounding of his heart. He was hugging me so hard I could barely breathe.

I didn't care. I needed his arms around me, needed to be assured we were both okay. My arms wrapped around him. His warmth was soothing, his so-familiar smell comforting.

"Baby, are you okay?" he whispered, his voice shaky. He straightened a little and pressed his cheek to the top of my head.

I nodded, unable to speak. He ran his fingers through my hair, an unconscious gesture that comforted both of us. I don't know how long we held each other, but eventually our hearts slowed to their normal rhythm. The pounding in my head dissipated, and my breathing returned to normal.

"You okay?" he repeated, rubbing my back.

I nodded. "Yes…Caleb, thank you," I said, hugging him tighter. "You saved us both."

He blew out a breath, relief evident in his eyes. "I'm just glad you're okay. You didn't hit your head or anything, did you?"

He gently returned me to my seat, his eyes scanning my face before moving down to my lower body, checking for signs of injury.

"I'm okay, Caleb. Are you?" I asked, giving him the same inspection.

His eyes were still glinting from the rush of adrenaline, but he looked unharmed. Thank God. If something bad happened to him... I took a deep breath and refused to think about it.

He tried a smile, but it was forced. "I think I just lost ten years of my life, but I'm good. Next time we visit, we're definitely going to a hotel and staying the night."

I agreed. Suddenly, I felt very weak and thirsty, my body slumping in my seat.

"Stay inside. I'm going to check the car, make sure the tires are okay," he said.

I nodded, praying we weren't going to be stranded in the middle of nowhere. I watched Caleb as he walked around the vehicle. He crouched to check the tires, disappearing from view. I felt the car rock as he opened the trunk. He returned a few minutes later, assuring me everything was okay and handing me a can of orange pop. He must have had some stored in the trunk. I smiled at him in gratitude.

After that, he drove at a slower speed, with both hands on the wheel this time. He was more alert, paying attention to the sides of the road.

When we reached Caleb's building, I was exhausted and

found myself leaning into him as we walked. The concierge greeted us as we passed. Caleb chatted with him for a moment before we made our way to the elevator. When the door opened and we stepped in, Caleb scooped me up in his arms. I yelped in surprise.

"Caleb! What are you doing?"

The doors closed, and the elevator ascended.

"You were about to pass out. I can't let that happen," he replied, leaning against the wall with a long sigh.

He must have been exhausted too since he could barely stand up. Today had been incredible, but it had been a long day.

"I'm okay now, I promise. Please put me down."

"Nope." He squished me closer to his chest, brooking no argument.

Suddenly, the doors opened and I stared in horror as an older woman stepped in, shock on her face. When she recovered, she glared at us and then stood as far away as possible inside the cramped space.

"Young people nowadays," she muttered under her breath in a disapproving voice. "So disrespectful, so disgusting."

I slapped Caleb on the arm. He was grinning, the bad boy! I pinched him, but he wouldn't put me down. In fact, he hitched me up higher in his arms and dipped his head to kiss me.

The lady's muttering grew louder.

"What have we planned for tonight, love?" he asked, his lips still hovering over mine.

He was probably going to say something that would shock this older woman into an early grave, but that wasn't why my heart started pounding. My lips were still tingling from his kiss, and he had never called me "love" before.

Oh no, Caleb… What was he going to say now?

"Whips and chains on the menu tonight? No? Ball gag, then. You can tie me up."

I groaned. Oh good Lord.

He started humming "S and M" by Rihanna. Bobbing his head up and down, making his voice sound rough as he growled a little bit.

Mercifully, the doors opened and the woman ran out, glancing back to give us a look of revulsion before the doors closed.

"You're crazy," I whispered, giggling.

"I don't like it when people judge others."

"You *did* mention whips and chains," I reminded him.

"Yeah, but I only did that because she was complaining about me carrying you in the elevator. What's so disrespectful and disgusting about it? What if I was carrying you because we just got married? Or maybe you hurt your ankle, and I—as your husband—was carrying you so you didn't have to walk."

Your husband. I had to let that pass so I could concentrate on the other things he was saying.

"People shouldn't be so quick to judge. She could be guilty of doing the same things she criticizes other people for…or worse. It's so hypocritical." He blew out a breath.

"You know her?"

"She used to teach at a prestigious school. Let's just say she won't be teaching any kids in the future because of what she's done." He shook his head. "Just because they're older doesn't mean they're always right. I automatically give respect to people I meet unless they do something to take that away. I won't disrespect them, but I can be blunt."

Oh, Caleb.

The doors opened and he walked out, still carrying me. He glanced down at me with a puzzled smile on his lips.

"Why are you looking at me that way?" he asked.

I dropped my gaze, blushing. Thankfully, he didn't comment on it.

He had to enter the code to his apartment, and I expected him to put me down once we reached the door, but he didn't.

I cleared my throat. "Aren't you going to put me down?"

"No."

He leaned down—crouched, really—while I was still in his arms. I was blocking his vision, so he moved his head from side to side, trying to see the numbers on the keypad.

"Caleb!" I giggled, holding on to his arms to keep from falling.

We were both laughing. My hair was in his mouth as he tried to press the numbers.

"This is silly… Oh my God!" I squeaked as he lost his balance, tipping backward.

He landed on his back as I sprawled on top of him, his arms protecting me as we fell.

"Ouch!" he moaned, but he was laughing.

"We're going to wake the neighbors." I chuckled, too tired to move.

I was on top of him, my head on his chest.

"We can just sleep here," I murmured, feeling so comfortable and relaxed that I closed my eyes.

"I'm not tired at all," he answered, raising his head so he could look at me.

My eyes snapped open.

"Um…" I suddenly felt awake, my nerve endings coming to life.

I pushed off him, then awkwardly stood up.

He sighed. "Help me up, please." He stretched out his arm so I could pull him up.

I pursed my lips, grabbing his hand. I squealed as he jerked me down on top of him again.

When I landed on his hard body, he started laughing.

"Caleb!" I scolded.

"God, you feel so good," he whispered in my ear.

I blushed, trying to keep my wits about me since I was very aware of his solid body beneath me.

"Caleb, let's go inside."

"We will." The sudden change in his tone—from playful to somber—alerted me. He was serious all of a sudden, his green eyes filled with fear. "I just need…"

"Caleb…"

He pulled back and reversed our positions so that I was lying beneath him. His touch was gentle, almost reverent, as he caressed my cheek with his fingers, his eyes searching mine for reassurance that I was okay.

"If I lost you… If something happened to you, I wouldn't be able to… I wouldn't know what to do," he said, his voice rough.

I reached out to touch his face, pressing my lips to his for a soft kiss before pulling away.

"I'm right here. I'm okay," I said gently, placing my palms on his chest.

"My Red…"

His eyes focused on my mouth, and he reached out a finger to trace my top lip, dipping down on my Cupid's bow.

He went on to trace my bottom lip, rubbing the pad of his finger against it. I held my breath as his thumb lightly pressed the side of my mouth, dragging down my bottom lip so that my mouth opened a little. He was touching me softly, teasingly, deliberately, and I'd never realized just how sensitive lips were.

I started panting.

I saw the struggle in his eyes before he closed them, as if he needed a moment to gather himself. When he opened them again, they were a little calmer. "I'm sorry," he murmured. "I just can't help it."

Like a cat, he jumped up in one smooth move and pulled me up with him. I blinked, needing a few moments to recover, but he was already opening the door and guiding me inside.

We stopped in front of my bedroom. He turned me to face him, holding my hand in both of his, slowly rubbing my palm. I didn't think he was even aware of the action. His eyes were looking at our joined hands, a small frown creasing his brows.

I waited for him to speak. After a moment, he said, "I have to say good night right here."

I studied his face, puzzled. His gaze was intense and troubled.

"You don't know how much I want to go in there with you."

My heart skipped a beat.

He looked down, shook his head, and looked back up at me again. "Thank you for a lovely night." He leaned closer to me, our noses touching. "Sweet dreams."

Then he walked away.

The soft glow of the lamplight greeted me as I woke up. I never turned the lights off when I slept. Something bad always happened when I did.

So Caleb was right when he said I slept with the lights on. But how did he know that? I locked my bedroom door every night. It was habit. He couldn't have come in while I was asleep. Unless he had a key.

Of course he had a key, I thought, mentally *duh*-ing myself.

But I was a very light sleeper, and I was positive I would have heard the door open if Caleb had decided to come in. Then again, if he'd passed my room, he would have seen the light from under my door.

I squinted to check the time—3:00 a.m. I groaned. I hated 3:00 a.m. It was the time when bad things happened—at least in my experience. But I was feeling really thirsty and had to drink some water.

I was exhausted and dehydrated from drinking with Kara and Beth the other night, and then going out on that incredible date with Caleb. I was surprised I could still walk.

My eyes were still half closed as I padded to the kitchen. I groped for the lights, but I couldn't find them.

What the hell?

Still half asleep, I decided to abandon the search for the switch. Opening the fridge, I grabbed Caleb's carton of orange juice and moved it to its designated bottom shelf. I chuckled, thinking of how much orange juice he drank as I fished out a can of coconut water.

I popped open the top, the sound piercing the silence of the room. It woke me up a little, enough to make my senses adjust to the dark.

There was something in the shadows...watching me.

I narrowed my eyes, trying to make out if anything or anyone was hiding in the darkness.

There was nothing. My mind was clearly playing tricks on me. I turned back to the fridge, intending to close it, and then I heard the sound behind me.

The hair on my arms stood up as fear rushed through my veins, numbing my limbs. The can fell from my hand, and the sound of it hitting the floor broke the maddening silence. It was like the sharp crack of a whip, waking me from my frozen state.

I ran. Ran as fast as I could, but everything was cloaked in darkness and I could barely see anything in front of me.

I could feel the figure's hate, creeping in the air to smother me. It wanted my pain. It was chasing me now, enjoying the hunt. Its quiet chuckle was pure evil.

I cried out in alarm as I tripped, my palms flattening with my weight as I made contact with the cold floor.

I heard sadistic laughter behind me. Something sinister that belonged to the darkness. Something very, very familiar.

I scrambled up, spinning around so that I could see what was chasing me. Screams bubbled out of my throat as I heard footsteps thumping toward me. Instinct screamed at me to run, but I was too petrified to even turn my head away.

"Run, little girl," the specter taunted. "I'm gonna get you." Its voice hissed like a snake.

I forced myself to move, glancing back to see nothing but darkness.

I wanted to scream, but my throat refused to work. Something was choking me...and I realized it was fear.

"Do you think I won't find you?"

No! No, please!

I ran faster, pumping my legs as fast as I could. I let out a scream when I crashed against a solid object.

"Red! What the hell?"

Caleb!

He gripped my arms, his eyes alarmed. My eyes were wide with panic as I tried to tell him what was going on. I opened my mouth, but I couldn't speak.

I shook my head and reached for his hand, frantically pulling at him to run.

Please!

"Red, calm down. What's wrong?"

He cupped my face, forcing me to look at him. "It's okay. You're having a panic attack. Breathe slowly. In through your nose now, come on. Out through your mouth. Focus!"

His authoritative command pulled me out of my panicked state. I took slow, deep breaths, in and out, in and out.

"What happened? Why were you running?" he asked. His gentle eyes and controlled voice calmed me.

Am I going crazy?

"The-there was something b-back in the kitchen," I stuttered.

Without warning, Caleb fell to his knees, shock on his face. My mouth opened in a silent scream as he stared at me with fear and incredulity, his hands covering his stomach. I watched as blood seeped through his shirt.

"Go!" he begged.

I covered my mouth with both hands as I watched Caleb crumple to the floor. Unmoving. Lifeless.

No! No, no, no!

Before I could reach out to him, the evil thing stepped out from the shadows. The dark figure had a malicious smile, and its gaze bored into me.

"Hello, Daughter."

I heard screaming, so loud and sharp it hurt my ears. I realized it was me, and the sound pulled me out of my nightmare. And then Caleb's voice came through the fog.

"Red! Wake up! It's okay, baby. I got you. Shh… I'm here now. It's okay."

I was shaking. My bones were cold and my lungs felt full, choking on too much air—or not enough. Caleb's arms were around me, rubbing my back, comforting me. He was still murmuring soothing words in my ear, but I wasn't hearing them.

All I could register was his voice.

Caleb was okay. He was here. He was alive.

God.

My arms wrapped around him as I buried my face against his chest, sobbing. I was soaking his shirt, but I couldn't stop the tears from flowing.

I didn't know how long we stayed like that, but eventually my sobs diminished to just hiccupping. Caleb was still rubbing my back, softly humming a song. I closed my eyes, letting his voice soothe me.

"Want to talk about it?" he asked quietly.

I shook my head. I felt him nod, and then he kissed my hair. The memory of the nightmare was already escaping me, like dust in the wind. I reached for it, concentrating hard to catch it, but then it was gone.

"Caleb?"

"Mmm-hmm?"

"Will you stay with me tonight? Please."

His intake of breath was audible. "Yes," he said simply, pulling me closer so the top of my head was secured under his chin.

Just like that. No questions asked.

Had anyone besides my mom cared for me this much?

No, not like this. Never before Caleb.

"I almost broke your door when I heard you screaming. I hope you don't mind that I opened it. I have a key."

I shook my head and burrowed deeper against him.

I noticed the soft patter of rain blowing against the windows. It consoled me, steadied me. I've always loved the sound, even when I was a child.

"Do you like the rain?" he asked softly.

I snuggled closer to him, held him tighter. "Yes."

"Tell me why you like it," he whispered.

"Do you like it, Caleb?"

I felt him smile. He probably thought I was avoiding his question, but truthfully, I wanted to hear his answer.

"Yes, I do. When I was young, I would run outside every time it rained so I could play. I loved the smell of it, loved the way it hit my skin. It tasted like the ocean."

Thunder rumbled outside, the sound booming through the room. Thunder didn't scare me. I loved it. Caleb didn't seem to mind it either because he let out a contented sigh.

"To me, it symbolizes new beginnings. I don't know if you believe in God or in a higher being, but I do. I was an altar boy growing up, you know." He chuckled. "That white robe was my Sunday attire for years."

I smiled. "You said the rain symbolizes new beginnings to you."

"Yes," he answered after a moment. He seemed lost in his thoughts as he absently stroked my arm.

I closed my eyes. His touch felt so good.

"I feel like God is washing off the dirt from the world," he explained. "Wiping the slate clean. Handing you a new beginning. Washing away all the sadness, the sorrow, the nightmares."

I didn't know why I felt sad all of a sudden. "Some bad things can't be washed away, Caleb."

"See now, that's just sad. True enough, there are some bad things that are just part of your landscape, and you can't simply wash them away. But you can learn to accept them and not let them define who you are," he continued, his voice turning deeper. He tipped his head back so he could look into my eyes.

"It's what you learn from the bad things that can determine the path you choose. If you embrace your scars and let them make you stronger, you might be able to open up and move beyond the pain."

I swallowed the lump in my throat. What if the scars were so deep that they were all I could see? All I could feel?

"Tell me a story, Caleb."

"All right, but let's get you under these covers first."

We settled under the blanket, facing each other, and he wrapped his arms around me. He was quiet for a moment, but the silence was comfortable between us. Warm. Caleb was so warm. I hadn't realized how cold I was until he came into my life.

"All right, I'll tell you a story," he began, tucking my right leg between his and wrapping my arm securely around his waist. "Once upon a time there was a handsome caterpillar—"

"A handsome caterpillar?" I laughed.

"Shh. This handsome caterpillar had everything in life he could wish for. Green leaves to eat all day, green branches and green grass to crawl on, green skies and green friends he could enjoy. And then he started to notice that everything was green. Different shades of green, but all around him was green just the same."

"Even the sun?"

"Even the sun. He started to question: *Is this all that life has to offer?* He started to feel dissatisfied. He survived, but he never really *lived*. Soon, he felt green was suffocating him. Green was his prison. Green to him was black; it was darkness. So he crawled through the green world, searching without knowing what he was looking for."

I looked up at him when he didn't continue. "What was he searching for?"

"Color." He looked in my eyes. "You're my color, Red."

My heart was in my throat. His eyes were intense, pulling me in.

"And so," he murmured, snuggling closer and resting his chin on top of my head. "The caterpillar found his butterfly. She was so lovely, so colorful, and so full of life. Her beauty and love filled his heart to bursting every day of their lives. And they lived happily ever after."

My lids felt heavy and I sighed against him, comforted by his familiar scent and warmth.

"I won't let anyone hurt you. Sleep," he whispered.

I did. I slept with no nightmares tainting my dreams.

I woke up with Caleb's arm across my chest and his legs tangled up in mine. He had kicked the covers to the floor. He was lying on his stomach, his head turned toward me. The sun was on his face, but it didn't wake him.

I never had the opportunity to look at him without him knowing, so I just stared. The soft morning light bathed his lightly tanned skin, making it glow. His white T-shirt was hiked up and his sweats rode very low, revealing the lighter skin on his lower back that was usually covered. His bronze hair was mussed and covered his forehead. I smoothed it away and noticed his lashes.

How could a guy have long lashes like that?

I reached out my finger to trace the shape of his nose, then the square of his jaw. His skin had a light sprinkling of stubble, tickling me as I caressed his face.

Suddenly, he opened his eyes. My hand froze, and I stopped breathing.

His eyes, already twinkling, told me he had been awake all along. He knew I had been staring at him, touching him.

"Good morning," he said, his voice rough from sleep. "I dreamed of you."

CHAPTER
twenty-three

Caleb

WHY DID DAD HAVE TO DRAG US TO SMALL TOWNS EVERY weekend? Why couldn't we just go to McDonald's—or better yet, Dairy Queen?

I slumped on the stone bench in front of a big, old garage, kicking my feet, which barely reached the ground. There was a forest out back that reminded me of that horror movie *The Blair Witch Project* I'd seen with Ben the week before... Ben, my older brother who wasn't with us this time. I sighed.

My dad had disappeared inside. What if he died in there? What if there was an ax murderer inside?

I snorted. That was only in the movies. Things like that didn't happen in real life, did they? But if they did, that would be pretty cool. I could be a detective who strapped guns underneath my long, black coat to hide them.

I would have stayed home and played the new *Crash*

Bandicoot game on my PlayStation, but Dad had promised he would buy me that new bike we saw on TV the other day if I tagged along.

A real mountain bike, not the girlie bike my mom got for me. Ben teased me all the time when we went biking, and now I refused to ride it. It was green too. Why couldn't it be black or red?

"Caleb!"

I turned and saw my dad standing beside a fat, old guy who was drinking beer. The guy looked like Santa Claus, with a cloudy white beard and a potbelly. I was waiting for him to spit out a booming laugh and shout *Ho, ho, ho!* But he just stood there smiling at me.

"Why don't you walk around and find someone to play with?" my dad said. "But don't go too far."

I jumped off the bench, slightly offended. He wanted me to look for a playmate in this old town where only *old* people lived? There was no way kids lived here. The houses were old and scary looking, with peeling paint and weird rocking chairs on the porches. I didn't see a McDonald's anywhere.

I walked along the trail behind the garage. I was just going to walk straight so I wouldn't get lost. Besides, the sun was up. In the movies, bad things only happened at night.

I picked up a broken branch from the wet ground and wished I had a dog to play with. My ears perked up when I heard running water. I followed the sound and cried out in happiness when I saw a long, wooden bridge at the end of the trail. I ran to it, my footsteps making a hollow thumping sound on the wood planks. I stopped to stare at the water rushing under the bridge.

"Cool!" I yelled. I crouched and saw a bunch of fish gathered behind some rocks, protecting them from the current.

I jumped and nearly fell in the river when I heard a small voice. "You're going to fall just like that stupid boy."

I looked up and didn't see anyone.

"He didn't even know how to swim," she added, as she leaned back and looked at me from behind one of the thick wooden posts. That explained why I didn't see her right away.

First thing I thought was that her eyes were like a cat's. I'd never seen eyes like that before.

"Who are you?" she asked, tilting her head to the side. Her long, black hair fell across her shoulder.

"Caleb. Who are you?"

Her mouth broke into a grin, showing a gap between her front teeth. She must have lost a tooth recently. "I'm Batgirl today."

I noticed she was wearing a Batgirl costume but didn't have the headgear for it.

"Batgirl?"

"Yep. She smacks and kicks and always, *always* wins against the bad guys. I want to be like her!"

She was weird.

Her face scrunched up. "I'm hungry. Do you have any food?"

I suddenly remembered the sandwich in my pocket that my

dad had made for me that morning. I walked toward her, glad to have found someone to play with.

"Here." I sat beside her, offering her the sandwich. "It's peanut butter."

She didn't take it but eyed it suspiciously instead, scratching her chin. "Oh."

"You don't like peanut butter?"

She shook her head. "Nuh-uh. I never had it before. The bad guy in my house hates it, so we don't have it."

The bad guy? "Well, I'm allergic to it."

Her cat eyes narrowed suspiciously. "Why do you have it in your pocket, then? Is there poison in it?"

I stared. Her eyes were really pretty. I blinked when she waved both her hands in front of my face, trying to get my attention.

My cheeks felt hot. I shrugged. "My dad forgets I'm allergic to it."

She nodded as if she understood.

We sat together quietly. Girls were usually weird and a pain in the butt to play with, but she was…nice.

"How old are you?" I asked.

She wiggled four fingers. "Five."

"This is five," I corrected, wiggling five fingers. She didn't look interested. "I'm seven."

"Are you still going to give me that sandwich?"

I chuckled and handed it to her. She looked at it for a moment, sniffing it before she unwrapped it and took a small bite. Her eyes widened. "Mmm…peanut butter is my favorite sandwich forever starting today."

I laughed.

Facing the water, I dangled my feet low enough to touch the surface. When I turned to Batgirl again, I saw Red's face.

She smiled at me and reached for me, tracing my eyebrows, my nose, my lips with her fingers. "Thanks for the sandwich, Caleb."

When I opened my eyes, there was Red's beautiful face, her dark cat eyes staring at me in surprise.

Veronica

"Good morning," Caleb murmured, his voice rough from sleep. "I dreamed of you." Then he flashed a naughty I-am-going-to-get-you-in-trouble smile. "Wanna know what it was?"

The sunlight reflecting in his eyes made them almost seem transparent. His arm was still draped across my chest, his leg pinning me to the mattress. Even through my tank top and bra, I felt the heaviness of his arm and the warmth of his skin. A blush crept onto my cheeks, and I knew I probably looked like a ripe tomato.

I yelped as his arm hooked around my waist and pulled me closer. I quickly scooted away and jumped off the bed.

I didn't want him to smell my morning breath.

I darted to the bathroom, glancing in the mirror and groaning when I saw that my hair looked like a bird's nest. After a storm. Grabbing my brush, I attacked my hair, desperately trying to tease out the snarls and twists. It was so thick and long that it took me a few minutes to make it look presentable. I washed my face and brushed my teeth as fast as I could. Just as I was drying my mouth with a towel, Caleb came in.

His hair was mussed from sleep, his eyes bright and happy and *so* green as they met mine in the mirror. His sweatpants were riding low on his hips as he lifted his T-shirt and scratched his flat stomach.

I took a step back when he started toward me. He raised his eyebrows.

"Can't handle me in the morning, can you?" he drawled, his eyes dancing with mischief.

He kept walking closer, and I kept backing away until I hit the wall.

He grinned. "Nowhere to go?" His voice was as dangerous as the big, bad wolf's.

A very sexy big, bad wolf.

He was so close that I had to tilt my head up to see his face. Good Lord, he looked so good he should be illegal.

"Want to shower with me?" he whispered.

I gulped and shook my head. My voice seemed to have left me.

"Is that a no?" he teased.

I nodded, then shook my head again.

What the hell is wrong with me?

He stepped closer and lowered his head. His lips brushed the side of my ear as he murmured, "What do you want to do with me, then?"

I shivered. I smelled mint on his breath. I realized he must have gone back to his room to brush his teeth—the devil.

"I know you're not ready but we can do...other stuff," he said in a husky voice.

I had been thinking about that a lot...the *other stuff.*

"Red?" I felt him take a deep breath, his nose nuzzling my neck. "Wanna?"

Oh God.

I nodded weakly.

I do. I really do.

I blew out a breath as his hands gripped my hips, pulling me closer. My eyes widened as I felt the hardness below his hips.

Holy crap. Is that—

Caleb's voice cut into my thoughts. "I haven't kissed you yet, and you're already trembling."

My knees felt weak and rubbery. I had to place my hands on his shoulders so I wouldn't fall.

His intake of breath was audible as I touched him. He slowly rubbed my hips with his hands, shifting me so that I was cradling his hardness between my legs. I clamped my lips tightly to prevent myself from whimpering.

Those big, wonderful hands pressed against the small of my back, then traveled down to cup my ass. He squeezed and gently thrust his hips against mine.

I closed my eyes and moaned.

Hot. I felt so hot, but the burn felt really good.

His hands traveled to my waist, his thumbs leisurely stroking the exposed skin just above my shorts. Then they moved under my shirt, slowly caressing my ribs, just below my bra.

My heart started pounding.

"Look at me," he said, his voice low.

I opened my eyes and noticed he was clenching his teeth, the skin on his cheeks stretched taut. I held my breath as my eyes traveled up to his and I saw the desire in them.

"I remembered how you tasted in the morning," he whispered.

My lips parted as his thumb slipped inside my bra, caressing the side of my breast.

He lowered his head, then paused, his lips hovering an inch from mine. "I want to refresh my memory."

My head spun as his thumb lightly brushed my nipple.

"Oh God, Caleb," I moaned, leaning into his touch.

I heard a growl at the back of his throat before his mouth devoured mine. He took what he wanted, and I gave it to him—because I was helpless not to, and because I wanted to.

His kiss was hungry, his hands squeezing me gently. I whimpered as he released me, then gasped as he lifted me up. My arms wrapped around his neck, my legs around his waist. He cradled my ass, grinding against me.

I bit back a cry as his mouth dragged along my cheek and down to my neck, where he licked and sucked. My hands plunged into his hair, gripping hard as I felt his teeth bite me lightly.

He pressed me against the wall, and his lips found mine again. The kiss was wilder, more passionate. I felt myself giving in, letting my senses overtake me as I jumped blindly into madness.

I felt him lowering both of us onto the bed. I was drowning so deeply in his kiss that I hadn't even noticed he had walked us to the bedroom. His weight was delicious as he climbed on top of me, all the while never breaking our kiss.

I heard him growl again as he wrenched his lips away from mine, raising himself up. Wide-eyed, I watched as he reached back and pulled off his shirt one-handed and tossed it on the floor. There was nothing soft about him. The strong muscles in his arms rippled, his stomach flat and hard. My hands reached out to touch his naked skin, and his muscles tightened beneath my fingers.

And then his warm, hard body was rubbing against mine again, and he was kissing and biting my lips.

"Touch me," he pleaded, his voice hoarse. He shifted his weight to his forearm. Reaching for my hand, he placed it on his chest. "Please."

His skin was burning; it felt so good under my fingertips. Instinctively, my other hand followed, fingers exploring. I wanted to taste his skin, but his mouth grazed beneath my jaw and then his teeth lightly scraped my neck. My hands roamed over his chest, my fingers digging into his skin as sensations flooded me.

Was there a part of his body that wasn't hard? He was all sinewy muscle and warm skin. I felt consumed. Consumed by him.

In one fluid motion, he pulled back, taking me with him. An alarmed cry escaped my throat as he lifted me up and wrapped my legs around his waist. He kneeled back on the bed, settling me on his lap. With me straddling him, our gazes were now even. His nostrils flared, and the hunger and heat I saw in his eyes crackled through my body. I groaned, involuntarily grinding against him. I could feel all of his hardness.

"Red," he murmured. "Shall we get rid of this?" He tugged at my tank top, raising his brows in question.

I bit my lip and nodded. I could do this. I wanted this.

Holding my gaze, he lifted my shirt and discarded it on the floor.

His eyes were possessive as he took in my near-nakedness. I still had my bra on, but I suddenly felt shy, my arms instinctively covering my chest.

"Wait," he implored, touching my shoulders. "Let me look at you."

My heart was beating so fast that I wondered briefly if he could hear it. I lowered my gaze as I slowly moved my arms to my sides, my hands balling into fists.

I'd never done this before, and I thought I'd never meet anyone I would *want* to do this with. But with Caleb—only with Caleb—I wanted to. God, I wanted him.

"You're the most beautiful woman I've ever seen."

He tipped my chin so I was looking straight into his smoldering eyes.

"The most beautiful," he repeated, his lips softly kissing the side of my mouth.

His hands slid down my arms and gripped both my wrists. He leaned forward, locking my arms behind me and making me arch my back. A harsh breath left my lips as his tongue glided on my skin.

"Caleb!" I cried out, then moaned as he sucked on my breast through the fabric.

My arms strained against his grip as he kept on sucking, biting lightly. My legs tightened against him as he ground between my legs. The sensation was so intense that I thought I was going to faint.

"Do you want me to stop?" he asked as he dragged his lips between my breasts, then up my neck.

I don't want you to stop.

"Tell me"—he licked a sensitive spot on my neck, and I shivered—"to stop."

He released my wrists. His long fingers streaked up my back. He curled one finger under the left strap of my bra, tugging it toward my shoulder.

"Red?" His eyes sought mine. "Do you want me to stop?"

I wanted this. I wanted him.

"Don't stop," I answered.

His pupils dilated, his lids lowering.

"Are you sure about that?" He pulled the other strap of my bra.

I bit my lip. He started releasing the hooks of my bra behind me. No one had ever seen me naked before. My breathing hitched, my heart pounding against my chest.

Was I ready to do this?

"Wait!"

He froze, his eyes lifting to mine.

"You want to stop?"

I nodded.

His jaw tightened, his body straightening. His hands drifted down to his sides.

Lowering my gaze, I lifted my hands to cover my breasts and

keep my bra in place. I suddenly felt very naked. I wanted to grab a blanket and hide myself, wanted the floor to open up and swallow me.

Embarrassment flooded my whole being as he stared at me for what seemed like an hour, though I knew it was only a few seconds.

He dipped his head, letting out a breath. When he lifted his head, he was smiling. "I understand, baby."

He sounded like he was in pain. "Here. Let me." He reached around and hooked my bra closed, pulling up the straps on my shoulders. I kept worrying my bottom lip as he blew out another breath and rubbed his hand over the stubble on his chin.

Silence.

"Please stop doing that," he said in a hoarse voice, his thumb gently pressing on my bottom lip.

I released my lip once he removed his thumb. My skin tingled where he'd touched me...which was everywhere.

"Never hesitate to tell me when you're not ready," he said. "Understood?"

He was still hard. I could feel him beneath me.

I nodded, lowering my head. I felt like a killjoy, a prude, unable to give Caleb what he wanted, what *I* wanted.

Because I wanted to...make love with him, but something was stopping me. I just couldn't do it.

"Hey." He cupped my face and urged me to look at him. "What's wrong?"

I shook my head, closing my eyes.

"Do you feel bad that you stopped me?"

My throat felt thick, tears threatening to flow. "Caleb…"

"Open your eyes."

I did. His gaze was sincere as he looked at me.

"Don't ever feel bad when you tell me to stop. I'm a guy. I'm attracted to you. This may not be the only time you'll tell me that, so you might as well get used to it, okay?" He kissed my forehead. "*I* better get used to it," he added, frowning in thought.

He gently lifted me off his lap and set me on the bed. Then he stood up and raked his hands through his hair. "But now I need a very cold shower."

He paused as he reached my door, turning to look at me. "Wanna join me?"

I laughed and shook my head. And just like that, he made me feel better.

CHAPTER

twenty-four

Caleb

OTHER STUFF? WHAT THE HELL WAS I THINKING?

I couldn't just do "other stuff." I wanted *all* of it. All of *her.*

Stop.

Damn, I hate that word. How the hell I'd stopped when she'd told me to a few minutes ago, I had no idea.

Alone in the shower, I lowered my head and braced my hands against the tiles, letting the cold water beat against my back. An image of her filled my head, and I groaned.

The sexy moans she made drove me crazy. She had a mole just above her left breast that I desperately wanted to lick. She was so...

Damn it all to hell. I needed to stop thinking about her. This was getting out of hand.

The water was cold, but I adjusted it to freezing.

Think of something else, moron.

I tried to imagine the smell of the locker room just after a game. Smells of sweat, feet, and piss. Yeah, that should calm me down.

Her long legs felt like heaven when they wrapped around me.

The freezing shower was not helping. Frustrated, I turned off the shower, grabbed my towel, and dried off. I headed straight to my gym room—a few doors down from her room—for a serious workout. It felt like I spent all day in there, not just two hours. Another cold shower in my gym bathroom and a quick hand job calmed me. But as I exited the shower, just the thought of her beneath me worked me up again.

Damn blue balls.

I had to get out of here before I did something crazy. Like take her against the wall. Or on the kitchen table. On the bathroom counter. In my bed. Anywhere.

It wasn't just that I hadn't had sex in a long time, or because I desired her so much it hurt. Making love with her was a way for me to express my feelings for her—and, if I'm being perfectly honest, it was also a way to mark that she belonged with me. I exhaled.

Slow. She wanted it slow. Slow was good. I could do slow. I was capable of waiting for her, but that didn't mean I couldn't do my best to show her how I felt about her and convince her that we belong together.

Looking around the bathroom, I realized I didn't have any clean clothes to wear. Wrapping a towel around my hips, I grabbed my phone and saw a text from Justin inviting me to a party at his place tonight. Ignoring it, I was heading back to my room when I stopped in my tracks.

I saw Red dressed in my bathrobe, her ear plastered to my bedroom door, and I bit my lip to keep from laughing. Was she trying to eavesdrop?

Damn if that didn't make me smile.

The bathrobe was too big for her. It covered her from neck to toes, the hem trailing on the floor. She must have found the robe in her room. I had a few clothes in there.

I watched her as she straightened up, clutched her hands together, and took a deep breath. Raising her fist, she was ready to knock on my door, but she paused and shook her head. Then she pressed her ear against the door again.

"Anything interesting?"

She gasped and jumped as she spun around and saw me, her hand flying to her chest.

"Caleb!"

I laughed. Not just because I caught her, but because I was remembering the time Cameron caught me doing the same in front of her bedroom door.

Her eyes glazed over as she took in my naked chest. She was as affected as I was. Good. When she looked at me like that, I felt like I needed to go back to the gym and work out again for another two hours.

Damn. I really needed to stop thinking about worshipping her body for an hour or two. Maybe I should go to Justin's party. I couldn't stay here with Red when just the sight of her put me on edge.

"Look," I started, raking my hair with both my hands. "I need to get out of here for a few hours."

She dropped her gaze, but I caught the flash of hurt in her eyes. I closed the distance between us, lifting her chin with my thumb and forefinger. I couldn't help but notice how big my hand looked next to her beautiful face. She looked delicate, vulnerable.

"Red, I can't be here with you right now. It's not because I don't want to be with you. It's because I really, really want to."

Her eyes cleared. She understood. I wanted to kiss her right there, but I didn't trust myself. I *had* to leave.

I got dressed quickly and texted Cameron that I'd pick him up to go to Justin's party. I stopped when I passed the kitchen and spotted Red seated on one of the barstools, still wrapped in my robe. I loved seeing my clothes on her.

She was gazing out the window, her palms cupping her face. My hands fisted to keep from touching her. I must have made a sound because her head turned toward me.

Her expression was uncertain and a little sad. Her eyes were pleading me not to go. I really didn't want to leave…but I craved her so much that it was better for me to go. I needed to clear my head.

"Are you feeling better?" I asked. When she looked at me in confusion, I added, "You had a nightmare last night. Want to talk about it?"

She shook her head. "I'm okay. I don't even remember it." When she moved on her seat, the robe opened, exposing a shapely leg.

Damn. I have to get the hell out of here.

"Will you be coming home tonight?" she asked quietly. So quietly that I barely heard her.

"Yes."

She nodded. "Caleb…"

Jiggling my car keys in my pocket, I waited for her to finish what she was going to say. She just stared at me, biting her lip.

I wanted to bite her lip.

Instead, I gritted my teeth, nodded, and left.

I drove to Cameron's house to pick him up and then headed to Justin's party. It was at his parents' cabin just a few minutes outside the city. His closest neighbors were miles away so he had the music cranked up high, obviously not worried about noise complaints.

Cameron and I headed to the basement, where it was considerably less noisy and less crowded. That's where we found Amos sitting by himself, busily texting on his phone.

"Hey, bro, 'sup?" I asked, giving him a fist bump.

Amos's clenched fist spread wide, fingers wiggling as I moved away.

I groaned and shook my head. "Bro, you do *not* explode the fist bump. How many times will I tell you this? It's a sacred rule."

He smirked in response and did the same to Cameron, this time with both hands.

"Asshole," I quipped.

He grinned. "Cocksucker."

"So where is everyone?" Cameron asked.

Amos swatted his bangs away from his eyes and leaned back on the couch. "Probably setting up a big bonfire out back. Justin's getting laid or pretending he's passed out on the floor again so he can peep up girls' skirts. You know, the usual."

Justin should really stop doing that.

I took the seat next to Amos, grabbed the two beers he handed me, and passed one to Cameron.

Amos gestured with his beer. "Haven't seen you pussies lately. You been busy getting your eyebrows plucked or what?"

I laughed and answered, "Yup. Had my legs waxed."

"Had his nails done too," Cameron added, popping open his beer.

"Aw." Amos winked. "You should have worn a dress tonight to show them off, bro."

"I will once you ask me out on a date."

He chuckled and cleared his throat nervously. "I would if I didn't have a girl."

I blinked. "What? You don't have a girl."

He cleared his throat again. "I haven't told you guys till now because I wanted to make sure, you know?"

"You're serious," Cameron commented.

"Yeah. Been living with her for two months now."

I had managed to move Red to the back of my mind, but Amos's confession brought her straight to the front row. I grunted in answer, waiting for him to tell me more.

"Driving me fucking crazy," he mumbled after a moment, his face looking tortured. "I can't figure out what the hell she wants. What's going on in a girl's head, anyway? Seriously I want to know."

Ditto, I thought. "What's wrong?"

His eyebrows shot up. "That's what I asked her. She said *nothing*. But obviously there's *something*. I asked her if she's okay, and she said everything was *fine.* So I thought okay, maybe she wants some space. So I told her I was going to see you guys tonight, and she said, *Fine, have fun!* But she didn't sound like she meant it. She sounded like she wanted to chop my balls off. What the fuck is wrong with her? She's driving me nuts."

I handed him another bottle. "Here, drink more beer."

"Thanks." He popped the top open and guzzled like he hadn't drunk in a week. After burping like a train, he continued. "Then I asked what she wanted for her birthday, and she said she didn't want anything. I kept asking her what she wanted, but she said not to give her anything. So I didn't." His face mirrored bafflement. "She didn't talk to me for a week. What the hell?"

Poor guy. Even I knew about that one. You should always give someone a birthday present no matter what they said.

"Have some Doritos." Cameron handed him a bag.

Amos opened the bag, munching chips like a monkey. "Why doesn't she just tell me what she really wants? I'm not a fucking psychic."

I nodded. "It's a trap, dude. It's the same as when they ask you if they look fat in a dress, or if you think their friend is pretty."

Cameron laughed. "Or what shade of color is on the wall."

"Huh?"

Cameron shrugged. "Nothing."

"Shit." Amos hissed, looking frustrated. "Do you know how long I have to wait when she gets ready? She says five minutes, and five minutes in girl language could be half hour to an hour. I'm not joking, dude. What the hell do they do?"

"It's a mystery," Cameron replied, a small smile on his face.

Red didn't take two hours to get ready, I thought, remembering our first real date last night. Less than half an hour, and she was done. I was pretty lucky.

Amos nodded and let out a huge breath. "But damn, I'm crazy about this girl."

I know how you feel, I thought.

"I love her hair. It's down to her ass," Amos continued. "Sexy as hell, but she sheds hair more than my dog does."

I laughed. I'd found a strand of hair on the couch that could only be Red's. I remembered picking it up and placing it between the pages of my book.

God, I'm such a creep.

Four hours later, I'd lost count of how many bottles I'd finished and was feeling drunk. Red had moved to the back of my mind again. Thank God. The other guys had joined us, throwing around insults and fake sex stories to make them look good.

"Hey, baby, come back for more?" Justin slapped a girl's butt as she walked past him. I thought I'd seen her with him earlier.

"Hey!" She slapped him in the face. "Asshole."

We hooted in laughter as Justin turned red, before a drunk, goofy smile appeared on his face. "She loves me," he declared, watching the girl walk away.

Amos threw a piece of food at him—pizza maybe. "Sure she does, buddy," he hollered.

Justin shrugged. "She's clingy anyway."

I stared at the beer bottle in my hand, my vision getting hazy.

I was drunk. I really couldn't remember how many bottles I'd had so far.

"Hey, Caleb."

I looked up when I heard my name and saw…Red?

What the hell was she doing here?

She was just a blur in front of me. I blinked twice to focus.

"I was wondering if you want to take a drive with me. It's nice out."

The voice was wrong… Red's voice wasn't that high. I blinked again, shook my head. It was Claire, batting her eyelashes at me. I must be solid drunk to mistake her for Red.

"He's in no shape to take care of you, babe. I'll do it for him if you like," I heard Justin offer.

"Kiss my ass, Justin."

"Hit me, baby, one more time," he sang. He must like getting slapped by different girls. He didn't get his wish since Claire huffed and left.

Okay, bye-byes, I thought. I wasn't interested in any girl except for one. But I silently praised Claire in my head for rejecting Justin. Last I heard, his girlfriend had broken up with him when she caught him on top of Lydia with his pants down.

Justin could be a real douche when it came to girls. If he couldn't make one girl happy, how did he expect to handle two or three at the same time? Moron.

Beside me, Cameron was slumped in his seat, his head resting on the back of the couch. He must be drunk too.

"What's the deal with you and Kara?" I asked, not expecting him to answer, so it surprised me when he did.

"She kills me. Just one blow." His hand fisted as if he were holding a knife and stabbed it in his chest. "And I'm dead. Fucking dead."

Amos shook his head. "What'd you do, bro?"

"Tried to save her."

"If I've learned one thing from living with my girl, it's that sometimes girls don't want to be saved," Amos said. "They want to do the saving."

Cameron chugged an entire beer. He leaned forward, propping his elbows on his knees and rubbing his hands on his face. He looked tired but remained quiet.

Hours had passed in a blur. I knew it was past midnight, and I had to go home. I didn't know if Red was waiting up for me, but I'd told her I would come home tonight. I'd given her my word, and I would not break it.

Driving was impossible. I needed to phone a cab, but I couldn't remember the number. In fact, I could barely hold my phone.

"I'll drive Caleb home." Was that Claire again? I wasn't sure, but the voice was squeaky…kind of reminded me of a mouse.

Wait, she was going to drive me home? No. Not her.

"Leave him alone," someone said.

Thank God.

The next thing I knew, Cameron and I were in the back of my car with Justin behind the wheel. He dropped off Cameron at home, and then headed to my place. Thinking about walking into the building and riding the elevator exhausted me. I could barely keep my eyes open, but I felt happy.

Justin helped me inside, and we sang in the elevator, my arm around his shoulders as he tried to keep me from falling on my face. He could be a moron most of the time, but he had his good moments.

I blinked slowly at him. Had he said something? "My what?"

He sighed heavily. "The code, dude. To get into your apartment. You weigh a ton. Tell me the fucking code so I can dump you inside."

"Gotta get home to Red. Gotta get home. I told her I would. Obsessed with my girl Red."

"Yeah, yeah. When were you ever obsessed with a girl?"

Seconds later, the door was pulled open and a shocked Red stood in front of us. She was so beautiful and I was so happy to see her that my smile felt like it was splitting my face.

"Caleb!" she exclaimed, her eyes wide with shock as she took in my drunken state.

"My girl Red. I promised I'd come home to you. Always."

The last thing I heard before passing out was Justin's confused voice as he stared at Red and said, "What the fuck?"

CHAPTER

twenty-five

Justin

THE IDIOT WAS HEAVY.

He definitely owed me one after this. That asshole Cameron owed me too. I didn't give shit for free.

What am I, a fucking food bank?

One of the perks of hanging out with Caleb was that I could get into circles that normally wouldn't welcome me. I hated kissing ass with spoiled rich sons of bitches who thought they shit gold and rainbows, but you gotta do what you gotta do.

It helped to have connections, especially now that our family business wasn't doing well.

The shit I gotta do, I thought darkly, grunting from Caleb's deadweight. He was singing in the elevator, the stupid shit.

"Sing with me, bro. It's Bon Jovi."

I glared at him. "I fucking hate Bon Jovi."

"What? Bon Jovi's a master. Fine, Aerosmith then."

He was such a loser.

He paused for a second, hiccupped, and continued singing. When he stopped, he said, "I miss her. I miss my Red."

He'd been talking about this Red the whole ride. Who was she? Or *what* was she? A dog, maybe? Was he hallucinating? As far as I knew, Caleb didn't have a girlfriend.

He had flings. Everyone seemed to love the guy. Everything seemed to be so easy for him, everything just fell into his lap without him asking for it. Girls, friends, money…the basketball captainship.

What the hell was I? A statue?

Sure, I wasn't as pretty as he was but I looked fucking hot. I went to the gym almost every day to get the mouthwatering body I had now. In fact, I had my own share of girls chasing after me. I even showed them who was boss.

Me. I was the boss.

No girl was going to pussy whip me.

The best girls were the girls who wanted Caleb. They always went running after him, and when he didn't want them anymore, they'd come to me.

But I was tired of getting his leftovers.

At last, we were at his front door. Stupid shit couldn't even think properly.

Probably should've asked the concierge to let us in, I realized.

Caleb had a sweet place here, the rich bastard. There were only him and another rich fucker living on this floor. The hallway was carpeted, with dark-green walls displaying abstract paintings that screamed money. There were these big-ass crystal light fixtures on the ceiling... What did you call those again? Chandeliers. Yeah, that was it. Show-offs.

I heard Caleb's grandfather had left a huge chunk of cash to Caleb when he died. That was probably how he could afford this huge place. Wish I had a rich, dead old gramps too who'd leave me everything.

It was fucking unfair.

"What's your code, dude?"

He mumbled again, but I couldn't understand a word he was saying.

I stared at him, debating whether to push him off me. Maybe he'd hit his head against the wall and break his neck. Maybe he'd die. I could always tell the police he was so drunk that—

The door was pulled open, and a hot girl stood on the other side, looking shocked.

"Caleb!" she exclaimed.

"What the fuck?" I asked.

I grunted when Caleb's full weight fell on me. The fucker had passed out. She looked at him with concern. I knew this girl.

"You're the girl from the club that night." I eyed her from the top of her hair to her cheap hoodie and yoga pants. She looked very uncomfortable but really hot. The kind of ass I preferred, unlike those boring blonds that Caleb seemed to like. Which brought me to *What the fuck was she doing here?*

"What the fuck are you doing here?" I demanded.

Caleb never let a girl stay at his place. From what I knew, he usually booted them out after sex.

"Why don't you mind your own fucking business?" She

glared at me and then grabbed Caleb's other arm as we muscled him inside and to his bedroom.

She seemed to know the way to his bedroom. Who the hell was she?

Red. Caleb was talking about Red. It was probably a girl, if not a dog, but this chick didn't have red hair.

"I'm going to call the police if you don't tell me what the hell you're doing in Caleb's apartment," I threatened.

"Go ahead. You'll only look like an idiot."

We dumped Caleb on the bed. He moaned and turned on his side. "Red," he mumbled.

I turned to her and narrowed my eyes. "Will I?" I stepped closer than was normally polite.

She backed away, panic on her face. I saw her eyes dart around the room and fix on the lamp. I smirked. Was she going to hit me with it?

What a hellcat. She'd be really great in bed, I bet. Once Caleb was done with her, I'd come to the rescue. I would enjoy this one more than the others.

"Get away from me, asshole," she spat out, her dark eyes filling with fire.

Feisty. I liked them aggressive.

I smirked. "He's never had girls stay over at his place before." I leaned back against the bedpost, crossed my arms over my chest so she'd notice my big arms—if she hadn't already—and took a good long look at his crib.

It was fucking amazing, with a king-size bed covered in white sheets and gray pillows. In front of his bed was a giant window that showed the entire city. Prime view. Only the best for dear Caleb.

He even had a small living room in here with a sleek flat-screen TV and the latest Xbox model. I thought about my beat-up Xbox 360 and my tiny TV that wasn't even a flat screen, and it made me so fucking angry that Caleb had all these sleek new toys he probably didn't even have time to *use*, while I had to work my ass off for everything I got.

There was a door that I knew led to a big-ass bathroom and another door that led to his walk-in closet, where I really wanted to go.

I'd been in his apartment once before when Caleb invited us for drinks, and I'd snuck in his room out of curiosity. I'd even nicked a Piaget watch from his closet as a souvenir. He never noticed it went missing. He had a box full of expensive watches, and I really wanted to borrow that sweet Rolex I'd seen last time. Too bad this bitch was around now.

"You're not one of his stalkers, are you?" I asked. "Did you sneak in here while he was away?"

"I'm going to call security if you don't leave."

Not a stalker, then. Maybe Caleb had hooked up with her since the night at the club, and now they were together.

Quite a feat for you, Caleb, I thought.

"You're not his usual type."

I eyed her again. Despite the hoodie and yoga pants, her body was clearly rocking in all the right places. She shuddered, disgust on her face.

Gritting my teeth, I pushed away from the bedpost. This girl made me angry for some reason. The way she looked at me made me feel like a bug she wanted to squash with her foot.

What, did she think I wasn't good enough for her? She was just one of Caleb's lays. Who the hell did she think she was? She wasn't special.

He'd throw her out on her pretty ass soon, and then she'd come crawling to me. I'd give this bitch a good time and wipe that snobby look off her face.

"I know my way out, so don't bother. I guess I'll see you around." I paused by the door, turned, and looked at her. "Red, isn't it?"

She paled but didn't say anything.

"I heard he was dating some brunette at school. Or was it another blond? Didn't know it was you. Or maybe you're just one of them." I paused, waited for her reaction. Nothing. "I guess I'll see you at school then, sweetheart." I winked and left Caleb's bedroom.

I didn't leave the apartment yet, though. Caleb had a lot of expensive things I wanted. One day...I swore I'd get those too. One of the reasons I'd brought him home was to drive his sweet-ass ride. He wouldn't let me drive it if he wasn't drunk out of his mind.

I was still hung up about that Rolex. That gem probably cost twenty grand easy. It wasn't stealing if you were filching it from someone who didn't need it, as far as I was concerned.

All good. I knew he left some of his stuff in the guest bedroom. I'd just slip in there and take a look around while the bitch was busy taking care of him.

What the fuck? I thought as I quietly opened the door to the guest bedroom. There were girl things everywhere. The room even smelled like a girl, like freaking strawberries.

Was she living here with him?

What the hell?

Looked like Caleb Lockhart had let someone in…for the first time. This girl must be really great in bed if Caleb was keeping her.

This was *very* interesting. I knew several of Caleb's exes who were still hung up on him and would totally enjoy having some good ole fun with this girl. Those girls could cause a lot of trouble for little Red, particularly one blond I knew. The faster Red left Caleb, the faster she'd be in my bed.

When I left her room, I almost cried out in glee when I spotted gold cuff links carelessly thrown on a table in the hallway. They were almost hidden by a porcelain vase. Before someone could see me, I pocketed them.

I passed Caleb's room again and stopped when I heard her talking. "Caleb, what were you thinking?"

"I miss you, Red."

Whoa. This guy sure knew how to make girls fall in love with him, even when he was drunk.

I was going to leave when I heard her say, "I miss you too."

Sounded like she was already in love with him. Typical.

"Lie down with me, Red?"

Seemed like she meant something to Caleb too. He sure sounded pussy whipped. Good. It would hurt more than his pride to see her with me. Even better.

Damn. This was going to be fun.

CHAPTER
twenty-six

Veronica

"YOU'RE SUCH A BIG BABY WHEN YOU'RE HUNGOVER," I TEASED Caleb. He was in his bed, wrapped in a heavy white duvet with a fat gray pillow on top of his face, groaning and moaning in pain.

I'd woken up this morning in his bed, wrapped in his arms. That was the second time I'd slept beside him, and I realized that it felt…good. Really good.

The feel of his warm, hard body behind mine was getting familiar.

Caleb loved to spoon, I thought with a smile as I sat beside him gently. He groaned as my weight disturbed the bed.

"You stink, Caleb."

He made a noncommittal sound.

"Please sit up so you can take this aspirin."

"Why are you screaming at me, Red?" he moaned, his voice muffled by the pillow. He didn't move.

"I'm not screaming." I couldn't help smiling. After the awkwardness of yesterday, it felt really good to be back to normal. "Do you know the cure for a hangover?"

He grunted.

"Stay drunk," I answered.

This time, he moved the pillow so that one green eye looked at me with amusement. "Did you just make a joke?" He sounded like he was laughing at me.

I felt myself blushing. The only time I'd made a joke, and he had to make me self-conscious about it. He could have faked a laugh. I never told jokes, and this was why. This was so embarrassing!

He started laughing silently. Not at my joke, but at me.

"Ah! You're being a jerk." I pushed the pillow into his face and stood, making sure that the bed shook a lot.

"Ow. Ow. Ow. Why you so mean to me, Red?"

I smirked. He deserved that! When his moans subsided, he just lay there like the dead. Not moving, not talking.

Oh no. I shouldn't have done that. But he was teasing me... and I had just reacted. I felt bad.

"I got you orange juice," I said. Nothing. "I'm going to work. Make sure you take the aspirin." He didn't respond. "Caleb?"

Still nothing. He must have fallen back asleep. His arm was covering his eyes, the pillow having fallen away from his face. The light must have been bothering him, so I closed the drapes silently. I didn't want to wake him up.

I hadn't really been in his room before. It had pretty much the same layout as my room, only bigger. And messier—not dirty, just messy. An oversize chair he'd been using as a catchall for his clothes and little knickknacks sat nearby. Textbooks were thrown haphazardly on the floor, as if he'd opened them and decided they weren't worth his attention. He had a bad habit of leaving a trail of clothes on the floor, but I noticed that his DVDs and CDs were stacked neatly on his computer table.

We hadn't watched a movie together yet. That was on his list, I thought, smiling like a lunatic. *Our* list.

He was already snoring, so I mustered the courage to lean down and place a kiss on his cheek.

What is he doing to me?

"Feel better, Caleb. I'll see you later," I whispered.

I was about to leave when my eye caught something on his desk. It was a small black box with the lid slightly open and a neon-green Post-it Note hanging off it. I probably shouldn't have snooped, but I wondered if it was...

I turned around to check if he was awake. He was still snoring softly. I opened the box silently, and my heart jumped when I saw a stack of the Post-it Notes I had stuck to the fridge for him.

Warmth traveled from my heart to my toes.

He'd kept them all, even the ones from the first day.

Oh, Caleb.

I put everything back in its place, gave him one last glance, and left for work.

As I boarded the bus, I wondered whether I should tell Caleb about his friend from last night. The creep said he'd see me at school. I'd rather eat scorpions and tarantulas than see him again.

The hair on my arms had actually stood on end while I was talking to him, as he was eyeing me like I was a piece of meat.

The college was huge. He wouldn't find me. Plus, I had a knack for hiding from people.

He might have driven Caleb home, and he might've had the face of an angel—with his dirty blond hair, blue eyes, and boyish looks—but I didn't trust him. Looks could be deceiving, and his definitely were.

I wondered what assumptions he'd made when he saw me at Caleb's last night. I didn't want everyone on campus to find out that I was living with Caleb.

Poor people might not have money, but they have their reputation to take pride in. A good, clean reputation. And morals. You can't buy that with money. Remember that, Veronica.

That was what my mom had said. What would she say, I wondered, if she were still alive and found out I was living with a guy? She'd skin me alive.

But I was desperate when I met Caleb. Living at his place had seemed like the best choice at the time. And now everything had fallen into place. Somehow it just felt right to be with him.

It wasn't like we were having sex.

I closed my eyes and suddenly felt hot as a memory shot into my head. When he was licking my skin, kissing, tasting.

Oh God. Stop. I must not think about it. Must not think about it.

Kara had taken today off to help Beth shop for a dress for her graduation, so I opened shop by myself when I arrived. It was busier than normal since it was Saturday and I was alone, which was perfect. Didn't give me time to think much about Caleb.

When the office phone rang and the caller ID showed Beth's name, I grinned as I answered it.

"When are you going to get a phone, homie?" she greeted me.

"I have one. It's just for emergencies. How's shopping?"

"I'd rather have a root canal."

"That bad?"

"Kar's dragged me to every freaking consignment shop in the city. Listen, Ver, you know I was born smart. Very, very smart. School made me dumb. Ya feel me?"

I laughed. "What happened?"

"There's a sale going on. Anyway, it says seventy percent off, right?"

"Uh-huh." I glanced at the clock. Half an hour more until closing time. I'd better start cleaning up, I thought as I shuffled papers and started filing.

"You know when stores add another red sticker on top that says take an additional percentage off?"

"Uh-huh."

"This one says take an additional thirty percent off. Am I dumb, or doesn't that make it *free*? Seventy percent plus thirty percent is one hundred percent! Free!"

I laughed, reaching for the stapler. "No. Let's say the original price is one hundred dollars. Take seventy percent off, and you'll end up paying thirty dollars. Then if there's another additional thirty percent off on top of the seventy percent off…" I bit my lip, crunching numbers in my head. "Thirty percent of thirty dollars is nine dollars. You subtract nine dollars from thirty dollars. Total price is twenty-one dollars. Got it?"

There was silence on the other end of the line.

"Beth?"

She cleared her throat. "I'm sorry, Ver. I think my brain just exploded."

I rolled my eyes, laughing while I stapled receipts. I was sure she was joking. "Check with Kar. She knows this. Or an employee there. They'll tell you."

"There's only one here, and she hates me. I was only trying to be friendly and asked how many months pregnant she was."

"Okay?"

"Well, she wasn't. How the hell would I know? Her stomach was pretty round. Like pregnant round."

I shouldn't have laughed.

"Try this one on! Is that Ver on the phone?" I heard Kara say. "Gimme."

I heard clothes rustling and a door slamming shut and assumed that Kara had locked Beth in the dressing room.

"Hey, Ver. Hold on. I'm going to try on a dress." She was trying on a dress? I thought this was a shopping day for Beth. I chuckled, knowing that Kara couldn't help herself. She loved shopping. "I'll take a picture and send it to you—"

"You can't. My phone isn't high tech enough to view your pictures. Besides, that probably costs a dollar."

"Seriously, get a damn smart phone! You can definitely afford it now." A clicking noise indicated she was taking a photo. "Why do I look beautiful in the mirror but ugly in pictures today? Seriously! Dammit!" I heard her sipping loudly from a straw.

"You're drinking a milk shake, aren't you?"

"You know me so well. Damn, I look fab."

"Yes, you do," I said.

"I love you, even though you have no idea what I look like right now." She sucked on her milk shake. "Anyway, how'd your holiday go yesterday?"

When I didn't respond, she gasped dramatically. "Did you let him pop the cherry?"

Silence.

"Ver, did you offer him the nectar of the gods?"

I choked. "No."

Silence.

"Huh," she grunted. "BJ?"

I face-palmed. "No!"

"Oh-kay." I heard her clucking her tongue. "Ate you ou—?"

I groaned. "*Stop!*"

"Blue balls then."

Silence. How the hell did she know these things?

"Yes," I admitted sheepishly.

She chuckled. "Aw, Ver, you cock blocker. Aww...poor Caleb."

"What kind of best friend are you? I just saw a customer come in. I have to go. Talk to you later?"

"All right. I have fat-ass emergency foods at home for occasions like these. Come on over tonight or tomorrow. We can fat-ass with Beth all night, k? Talk about that wonderful, wonderful man you seem to enjoy torturing." We said our goodbyes and hung up.

Wonderful, wonderful man. Caleb was that, I thought, smiling as I served the customer.

I knew that sex came easy for him before he met me, and he was being very considerate and understanding about us.

Yes, but until when?

There go my doubts again, I thought darkly. As the customer left, I sat back down on my chair.

Would he cheat on me eventually if I didn't have sex with him? Was there a rule for this? Like a three-month rule or something stupid like that? Because I wasn't all for it. Not at all.

What was I waiting for? What more did I want from him for me to believe and trust him?

I was filing with my back to the entrance when the bell above the door jingled.

"Hey, Red."

Surprised and delighted, I turned around with a huge smile on my face.

"Caleb." I hated the breathlessness I heard in my voice. "What are you doing here?"

"Picking up my girl, of course." He winked at me. He looked pale and had dark circles under his eyes, but he was still gorgeous—and he'd still come to pick me up.

He always made me smile, made me feel special.

It was the little things he did that chipped the walls around my heart bit by bit until he had all of it in the palm of his hand.

He grinned at me boyishly. "Any new jokes for me?"

"Dammit. Stop teasing me!"

He laughed. I glared.

"Come on, Red. Don't be mad. I really liked your joke."

He grinned. I still glared.

"Okay, your joke wasn't funny, but I love that you said it anyway. Come on, give me another one," he cajoled.

"No way—"

Suddenly, the door from the garage opened. "Hey, Caleb. How's it going?"

"Dylan! I'm great, bro. How're you doing?"

Kara's brother looked so different from her that no one would guess they were siblings. I watched as Caleb slapped Dylan's back and they gave each other the man version of a hug. I let them chat while I closed up shop. By the time I was done, Dylan was saying goodbye.

Caleb turned to me. "So, where to, Red?"

I studied his face. He still looked hungover but definitely better than this morning.

"Let's just go back to your apartment and have a quiet night tonight."

"Aw." He batted his eyelashes and placed his hand on his chest. "Red, are you thinking about me? I feel fine already. Just a slight headache, but it's barely there." He grinned, offering me his arm.

I smiled back and wrapped my hand around his strong forearm.

"We can go on a date, if you like," he continued as we walked out. "Tell me where you would like to go. Your wish is my command."

I couldn't stop smiling. "Just home."

He stopped all of a sudden, and I would've tripped if he hadn't caught me. He smiled from ear to ear. "Home."

We had just arrived inside Caleb's apartment when his phone started ringing. He just stared at the screen, looking reluctant.

"What's wrong?"

"It's Beatrice-Rose."

Beatrice-Rose. Last time she phoned, I blew up like a cheetah on crack, as Caleb had put it. Truthfully, I felt guilty. They were just friends. Childhood friends, he told me. And I had overreacted.

"Please answer it," I urged.

He raised his eyebrows.

I bit my lip, trying to hold my laugh in. "I promise I won't overreact this time. I feel so bad. Please."

He nodded.

"Hello? I'm good, you? Right now?" His eyes turned to me. "Hold on." With a quick tap, he muted his phone. "She said she's on her way over. Is that okay with you?"

I worried my lip.

"If it's not, I can always tell her no. It's up to you, Red. It's not a big deal," he assured me, his thumb rubbing my elbow.

For some reason, I didn't want her to come. I didn't want... Whatever. I was overreacting again.

"No, let her come. I can just leave and give both of you some privacy. I've imposed on you too much already."

"What?" He frowned. "Where'd this come from?"

I shook my head. "Caleb. Tell her to come."

"No," he replied, his voice emphatic. "If you feel this way, it's better if she doesn't."

"Feel what way? She's waiting." I gestured to his phone.

He shrugged.

"Fine." I crossed my arms. "I'll stay."

He tilted his head, a knowing smile on his face as he unmuted the phone and placed it against his ear again. "Okay, come on over."

When he hung up, he curled his hands around my shoulders and turned me to face him. "There's nothing to worry about, Red. You're my girl."

I held my breath as his thumb played with my bottom lip, rubbing it softly. "There's only you," he whispered before he dipped his head to kiss me, and all my doubts were forgotten.

CHAPTER

twenty-seven

Caleb

"ONLY YOU," I TOLD HER SOFTLY, HOLDING HER FACE IN MY hands.

My thumb caressed her cheek, marveling at the softness of her skin. Her dark cat eyes were wide as they took in my face, revealing an innocence that I wanted to grab and hold on to… and keep.

Beatrice-Rose was going to be here in less than an hour, but I couldn't stop myself from pulling Red close and kissing her lips. I hadn't kissed her since this morning.

She was like an addiction. A drug pumping through my bloodstream.

I kissed her hungrily, my hands roaming all over her body. The dip on her back just above her ass drove me insane.

Her taste was turning me on. Her *breathing* was turning me on.

Her lashes fluttered as she closed her eyes, and she sighed as my tongue glided over her skin, down the long line of her neck to that sensitive spot just below her ear. When I placed my lips there, she shivered.

Damn, we had to stop.

Just a few more minutes, I told myself. But when she plastered her body against me, her breasts pressing against my chest, I lost all reason.

I plundered her mouth, exploring it with my tongue. When her tongue touched mine, I exploded. My hands claimed her body, her full breasts fitting perfectly in my palms. I wanted to see her bare breasts, to suck on them until she cried out again.

I held her close, backing her up until she hit the wall. I grabbed her leg and hooked it around my hip, grinding myself against her heat. Her hands wrapped around the nape of my neck, her fingers tightening in my hair, pulling hard enough for it to hurt. I loved it. And then she moaned. Drove me fucking wild.

"Jesus," I said breathlessly.

I'd only wanted a taste, a sip. But now I wanted to drink. Swallow her breathy sighs. Savor her creamy skin. I was lost in her…lost in my Red.

When she bit my lip and sucked, I growled. She nibbled my lips for a few moments before biting. So fucking sexy.

"Want you so fucking bad," I whispered in her ear.

I scooped her up in my arms, my lips never leaving hers.

The bedroom, I thought, struggling to think. Too far. I spotted the couch a few feet away and hurriedly carried her there without breaking our kiss. I roughly laid her on the cushions.

I straddled her, pulling my shirt off, and then I froze and looked at her.

Fuck me.

Her lips were red and swollen, her pupils dilated. She was half lying, half sitting up with her elbows supporting her weight as she stared up at me.

So fucking beautiful.

My eyes widened as she sat up, shyly placing her hands on my thighs.

My muscles tensed. I swallowed nervously, watching her raptly as I waited for her next move. Waiting…waiting…

I thought I'd died when she reached for her shirt, took it off.

Holy Jesus…

So lost. I was so lost in her spell… I watched as she reached for my hand. I leaned down to accommodate her as she slowly placed my hand on her cheek. She stared at me with those dark mysterious eyes, kissed the palm of my hand.

There were very few moments in my life that I knew would stick with me forever—lasting only a few seconds but irrevocably staying with me, finding a spot in my heart and burrowing in there, changing me for the rest of my life.

This. This was one of them.

I was always surrounded by people, always thought I belonged with them. I was never lonely, but I was never really happy either. I didn't realize until now, as we stared into each other's eyes, that I had never really belonged with anyone.

Until Red. Until she came into my life.

She was home. My home.

"Caleb." Her voice was whisper soft, a siren's call to my senses.

My mouth opened in surprise as she placed her hand on my chest and pushed me onto my back. When she climbed on top of me, my brain stopped functioning.

She kissed my neck softly, her lips drifting down to my chest, to my stomach. When I felt her tongue flick against my skin, I nearly came in my pants.

I knew lust, had acted upon it more times than I cared to count. But this…this was something else. It was painful, almost unbearable. But it was the good kind of pain. The best kind of pain. I wanted to possess her just as she possessed me.

She was fire, and I wanted her to burn me…consume me.

Like a moth to a flame, I could not resist.

I took over, kissing her with an abandon and a wild hunger that shook me.

"Bed," I murmured, my voice gruff and heavy. When she nodded, I stood and scooped her up in my arms, still kissing her while heading to my bedroom.

When the buzzer sounded, I nearly snarled.

"Caleb, wait. Stop."

She was telling me to stop, but we were both still kissing each other.

The buzzer sounded again.

"Fuck."

When she tucked her head under my chin, I closed my eyes. My body was on fire, but my heart was melting.

With that small gesture she destroyed me.

I love you.

My heart was beating like it was going to explode in my chest. I'd never said that to anyone before. Never felt it before her.

I waited for panic, fear, denial to come—but none of those did. It just felt...right. As if I had loved her from the very beginning without realizing it.

I wanted to tell her, but I kissed the top of her head instead, smelled the sweet strawberry scent of her hair. Her heart was beating fast, her breathing shallow. Her hands came up to my shoulders, shaking me slightly.

"Put me down, Caleb. Answer the intercom."

I blew out a breath. "Damn."

I put her down, made sure her body slid tantalizingly against mine. Her head was down, avoiding my eyes. She was embarrassed again.

It was one of the many reasons I couldn't get enough of her. She was passion and fire one minute, shy and sweet the next.

"Hey," I said softly, lifting her chin with my finger. Her eyes met mine, and for the second time in less than half an hour, she took my breath away.

She slays me, I thought, *with just one look. One goddamn look.*

She smiled at me, and then gave me a quick kiss on the mouth. "Answer the intercom. I'll just...fix myself a little bit."

When she turned away, I reached for her arm, pulling her to my chest and wrapping her in my arms. I heard her gasp, her body tensing, then relaxing as she settled comfortably—and with sweet familiarity—in my embrace. As if we'd been doing this for a long time.

"You're my home, Red."

She didn't respond with words. But her arms gently but firmly wrapped around my back. She rested her cheek on my chest, her ear perfectly aligned with my heartbeat. As if she was listening to it and found the sound beautiful, she let out a contented sigh and held me tighter.

Yeah, I realized, *I'm home.*

CHAPTER
twenty-eight

Veronica

RELAX. RELAX. RELAX.

It became a chant as I put on a white tank top, then quickly fished out my lip gloss from my purse and applied it.

Dammit. My hair was a mess. Caleb liked to run his hands through it. It always needed a hell of a brushing after every time we kissed.

God. That had been so very, very close. I still wasn't ready to do it with him, but I loved it when we kissed. He made me feel strange things...with his hands...his mouth... I shook my head to clear my thoughts. *Focus.*

I had no time to play with my hair, so I just pulled it up in a bun on top of my head.

Breathe in. Breathe out.

Everything was going to be fine. It was just Beatrice-Rose. Caleb's childhood friend. It was nothing.

I quietly walked to the living room, listening. I stopped in my tracks when I saw Caleb doing push-ups on the floor.

"Caleb?"

"Yes, baby?" he huffed, raising his head to look at me.

"What are you doing?"

He placed one hand behind his back and was doing one-arm push-ups now. He winked. It reminded me of my second day in his home, when he was showing off his arms and butt to me. It felt so long ago. I pursed my lips, trying to keep from laughing at the memory.

"You got me so hot that I had to cool myself down. Don't want anything sticking up when Beatrice-Rose comes in, now, do we?"

My laughter disappeared. Heat rushed up in my cheeks. The things he said…

"That was the neighbor, by the way, but Beatrice-Rose is coming up now. Did you do something with your lips?"

Did he notice everything?

"And that top." Suddenly, he jumped to his feet, still shirtless. "Red, you're not helping." His voice was turned low—the I'm-going-to-kiss-you kind of low.

"Caleb, she'll be here any second!"

I picked up his shirt from the floor and tossed it at him. He caught it easily.

"So?" he challenged, stalking me. I backed away, laughing now. "Can't I get a kiss?"

He kept on coming, and I kept on backing away. This reminded me of what had happened in the bathroom when we—

Focus!

He seemed to enjoy stalking me like this.

"Caleb," I warned, looking behind me, ready to bolt.

He paused, blinked, and then blew out a breath. "You're right. What the hell. Red, I swear, you've made me a walking hard-on."

I rolled my eyes. "Is that all you can think about?"

"Yes." He grinned. "If *all* meant you, then yes."

When the soft knock sounded at the door, Caleb let out a sigh and put on his shirt. My insecurities fled as he grabbed my hand and led us to the front door.

When Caleb opened the door, I caught a flash of light-blond hair and a whiff of expensive floral perfume as a body catapulted through. I heard Caleb's *oof!* and his hand was wrenched from mine. I turned to see Beatrice-Rose pressed against Caleb, her hands wrapped around his neck like an octopus's tentacles. That was mean, I scolded myself. She hadn't done anything bad to me. *Not yet*, my subconscious added. I ignored it.

"Cal! I missed you!" she cried out, delighted.

My insecurities came flooding back with a vengeance as Caleb hugged her back before pulling away from her. He looked at her and smiled.

"Hey, B. How are you?"

She was petite. And very beautiful, with classical features that reminded me of the princesses in fairy tales.

The first thing I noticed was her hair. It was light blond, straight as a pin, and ended just below her jawline in a perfect bob. Ruler-straight bangs framed her big blue eyes.

It was hard not to appreciate the white satin blouse she had on, with a loose bow tied around the collar. She paired it with black leather shorts that showcased long legs and a pair of royal blue pumps. She exuded class and expensive things.

I felt like a character in "Jack and the Beanstalk." The giant, to be specific.

She placed her hand on Caleb's arm. Squeezed. "I'm good. I was just in the neighborhood and decided to drop by."

"It's fine," Caleb said, steering her toward me. "I want you to meet my girlfriend, Red. Red, this is Beatrice-Rose."

Girlfriend. Just hearing him introduce me like that sent the butterflies skittering around my stomach.

Beatrice-Rose's eyes widened as, for the first time, she finally noticed me. The hand that was on Caleb's arm fell to her side when Caleb reached for my hand again, lacing our fingers together. Her blue eyes followed the movement, and stared at our intertwined fingers.

Something there, I thought, as an emotion flashed in her eyes, so fast I wasn't sure what it was. Then she smiled at me.

"I'm so sorry. I didn't mean to intrude. It's so nice to meet you, Red. I'm Beatrice-Rose."

She offered her hand. Her nails were unpainted but tastefully manicured. My nails were chipped and untrimmed as I shook her smooth, soft hand, and I wondered what she thought of mine, rough from dishwashing and cleaning. I didn't like this self-conscious feeling. Didn't like it at all. I let go as fast as I could.

"Veronica, actually," I clarified. "Caleb calls me Red. It's nice to meet you too."

She threw her head back and laughed. Did I say something funny?

"Cal, remember when we were kids and you used to call me Yellow? Glad you kept the habit."

Her hand reached for his arm again. She touched him so casually, as if she'd had a lot of practice over the years.

Yellow.

Cal.

B.

Yellow…

Caleb nodded, smiling fondly as he remembered. My stomach knotted.

Beatrice-Rose's eyes shifted to me. "It's my hair," she explained, pointing at her shiny locks.

I slowly removed my hand from Caleb's, needing some space. He noticed, a frown marring his forehead.

"I called Ben Blue too," he said, stubbornly reaching for my hand again. I tugged, but he only held it more firmly.

I didn't want to hold his hand. I wanted to stomp my foot and walk away…but she was there and I didn't want to appear to be a spoiled kid.

Beatrice-Rose let out a laugh. "Oh God, yes, I remember. Our families went on a lot of trips when we were younger. We got in trouble a lot. And Ben… Well, let's just say he was less serious at the time. He had an obsession with dyeing his hair blue."

Caleb laughed. "Yeah. He's too busy with work now."

I got it. They had a lot of memories together. They were close. They had a bond.

But more importantly, Caleb named people colors that he associated with them. It wasn't just me. It wasn't *our* thing. My heart fell into my stomach.

"I'm so sorry, Veronica. I didn't mean to…" Beatrice-Rose laid her hand softly on my arm, a sign of comfort, as if we'd been friends for a long time. Maybe she just liked to touch people. But I didn't like being touched by strangers. It wasn't *my* thing. I stepped away.

"It's just that…I haven't seen Caleb in months," she said. "I've been away, in Paris. And he's family. I don't…really have much family."

I heard the genuine sadness in her voice. I felt bad. I shouldn't have judged her so quickly. She and Caleb must be really close, and she must have missed him a lot.

But there was something there… I knew it wasn't just sisterly affection she felt for him. She liked Caleb as more than a friend. I could see it in the way her eyes lingered on his face, the way her hands stayed on his body. I knew, as only a girl would, that she had feelings for Caleb.

"You ladies want to hang out on the balcony or in the living room?" Caleb asked, but he was only looking at me. I didn't answer.

"Living room is fine," Beatrice-Rose answered, walking ahead of us. "Dinner will be here in ten. I ordered our usual." She grinned, kissing her palm and blowing it in Caleb's direction.

"Perfect."

Our usual.

Just how many times had she stayed over here to have a

usual? And how close were they? Were they...*together* before? Oh God, what if they were? This was so awkward. And if they were, why hadn't Caleb told me? I hated these thoughts. This was why I didn't want to get close to a guy.

Jealousy.

Such an ugly feeling. I hated it. I hated Caleb for making me feel it.

He pulled me on the couch beside him as he chatted with Beatrice-Rose. I asked them if they wanted drinks, and they both refused. She talked about her trip to Paris, how she had to go back this summer because her best friend was getting married there.

Paris. Someday, I promised myself, I'd go there too. I would love to go around the world.

With Caleb, my subconscious whispered. Again, I ignored it.

She went down memory lane with him, asking if he remembered that time when they went camping and he had to carry her back to camp because she'd sprained her ankle. Or those times he gave her peanut butter sandwiches. With no jelly. Her voice just held a hint of disgust. I loved peanut butter sandwiches. And yes, with no jelly. Those were my favorite. But I didn't tell her that.

What was I doing here? They didn't need me here to keep them entertained; it looked like they were having a lot of fun talking by themselves. I should leave. Suddenly, I felt Caleb reach for my hand, squeezing it gently. My eyes flicked up at him, but he was still talking and laughing with her. He squeezed my hand again.

A feeling of warmth settled in my chest. I smiled. Somehow he knew when I needed comfort. I was still anxious, but his hand in mine served as a Band-Aid to all of it. *He* was my Band-Aid. I noticed that Beatrice-Rose looked at our joined hands, then quickly pulled her gaze away.

When the intercom buzzed, Caleb got up. "Finally. I'm starving!"

Beatrice-Rose chuckled, shaking her head so her hair swayed with the movement. "You're always starving."

"Yes, I am." He leaned forward and gave me a quick kiss on the mouth. "Starving for Red."

CHAPTER

twenty-nine

Veronica

"STARVING FOR RED," HE WHISPERED BESIDE MY EAR, THEN stepped away to answer the door.

I turned red. I knew he said it loud enough for Beatrice-Rose to hear. My face grew hot and I felt giddy, like something was tickling my stomach.

"He's like a kid, isn't he?" Beatrice-Rose motioned with her chin to where Caleb was chatting with the delivery guy. Caleb was saying something that made the guy guffaw.

She toyed with the pendant on a chain around her neck. "God. I missed him so much," she whispered so quietly that I almost didn't hear it. But I did.

Her eyes widened, as if she couldn't believe she'd just said those words. "I'm so silly." She let out an embarrassed laugh. "I'm so sorry, Veronica. I was thinking out loud." She lowered her eyes, and I could see two pink spots on her cheeks.

It hurt to look at her. She was like a double punch to my already sore bruise. She was beautiful and rich, and had a history with Caleb. And she was obviously in love with him. Was Caleb in love with her too?

"He was my first, you know. You never forget your first. I was his too." I noticed the death grip she had on the pendant around her neck, her knuckles white.

What did she mean? *First love?* I felt nauseated.

And why the hell was she telling me this? Did she really think that I wanted to hear this?

"Please don't take it the wrong way," she said. "I don't know why I even told you that."

If her intention was to make me jealous, to show I could never have the connection she had with Caleb, then she was winning. If she'd been mean about it, I would have lashed out already. But she wasn't. She just sounded…sad.

Either way, I wasn't going to play along.

"I think…" Beatrice-Rose paused as if she was trying to find the right words. "Today was just a shock for me, seeing him with you. I've never seen him this way with anyone else."

I really didn't want to hear any more.

"I'm sorry, Veronica. Please don't be upset with me," she murmured softly.

I blinked, searching her face for deceit. It was hard to tell. She looked and sounded vulnerable and sincere. How was I supposed to respond to that?

"Have you met Miranda?" she continued, smiling radiantly.

"No." I didn't ask who Miranda was, didn't really want to talk anymore.

She touched the back of my hand again. I gritted my teeth, trying to stop myself from pulling away from her touch.

"Food's ready in the kitchen." Caleb called. "Ready when you are, ladies."

I let out a relieved sigh and headed straight to the kitchen with Beatrice-Rose following behind me. Caleb had laid out the food on the counter where he liked to eat. I glanced at it, my stomach in knots.

This was rich-people food. Caviar, truffles, goat cheese on crackers with some kind of fruit on top. Then I spotted a cheesy lasagna, which made me feel slightly better. Real food.

I opened a cupboard, grabbed three plates, and set them on the counter. Caleb handed me two forks, which I placed on top of the napkins beside our plates. He opened the fridge, and I knew he was going to grab his orange juice so I got two glasses. By the time I turned around, he was in front of me, waiting for me to hold his glass steady as he poured his beloved orange juice in it. This was our routine. We could do this with our eyes closed.

"Want some too?" he asked Beatrice-Rose.

She was watching us with an expression I couldn't decipher. "No, thank you. I'll have wine if you have some."

"Of course. Hold on, gotta get Red's drink first." He opened a can of coconut water and filled my glass. This was routine too.

I could either sit beside Beatrice-Rose or across from her. I chose the seat across from her.

"Here you go." Caleb handed her a quarter-full glass of red wine, then sat beside her. She was looking at him like he was Superman and Batman rolled into one.

I placed my fork in my mouth because I wanted to bite something. Preferably Caleb's hand so he'd stop smiling at her.

"Could I get a fork too?" she asked, looking down at her plate.

Great. I hoped she didn't think I deliberately didn't get her one. Caleb was so used to our routine that he had grabbed two forks, forgetting there were three of us tonight. It was mean and petty, but it made me slightly happy. I stood up quickly to get her a fork.

"I was just asking Veronica if she had met your mom yet," Beatrice-Rose said.

I stopped in my tracks.

What the hell?

"She hasn't." He looked at me. "As soon as Mom gets back from her business trip, I'll take you to meet her, Red."

What?

In a daze, I placed Beatrice-Rose's fork on her plate. I cried out when I realized that instead of the clean fork I got for her, I'd stupidly given her the fork that had been in my mouth.

"Omigod. I'm so sorry!"

Caleb laughed. He was such an ass sometimes.

In a rush to fix my mistake, I reached for Beatrice-Rose's plate and accidentally knocked her hand just as she lifted her glass of red wine. The glass hit the floor and shattered.

"Oh no!" She abruptly knelt on the floor, hurriedly picking up the broken pieces of glass with her bare hands.

Caleb stopped laughing. "The hell are you doing, B? Stop."

Her hands were starting to bleed, but she didn't stop.

"Beatrice-Rose." Caleb's voice turned hard. She stopped and looked up at him. My mouth opened in shock as I saw tears running down her cheeks.

Silently, Caleb helped her up and led her to the sink, gently shaking her hands. I heard the pieces of glass as they fell in the sink.

"Let's go to the bathroom," Caleb said softly. "I'll clean you up."

She nodded imperceptibly, looking like a broken doll. Caleb wrapped his arm around her shoulders.

"Red, could you grab the first aid kit, please? I think it's in the—"

"It's okay. I know where it is. Just clean her up."

He gave me a grateful smile.

What the hell is going on?

Was she crying because she cut her hand? But the way Caleb spoke to her told me it was something else.

Not my problem, I thought. I got the first aid kit from the laundry storage room and headed to the bathroom. I froze in my tracks as I heard Beatrice-Rose's soft voice.

"I'm sorry I broke down in there. She must think I'm insane. Your Red."

"No, she's not like that."

"What is she like?"

It was a moment before Caleb responded. "Everything."

Silence.

"Don't move," he continued. "I still have to remove some glass from your skin. What were you thinking?"

"My dad's dementia is worsening, Cal. I don't even want to go home anymore. My mom takes it out on me. It's hard. I don't want to watch my dad... It hurts to see him like that." She sobbed.

"Shh. It will be okay."

"I need you. Don't leave me. You're the only one who understands me, Caleb."

I felt awful for her. Dementia was a debilitating illness I wouldn't wish on anyone. But...was I rotten to wish she would leave? Did Caleb have to be the one she turned to for comfort?

It wasn't like Caleb was mine.

But he was.

He was mine.

Oh God. When did I start thinking he was mine? Caleb was sneaky, slithering unnoticed under my skin, where he'd set up camp and claimed a part of me.

Like a virus, I thought darkly. Caleb was a virus. And he'd better not be thinking of doing anything other than *comforting* Beatrice-Rose or else...

I cleared my throat to alert them of my presence.

"Red?" Caleb asked.

Yellow. I couldn't get over it yet.

"Hey. Here's the first aid." I handed the kit to him and turned to Beatrice-Rose. "How are you?" She sat on the toilet seat with Caleb kneeling in front of her. He was holding her hands.

I clenched mine. I'd never seen him hold anyone else's hands except mine. I knew he had to clean her cuts but still. It was unreasonable, but I wanted to pull him away from her.

"I'm better. I'm sorry you had to see that. I'm not usually like that around strangers."

I nodded. I *really* didn't want to see them so close together. "I'll just clean up in the kitchen."

Sweeping the floor was a mindless task that gave me room to be alone with my thoughts. I didn't like it, but I swept the floor twice. Caleb liked to walk barefoot in the apartment, and I didn't want him to step on broken glass.

"Red?"

I turned around and found Caleb standing beside Beatrice-Rose, his arm wrapped around her shoulders again. She leaned against him, her head lowered so I couldn't see her eyes.

"I'm just going to drive Beatrice-Rose home. I don't think she's in the right condition to drive herself. I'll be back soon, okay?"

No, it's not okay.

I ignored him, looking at Beatrice-Rose instead. Whatever game she was playing, I still felt bad about her cuts and what was happening with her dad so I said, "I hope you feel better."

She looked up and gave me a strained smile.

Caleb stepped toward me. He was removing his arm from Beatrice-Rose's shoulders when she squeezed his arm, stopping him. He looked at her with exasperation and then sighed.

"Let's go," she pleaded quietly. "Please, Cal."

Before they left, Caleb looked back at me, clearly hesitant.

"I'll be home before you know it."

But he wasn't.

He didn't come home that night.

CHAPTER
thirty

Caleb

I SHOULD HAVE KISSED HER GOODBYE BEFORE I LEFT.

This was not good. This was not how I'd imagined my night would go. Damn.

I just wanted to spend the night with Red. Alone. Watch one of those scary movies on "our" list. Order pizza. Kiss her, touch her if she'd let me again. I couldn't get enough of her.

I wondered if she was one of those girls who covered their eyes and squealed while watching horror movies. Or did she stay silent, staring at the screen unblinkingly. Whatever her reaction was, I wouldn't be finding out tonight.

I glanced at Beatrice-Rose, who stared out the passenger window silently, a small smile on her lips. "Are you feeling better?"

She smiled at me. "Yes, Cal. You're here now. I'm feeling much better, thank you."

I frowned. Something in her words didn't sit well with me. Maybe when she said, *You're here now.*

"I miss you," she murmured.

I felt uncomfortable. I wasn't sure if I should tell her to stop talking to me that way. If some other guy was talking to Red like this, I would go ballistic.

"I miss my best friend," she clarified.

I wasn't even aware how hard I was gripping the wheel until I relaxed my hands. Yeah, she thought of me as her best friend— though I wasn't sure how well she understood the new dynamic in our relationship. She had always been possessive of me.

Girls came and went in my life, but Beatrice-Rose was a constant. She had learned to depend on that. In a way, that was my fault. I had let her depend on me. It became a habit for her. And for me.

But it was different now. I had not anticipated Red coming into my life. She'd blindsided me, and now all I wanted was her.

I could say that Beatrice-Rose was the first girl who fascinated me. As kids, we were forced to spend time together in the playroom. *Sleeping Beauty* was her favorite movie. I thought it was because she was blond and because of the similarities in their names—Briar Rose to her Beatrice-Rose.

I could not count how many times I had watched that damn movie with her. I'd bet my left nut I could still recite the lines, even in my sleep. Not that I would tell anybody, obviously.

It didn't escape my young mind's notice that Sleeping Beauty was vulnerable, fragile. The type of girl who could draw out the protective instinct with just the way she looked, the way she spoke. Like a meek lamb, a little kitten. And after you had slain her dragon, she would gaze at you and make you feel like a hero.

In a lot of ways, Beatrice-Rose reminded me of Sleeping Beauty. She always came to me for protection, for safety, which made me feel like a hero. It made me feel strong. It might have been caveman thinking, but sometimes it's really good to feel like a hero.

Beatrice-Rose was very, very good for my ego.

Reflecting on it, I realized those were the types of girls I always went for. Girls who needed saving, who needed protection, who made me feel *needed*. This desire to feel needed might have come from my childhood when no one needed or wanted me, but that didn't really matter in the end, did it? Because now I felt ashamed, embarrassed, stripped. It seemed so shallow to date those girls just because they fed my ego.

Maybe that was how Red had captured my attention. She was different from all the girls I knew. She seemed fearless and strong, then seemed so helpless, so vulnerable when I found her at the parking lot. I'd wanted to save her. But she'd proved me wrong.

Because in the end, she was the one who saved me.

Red made me bare my soul, made me aware of what was lacking in my life and what I wanted to be. She made me want to do more, be more. Be a better person.

Yellow—that damn nickname. When I saw Red's face after Beatrice-Rose told her that, my first thought was *shit*. She might think that calling her Red wasn't anything special. When she was the most special person in my life.

It was an old habit, naming people after colors that reminded me of them. What Red didn't know was that I'd stopped doing that when I turned eight. She'd just brought it out of me that night when I met her.

That night.

She'd danced on that floor like she owned it, with her killer red dress, red lips, and sheer presence. I *had* to stop and stare. It felt like a siren's call. I was unable to look away for fear I would miss something important. That I would lose a chance I could never get back again.

It wasn't just lust. It was a pull I couldn't explain.

And when she approached me, kicked my ass, and rejected me…I *knew*. She was red. My Red. She was fire, passion, strength…

Love.

I love her.

I hadn't told her yet, because I was waiting for the right moment. I knew she loved me. I just didn't know if she was ready to admit it to herself yet.

"…so there you go. Right, Cal?"

I blinked. What? I'd missed everything Beatrice-Rose had just said. I grunted, letting her interpret that for herself. I changed the subject quickly so she wouldn't notice I hadn't been listening for the last ten minutes.

"I thought you got over your panic attacks," I said. "What happened in my apartment?"

I heard her sharp intake of breath. "They came back after Dad got sick."

"Aw, B."

She sniffed. "It's gotten really bad, Cal. Sometimes he thinks I'm grandma or his sister. Sometimes he doesn't know me at all. I can't take it. I can't."

I reached for her uninjured hand, offering her comfort. "I'm sorry."

She nodded, tightly holding my hand in hers. I squeezed her hand again and let go.

I felt horrible for her. She'd started getting panic attacks in high school. It wasn't easy for her. And for some reason, I was the only one who calmed her down.

I remembered one time when I was in the middle of a heavy make-out session with a senior named Sakura, remembered how excited I was because I had been pursuing her for quite some time and she was playing hard to get.

That night when she finally gave in, Beatrice-Rose had phoned me in a panic, saying she couldn't breathe. That freaked me the hell out. I left Sakura and went to find Beatrice-Rose. It took fifteen minutes to calm her down and help her breathe properly again. Since then, she phoned me every time she had an attack, and I was always there.

"It's all right," Beatrice-Rose said now. "Like I said, you're here now. Everything feels better."

I parked my car in their circular driveway. "I can't stay. I have to go home to Red."

"Please, Cal. Stay." Her blue eyes were wide and pleading. "Please."

She rested her hand on my thigh, making me squirm. She removed it.

I let out a sigh. "Okay," I relented, thinking of the crap she must be dealing with at home. The least I could do was lend her a little support. "Half an hour."

She pouted. "Three hours."

"Forty-five minutes."

She shook her head. "Two hours."

"An hour."

"Deal!" She grinned at me like the cat that ate the canary— like she'd wanted an hour all along. I should have known. I always seemed to underestimate her.

"I feel tired, Cal. But I'm hungry. Don't start the timer until after we're done eating. Okay?"

"Beatrice-Rose," I warned.

"Caleb." She giggled.

I knew Red was going to wait up for me. I had to phone her, let her know. When I reached for my phone, I panicked. It wasn't in my pocket. Did I forget to bring it? Dammit.

"I forgot my phone. Can I borrow yours? I need to call Red and tell her I'm going to be an hour late."

She pouted again. "My battery's almost dead. I need to charge it first."

Nodding, I got out of the car and opened the door for her.

Their house was a long, modern, rectangular building, with three floors of clear glass walls that reminded me of an aquarium. I could see everything in their house from where I was standing. Granted, they had a gate and a long driveway, so the house wasn't necessarily exposed to the streets.

All I could think was that they couldn't walk around naked

or scratch their asses whenever they wanted to. I would rather live in a mud hut than expose myself that way.

The inside of the house was pretty much the same as the outside. Expensive antiques, classy furniture, paintings. It was elegant, beautiful…and cold. It lacked the warmth of a home. My eyes locked on the naked Greek god statue in the foyer. That was new. I had no problems with statues, but this one was ugly as sin. What the hell was the artist thinking? Were those horns sticking out of his—

"Good evening."

It was their butler, Higgins. He'd been working for them for as long as I could remember. He always seemed to magically appear whenever there were visitors.

"Higgins! How's it going, bud?"

"I'm well, thank you for asking, sir. Yourself?"

"Caleb, my dear!"

Katherine-Rose, Beatrice-Rose's mom, descended the stairs like a queen in a purple dress. She always loved dramatic entrances. I didn't miss the glass in her hand—brandy, probably. She had grown fond of drinking since her husband's health started declining.

She kissed my cheek as soon as she reached me. I tried not to recoil when I smelled the alcohol on her breath.

"It seems that every time I see you, Caleb, my dear, you grow taller. And more handsome each day."

"Any taller, and he'd hit the ceiling."

"Beatrice-Rose! Mind your manners, please!" Katherine-Rose glared at her daughter, disapproval dripping in her voice. "How juvenile."

I could feel Beatrice-Rose shrinking beside me. She reached for my hand, seeking comfort.

"Definitely not. I find her quite charming. After all, where else would she get it but from you?" I said easily, wanting to diffuse the tension in the air.

Katherine-Rose's eyes widened with pleasure, and she let out a trilling laugh. "Oh, you handsome devil—"

A loud wail cut her off. "No! Thief! Get away! She stole my money! Help! Help!"

I spun around at the commotion behind us. My jaw dropped as I took in Liam's decimated form standing in the hallway. He looked terrible. His clothes and hair, always immaculate, were in disarray. His cheeks were sunken, the sharp bones of his face in stark relief against pale, taut skin.

"Please, let's go back to your room, Liam," the nurse pleaded.

"Get away from me!" he shouted, the look in his eyes reminding me of a trapped animal.

"Dad!"

Liam's eyes focused on Beatrice-Rose and narrowed infinitesimally. Suspiciously. "Who are you?" he hissed. "What are you doing in my house?"

"Dad," Beatrice-Rose choked out.

"Who the hell are you? There are strangers in my house! Someone call the police!"

When the nurse reached for Liam's arm, he panicked, shoving her away from him.

"Get him away from here!" Katherine-Rose snapped. "I'm paying you to take care of him! Oh God!" Her hands shook as she brought her glass to her lips and took a long drink. She hurried away without saying goodbye.

Beatrice-Rose stared as the nurse struggled to take her screaming father back to his room.

"Haldol," Beatrice-Rose whispered. "They give him Haldol to calm him down. I think. Or maybe that's changed. I don't know..." She trailed off into unintelligible muttering. And then slowly, she slumped to the floor, weeping, dejected.

"B." I lifted her to her feet, and she leaned heavily on me, burrowing her face in my shirt, still weeping.

I took her to her room and helped her get into her bed. Picking up a chair from her sitting area, I carried it over and placed it beside her bed. I sat.

"He doesn't know who I am anymore, Cal." She curled herself into a ball but had stopped crying. "Cal, don't go."

I felt a headache coming on. Red was waiting for me, and I hadn't even phoned her yet. But I couldn't possibly leave Beatrice-Rose in this state.

"I need you," she begged. "Please."

"All right. Let me phone Red first. Where's your phone?"

She pursed her lips. "In my purse."

I got up, plugged it in the charger, and phoned Red. When she didn't answer, I called my apartment. No answer. I tried again. No answer.

"She's not answering. She must be in the shower," I said, returning to my seat. "I'll try again in five minutes."

"Where did you meet her?" Beatrice-Rose asked after a moment.

"Red?" I leaned back comfortably in my chair, smiling at the thought of her. "At a club."

"Oh." She paused. "How long have you known her, Cal?"

"A few months."

"That's not very long."

I shrugged. "Long enough." It didn't matter to me if I'd known her for a day, an hour, or only a moment. I was hers.

"Will you stay with me tonight?"

"Until you fall asleep," I replied.

"No, Cal." She held her hand out. "Stay with me."

She took my hand in hers, squeezing. I squeezed back but didn't answer.

"Tell me about her."

Thinking about Red made me feel good. "She's…different. Tough, very independent, a good heart. Difficult sometimes," I added, grinning.

"You say that as though it's a good thing."

"I love it when she gives me a hard time."

Silence.

"Where does she live? Is she in college?"

I ignored her first question because I was sure Red wouldn't appreciate me telling anyone she lived with me. "She attends the same college. Lost both her parents as far as I know. She didn't grow up as privileged as us, had to work hard for everything."

"Being able to afford anything doesn't mean things are easy, Cal. You of all people should know that."

I looked around me, noting that her room looked just like the rest of the house—not a thing out of place. She didn't even have books on her night table like Red did. Or a colorful blanket that showed her personality. The colors in her room were different shades of beige. I found it…boring. I didn't before. Since Red, I needed color. Color was interesting. It gave life.

Everything in Beatrice-Rose's room looked like it was ready for a photo shoot. Yes, she and I did have the luxury to buy anything we wanted. That didn't guarantee happiness, but not having to worry about money sure helped a lot.

"You know it's still easier than for most people," I said. "Red had a rough childhood."

"Does she hate me?"

My mouth opened in shock. "What?" Why would she ask that?

"She seemed unfriendly. She gave me the fork from her mouth, Cal. How rude was that? She hates me."

I laughed. "That was your fault for dropping that bomb about introducing her to my mom. Way to beat me to it. I was waiting for the right time to ask her."

She curled her small mouth into a snarl. "She knocked my glass out of my hand on purpose. I just think—"

Irritation filled me, and I cut her off. "She's not like that. Why would you say that?"

"I'm just saying, Cal. What do you really know about her?"

Now I was getting angry. "Don't be ridiculous." I stood up, ready to leave. "I don't want to hear about this anymore."

"I'm sorry," she apologized, sitting up on the bed. She grabbed my arm. "You know how protective of you I can get… Cal, don't be upset. I don't think I can take more tonight."

My anger deflated. I felt like a douche, adding to her problems. I blew out a breath and sat back down.

"Can you lie down beside me?" she asked quietly, tucking her hair behind her ear. She looked like a defenseless kitten.

"I can't do that anymore."

She frowned. "Why not?"

I raised my eyebrows.

"You didn't have a problem with it before. It's not like we're going to have sex. We grew up together. We're best friends. I just need you. Like old times."

"I told you this time it's different."

She fell silent, lowering her head and clutching the pendant I had given to her so long ago. I couldn't believe she still had it. "She's taking you away from me."

"Don't be dramatic."

"Just for a few minutes," she begged. "Until I fall asleep. You can leave once I do."

I hesitated. It didn't feel right.

"You know it'll help me fall asleep, Cal. I don't want to take more pills to help me sleep. Please."

She was taking sleeping pills again? Or did she mean antidepressants? She took them before, a long time ago.

"Cal, I want to stop thinking about my dad tonight. He can't even remember me anymore. You don't know what it feels like. It hurts so much."

I sighed. "All right. But just for a few minutes. Then I have to go."

She scooted back to make room and patted the spot beside her, smiling innocently.

I stretched out beside her, and it immediately felt wrong. But I didn't want her to take any more pills or worry about her dad. It seemed so inconsequential to give her this simple thing. Besides, we both knew she'd be out like a light in a few minutes once I lay down beside her. The faster she fell asleep, the faster I could get back to Red. Beatrice-Rose snuggled closer to me, her arms wrapped around my torso, resting her head on my chest.

I'd never had a problem with this before. Why did it feel wrong this time?

I needed to call Red again, but I didn't want to get up right away and disturb Beatrice-Rose. I listened to her breathing, waiting for her to fall asleep. Suddenly my eyes felt heavy, my body exhausted. I hadn't slept properly since the party at Justin's house, and this bed felt really comfortable…

I need to call Red was my last thought before I fell asleep.

Red was so soft, like silk in my hands. Her kisses drugged me, made me feel high, made me crave more. I kissed her back as hard as she was kissing me. I moaned, wanting more of her touch. But something was not right. She tasted different.

Then she reached for my jeans…

"Cal."

Red never called me Cal. My eyes snapped open.

"What the fuck!"

Beatrice-Rose was on top of me. I pushed her away and jumped out of bed. My eyes widened in horror as I realized she didn't have her shirt on. What the fuck. I was dreaming of Red and…

God.

"I have to go."

"Cal—"

"I was dreaming of her, goddamn it."

She reached for the blanket, covering herself with it.

"I don't cheat," I snapped. "You know the rules."

"Cal, I'm sorry. Please, don't go. I just need... *Please.*"

I rubbed my hands over my face. "This can't happen again. I'm sorry. This was my fault."

I didn't know what time it was, didn't care. I had to get the fuck out of here. I had to get home to Red.

Red...

My God.

What have I done?

CHAPTER

thirty-one

Veronica

STAY.

But asking him would be selfish, wouldn't it?

I impatiently flung back the hair that fell on my face and continued scrubbing the counters—hard. I was in a cleaning frenzy, as my mom had called it. Whenever I was working something out in my mind, I ran around the house cleaning like a shopaholic on Black Friday.

Beatrice-Rose was Caleb's childhood friend. A *close* friend who was in need. Of course Caleb would do the decent thing and help her. She'd looked like she was almost going to pass out earlier. But...

He could have called a taxi for her, phoned another friend to pick her up...something.

Maybe he's in love with her.

No, no. Caleb was just being a good friend. He said he'd never been serious with anyone until he met me.

But was he telling the truth?

And he didn't even mention that they had been together. Why did he have to hide it?

I didn't know.

I moved to the next counter, scrubbing like hell. But the black thoughts continued snaking through my mind.

She said he was her first love, and she was his.

She could be lying. Even if that was true, that was in the past. That was over.

Are you sure? Looks like he still has feelings for her. Why would he leave you and take her home if he doesn't?

She needed his help.

Wrong. He picked her. He's way out of your league. You're fooling yourself if you think there's a future for both of you. Leave now before he leaves you. Leave him before he hurts you.

Do you really think he's going to stay with you when you can't even give him what he wants? Do you think Beatrice-Rose would hesitate to give him what he wants?

Stop it! I shook my head and began attacking the stove top.

All men lie. All men cheat. Just look at your father.

No.

You're pathetic. Look at yourself, cleaning his apartment when he's with another girl. Pining for him like a lovesick fool. Just like your mom.

I'm nothing like my mom.

Run. Isn't that what you're good at? Running away?

No, no, no. I was going to try. I had told Caleb I would. I would trust him, believe him. He was nothing like my father. He would not cheat on me. Hadn't he proved himself enough?

Suddenly I had to get out of here—had to clear my thoughts.

When I stepped out of the building, the late-evening air was cool and damp. It felt like it was going to rain, but I just couldn't stay inside. Maybe I should get a phone now—an honest-to-goodness smartphone with a two-year plan like Kara said. I was long overdue for one. I decided to head to the nearby mall.

How long is he going to stay at Beatrice-Rose's?

I would not think about it anymore. He'd be back soon enough. I didn't leave him a note. If he came back before me, I'd let him worry. He deserved it.

So this is what being in a relationship is like, I thought as I walked inside the mall, heading over to one of the cell phone shops. It only took me half an hour to select a phone, choose my plan, and set it up. I had a bit of savings now from working at Kara's.

Was Caleb home yet?

If he was, I wanted him to wait for me a little longer, so I went window-shopping. I knew it was petty, but I didn't like how I'd felt when he left with Beatrice-Rose. I also didn't like how pathetic and whiny I sounded in my head. Was I punishing myself or him by not going home yet?

Suddenly, I stopped in my tracks and stared. In a shop display window, I spotted a miniature key chain of a stack of pancakes with whipped cream and strawberries on top. Caleb would get a kick out of it. Feeling giddy, I entered the store and homed in on my prize. I lifted the key chain and checked the price. Not too expensive. Grinning, I bought the key chain and had it boxed and wrapped.

I was changing, I thought, as I stepped out of the mall and

into the rain. I was opening up more because of Caleb. He made me feel safe.

People started to run inside buildings, seeking shelter from the wet. Caleb said he used to play in the rain when he was a kid. To protect them, I wrapped the gift and my new phone securely in the plastic bag and stuffed it in my jacket pocket. I decided to walk and let the rain drench me. I wished he was here.

The rain washing over me made me feel calm, but something was off. My skin prickled, the hair on the back of my neck stood up, and I was just *itching* to look around me and sweep the area for any suspicious figure. It wouldn't be the first time.

When Mom passed away, I moved into a rented room in a boarding house. The rent was cheap, and I had to share the room with two other people. There was a guy renting the room across from ours who had stalked me…

I slowed my steps, feeling uneasy. It felt like someone was following me. Damn it, I'd forgotten to bring my pocketknife. I was too distracted earlier to remember to bring it.

No use feeling sorry about that now, I thought, as my heart started to accelerate. I balled my hands into angry fists and got ready to attack. But when I looked back, there was no one behind me but a few pedestrians crossing the road and three people in the bus shelter.

It was getting dark fast. I should have called a taxi earlier, but now it was only two more blocks to Caleb's building. I could make it. Besides, there were still people around. I could call for help if there was trouble.

I walked faster. When I heard footsteps getting closer behind

me, I spun around and screamed as a dark figure brushed past
me. Panicked, I tripped over my own feet at the stranger's slight
push and sprawled to the ground. I scraped my palms on the
asphalt as I tried to catch myself.

The dark figure didn't even look back.

False alarm, I thought, my heart in my throat as I slumped in
relief. I glanced at my palms and saw they were bleeding. Damn
it. I got up slowly and checked to make sure I wasn't bleeding
anywhere else. Other than my scratched palms, I was okay. I
pulled my sleeves down, wiping the blood on them.

I squawked in alarm when I remembered Caleb's present.
Frantically, I reached into my jacket pocket, blowing out a
relieved breath when I felt the box's intact shape.

It didn't escape me how ridiculous it was to be more concerned
about a key chain than my expensive new phone. Maybe because
it was a present for Caleb. I'd never given him one before.

When I spotted Caleb's building, I quickly ran inside, hoping
Caleb was home. I realized how much he'd always been there
for me. How I never had to look for him because he was always
there. But now that I'd arrived at his place and realized he wasn't
home, I felt anxious.

My heart felt a little empty.

Should I call him?

That would be nagging, wouldn't it? What were the bound-
aries in a relationship? The rules? I sucked at this.

I argued with myself as I took care of my cuts, cleaned around
the house a bit more, showered, and changed. He'd be home
soon enough.

I held the small present in my hand, feeling slightly embarrassed. How do I give it to him? What should I say? Too
cowardly, I decided to leave it on his bedside table instead, with
a quick thank-you note tucked under it.

Grabbing a book, I stretched out on the couch and decided
to read while waiting for him.

Wait…was it too lame to give him a key chain? Maybe I
should just keep it for myself. I'd never given a boy a present
before, and I doubted Caleb wanted a key chain. What gift did
you give someone who already had everything?

What was taking him so long? Something must have
happened.

He's not going to come home, you know.

Yes, he will.

I glanced at the clock. It was already half past midnight. The
hours felt so long.

Where was he?

My lids felt heavy, and I knew I was going to fall asleep soon.
The last thing I thought before darkness claimed me was that I
wished he would come home.

I woke up disoriented. It took me a minute before I realized
I'd fallen asleep on the living room couch. My book was on
the coffee table, and something slid off me and onto the floor. I
reached down to discover a blanket. I didn't remember getting
a blanket…

The only light was the soft amber glow from the lamp. My

heart jumped into my throat as I saw a dark figure against the wall. I sat up.

"Caleb! You scared the hell out of me!"

It was dark, but I could make out his shape. A sliver of light from the window illuminated half of his face. He sat on the floor, his back against the wall. His long legs bent in front of him, his elbows resting on his knees, his head bowed.

It was a moment before he finally spoke. "I'm sorry, Red."

It occurred to me that Caleb never sat far from me. He always wanted to be close. Holding my hands, touching my shoulder, smelling my hair...so why was he over there?

Something was wrong.

My heart started to thunder against my chest. At first, I panicked and worried that he was hurt. I almost stood up and went to him, but then he stopped me when he spoke again.

"I'm sorry I scared you," he whispered, his voice so quiet. "To start."

To start? What is he talking about?

"I phoned, but you didn't pick up."

I opened my mouth to answer him, but no words came out. I felt cold. So cold. I grabbed the blanket and slowly wrapped it around my shoulders, gripping it in my fists. I realized Caleb must have covered me with it while I was asleep.

"I came home as fast as I could," he continued, still whispering. I could hear every nuance in his voice. He sounded different—sad, pained.

Guilty.

"I'm sorry I was late."

I wanted to tell him it was okay, but my throat had closed up. I couldn't shake the feeling that something was wrong, and that he would tell me what it was very, very soon.

"Red…" He finally raised his head, leaned back on the wall, and looked at me.

I inhaled sharply.

The sun was rising, an enormous beacon of light to those who had lost their way, adrift in their own pain and misery. Would I be one of those people tonight?

The sun's soft rays now penetrated the window, providing enough light to see all of his handsome face. Caleb looked exhausted. I took in the shadows under his eyes, eyes so dark that the green was gone. His mouth was set in a tight, severe line, his jaw hard. It looked like he had run his hands through his hair many times.

And then I noticed his clothes. Why were they rumpled? I shut my eyes.

No. No. Please…

"She asked me to stay, and I did. I meant to stay just for an hour, but I fell asleep."

I let out the breath I hadn't known I was holding. All right, he fell asleep there. He was exhausted, probably still had a headache from his hangover. It made sense. But why was he speaking like he still had something…bad to tell me?

"Her dad has dementia, Red. I didn't know it was that bad. He didn't even recognize her. She didn't take it well, broke down in front of me. Her mom was yelling at the nurse to take him away. It was awful." He shut his eyes and pressed his fingers against them, as if to wipe away the memory of what had just happened.

I wanted to go to him, comfort him. But I didn't.

There was more. I knew there was more.

"Red."

This is it. He's going to tell me. God. Please.

I lowered my eyes, refusing to look at him. Whatever he was going to tell me was not good. I could feel it in the air, almost taste it. Dreaded it.

"Red," he repeated. "Please look at me."

I clenched my fists, unclenched them. Then slowly, I raised my eyes and looked at him.

"Do you trust me?"

Four words. Four words that sounded so simple. But nothing held more meaning than those four little words at that moment.

Trust. It always boiled down to trust, didn't it? Giving your trust to a person meant handing them the dagger to stab you. To hurt you. To destroy you. And I had given Caleb that weapon.

I shut my eyes again, feeling my heart break. I wanted to throw up.

"Red, do you trust me?"

God. Please not him. Not him. Please, don't let him betray me. Anyone but him.

What did I tell you? my subconscious mocked. *All men lie, all men cheat. Leave him before he hurts you.*

Words spilled out of my mouth without thinking. "Did you sleep with her?"

Caleb pulled himself to his feet with deliberate slowness, as though trying not to scare me. As though I were a frightened animal, ready to bolt. Anguish reflected in his eyes as he watched me.

"Answer me, Caleb." I said it calmly, not betraying any of the turmoil I was feeling inside.

His face twisted in pain. "It's no, isn't it? You don't trust me."

It was like witnessing a building about to collapse, and I was inside it. I knew what was coming, could see the cracks in the walls, hear the screech of stone against stone. No matter how hard I tried to escape, how hard I tried to run away, I couldn't. All the doors were locked, and I was trapped.

And Caleb had the key.

He started toward me.

"Don't!" I snapped. I was barely holding it together. If he touched me, I would unravel.

I stood up on wobbly legs, went to my room, shut the door, and began to pack. My hands were shaking as I shoved books and clothes in my bag.

What did I tell you? He's a liar, a cheat. All men are. Don't be like your mom.

Yes. I should have known… I wished I had the energy to slap him, kick him…but I didn't. I just felt…crushed. Heavy. My limbs weighed down by pain and betrayal.

I swallowed the hurt, buried it deep. I wouldn't show it to him. He had crushed a part of me, but I wouldn't let him take my pride. He wouldn't see my tears. He didn't deserve to see them. He wouldn't… He wouldn't…

But my feet gave out on me, and I slid against my bed to the floor. Buried my face in my hands and cried silently.

How could he?

I don't know how long I sat there, staring into space, lost in thought. Eventually, I forced myself to get up.

It was time to leave. I shouldered my bag.

There was a hitch in my stride as I opened the door and spotted Caleb seated on the floor outside my room. When he glanced up, I noted the dark shadows under his green eyes, the dejection in them. He looked exhausted and vulnerable.

But I knew now that he was a great pretender.

Everything was a lie.

I ignored him, turning to walk toward the front door. I had to leave *now*. I gritted my teeth as he stood in front of me, blocking my way.

"You don't trust me. You never did, did you?" he asked.

He waited for me to answer him, but I didn't. I wouldn't.

"Whatever I say to you now, it wouldn't matter. Because you've already made up your mind," he continued, his voice thick with emotion.

"Red."

His green eyes were pleading, compelling me to stay.

But I can't. I can't. I can't.

"Without trust, you and I are nothing," he whispered.

Trust him? So he could feed me lies… No, I wasn't going to stay for that. My hand reached for the doorknob. I was breathing hard.

Silence.

"Red?" He extended his hand, palm up, silently asking me to take it. "Don't go."

I looked into his eyes, and I *wanted* to believe him. My breath was shaky as I dragged air into my lungs, and I smelled Beatrice-Rose's floral perfume on him, leaving me no doubt in my mind. I bit back my tears and hardened my heart. "I can't do this. Goodbye, Caleb," I choked out.

I rushed blindly past him. I was losing it, and I couldn't allow him to see me fall apart. I opened the door and stepped out, refusing the urge to look back. I had packed everything I brought with me when I came to his home...

So why did it feel like I was leaving everything behind?

CHAPTER
thirty-two

Veronica

VULNERABILITY WAS AN INVITATION FOR PAIN.

Betrayal was like a rabid wolf, able to sense even a whiff of weakness. Its purpose was to devour and destroy the fainthearted.

How many times did our paths need to cross before I learned?

I showed the world what it hated to see: someone strong and unaffected, but inside I was nothing but a heartbroken disaster.

I was moving but I wasn't feeling, looking but not seeing. I boarded the bus to Kara's place and walked the distance from the bus stop to her place. I was so immersed in pain that it took all my strength to keep it inside. I was in a complete daze. When I crashed into a solid object, I didn't even react. I just crumpled to the ground.

"I'm sorry. Are you all right?"

A deep masculine voice spoke. Someone knelt in front of me, but I couldn't see. My vision was blurry.

"Damn." A low curse. "Here, I got you."

I felt strong arms pull me up, then push a cloth into my hand. I looked at it, bewildered.

"For your tears," he said. "You're crying, Angel Face."

I was? My hand reached for my cheek, feeling the wetness there.

"Kar," I choked. "I need Kar."

"Kar? You're out of luck. She's not here, but she'll be back soon." He steered me onto Kara's porch. He sat on the white bench, looking at me expectantly. I followed and sat on the opposite end, as far away from him as I could.

"I'll just wait with you here until Kar comes back. Okay with you?"

I nodded, shutting out everything.

When I heard the strum of a guitar, my head turned toward the sound, and I found him playing the instrument. His long, nimble fingers strummed the strings with expertise.

He was playing "Let Her Go" by Passenger.

Oh, isn't it ironic? I came here to forget, but I was getting salt rubbed into my wound.

His voice was deep and raspy. I closed my eyes, feeling a pang in my chest as I listened to the lyrics.

We sat together without talking. I listened as he played songs. He let me be, didn't ask what was wrong. I was grateful for that.

After a while, I glanced at him. I'd seen him before. I was sure of it. His hair was thick and dark brown, almost black. It was slightly curly and long enough to touch his shoulders. It looked disheveled, as if he ran his hands through it several times. His features were sharp and beautiful, reminding me of a statue of a warrior angel I'd seen once.

He wore an ancient short-sleeved black shirt, a pair of old, faded jeans that had holes on the knees, and Converse sneakers. Sitting comfortably, one leg crossed over the other, with the guitar propped on his knee, he continued to play. He looked at ease in his own body.

He impatiently swatted the hair that fell on his face, revealing three silver stud earrings in his right ear. Around his wrist was a black leather band that was fraying at the edges, like he hadn't taken it off in years. I spotted several rings on his fingers.

He stopped and pulled a black hair band out of his back pocket. Placing it between his teeth, he reached back and gathered his long, dark hair in his fist and quickly tied it in a messy bun. Then he started to play again.

There was something wild and masculine about him, I observed as I studied him—something free. He had an I-don't-give-a-damn air about him. I envied that.

Startling light-blue eyes looked at me curiously, deep dimples popping out as he smiled.

"You still have my towel?" He had a twinkle in his eye that I assumed warned everyone he was trouble. And I'd had enough trouble.

Towel? What was he talking about?

He had a slight accent that I couldn't place. I realized I didn't even know his name or what he was doing here when I heard someone call my name.

"Ver?"

Kara. I willed myself to calm down, get a grip. My gaze was steady as I turned to look at her, but then she asked, "What's wrong?"

I thought I had it under control, but just one look from my best friend—the look that told me she knew something bad had happened, knew I was hurting—and all the emotions I was desperately trying to keep inside spilled out. "Kar," I sobbed.

"Oh, sweetie." She wrapped her arms around me as the tears began to flow.

"Damon! What did you do to her, you bastard! You always make girls cry. What did you say?"

He raised his hands in surrender. "I'm innocent."

Kara shook her head. "Come on, let's get you inside."

She led me to the kitchen. "Sit down, Ver." She filled a glass with ice water and handed it to me. "What happened?"

The water was cold as it slid down my parched throat. I concentrated on that feeling, wishing my heart was as hard and cold as the ice that clinked against the glass.

My eyes darted to Damon, who was now lying on the floor, half of his body disappearing under the sink. His hand reached blindly for the toolbox sitting beside his hip. Kara kicked it closer to him.

"Don't mind him. He's here to fix a leak." Then she pointed at her ears. "He's always got his earphones in when he's working so he won't hear us. Now, Ver, you better tell me what happened before I explode and kill someone. Caleb will be the first on my list. How did he fuck up?"

I shook my head. I didn't want to talk, didn't want to rehash it. I just wanted to curl into a ball and forget about it. *Maybe I should sleep, and when I wake up, it will all be a dream.*

Kara shook my shoulders when she didn't get a response.

"Kar, I just...want to sleep for now. Can I use your spare bedroom? I'll tell you everything when I wake up."

"No. You tell me now."

I jumped in my seat when I heard the doorbell.

"Stay here," she ordered. "I'm expecting a package. When I come back, you better fess up."

When she was gone, I stretched my arms on the table and buried myself in them.

I hated the hope and fear that had sprung into my chest when I'd heard the doorbell ring. How pathetic was I to expect that it might be Caleb? Of course he wouldn't follow me. Why would he? Did I even want him to?

No, I didn't. In fact, I never wanted to see him again. If he had the power—the *carelessness*—to hurt me this much, I didn't want him in my life. He never should have been in it in the first place.

When I heard a commotion in the living room, I smashed my hands against my ears. I just wanted to be left alone.

"Red."

I froze.

No. No. No.

My heart was thundering against my chest, but I dared not move.

It was his voice. Caleb's voice.

"Red," he repeated, his voice soft.

It was really him. He'd followed me.

I felt mixed emotions—relief because he had come after me, anger at his betrayal.

I curled my hands into fists, wishing I was somewhere else. Wishing last night hadn't happened. That Beatrice-Rose had never come... But she had. If it hadn't been last night, it would have been another night. It still would have happened.

When I felt his hand on my shoulder, I flinched. I pushed away from the table, the scrape of the chair against the floor hurting my ears. "Don't touch me!" I shouted. His touch burned.

My breath stuttered when I took in the raw pain on his face. I thought I would be unbreakable when I saw him again, but the sight of his handsome face and the wounded look in his eyes cut me deep.

Caleb always appeared put together, but as he stood in front of me, he looked rough. His clothes were disheveled, his hair tousled.

"I shouldn't have let you leave," he whispered.

I closed my eyes tightly for a moment, composing myself. I bit my lip as hard as I could. Maybe if I bit hard enough, that pain would eclipse what I was feeling in my heart.

"Please leave," I choked out.

"Hear me out. Then I will," he begged. "Please."

"Do we have a problem here?" Damon interrupted, suddenly standing beside me.

Caleb's eyes hardened as he glowered at him. "Back off, Damon."

"Last time I checked, I don't answer to you, Lockhart."

My eyes widened in alarm as I watched Caleb take a threatening step toward Damon. Flexing his arms, Caleb curled his hands into fists, ready to hit Damon.

"You do now," Caleb snapped. "Get away from her."

I had never seen Caleb so hostile and angry toward another person.

"Stop!" I shouted, stepping between them and thrusting my palms against their chests. It felt like I was trying to stop two speeding trains about to collide.

"Stop!" I repeated, glaring at Caleb. "I'll talk to you outside."

"Damon!" Kara rushed in the kitchen, grabbed Damon's arm and tugged. "Save your hero complex for another time and leave them alone. Let's go. I forgot something at Dad's."

I threw Kara a grateful look. She mouthed *Call me* and then left, tugging Damon behind her.

Not waiting for Caleb to answer, I slammed open the screen door that led to Kara's backyard and stepped out. I had walked a few steps when I felt Caleb behind me. I needed space away from him.

The sun was glaringly bright and high in the clear azure sky, the wind whooshing musically through the trees. Birds crooned their cheery tunes.

It seemed cruel that the world was moving on when I wasn't ready. The world didn't wait for anyone. Even when someone had fallen on their knees, screaming and hurting, it continued its course, unblinking and pitiless. It didn't care.

I knew this. I knew this before I met Caleb. Whatever pain I felt was my fault. I should never have trusted him.

I stiffened when I heard his footsteps behind me. He stood close enough that I could feel the heat emanating from his body.

"I didn't sleep with her last night, Red. I would never deliberately hurt you."

I spun around to face him. "Then why didn't you answer me when I asked you?"

"Because when I asked if you trusted me, you didn't answer. And I knew by the look on your face that you didn't... You don't. And that fucking hurts."

I looked away from his eyes. It hurt too much to look at him.

"I fell asleep. I didn't mean to. I fucked up, but it's not what you think."

I didn't know if I believed him. I wiped my face free of any emotion.

"She said she was your first."

He sucked in a sharp breath. "Yes, that's true."

It felt like someone had punched me in the stomach. I wrapped my arms around myself, my shoulders hunching.

"You already know we grew up together. At that young age, I wanted to have someone to protect. It felt good. I was always there for her, and she came to depend on me. It became a habit. And I felt...responsible for her.

"I'm not sure when it started to change," he continued. "In high school, I guess. We were on vacation in Greece with our families. Beatrice-Rose wasn't feeling good, and she asked me to stay with her at the hotel. She kissed me, and I...responded."

"You mean you had sex with her."

It was a moment before he answered. "Yes. My relationship

with her was complicated. We'd hook up on and off for years. It never meant anything more than sex—"

"It sure as hell meant more to her." I glared accusingly, fury coloring my voice. "And if you didn't know that, you're not just stupid, you're insensitive. It's so obvious she's in love with you."

The look of pure shock on his face made me realize he had no idea Beatrice-Rose was in love with him. My heart ached. Now that he did, would he…would he do something about it? Go back to her?

"Red. I stopped sleeping with her more than a year ago. I told her we had to stop. I didn't want to ruin our friendship. It wouldn't matter if she's in love with me. I'm not with her. I never was. I'm—"

I cut him off. "What happened last night?"

His nostrils flared. "Last night, when she started to cry, I knew she was close to having a panic attack. She's had them since high school. After her panic attacks, she'd have a hard time falling asleep, so she'd call me. And I'd…"

When he trailed off, I said, "And you'd have sex with her."

He clenched his teeth. "Yes, but I told you we'd stopped a long time ago. After that, she'd still call me and I'd just lie in bed with her. For some reason, I always calmed her down."

I swallowed past the lump in my throat. "And last night?"

"She wanted me to stay the night, but even if I hadn't promised you I'd come home, I wouldn't have stayed the night with her. It's different now. *You* made it different, Red."

He breathed deeply and continued. "I was only planning to stay until she fell asleep. But she asked me to lie down beside her—"

No.

I closed my eyes tightly, pursing my lips so that no sound came out. But I wanted to shout, to lash out at him, to hurt him the way he was hurting me now.

"It was habit." His voice shook. I opened my eyes and saw his anguish. "I wanted to get home to you. I knew the faster she fell asleep, the faster I could leave. But it felt wrong. I shouldn't have done it. I screwed up, Red, and I am sorry. It was a mistake. I fell asleep beside her and was dreaming of you, and I—"

"Stop." I said it calmly, although inside I was screaming. "Just stop."

How could he expect me to believe him when he just unknowingly admitted his betrayal to me? He'd said he calmed her down by having sex with her. What made him think I would believe this time it was different?

He drove her home and stayed with her last night. *Slept* with her last night.

Did he really expect me to believe nothing happened? Especially with his track record, his blasé attitude toward sex...

"Red—"

"Don't call me that!" My eyes burned with unshed tears I refused to let him see. "I don't want you to call me that ever again." I was breathing fast, my chest heaving. "I want you to leave."

I turned away from him and walked toward the house.

"Goddamn it!" His hand slapped the screen door to prevent me from opening it. "Goddamn it. Don't go."

When I heard his voice break, I crumpled inside.

"Is it a crime for me to ask for…to *want* your trust? It hurts me that you don't trust me. It hurts a fucking lot."

My grip on the doorknob loosened, and I let my hand fall to my side.

"What am I to you?" he demanded painfully. He turned me around to face him.

My throat tightened and burned. Even if I'd wanted to answer him, I couldn't have. When he reached for my face, I turned away.

"Don't," I choked out.

"Am I… Am I not even worth a fight?" he whispered. "Red?"

"I said—" I bit the words out, feeling angrier when I heard my voice quiver. "Don't. Call. Me. That."

I'd known from the start that he would hurt me if I let him in. I had let him in, and he had hurt me more than I could possibly imagine. I wanted to hurt him just as much before he could do even more damage. So I lashed out and hurt him as deeply as I could.

To protect myself.

I looked him in the eyes. "I want you to leave me alone from now on. I don't want to see you. I don't want to hear from you. It's not going to work out between you and me. It never will."

"Liar."

"I was desperate," I said. "You were convenient."

He grabbed my upper arms, his eyes full of rage as he stared at me. "I don't believe you."

I gave him a careless shrug and shook off his hold on me, showing him I didn't care. But my heart was breaking. Because

I was so afraid of getting hurt, so terrified of being weak like my mother, that the panic was a constant threat in my chest. My dark thoughts about him had been right all along.

"I don't care what you did with her, what you do with her. *I don't care.* You can sleep with whoever you like. That's what you're used to anyway. That's who you really *are.*"

His eyes blazed with anger. Without warning, he gripped my shoulders and yanked me to him, burying his face in my hair with a ferocity that took my breath away.

I felt my resolve weaken.

"No!" I pounded his chest with my fists, trying to push him away. "Let go of me!" But he held on tighter.

"Don't ask me to let go of you. I can't," he said against my ear. "I can't."

My body sagged against him, all the fight draining out of me. I was horrified as the tears I'd bottled up started to flow.

"I have given you more of myself than I have given anyone, Caleb." I sobbed, the ice around my heart cracking.

"I'm sorry," he said softly, leaning his forehead against mine. "I would never hurt you. You are the only one."

I closed my eyes as his hand caressed my face. "God," he whispered. "Don't cry. Please, don't cry."

His lips found mine, coaxing and gentle, breaking down my defenses.

"I want more. Not just scraps. I want all of you," he said desperately.

As if he sensed I was softening, his hands gently held the sides of my neck, his thumbs tenderly stroking my skin. When his arms wrapped around my waist to pull me closer, I gave in to his kiss. I forgot everything as his tongue delved deeply in my mouth, claiming me. His body was hard, his hands hot on my skin.

And then my sanity returned.

"No!"

I pushed him back, but he held on to me.

How many times had I seen my mother give in to my father just like this? I was so scared I would give in, forget what he did, and forgive him over and over again. Until I lost myself. He *couldn't* have all of me. That was the point.

"Let me go!"

When he finally released me, I swiped my mouth angrily with the back of my hand, erasing his kiss. Erasing him.

"Just stop it!" I yelled. "How do I get rid of you? God, you're like an annoying stray dog!"

He took a step back, his eyes wild and hot with anger. "Is that what I am to you?"

No, but I have to hurt you now.

I was like an injured animal, cornered with no other option but to lash out—lashing out in fear as my heart was breaking. To protect myself, I had to. It was like watching my own train wreck, and there was nothing I could do to stop it.

The rope is fraying. It just needs a little tug to sever it.

"You only think about what *you* want. What about what *I* want? This, us." I waved a hand between us. "It all happened so fast. I told you I wasn't ready, but you kept pushing for more. I can't give you more, Caleb. I'm done. And I want you to leave me the hell alone."

I stared at him, at the naked misery on his handsome face, and destroyed what was left. Of me. Of him. Of us.

"I. Don't. Want. You," I said.

Liar.

His eyes turned cold as they narrowed at me. My heart, already broken, cracked in two.

"You're a coward." His voice was just as cold. "Do you remember when you told me you refuse to be weak? That you won't give up?"

I did. I remembered.

"You're giving up now. You're weak because you're too afraid to get hurt. Well, you know what? You have to fight for something if you really want it. I have been chasing you—fighting for you—since the moment I met you. You kept pushing me away, but I never gave up. I wanted you to fight for me, just as I fought for you. But you wouldn't."

He took a deep breath, his hand shaking as he rubbed his face.

"You told me to let you go. And because I have *always* given everything you asked of me, I will leave you alone. I will let you go."

The grief came in waves, but I held it all in.

He turned, stepping away from me. He reached for the screen door and stood there with his hand suspended above the doorknob.

I held my breath as I watched him slowly drop his hand to his side, lowering his gaze to the ground. Then he turned and looked at me with eyes as cold as ice.

"Goodbye," he said softly. "Veronica."

CHAPTER
thirty-three

Caleb

As I ran through the streets, I rode on a wave of anger.
It became my friend, blinding me to my other, deeper wound:
the truth. The truth made you face the ugly reality; it brought
you pain. Maybe that was why people held on to their anger.
They preferred it over feeling pain.

My lungs burned, and my legs were about to give out. I'd
been running for two hours straight, trying to exhaust myself,
trying not to think about *her*.

*How do I get rid of you? God, you're like an annoying stray
dog!*

I ran faster, my sneakers pounding on the pavement.

I don't want you.

I could hear my breathing, harsh and loud. My chest felt
tight, and my heart hammered against my ribs so fast I thought
it would burst.

*I don't care. You can sleep with whoever you like. That's what
you're used to anyway. That's who you really are.*

Sweat dripped down my face, stinging my eyes.

Fuck.

Had I ever felt this kind of pain before? No, I realized,
because I had never fallen in love. Until Red. And look where
that had gotten me.

There was a reason I didn't commit myself to any girl: because
I didn't want to experience this. I knew I wasn't a saint before I
met her, but—dammit all to hell—I very nearly was after. From
the moment I laid eyes on her, I never wanted anyone else.
She never trusted me, never gave me—*us*—a fighting chance.
I knew I had a reputation, and she had trust issues. But I had
fought hard to prove myself, to show her she was the only one.
But that hadn't meant anything. She'd always expected the
worst from me.

That's who you really are, I thought bitterly as I entered my
apartment.

I was better off alone. I wished I could go back to the days
when I didn't care about a girl who could slash me so easily
with a look, cut me so deeply with her indifference and her
lack of trust.

Anger building, I showered and got dressed. I'd show her
who I really was.

I smelled a mix of various perfumes and body sweat, fried food
and whiskey as I entered a new club down the street I hadn't

been to before. Techno music blasted my ears, and blinking neon lights blinded me as I waded through the dark club to find a seat. The dance floor was already packed with people.

If the scene didn't excite me like it usually did, like I expected it to, I ignored the feeling and looked for an empty table. When I didn't find one, I went to the bar and sat on one of the backless stools there. I caught the bartender's eye and ordered a beer.

"Rough night?"

I glanced to my right where a pretty brunette occupied the seat next to mine. A tight, black dress showcased her body, revealing a lot of skin. Her eyes gleamed with the confidence of a female who knew her own allure.

I knew this game, had played it countless times.

"Not anymore," I replied, but my comment lacked enthusiasm. She didn't seem to notice as she flashed her perfect white teeth at me, smiling prettily.

If I remembered correctly, this would be the perfect time to ask if she wanted to go somewhere else.

Some girls needed flattery to make them feel better about sleeping with a stranger, and some girls needed to be bought a few drinks or maybe share a few moves on the dance floor.

It was all a game. A sick game where no one really came out the winner.

Because in the end, we'd both still feel hollow.

Red had made me feel…

"I'm sorry," I said, smiling at her apologetically. "I can't do this."

The thought of being with another girl made my stomach churn. I pushed away from the bar.

You only think about what you want. What about what I want? This, us, it all happened so fast. I told you I wasn't ready, but you kept pushing for more. I can't give you more, Caleb. I'm done. And I want you to leave me the hell alone.

Fuck that.

I walked blindly toward the exit, not caring if I bumped into anyone. I heard a woman yell and ignored it. I just wanted to get the hell out of there.

"Are you fucking blind, asshole? You spilled my girlfriend's drink, and you think you can just walk the fuck out?"

The guy yelled in my face, his spit flying. He moved really close, grabbing my arm.

"Get your hand off me," I said quietly.

He shoved me, and I lost it after that. I just started swinging. The next thing I knew, I was being hauled out of the club.

"Don't come back here, dumbass."

My ribs hurt and my jaw throbbed as I stumbled into the parking lot. I looked down at my fists and noted the blood on them. It wasn't mine.

When I got in my car, I thought of *her*. This wasn't the club where I met her, wasn't the same parking lot. But I thought of her anyway.

I thought of her red dress, her red lips, her intense dark eyes that stripped my soul. Eyes that looked older than her age, eyes that said she had been through a lot.

I have given you more of myself than I have given anyone, Caleb.

I closed my eyes and rested my head on the steering wheel.

She could have opened up my chest and ripped out my heart, and that would have been better than what I was feeling now.

I drove aimlessly, turning up the volume on the radio to block my thoughts. I didn't realize until I was slowing down that I was on Kara's street.

Red told me to let her go. What was I doing here?

Hadn't I had enough of chasing someone who didn't want me?

Why can't I let her go?

I knew I should leave. But I parked on the street, staring at the light in the living room window. I was still angry, hurt, but like the loser I was, I hoped to catch a glimpse of her.

My eyes narrowed as I spotted a familiar figure on a motorcycle stop in front of Kara's apartment. He was clad in a black leather jacket and black pants. His helmet covered his face, but I knew who it was.

His head was turned toward the door. He stayed there, his body tense, as if debating whether to go in or ride away.

I rolled down my window. "Want a beer?" I shouted.

He lifted his visor and nodded at me. "Back at my place."

I nodded and followed him.

***

"Stalking your ex?" I asked Cameron when he stepped out from the kitchen into the backyard. It was almost two in the morning when we arrived at his place. I waited for him in his backyard while he got us some beers.

He handed me one and nodded, not even trying to deny it. "Now and then."

"I'm ashamed to tell people that I know you." I let out a breath. "But I can top that."

"I don't think so," he scoffed, taking the seat beside me. "What were you doing at my…" He cleared his throat. "At Kara's?"

It was easier to tell him since I'd caught him there first. "Same thing you were doing. Red…" My voice trailed off. Her face swam in my vision—angry, hurt, and then closed off as she told me not to call her that anymore. "Veronica," I corrected, "is staying at your girl's place. She ended it between us."

Her name felt foreign on my tongue. Veronica. I loved her name. It was strong, beautiful. But she was Red to me.

"Sorry, man."

Restless, I got up from my seat and walked to the edge of the pool, staring at the lights reflecting on the water.

"Yeah. We were doing good. No, fuck that. We were doing *great*. Or I thought we were. And then I fucked it up." I chugged my beer. "Beatrice-Rose came over to my place."

"Damn. Did your girl know about you and Beatrice-Rose?"

I could feel the headache coming on, so I pressed my fingers against my eyelids.

She isn't my girl anymore.

"No. That's another piece of crap on my shitty pile of things-I-should-have-told-her."

He nodded. "I wouldn't have told her either, if it's any consolation. You didn't necessarily lie to her. You just didn't tell her."

I nodded, pleased that he understood.

"But she wouldn't see it that way, you know? Kara…" He cleared his throat. "Let's just say I know how a girl gets when she finds out about your ex from another source. It's not pretty." He stood beside me, handed me another beer.

"I don't know why women want to dig up the past. It's like a freaking obsession for them." Cameron chuckled. "She said she didn't care about the one-night stands. They didn't count as far as she was concerned. But the ones that lasted more than a couple weeks—the ones that came close to relationship material—she *demanded* to know about." He took a long pull on his beer. "Like it was the cure for cancer or something. Like it would change what I felt for her." He wiped his mouth with the back of his hand. "She was it for me."

Cameron rarely talked about Kara. I glanced at him, surprised. He was looking out into the darkness. Pensive, lonely.

"You and Kara—" I started.

He shook his head. "I didn't ask you to come here to talk about Kara, man. I can't…can't talk about her more than that."

I recognized the look in his eyes. It was pain, like he was being tortured. Maybe that was why he'd opened up to me about Kara. He'd recognized the same look in my eyes.

It hurt to talk about the girl you loved most…and lost.

"Fair enough," I conceded.

"So you going to tell me what happened?"

"Do you remember in high school when Beatrice-Rose used to get panic attacks?"

"Yeah. You always came to her rescue. That girl played you like a violin."

I stopped and stared at him. "What?"

He shrugged. "Tell you later. Keep going."

Cameron had never liked Beatrice-Rose.

"Yesterday she came by my place, and I introduced her to Red." I shook my head, remembering. "Her wineglass broke and Beatrice-Rose nearly had a panic attack, so I drove her back to her place. It was a mess. Her mom was drunk, and then her dad showed up. He is…really sick with dementia, and it was bad, really bad. Screaming, swearing at them. He didn't even recognize Beatrice-Rose." Restless, I rubbed my face. "She broke down after that. She asked me to stay. I didn't want to; I felt uneasy. I just wanted to get back to my girl. But how the hell can I refuse Beatrice-Rose after seeing that? She's my friend, and she needed me. What kind of a friend leaves a friend in need?"

Cameron nodded.

"She said she's taking pills again. I don't know what pills, but if they were anything like the ones she took in high school, they're bad news. She asked me to lie down beside her. And I fucked up, Cam. I fucked up because I didn't think. I lay next to her, thinking only of helping her go to sleep. Thinking she'd fall asleep faster that way, because we used to do that. She'd be out like a light if I did. Then I could get the hell out of there and go back to my girl. The next thing I know, I wake up and she's on top of me. She was kissing me. And her top was off. Fucking hell."

I gulped beer, feeling sick to my stomach.

"Damn" was all Cameron said.

"I know."

He raised his brows. "Did I tell you why I never liked her?"

"I think so, but I probably wasn't paying attention."

He gestured with his beer. "That's your problem, man. You always turn a blind eye to the people you love. She's manipulative. A great actress. Did you know she's sleeping with Justin?"

"What?"

"I was going to tell you at school tomorrow, but hell, you're here now." He sighed as if telling me was a big burden. "I had a drink with Justin last night, and he was juiced. Running his mouth off about Beatrice-Rose."

"What'd he say?"

"Everyone thinks she's your on-and-off girlfriend. I knew better. She was your booty call." He shrugged. "But when she wasn't with you, she went to Justin to get what you weren't giving her. Still does, apparently."

"We weren't exclusive. She can go out with whoever she wants."

I cared for Beatrice-Rose, loved her as a friend, but I never felt for her anything even close to what I felt for…Red. Dammit, I was calling her Red, and that was that.

"Yeah, but there were other things too."

I frowned. "What other things?"

"Justin said she was faking her panic attacks."

"What are you talking about?"

"She played you, man. She's been faking them to get you to go to her."

"Why would she do that…" My voice trailed off, my eyes widening in horror. I immediately thought of last night, the events playing in my head like a movie.

She's in love with you, Red had said.

My heart thundered in my chest. Had Beatrice-Rose planned what happened last night? Had she pretended to have a panic attack to get me to drive her home? To get me to stay with her?

I went numb. She knew me well enough to know I was different with Red. Maybe she'd even figured out that I was in love with Red, but she still kissed me while I was asleep. Did she deliberately do that to…break us up? Beatrice-Rose knew me, knew what buttons to push to make me stay.

She wouldn't dare.

The information came from Justin, and everyone knew he got off on spreading lies about people. But what if it was true?

The headache was drilling a hole in my head now, and anger was filling it. If Beatrice-Rose had manipulated me, I didn't know what I would do to her. Last night had cost me the only girl I loved.

I had to hear the truth from Beatrice-Rose. But not tonight. I'd had enough. I was drained.

"I need to shut down for a while. Got anything here I can demo?"

He laughed. "Sorry, no. Got a new video game, though," Cameron offered, clapping me on the back.

"Thank God."

"Let's go, then. If you're going to be in my crew, try to keep up this time. I'm tired of covering your ass."

I raised my brows. "You'll be covering this ass with kisses when we're done."

"That's what I told your mom last night."

Thank God for best friends.

———

I didn't go home. There were too many memories of Red at my apartment, and I wasn't sure I could handle them tonight. Video games helped me shut off my brain.

When I'd lost count of how many beers I'd had, I told Cameron the rest of the story. I didn't really expect him to say anything, but then he spoke.

"Some people are more work than others, but hell, if she's worth it, then go back and fix it."

"Then why didn't you fix things with Kara?"

He was silent for a moment.

"Because," he said quietly, "*I'm* not worth it."

He got up and told me he was going to bed.

I stared at the ceiling for hours, torturing myself with thoughts of her. Thinking about what Cameron had said.

Red was, without a question, more work than anyone I knew.

Was she worth it?

Hell, yes, she was.

But I still had my pride, and she'd stomped on it pretty bad.

She always had a shield that pushed people away, made her look distant, like she didn't give a damn. But she did care.

I had a bad habit of losing my keys, never remembering where I put them. But Red had placed a pretty bowl beside the umbrella stand in the living room, and she'd put them there for me. I felt how much she cared every time I saw those keys in the bowl.

I felt it when I woke up in the morning and walked into the kitchen and saw her cooking pancakes. I felt it when she looked at me like she couldn't figure out what to do with me. Her eyes would be confused and wary at first, and then they'd clear up and grow warm, as if she was telling herself it was okay to be happy. She'd smile at me sweetly, and I'd feel a squeeze in my heart.

Then go back and fix it, Cameron had said.

The next thing I knew, my alarm was going off. I didn't want to get up—I'd hardly slept a wink—but Red might be at school. Maybe I could...start fixing it.

I borrowed some of Cameron's clothes and drove us both to school.

The guys were talking and laughing as we joined them, but I couldn't tune in. We were walking in the hallways, and my eyes couldn't help scanning the crowd for *her.*

She wasn't there.

"You look like shit, dude," Justin commented.

I narrowed my eyes at him. I shrugged—and then froze. I would have missed her if I hadn't looked up at that exact moment. Red looked like she was in a hurry as she entered the washroom.

Did she see me? Was she hurrying because she didn't want me to see her?

I walked past the washrooms, my heart pounding. If she wanted to hide from me, that could only mean there was no chance of her listening to what I had to say. I kept walking with the guys, lost in thought. The look on her face pulled at me. She'd looked sad and tired, like she'd had trouble sleeping last night. Was it because she was thinking of me? It had to be.

"So, Caleb, tell me: Was it pussy?" Justin asked. "You're not getting it enough from your old lady? If you were, you'd look a hell of a lot more relaxed than—"

I shoved him, wanting to smash his face in. "Don't you fucking talk about her like that!"

"Hey!" Cameron held me back. My shoulders were tense, my body ready for a fight.

Amos glared at Justin. "That was a dick move, bro."

"I was just fooling around, dude. Chill." Justin held up his hands. "Sorry. Won't happen again."

I ignored him and turned to Cameron. "I'll catch up with you later."

He nodded.

I walked back to the washroom and leaned against the wall like a creep, waiting for her.

Veronica

Clad in her fluffy white bathrobe, Kara prepared a sandwich for me, taking the opportunity to explain a few things. "Loyal men are like unicorns. You've heard of them, seen them in movies, read about them in fairy tales, but I'd have a better chance of shitting one than finding one in real life," Kara declared, closing the ziplock bag containing the sandwich. "Here ya go, luv. Eat this. I only cook for people I love. Don't waste my love because it *don't* come cheap." She sang the last part.

She hadn't cooked anything. It was a peanut butter sandwich, which she knew was my favorite. I love Kar.

She leaned against the kitchen island as she sipped her coffee, studying me. "Why don't you stay in today? You and I didn't get any sleep last night." She choked on her coffee. "Boy, that came out wrong."

Laughing, I grabbed the sandwich and placed it in my bag. I shook my head and slung my backpack over my shoulder. "I can't, Kar. It's…it's just better this way. I *need* to stay busy."

Her eyes filled with understanding. Last night, she and Beth had stayed up late with me, watching movies and eating ice cream like it was going out of style. Nothing beats girls' night.

"I still think there's more to this story."

"Kar," I warned.

"He told you he didn't sleep with Beatrice-Rose, right?" she asked. "She's fast-food sex. That's what she is."

I burst out laughing. One of the things I loved about Kara was that she understood me, but she didn't mollycoddle.

"Fine," Kara continued. "But when you come back, you better make me some *pancakes*," she said, winking.

She knew *pancakes* was a code word between me and Caleb.

I bared my teeth at her before I opened the door. "Can you see the *fuck you* in my smile?"

"Always. You love me anyway. See you later, bitch." She blew me a kiss. "Oh, and I love you too."

I really wanted to stay in with her, but if I did, I would just think about Caleb. And I was bone-tired of thinking about him. Having a broken heart was a full-time job.

***

With my head down, I walked through the hallways to my locker. I was afraid I would see him, but I knew his usual hangouts. I just needed to avoid those places.

I felt my skin prickle, and I looked up. I froze, my heart jumping into my throat.

It was Caleb. He was a few feet away, walking toward me with his entourage. He was wearing a black college sweatshirt with the hoodie up, his sleeves rolled up his forearms, and cargo pants and black boots. He looked...exhausted but so handsome.

It hurt to look at him.

I darted inside the washroom before he saw me. Running into one of the stalls, I locked it and sat on the toilet cover, wrapping my arms around myself.

This is pathetic, I thought sourly, but I didn't leave.

So what if he saw me? I would have to face him sooner or later. I couldn't hide from him forever. But I couldn't see him...not right now. Not even tomorrow, or next week. Or next month.

I think I'm ready to move to Japan now, or Indonesia, maybe. I hear it's a very beautiful country.

I stiffened when I heard the bathroom door open.

"Veronica?"

What the hell?

"I know you're in there. Please. I just want to talk."

I don't. I really don't.

I took deep breaths, trying to calm myself. It was impossible. Adrenaline had already flooded my system.

When I opened the door, Beatrice-Rose was waiting for me.

The sight of her made me angry, with her innocent-looking eyes and her beautiful face. Her face was her weapon, I realized. She used it to dupe people into thinking she was harmless, when in truth she was as cunning as a snake.

"Hi." She spoke softly, biting her lip. She looked...guilty.

I narrowed my eyes at her.

"I just want to apologize for last night. I'm so sorry," she pleaded, looking contrite. "It was my fault. Caleb had nothing to do with it. The kiss...last night...wasn't his fault. It was mine."

The kiss.

What kiss?

Caleb told me he didn't sleep with her... *Oh my God.*

"It was only going to be a kiss, I swear. But...one thing led to another, like it always does with me and Caleb, and before we knew it, we were all over each other. I'm so sorry, Veronica. Caleb and I...he and I...had sex last night. I don't hold him responsible, and you shouldn't either. I'm so sorry. I didn't mean to hurt you. I didn't mean to ruin your relationship. It just happened. It *always* happens."

My throat closed up, and my limbs felt cold and numb. I

stared at her unblinkingly, at her eyes filled with apology and sincerity.

It lasted only a second, and I would have missed it if I had blinked, but the side of her lip lifted in a triumphant smirk.

My palm tingled.

"Veronica, I hope you now understand that Caleb and I will always—"

She didn't finish what she was going to say because I walked right up to her, lifted my hand, and slapped her across the face—hard. Her head snapped to the side.

I could see the red mark and the imprint of my fingers on her white cheek.

Her mouth opened in shock, her hand covering the spot where I'd slapped her. When she turned to face me, her eyes were filled with hate.

"Drop the act," I said quietly.

"I-I don't know what you're talking about, Veronica."

Her innocent mask was back in place. I dug my nails into my palms, resisting the urge to punch her. Maybe knock out a few of her teeth.

"I know your type," I said. "You may have fooled everyone, but you don't fool me."

Beatrice-Rose licked her lips, shaking her head. "You're mistaken. I know you're hurt that he broke up with you last night, but he and I... We loved each other even before you came in the picture. Caleb is—"

"You're pathetic," I bit out. I realized at that moment that I'd had enough. This girl wasn't worth another second of my time.

I forced myself to walk away steadily. I was so angry I started to shake.

I pushed open the door and stepped out of the washroom. My vision was fuzzy, but I kept going.

"Red."

I whirled around so fast that Caleb had to grasp my arms to steady me. Shocked, hurt, and confused, I stared at him. What was he doing here?

And then it hit me.

He'd called me a coward when *he* was the coward. Did he send Beatrice-Rose inside to talk to me while he waited outside? He didn't even have the courage to tell me himself.

In the back of my mind, I was hoping he hadn't lied, that he'd told me the truth yesterday…but I was right all along. Caleb had lied to me.

He said he didn't sleep with her. But he did. He did. He did.

Furious, I pushed him away. Then I slapped *him* in the face. Hurt and confusion reflected in his eyes as he looked at me.

"I hate you," I lashed out at him. "I fucking hate you."

I turned away from him. When I heard the washroom door open and Beatrice-Rose's shocked voice calling for Caleb, I ran.

My vision blurred. I didn't know where I was going. I just wanted to get the hell away from him. From them.

I lost my breath when I collided with a hard object and strong arms wrapped around me.

"We have to stop meeting like this, Angel Face. Hey, what's wrong?"

Damon.

"I'm going to start bringing tissues with me if you keep this up," he teased.

"Get your fucking hands off her!"

I spun around when I heard Caleb's furious voice. Damon's arms only tightened around me.

"I said, get your fucking hands off her," Caleb repeated, his voice sharp with warning. His eyes were wild and blazing with anger as they zeroed in on Damon's arms around me.

"What if I don't want to?" Damon challenged.

"No," I murmured. "Just let go, Damon. I don't want trouble." I tried to pry open his arms, but he wasn't budging.

There was a daredevil gleam in his eye as he whispered, "Oh, I think trouble is your middle name."

I watched in horror as Caleb threw the first punch, snapping Damon's head back. Damon relaxed his hold on me, and I stepped away, horrified.

He cupped his jaw, moving it from side to side, checking if anything was broken. "You're going to pay for that, Lockhart."

He lunged at Caleb, punching him in the stomach. They both went insane after that. I tried to get between them to stop them, but someone yanked me away.

"Stop! Stop! Get your hands off me!" I screamed.

"Sorry, but I'd pay to see this." The sadism in the voice made me look behind me.

"You!" I spat out.

It was Caleb's teammate who had brought him home the other night. The creep. He held me too tightly, my back facing him.

"Me." He winked. "I'm Justin, by the way. I don't think we were properly introduced last time."

"I don't care who you are." I struggled against his hold. "Stop them!"

Damon grabbed Caleb from behind in a firm choke hold. Caleb responded by driving his elbow into Damon's stomach. I shut my eyes.

"Why?" Justin asked.

Was he serious?

"Let go of me!"

"You're not breaking this up. I've never seen Caleb this mad before. You sure did a number on him, sweetheart."

My skin crawled as I felt his hot breath on my neck.

Inspired, I relaxed my body, indicating I wouldn't struggle anymore. When his hold on me loosened, I clenched my fist and elbowed him in the stomach as hard as I could—just like I'd seen Caleb do.

He let go of me, clutching his stomach in pain. "You bitch!"

"You'll get more than that if you touch me again, asshole."

I refused to rub my arms to ease the pain from his hard grip. I could feel bruises forming already, but I didn't want to give him the satisfaction.

When I spotted security coming to break up the fight, I let out a relieved sigh. But my mouth dropped open when I turned and saw Caleb. He looked livid, his mouth formed into a snarl as he glowered at Damon. I could see a bruise forming on his right eye.

Damon was sprawled on the floor, propping himself up on

one elbow, his hand massaging his jaw. He had a lopsided grin and blood on his lips.

My first instinct was to go to Caleb. Stepping toward him, I froze when I saw Beatrice-Rose run to him.

Something inside me cracked. I looked away.

"You okay, Angel Face?" Damon asked from behind me. I should be the one asking him that. He got into this because of me. I turned to face him. He rose, still massaging his jaw.

"Damon, I'm so sorry."

"Red."

Caleb. My back was to him, but I could just picture the pleading look on his handsome face by the sound of his voice. I closed my eyes tightly, blocking the image. I had to walk away.

"Let's go," I told Damon.

Caleb didn't follow me this time.

CHAPTER
thirty-four

Beatrice-Rose

"DAD?"

He sat in his wheelchair, staring through his window at a spot in the garden. Dazed with drugs, he didn't hear me. His eyes were glassy, his skin dry and pale. The nurse had tried to comb his hair, but it was all wrong. My dad never combed his hair to the side. It was always combed back.

Stupid nurses. We paid them so well, and yet they couldn't do their work properly.

I pushed myself up from kneeling in front of him and opened the drawer in his nightstand. He always loved his things in order. When I found his comb, I smiled and walked back to him.

"I'm just going to fix your hair, okay, Dad?"

I squeezed his hand, then I started combing his hair back. He used to have thick, dark hair, but it was now thin and graying. It terrified me how the people you love get old.

I didn't like old people. They scared me.

"Dad? Do you remember the pet rabbit you gave me when I was four? His name was Atlas, after that Titan you told me about who carried the world on his shoulders." I paused, feeling tears prick my eyes but held them back. "I miss your stories. You used to tell me all these fascinating stories, and I think Mom was jealous of me. Maybe that's why she always hated me, do you think?"

When I smoothed his hair back with my hand, his eyes fell closed. I kept at it until he relaxed.

"I know what you did, Dad. I never told you, but I saw you that day."

I studied his face for any sign that he understood what I was telling him, but his eyes were closed, his face calm and expressionless.

"I heard your car outside, and I was so excited to see you. But Mom was home and she hated it when I interrupted your time with her, so I stayed inside my room for a bit. I knew you'd come knock on my door soon anyway, bringing a present."

My dad always had big hands, but the ones in his lap now were thin and old, with spidery veins popping out under his skin.

"But I waited, and you didn't come. So I went looking for you. I went in your room. Mom told me I wasn't allowed there, but I really missed you. You'd been gone for so long. You were gone all the time."

I tried to keep the resentment out of my voice. I was an expert at hiding my real feelings, but sometimes I couldn't help *something* slipping through the cracks. My mom never loved me, but my dad did very much. I was his spoiled little girl. The only problem was that he was always away for business, for a party, for something. That was a long time ago and I had forgiven him for it, but the feelings of abandonment remained.

"When I saw your suit on the floor, I picked it up. There was a hole on the sleeve, and I knew, Dad. I knew Atlas had chewed it. I was so scared. So I went to search for him. He loved to hide in your garage. Did you know that? So I went there. And I saw it. I saw the blood and white fur on your worktable. I saw the hammer you used to kill him… It was still bloody. I knew you did it because I hid under the table when I heard you come in and I saw you clean it up and I saw your face. You were upset."

I was scratching my arms and I knew I was bleeding from them, but I didn't feel anything.

"That night during supper, when you told me you had bad news to tell me, I wanted you to confess. But instead, you lied to me and told me Atlas ran away. You lied to me, Dad."

My knees felt weak, and I squatted in front of him, holding on to the armrests of his wheelchair for support. I was shaking. I had kept this inside for so long, and I had never forgotten about it. Why did I decide to tell him now? Maybe because I was afraid he would leave me soon. He would die, and he would leave me. Again.

"But I want you to know that I forgive you. I understand why you lied to me. You wanted to protect me. You didn't want me to get hurt. You didn't want me to hate you. You didn't want me to see what you really were. Because we all have roles to play, right, Dad?"

He finally opened his eyes, but he didn't speak.

He didn't have to. I saw in his eyes that he had heard me, and that he was grateful and sorry. And that he loved me very much.

I got up and left.

———

We all had roles to play, and dealing with a lowlife like Justin was part of mine. I changed into a dark-red, long-sleeved dress to cover the scratches on my arms, and I told him to meet me at the photo studio on campus where I stored my equipment. I had a shoot later with a fat-ass socialite I'd met last week. She absolutely disgusted me, but she was friends with my favorite designer and she'd drop my name if I impressed her. Gotta do what you gotta do.

Justin had a role too. Someone I could use to keep tabs on Cal when I was away in Paris or wherever my mom wanted to send me. Someone who could get rid of the hungry sluts who wanted a piece of what was mine.

Caleb was mine. I was his first.

Everyone knew that he would marry me someday. We were perfect for each other. Our families were close, and we'd known each other our whole lives. Everyone knew—except that bitch Veronica. I hated her like I had never hated anyone in my life.

I was on my way to the photo studio when I froze in my tracks. I watched her now as she walked through the hallway, her head bowed low. Her face was sharp, almost fox-like, with big dark eyes and a wide mouth. She wore jeans and a white tank top that made her dusky-gold skin glow, but I knew she'd gotten those clothes from the Salvation Army.

The glow probably came from fucking Caleb day and night. I couldn't blame her. He was irresistible. I wasn't even jealous. He was just being a guy. Soon he'd cast her aside, and Caleb would be beside me again.

I watched as her long, dark hair swayed behind her back, reminding me of a cheap whore.

My mother's voice echoed in my mind. *Whores use their hair to seduce men, Beatrice-Rose. Don't be a whore. Tie your hair appropriately, or you will get the belt.*

What did Caleb see in her?

"She's fucking hot," Justin said, walking up beside me.

I eyed him with disgust. "You'd fuck anything with a skirt."

"You're not wearing a skirt, and I already fucked you."

"Well, I've had better." I smirked at him. He hated being looked down upon. "I need you to make sure Caleb doesn't see her. I need to talk to the bitch."

"Ooh. Catfight. Can I watch?"

I held my breath as I spotted Caleb in the hallway. If he kept walking, he would see Veronica. I couldn't let that happen.

Caleb was an honest person, and very protective. Even when we were kids, we'd get in trouble a lot. I always begged him to lie, to make up a cover story, but he never would. He'd tell the truth and take the blame.

And I knew he had told Veronica what happened. I knew, just from a single phone call from someone, that Veronica had left his apartment, crying her heart out. I barely stopped myself from giggling at the picture. It was a really good day for me. I would not let her steal Caleb from me again.

"He's going to see her," I hissed at Justin. "Do something!"

"He loves that ass. Not you. When will you learn to swallow it, babe?"

"I said, do something! Distract him. Pick a fight with him, but don't hurt him. What am I paying you for?"

"Yeah, yeah."

My fingers clutched the pendant around my neck as I watched Justin approach Caleb. I turned and saw Veronica rush inside the washroom. Perfect.

I walked in there, making sure to put on my fake I'm-so-sorry face. I just needed to make sure that she knew what happened last night. And of course, exaggerate a little bit. Just a little to push her to the edge.

The devastation on her face when I told her I had sex with Caleb made me want to squeal with glee, but I held it in. She absolutely believed me. And why wouldn't she?

I was an expert at this. I'd been at it since high school ever since Caleb slept with other girls and I had to get rid of them. Oh, how I loved this game. They were all pathetic and *so* easy to manipulate.

My work here was done. I should win an Oscar for this.

I was going to find Caleb and celebrate with him—comfort him, give him what he needed—it was me he needed. No one else.

But the bitch was smart. How the fuck did she know I was faking it? Who did she think she was, acting all righteous? She was nothing.

When she slapped me, I wanted to drag her to the toilet and drown her, but I couldn't let her see the real me. I had to be very careful with this game, especially when it came to my Caleb, so I let her go.

I followed her out of the bathroom and when I saw Caleb waiting by the door, I nearly had a heart attack.

When did he get here? Did he hear me?

Shit.

I ducked back into the washroom and took deep breaths to calm myself, thinking carefully about what I should do next. When I finally came out, I heard Veronica shout, "Stop them!"

It sounded like a fight down the hallway, and when I heard Caleb's name, I ran. I reached them just as the fight was over. Cameron was holding Caleb back. I went to him, ready to give comfort.

My baby needed me.

But he didn't even look at me. Instead, he walked past me and went to her.

Her!

A blade sliced through my heart as I watched him go to her, *begging* her. The desperation in his voice, the look of love in his eyes made me want to throw up.

Caleb! You're mine!

"Red," he whispered.

But she ignored him and walked away with some hot guy.

Caleb stood there for a moment, then stormed off down the stairs.

I followed him outside to the parking lot. "Caleb, please talk to me," I begged, trying to keep up with his angry strides.

Everyone has cracks and fissures inside them, and no one had fixed mine like Caleb did. No one understood me like he did; no one appreciated me and showed me love like he did. I needed Caleb almost as much as I needed air to breathe. I would not give up now.

His long legs ate up the asphalt with confidence, but there was an edge to his movements—an anger, a danger that turned me on every time I saw him move. I caught the glint of his bronze hair in the sunlight, his sweater stretched across his broad back and wide shoulders.

He was so beautiful. Everything about Caleb was sex and charm. The way he moved with style and purpose, the way he smiled, the way he looked at someone like they could light up his world. When he spoke, his deep voice made people want to shiver in pleasure. And the way he fucked made his partner forget her name.

I knew he was mad, still shaken from the fight. I was uncertain if he had overheard me in the washroom. I hoped he hadn't.

"I kept calling you last night, but you weren't answering my calls." He continued walking, ignoring me. "Cal, please, wait. Let's talk."

I stayed calm. Caleb always forgave me, even when we were kids. He always protected me, took care of me. And there was no reason for him to not do the same thing now.

When he reached his car and opened the door, I realized he was really going to leave without talking to me. I grabbed his arm.

"Cal, we need to—"

"Get away from me." He jerked his arm away.

He had never pulled away from me with anger before, had never spoken like this to me before. His voice was so cold. At first I wondered if he was being playful, but then I saw that his hands were curled into angry fists, his veins standing out on his forearms. My heart started to pound, and with a deep sense of foreboding, I slowly lifted my eyes to his.

I stopped breathing.

He was furious. The look of hate and disgust in his eyes was nearly paralyzing. I reached for him for reassurance, to make sense of it all, but he backed away.

No...

"I heard every word. Every fucking lie you told her."

I gasped.

All the years I'd spent socializing and cozying up to my parents' business associates had trained me to present the perfect face, the perfect gestures and responses. I was bred to be the perfect socialite. The perfect fake, the perfect liar. But as I stared at the absolute hate in his eyes, I panicked. I couldn't think of anything to defuse his anger.

I knew I had to say something, to repair this somehow. Tears usually got me what I wanted, especially from Caleb. I forced them out, and they cooperated beautifully.

"Cal, I don't know what you heard, but I only apologized to her. To make her understand that last night wasn't your fault."

"It was my fault," he whispered dangerously, glaring at me. "For trusting you."

"No." I shook my head. This wasn't happening. "You don't mean that. I only wanted—"

"We both know what you wanted. Congratulations, you've fucked up my life."

I swallowed my panic. Everything had been perfect between me and Caleb before *she* came into the picture. Now that I was back from Paris, I was going to get Caleb back in my bed—permanently. I'd had it all planned out, and she'd ruined it.

"Caleb, no! I just wanted to protect you. Can't you see who she is? What she's doing? She slapped me, Caleb! And she left you for that guy. She left with him. She knows how to manipulate you—"

"The only one who manipulates people is you. You played me. Tell me, was it hard faking your panic attacks?"

I paled. How did he find out about my panic attacks? Who told him?

I was shaking in fear. My world was crumbling right in front of me. I was going to lose him. I could feel it.

"You told her we're in love. I never loved you that way, Beatrice-Rose." The next words he uttered tore apart my insides. "I'm sorry if you thought I did."

Even though he was angry, I heard the sincerity in his voice.

The tears that poured down my face weren't fake anymore. It felt like someone had ripped my heart out. It hurt so fucking bad.

He was so cold now, so unreachable as he ignored me and opened his car door. He didn't even look at me again when he drove away.

What would you do if the only person you wanted to comfort you was the one who had caused you pain?

Caleb was just confused, blinded by his lust for that whore. Why else would he be obsessed with her, if not for sex?

Once he had sated his lust, he would come back to me. Like he always did. I had been patient and waited for him while he dated other girls, while he gave them his body. I knew I had his heart, and that was enough to reassure me. I had been with Caleb since the beginning, since we were kids. I knew him to the core. We had a history that *she* could never replace. Caleb loved me. He was just distracted. I'd make him remember. I'd make him remember how much he loved me.

Did he think I was going to let him get away from me? Never. He would come back to me. I'd make sure of it.

I have a lot of work to do.

CHAPTER

thirty-five

Veronica

I WISH THERE WAS A WAY TO TURN OFF EVERYTHING I FELT. Feeling pain all the time was exhausting. I was almost blind from it as I walked away from Caleb. I wasn't even sure where I was going as I pushed open doors and stepped outside the school building. I just needed to get away.

"Wait up, Angel Face."

Damon. I had almost forgotten that he was with me.

"I'm sorry." I stopped. A wave of dizziness hit me, and I would have fallen if Damon hadn't caught me.

"Whoa. You need to sit down."

I shook my head. "I'm fine."

"Sit."

His voice brooked no argument. My knees were weak, so he easily led me to a bench near the parking lot.

"You don't have to stay with me, Damon. Please, go."

He let out a loud sigh, sat beside me, and stretched his long legs out in front of him. "Your boyfriend can fight, I'll give him that."

"He's not my boyfriend." But I said it too quickly.

"Really?" His voice was light, almost teasing. "So was the blond his girlfriend, then?"

I gritted my teeth.

"Ah. Listen, I like you. You're tough, but Lockhart? He wants to kill me." Damon grinned like he enjoyed the thought, and then winced in pain. He cupped his jaw and moved it from side to side again. "Because I touched what's his."

I looked down at my hands, noticed they were shaking. I gripped them together.

"A guy like Lockhart won't fight for a girl if she doesn't mean anything to him," he said.

My chest felt tight.

"That guy is crazy for you."

I closed my eyes.

"I don't know what happened, but I've got eyes," Damon continued. "I saw you going to him, but you stopped when the blond reached him first."

"She...told me that Caleb... That they slept together."

"Did they?" he asked after a moment.

"Yes. No. I don't know."

He nodded. "I see."

"I have to go."

I stood up. He grabbed my hand quickly, pulling me down to sit with him again.

"There's no hurry. We have all day." He grinned, the picture of a happy-go-lucky guy. He placed his palms on either side of him and leaned back, looking up at the sky.

"Your lip is bleeding," I said.

He snorted. "So is his. I was going for his nose, but I didn't think you'd appreciate that." He winked. "Answer this for me: Did you get two sides of the story?"

I didn't answer.

"What did he say?" he prompted.

Damon was relentless. When I didn't answer, he let out another loud breath.

"When you have these strong emotions for someone," he said, his voice turning serious, "they tend to take over everything. If they're too strong, they could destroy you, eat you up."

He toyed with the ring on his thumb, a faraway look in his eyes, as if he was replaying a memory in his mind.

Damon was a stranger, but he had an air of openness and honesty that made me want to tell him everything.

"He said he didn't cheat, but he could be lying," I told him.

He nodded. "That's true. He's a liar, isn't he? He's a guy after all." He shrugged one shoulder. "Girls tend to believe other girls over us. She might be lying, but then again, she might be telling the truth. Do you think so?"

No...I don't think she was telling the truth.

When I found Caleb waiting outside the washroom, I'd assumed that he had asked Beatrice-Rose to talk to me because I didn't give him a chance to explain. And because...maybe he couldn't tell me what she had just said. That they slept together. But what if she was lying? Didn't I figure out that she was manipulative?

What if…

"Seems to me Lockhart doesn't even want her near him. Look." Damon motioned toward the parking lot.

I saw Caleb get in his car, leaving Beatrice-Rose behind. The squeal of tires echoed across the parking lot as Caleb drove away.

I don't know what came over me, but my chest felt tight and adrenaline coursed through my veins. I wanted Caleb.

I wanted him back.

I jumped up from my seat, and the next thing I knew, I was chasing after him.

"Caleb!" I yelled, running as fast as I could to catch him.

I want more. I want all of you, he had said, and I had turned him away.

I needed to talk to him. I needed him…

Don't go. I'm sorry! God, I'm so sorry, Caleb…

I ran. Ran as fast as I could to catch him, but he was driving away fast.

Am I not even worth a fight? Red?

His car sped up, turned a corner, and then—

He was gone.

I wanted you to fight for me, just as I fought for you. But you wouldn't.

I stood there, staring after him, tears pouring down my face.

I wanted him back, but I had hurt him so much, pushed him away so hard. I had let my past hurts take over me, destroy me. Had I pushed him so hard that he didn't want me back?

Oh my God. Am I too late?

End of Book One

Read on for a sneak peek of what's
next for Veronica and Caleb in

Coming November 2017

CHAPTER

one

Veronica

THIS WAS IT. THIS WAS MY CHANCE TO MAKE THINGS RIGHT. I just didn't know if I could take it.

Dread and anxiety chilled my spine as I stepped off the bus. I stood in front of Caleb's apartment building with my head bowed low, arguing with myself over whether or not I should go in. It had been a few hours since the fight in school, since I saw him drive away from the parking lot. It had been less than twenty-four hours since I packed my bags and left him.

This had been my home with him...before.

It wasn't anymore.

I knew good things didn't last. Every time something good happened, something bad followed. Maybe, just maybe, this time it would be good again.

Last time I entered this building, I had gotten a new phone

for myself and a present for Caleb. Had he seen it yet? Did he keep it or throw it away?

Heart racing, I clasped my hands together and tried not to wring them. Was he home? Would he let me in? What if he refused?

If Caleb rejected me, I didn't know if I could handle it...

You rejected him first. What gives you the right to ask him not to reject you?

Nothing.

Caleb's words burned in my mind. *I want you to fight for me just as I fought for you. But you wouldn't.*

I closed my eyes tightly. It hurt every time I heard his voice in my head. I hadn't been ready to hear everything he had to say before, but I was ready now. Beatrice-Rose said they had kissed and claimed they did more.

Caleb said they didn't sleep together. Now that anger wasn't clouding my thoughts, I realized that he had never lied to me before. If anything, he was too honest. Would he lie about something as serious as this? No, I realized, he wouldn't. And he...he was the only person who never gave up on me.

Don't ask me to let go of you. I can't, he had said.

But did he still want me? Had he let go of me after what I'd done?

My fears were nipping at my heels, waiting to pounce at my slightest weakness. I took a deep breath, pushing away my anxiety.

Gathering my courage, I stepped forward and entered the lobby. And froze. Beatrice-Rose was walking out of the elevator, her steps fast and determined. What was she doing here?

No one was allowed to go up unless the receptionist called

the tenant, and the tenant gave the go-ahead. So Caleb must have given her permission to go up. The thought made me take a step back to hide out of Beatrice-Rose's line of sight.

What if something was going on between them? What if Caleb had given up on me and realized I wasn't worth it?

No, no. Didn't you just say you believed him? You would fight for him?

Damn right I would fight for him.

Maybe Beatrice-Rose was trying to manipulate him again, pretending to be hurt and helpless to get what she wanted. If she tried anything with Caleb, she'd get more than a slap from me this time.

The kiss last night wasn't his fault. It was mine, she had said.

Did he really kiss her? I had to know, and the only person who could tell me was Caleb. I needed to talk to him.

I narrowed my eyes as I watched Beatrice-Rose get into a taxi. She had changed her clothes since I saw her a few hours ago. She wore a white baby-doll dress that ended above her knees. Her blond hair—now lengthened with expensive-looking extensions that bounced against her lower back—was swept off her beautiful face with a red headband. She had exchanged her heels in favor of white flats.

She looked as innocent as a dove. You'd never know that she was a snake behind that beautiful face.

Praying to God that Caleb hadn't removed me from the list of approved visitors who could go straight up, I casually strolled to the elevators, trying to avoid the concierge's hawk eyes. I froze when he spotted me, expecting him to call security to escort me out of the building, but he just smiled. I let out a relieved breath when the elevator doors closed.

As the elevator climbed up, my heart started to race. I felt nervous, my hands clammy and cold as I twisted them together. When the elevator stopped at Caleb's floor, I took a deep calming breath and walked out.

My steps were muffled by the carpet as I neared his door. It was so quiet in the hallway that I could hear my heartbeat in my ears.

Please don't hate me.

I stopped in front of his door, biting my lip. I had gotten used to going in without knocking, but I knew I had lost that privilege now.

Oh God. What if I lost him too?

Slowly, I raised my hand, forming a fist.

Just do it!

I closed my eyes tightly and knocked.

Acknowledgments

I was born and raised in the Philippines before we moved to Canada, and drama series are very popular there. I remember five days a week between 6:00 and 9:00 p.m., without fail, I would be in front of the TV with my parents, brother, and sister—sometimes even with my cousins and aunts—watching shows back to back.

I think watching all those shows inspired me to write. I've had these characters in my head for so long that it wasn't a struggle to write about them. Since I started writing, I've written different versions of all the characters in *Chasing Red*, and I realized all those stories were practice and led me to write this book.

To my Wattpad readers—there are so, so many of you to mention. Please know that I wouldn't be where I am without your positivity, your support, and your love. Thank you for the friendship, the endless encouragement, and the fangirling for Caleb and Red. There is no *Chasing Red* without you. I wake up grateful because of you.

Lianne, my twinks. Thank you for all the late-night phone calls and coffee dates as we brainstormed on the next chapter of Red and Caleb's story. We talked so much about them that they feel real to us. You are irreplaceable and I love you.

The amazing Wattpad team, especially Caitlin O'Hanlon—you

are my energy drink. I still remember that first email: it's legit! Ha-ha. Thank you for always taking care of me and replying to my crazy text messages. The sparkle in your eyes always makes me smile. Ashleigh Gardner—how many times you've clearly explained things to me so I can stop panicking. You are an amazing force of nature and I can't thank you enough for everything. Teach me the ways, master! Aron Levitz—I'm very grateful for your hard work and super cool glasses. Nazia Khan—I learned so much from you. I still have the notes you gave me and they will forever be pinned to my corkboard. And to Allen Lau and Ivan Yuen—thank you for creating Wattpad. You didn't give up on your dreams, and because of that, ours came true.

The Sourcebooks team, especially my editor, Cat Clyne. Because of you, *Chasing Red* is a better book. Thank you for your guidance and understanding my vision. You've taught me so much and I'm grateful! You are Wonder Woman. To Laura Costello—you're incredible. I'm so thankful for your valuable suggestions, and I'm glad you love Caleb's taste in scary movies! A very big thank-you to Heather Hall and Diane Dannenfeldt for all your hard work and feedback. Beth Sochacki—I still wear my pin, girl. Thank you so much for helping me promote *Chasing Red* on social media. Dawn Adams—you are a genius and I love the covers so much!

Tatay and Mama—you've worked so hard to raise us and all I want is to make you proud. I love you both so much.

My Adam. When I told you about my dreams and I know they sounded impossible—but you believed them because you believed in me. Thank you for the pancakes. You're my Caleb.

And to God. For making everything possible. For loving me despite all my faults, for never letting me forget what's important. For giving me all the people in my life. For being there always.

Love,
Isabelle

About the Author

Isabelle Ronin is a Filipino Canadian writer based in Winnipeg, Manitoba. Her Wattpad story, *Chasing Red*, has garnered over 150 million reads and was one of the most-read stories of 2016. As a result of the story's immense popularity online, several major publishers around the world have acquired the rights to *Chasing Red*.

When she's not writing, Isabelle can be found hanging out in bookstores, in cafés, and whenever possible, at the beach. You can follow her and read her stories on Wattpad. Visit her online at wattpad.com/isabelleronin.